THE YEAR OF OUR WAR

THE YEAR OF OUR WAR

STEPH SWAINSTON

An Imprint of HarperCollins*Publishers*

This book was originally published in 2004 by Gollancz, an imprint of the Orion Publishing Group.

HarperCollins books may be purchased for educational, business, or sales promotional use. For information please write: Special Markets Department, HarperCollins Publishers Inc., 10 East 53rd Street, New York, NY 10022.

FIRST U.S. EDITION

Eos is a federally registered trademark of HarperCollins Publishers Inc.

Designed by Jeffrey Pennington

Library of Congress Cataloging-in-Publication Data

Swainston, Steph.
 The year of our war / Steph Swainston.—1st ed.
  p. cm.
 ISBN 0-06-075387-0
  1. Human-alien encounters—Fiction. 2. Immortalism—Fiction. I. Title.

PR6119.W35Y43 2005
823'.92—dc22   2004056327

05 06 07 08 09 ❖/RRD 10 9 8 7 6 5 4 3 2 1

To Brian

Unnatural vices are fathered by our heroism.

—*T. S. Eliot*

ACKNOWLEDGMENTS

Huge thanks above all to Simon Spanton. Thank you to my Eszai-good agents, Mic Cheetham and Simon Kavanagh, for their vital help. My gratitude to Ben Jeapes for his excellent advice. Thanks and love to Brian, immovable object of my unstoppable force.

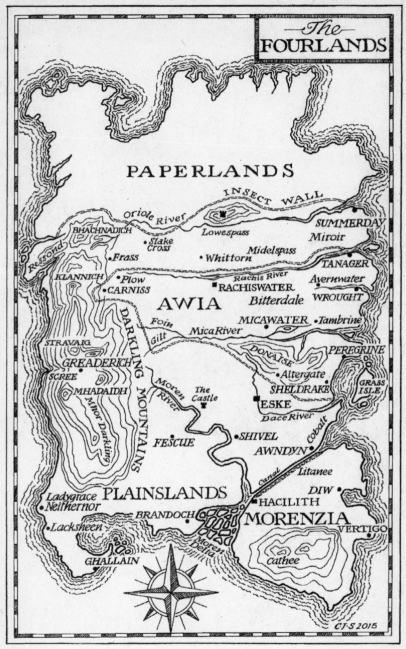

The FOURLANDS

PAPERLANDS

INSECT WALL

Oriole River

BHACHNADICH · Stake
Cross · Lowespass

SUMMERDAY
Miroir

Ressond

· Frass · Whittorn · Midelspass

TANAGER

KLANNICH · Plow · *Rachis River* · Ayernwater

· CARNISS · RACHISWATER · WROUGHT

AWIA · Bitterdale

Foin · MICAWATER · Tambrine

STRAVAIG · *Gilt* · *Mica River*

GREADERICH · *DONAISE* · PEREGRINE

· SCREE · · Altergate

· MHADAIDH · The
Castle · SHELDRAKE · GRASS
ISLE

*Moren
River* · ESKE

Mhor Darkling · *Dace River*

DARKLING MOUNTAINS

FESCUE · · SHIVEL

· AWNDYN

Cobalt

· Litanee

Ladygrace · DIW

· Neithernor · PLAINSLANDS · *Canal*

· Lacksheen · BRANDOCH · HACILITH

MORENZIA

*Moren
Delta* · VERTIGO

GHALLAIN · *cathee*

CJ-S 2015

Scale 1: 12 million

CHAPTER ONE

As soon as I arrived in Lowespass I bought a newspaper and read it in the shadow of the fortress wall—

CASTLE CALLS FOR REINFORCEMENTS—
RACHISWATER OFFENSIVE CONTINUES

The Castle has demanded eight thousand fresh troops to be raised from the Plainslands to join the Awian Fyrd on the Lowespass front. Awian soldiers led by King Dunlin Rachiswater have forced the Insects westward, exposing the remains of Lowespass town, which was lost in the Insect advance last year.

In a joint press conference held on Friday with Comet representing the Castle, King Rachiswater announced that five kilometers of ground had been recovered. He pointed out that this was the first time the Wall had been pushed back in twenty years. His Majesty appealed for "our brothers of the Plainslands" to send reinforcements so the advance could continue. Comet reported that the Emperor was "pleased" with the success of the Awian operation.

Lowespass town now presents a dramatic sight, shocking to those who have not seen the works of Insects before. To the scorched walls and timbers—the town was burned before evacuation—Insects have added their complex of gray paper constructions with pointed roofs resembling houses. The ground is riddled with their tunnels.

Awian losses in the last two weeks were heaviest in the infantry, with one thousand fatalities and as many injured. Five hundred of the cavalry were killed, while the archers, all under Lightning's command, suffered twelve injured. None of the immortals has been harmed, and they continue to encourage the troops. Veterans of the campaign have been promised settlements in newly recovered lands.

Comet said that despite such determined efforts the terror of an Insect swarm appearing remains significant. He reported that the buildings stretch for kilometers behind the Wall. He said, "Flying over it is like—

I knew my own words, however badly reported, so I flicked to page five, where there was a cartoon with a surprising likeness of Lightning. The cartoon grasped desperately at a beautiful girl who was carrying a guitar. Her figure dissolved like a ghost into little woodcut hearts. The caption underneath read: *Swallow? In your dreams.*

Giggling, I folded the newspaper and shoved it into the back of my belt. I strode away from the fortress wall toward the cliff, hearing the river torrent below. Two strides, and I started running. I forced at the ground, accelerating, faster and faster to the edge of the cliff. Three, two, one. I spread my wings and kicked over the edge as the ground fell away. I turned in a long calm arc down toward the camp.

By day the Lowespass outpost filled the river valley with sound and splendor. Tents covered the ground completely, colored like scales on a butterfly's wing. Troops patrolled the Insect Wall, covered wagons drawn by exhausted horses rolled in along the rutted road. They unloaded at the fortress, took the wounded away. From the air, carts were the size of matchboxes, parked in a line. Shouts carried from the soldiers at training; those at rest sat in groups on the grass, or in the canvas city, under awnings, around fires. Pennants, which marked fyrd divisions, twisted like vivid tongues on the blunted mountain breeze. They were blue with white eagles for the country of Awia, a scallop shell for Summerday manor, a clenched fist for Hacilith city, stars, plows, and ships for the Plainslands manors. The Castle's flag was set in the center of the camp, a red and gold sun-in-splendor. Our symbol of permanence now shines on land reclaimed from the Insects, and soldiers passing beneath it glance up, smiling.

I flew in at midnight, practically blind, trying to remember how deep the valley was. I hurtled down it, balancing on long wings. The river looked like a strand of silver mirror behind the slashed black hillside, and not too far distant I could see the Wall.

Too fast. I'm going too fast.

Good.

Dividing the valley, Lowespass Fortress on its rocky crag soared above me as I dropped. The dark ground was spotted with red, the campfires of the fyrd. Closer still, I could see pale faces surrounding them, but no more. I felt unnerved that Lowespass was populated with silent soldiers. I slowed, flared my wings, and landed neatly on a patch of ground not two meters from a cluster of sleeping bags, which yelped.

I made my way on the damp ground between bivouacs and tent pegs to the Castle's pavilion. Lamplight shone in a thin beam from the slit entrance. I stood for a while hearing the chatter coming from within, before remembering that those who listen outside tents rarely hear any good about themselves.

"Welcome back, Comet," said Dunlin.

"You can call me Jant," I said. As my eyes got used to the light I saw three men sitting around a thin table, playing cards. The pavilion was so large that the edges were in shadow; the central pole was wound with red and yellow ribbons. I bowed to King Dunlin Rachiswater, and to his brother Staniel, and I said hi to Lightning, the Castle's Archer.

Lightning nodded curtly at me. He was sorting his cards. "What's the news?"

"Diw won two-nil against Hacilith."

He gaped. "Can't you *ever* be serious?"

Dunlin leaned forward. "Have you been successful?"

"Of course. Your Majesty, there are five thousand soldiers on their way from the coast. They'll take a week to ride here. In addition to that, I went to the Castle and spoke with the Emperor, and he greatly favors what we've achieved and backs all the plans you asked me to report—"

"Wait, wait. Didn't we say eight, not five?"

"I can pull another three thousand from Awia if you give me time." I was slightly ashamed that I had spent the last few days at the Castle visiting my wife rather than working. King Dunlin Rachiswater is the only man I know who has enough stamina to remain at the front for weeks on end without feeling the need for a night with a woman.

He shook his head. "It has to be the Plainslands. Not Awia. Who'll feed us?"

"My lord, there are few soldiers left at the coast, and most of them are too young. There's no outcry as yet, but I think it's wrong to take so many."

"If my country of Awia gives all it can, then the Plainslands can too."

I said, "If I may venture a criticism, it's your campaign to push the Insects out of land where they're well established which is costing so many lives."

"So you'd rather remain in a stalemate for another two thousand years?"

I sighed. "The Castle aims to protect Zascai from the Insects. There's never a shortage of Insects. If you use up the fighting force of one generation, for how long can we guarantee that protection?"

"Immortals are so frustrating sometimes," he remarked to his brother. "We can beat the Insects. With eight thousand, we can control their movements. We can support each other!"

I told him, "I've seen a lot of action, and I think a hotheaded approach is wrong."

Rachiswater prepared to contest this but Lightning said, "Your Majesty, don't argue with Comet."

"Sorry, Jant."

"No, no. It's my fault. I've flown a long way. I'm a bit tired."

They fetched a chair for me to sit down at the table, and poured some red wine from a crystal decanter. The drink wasn't good on an empty stomach, and I began to feel very light-headed as the others continued with their card game.

"You look tired," Lightning said, tone dripping with suspicion. The Micawater manor insignia on his shoulder caught the lamp-light, a similar diamond design on the quiver full of red-flighted arrows dangling from the back of his chair. The arrows were hanging with a little state-of-the-art composite bow: gold-banded horn and polished strips of wood, curved back like pincers. This meant he must have been showing off because in battle he usually uses a longbow. He was a little taller than Dunlin, much broader than Staniel, and more muscular than me.

There was a resemblance between Dunlin and Staniel, but in it Dunlin had taken all the darkness and strength, whereas his younger brother was like a yellow reed.

Dunlin growled, "I want us to keep our minds on the *campaign*. Especially tomorrow, because it is going to be challenging. Archer, your command is vital." Lightning didn't say anything.

"And Messenger? Jant . . . ?"

"At your service," said I. Dunlin filled his glass, raised it, drank a toast to the Emperor. I clinked my glass to his, set it down after the briefest sip. I didn't want him to see my unsteady hand.

Dunlin's expression became thoughtful. "Out of the immortals apart from your good selves, Tornado, Mist, and Ata will join us. Rayne will stay in Lowespass Fortress. There hasn't been such a powerful showing of the Circle for . . . how long?"

"Just a hundred years," I said.

Staniel's pale eyes were starry with inward enthusiasm. His skinny hand stroked his little blond goatee. No doubt he planned to write about it later: Staniel Rachiswater fighting fearlessly against the Insects with the aid of the immortals.

In the Awian language immortals are called Eszai. Staniel's poetry portrayed us Eszai as divine, and his sturdy brother as a heroic fighter, and so his image shone with a little of our reflected light, but I had never seen him pick up a sword. His responsibility had been to make sure any wounded and food-poisoned returned to the fortress, and that fyrd on their way back to their manors did not linger and become highwaymen. He had delegated those tasks to me at the outset and now remained in the camp, scribbling in his notebook with a fountain pen.

"I have a straight flush in hearts," said Lightning. "Gentlemen? Oh dear. Pity. So—I acquire the Rachiswater amphitheater, and Staniel's library." He dealt, the red-backed cards pliant in his big hands. "I stake Micawater Bridge, which as you know is one of the seven wonders of the world, so please treat it kindly. Jant, are you playing?"

"You daft bloody Awians," I muttered unhappily.

"It's just a bit of fun. I'll let you have your manor back in the morning."

I declined; I don't see any point in card games. My reactions are faster than the Awians'; if I wanted to win I could cheat by sleight of hand. If I played without cheating, then Dunlin would beat me because he is a better, poker-faced strategist, and Lightning would beat him because Lightning has played cards for fifteen hundred years and can see through any strategy without trying. My thoughts strayed hard to something else. I was beginning to feel shaky, and in case my associates had noticed, I blamed it on fatigue. I stood up, pushing the chair back into damp grass. "Give me leave to leave?"

"See you at first light," said the King.

"Sweet dreams," remarked Lightning.

I found the gentle breeze revitalizing. It was the extreme feather's end of the mountains, and, with a little imagination, I could smell the high summits—glaciers and pine behind the reek of campfire cooking and unwashed soldiers. It was only fancy, but knowing that the breeze in Lowespass gusts down from the mountains made me feel nostalgic. I remembered bitterly that nostalgia is another symptom of withdrawal.

I don't have or need my own tent, so I hurried to Lightning Saker's pavilion where a bundle of chamois-skin blankets just inside the entrance marked my bed. He hadn't touched my maps

and clothes which were still piled as I had left them, though now
damp with dew. I managed to light a candle, gathered together
my works, and took a shot. I soon went to sleep, curled up,
racked with hallucinations.

Until golden dawn kicked me awake with big boots.

I yawned and stretched, decongealing. I lay cradled in the
blankets, comfortably warm and very relaxed, looking out down
Lowespass valley toward the Wall. The vale was filled with
blue-gray wood smoke from a thousand campfires, hanging in
horizontal stripes and softening the sunlight. Groups of soldiers
were gathering, heading toward the main source of the smoke,
where breakfast was being dished out. Food at the front was sur-
prisingly good—it had to be because very few of the General
Fyrd wanted to be there and it was better for Castle to tempt
them than force them. I watched soldiers striking low green
tents, which billowed down and were lashed to carrying poles. I
drifted for a while, observing the scene, pleasantly unfocused;
and then I thought about how good it would be to take another
fix. My needle was lying on an unfolded map. I reached out and
as my hand closed round it a boot descended on my wrist.

"No, you don't," said Lightning. He shoved a couple of folds
of crimson scarf over one shoulder, bent down, and retrieved
spoon, syringe, twist of paper. "I'll look after these."

"Oh, no. Honestly. Come on, Saker! Not *again*."

"Dunlin is calling for us. I need you to talk to Tornado. Up
you get."

I should have found Lightning's demeanor inspiring. He
wore armor—brass scale lorica made to look like covert feathers—over his chest and down strong arms to the elbow. He had
leather trousers laced up the sides, and a Wrought sword at his
hip. His scarf, embellished with the Castle insignia, stuck to his
wings—which were longer than the modern average—and ruffled the feathers. Other people would have been impressed with

such beautiful armor; I simply wondered how much the Wrought craftsmen were making from it, and whether I would see any of the profit.

Feeling rather diminished and dirty, I followed the embroidered sun on his mantle out of the pavilion and through the camp. Faces looked up from turfing ashy fires or pulling backpack cords tight, buckling cuirasses or blowing on hot coffee. The soldiers we met stood up, so that we went in a little wave of startled men standing, then settling down after we passed.

There was a difference between the soldiers of the General Fyrd and the Select Fyrd. The latter were proud of their warrior status, in competition with each other for the attention of governors and immortals; they kept their swords razor keen. They jumped quickly to their feet as we walked by.

Most of the archers were Select Fyrd, as it takes so long to train them; they were waiting by Lightning's pavilion and he nodded at a couple almost familiarly. His goldfish-armor shimmered.

We reached the area of the General Fyrd, soldiers who weren't trained, or new recruits who were much less well-equipped. The main armories were in Wrought, my wife's manor. On Castle's command they provided every man with shield, broadsword, and pike, but the drafted farmers in the General Fyrd could not afford more than this very basic equipment. They were dressed in worsted and muddied denim, hardly a glint of steel apart from ill-fitting battlefield spoils. These men and women shambled to their feet, still holding trays of food. Their camp was carelessly kept, their patched tents stood unevenly. Some tents were simply frames from which mosquito netting hung, weighted at the bottom.

It was one of Tornado's duties to direct the General Fyrd. Tornado was sitting cross-legged on the grass, stripped to the waist, sliding the edge of a battle-ax across a huge whetstone with a sound like sawing. A paunch hung over his cracked belt. At two and a half meters tall he was the biggest and strongest of the Castle's Eszai, unbeaten for one thousand years. He had brown hair shaved very close to the scalp. It looked weird together with the rug of hair growing on his chest and a little on his shoulders. The hair didn't cover pale scars, thick as my finger and long as a span, which crisscrossed his chest and stomach. Slabs of muscle shifted on his sunburned shoulders as he manipulated the ax. An ancient sunburst tattoo on his forearm undulated as the muscles moved.

Unlike most of the Eszai, Tornado had never owned anything—no lands, and no more wealth than beer money. His reputation hung on risking death in the very thick of the action. If he hadn't faced death so eagerly, so often, he wouldn't be so practiced at dealing with it. Tawny and I are similar in that our links to life are more tenuous than people expect.

Tawny's well-chosen girlfriend, Vireo Summerday, was also gigantic. She was scratching her leg by poking a stick through the joints of her plate armor. I couldn't fathom Vireo, she was neither terrified of nor attracted to me. She wouldn't call a spade a spade if she could call it a fucking bastard. Lightning bowed to her; she winked at me.

"Good morning," said Lightning.

"Yo," said Tawny. "All right, Jant?"

". . . Considering."

"I've been ready bloody ages and nothing has happened," said Tawny. "When do we get to fight?"

"You will be commanding the Hacilith men and those from Eske."

"The townies," I said.

"Nothing changed there then."

Lightning said, "When the Insects attack, fall back. There will be shield walls to channel them if necessary. We will drive them into the sixth corral. You should attempt to advance through the Wall. Dunlin believes it possible that we can breach their defenses and redeem more land."

"Whoa! Hang on. You what? Want me to go behind the Wall? No way, little one. I'll be on my own because townies are chickenshit, like you know. They'll run so fast they'll fly, by god! Behind the Wall, like, not bloody likely."

"It's Dunlin's main aim at the moment," said Lightning.

"If you thought with yer balls rather than yer heart you'd not let a soft bloody Zascai get in the way of how Eszai have always done stuff."

"Have we not recently decided to support the King of Awia?"

I interrupted, "But last time a thousand people died." If I had been on the field and not unconscious during the skirmish, the Castle might have fared better. Lightning seemed about to make that point, so I decided to keep quiet. Tawny complained for a while but accepted; he doesn't have enough willpower to argue with Lightning.

"Look, Tawny," I said. "The Emperor backs Dunlin, so we've got to do it. We can't guess why the Emperor makes such plans. They might come in useful a century from now."

He respected me; he knew that my experiences have given me calmness, a knowledge that sets me apart from day-to-day concerns. He sensed this, and he admired such steadfastness.

"Whatever you say, Jant." Tawny poked the bright edge of his ax with a grimy thumbnail. "But culling Insects should be a waiting game. I'm buggered if I want to stir them up." He used the ax to steady himself as he stood. I stepped back a little, over-awed by his size. He stretched and muscle on muscle tautened under fat.

"Be careful—" Lightning began.

"Get lost, lover-boy," said Tawny. "I'm doing my job which

is, like, cutting up Insects. I know I'll survive, behind the Wall
or underground or anywhere. Dunlin's trying to save civilian
lives. It's good that he cares for them, but he's trying *too hard*."
He buckled the ax to his chain belt, plucked at Vireo who had
been eavesdropping in the background. In Plainslands he said,
"Let's go, love. Everything round here with wings is crazy."

"What was that?" Lightning asked. I gave a loose transla-
tion; he watched them go. "Aren't lovers content in their own
little worlds?" he said.

In the pavilion, I was left alone while Lightning went to
address the archers' ranks and the neat phalanxes of Select
Awian infantry. They had blue plumes on their helmets,
heraldic creations of carved bone and cuir-bouilli and faience,
finely wrought iridium chain mail over their wings. I took the
chance to go through all his belongings searching for my drugs.
I found a couple of letters that would have been interesting if I
hadn't been so feverish. No cat. I called Lightning all the names
under the sun. Left a devastated mess behind. Sat down on the
grass. Started shaking with an advance on withdrawal—the
effect of panic.

Well. Plan B. I found my compass, pressed a button and the
silver casing clicked open like a shell. There was a twist of paper
inside, ripped from the edge of a map. It's vital to have more than
one stash. With a long thumbnail I cut a line of cat on the compass
glass, rolled up a five-pound note, and snorted it, north-south.

Oh, *yes*.

I let the worries dissolve, one by one, and drop from my
mind. Not even immortals are built to take so many misgivings.
Wiping my nose on the back of a hand, I considered the forth-
coming fight. I was wearing bangles, faded jeans, and a cut-off
T-shirt which read "Hacilith Marathon 1974."

I gazed at the heap of my silver scale armor, a byrnie adorned with smaragd and onyx, a helmet decorated with knot work, with a high white plume. It matches black-on-silver vambraces. A belt and a sword-hanger, a circular shield; my sword's grip has two snakes wrapped around it. I have pauldrons for my wings, inscribed "For god and the Empire." I have latten greaves. I have a black cloak, thin taffeta with a niello silver fastening. I have pinked black leather gauntlets, embossed with Castle's Sun and my sign, the Wheel.

Sod that. I strip my T-shirt off, shove my ice ax in the back of my belt, and consider myself ready to fight anything.

"Jant?" It was Dunlin, and he was looking amazed. I swept a low bow. "Your Majesty."

Dunlin said, "Comet, Tornado is already hacking at the Wall. You must be in the air as soon as possible." I was irritated until I realized that the true purpose of Dunlin's endless rallying and righteous enthusiasm was to make him feel better. "What did the Emperor really say?" he asked me. He was shrewder than I gave him credit for.

"San conceded the sagacity of everything you've done," I said.

"Did he have a message for me?" Dunlin's hand rested on an ornate sword hilt. "Am I valuable to the Emperor? Am I noticed by him?"

"There isn't time to go into details!"

"Then after the battle, Rhydanne. I know you remember court word-perfect and I have to know."

"Your wish." I shrugged. I wanted the bright air, not to be cornered in a tent by the Awian King. I didn't want this man I admired to make reference to my Rhydanne ancestry.

Dunlin regarded me carefully; cleverness would hide in the wrinkles round his eyes. His eyes were gray but not flecked—like silver coins—and he could outstare me, which few can do. He said, "You must remember to relate my Lord Emperor's opinion of our victory last week, in which Tawny and I were in the melee." There was a sheen of sweat on his red-brown neck.

His straightforwardness pushed me into telling the truth for once. "You want to join the Castle Circle, don't you?" I said.

"Good guess, Comet. More than you can ever know."

"Your Highness. There's nothing I can do."

He turned, sliding his blade in its scabbard, and with his broad back to me said, "In a lesser time I might have achieved a place, but not now. Over the years I have seen thirty of you fight and, to give an example, I can't wrestle as well as Tornado, I can't handle a longbow like Lightning, and I can't move as fast as you."

"There hasn't been a new entrant to the Castle for ninety years."

"Doesn't matter. Lightning says three might come along at once."

"We value your service in providing a link between the Castle and the common people," I recited, following him out of the tent.

"Oh yes. Allow us mortals our dream." All mortals dream, it seems, of joining the Castle Circle. Always pushing for immortality. Always seeking to stop the spin of the wheel of fortune, as it rips through their hands, leaving splinters. How splendid it would be to be eternal, and safe. But at the same time it is daunting to join such a fellowship. The dispositions of the other Eszai are unknown. Make the wrong move, and the pack draws together against you. A new Eszai wouldn't know that the most forbidding are the least dangerous.

The best I could manage was, "Immortality has its disadvantages." The Awian smiled like he didn't believe me. I told him I'd trade every minute of my long life to own, briefly, his lands and riches. There's no point in being eternal if you're eternally in debt.

"Immortal or not, you can fly," he said, longingly.

"Well, sometimes pleasure pays."

"Come on, Jant," he said, far more cheerfully. "Let me see you fly!"

The Sun standard's long shadow fell on tent-cleared ground. I heard the battering rams crash against the Wall. Their solid wheels squealed and jarred on the rubble, making the ground shake. Two battering rams, working in tandem. The jangled shouts of Tawny's fyrd got louder after each crash. The tightening sensation in every muscle as my drug kicked in twisted and heightened that already terrible sound.

"I'm going to take a closer look," I said. I began to jog, in a slight curve, into what little wind there was. Spikes on my boot soles held in the damp grass. I loped, leaned forward, started to run. To sprint. I charged downhill, and when I thought I'd reached top speed, I found a little more. A little more, a little more, till it was too fast to breathe.

Speed is a state of bliss.

I forced down half-spread wings. Feathers slapped the ground, but on the next beat I jumped and their downward movement pushed me up. I felt a meter of lift but the effort was agony.

I jump, and I keep going up.

My body took over, my mind dull with pain. Every beat tore at the muscles in my waist. I quickly made it up to a clear height. I looked down and saw tiny people. I started to climb more shallowly, settled into a gradual pace that rowed me upward, completed the curve into a wide circle so I was above Dunlin. I rejoiced in stretching the full length of my wings. I loved to feel the airflow as I pulled them down. At the end of a stroke, my fingers, long feathers, touched each other three meters beneath my stomach. I savored the resistance, which bent the wrists as I threw them back up through the air again. The air felt heavier than Tawny's weights. My wings are like long arms, and flat silver rings on the elongated fingers clacked together as I closed my hands for the upstroke. My weight hung from the small of my back. I kept my real arms crossed over my chest, sometimes spreading them to help with balance.

With great effort I fought my way up to a height where the fyrd had lost all individuality and were just areas of heraldic color. The General soldiers' ranks were dotted with movement as anxious faces turned up to see me.

Still the battering rams dragged back and surged forward, impacting against the Wall. Surly thermals formed above the Wall; I tried one long enough to get a close look. Five meters tall, the Wall stretched away east and west, a bright white ribbon against the forest canopy; it ran farther than I could see from cloud base on a clear day. Close up, the surface was uneven, and it was not built exactly in a straight line—irregularities showed where previous battles had scarred it and where the Insects had encountered difficult ground. Although mostly creamy white, the Wall varied in texture because it was built from anything the Insects could carry or drag.

So it's best not to look too closely. The sweating soldiers on the battering ram had a close view, as the Wall fell apart in fist-sized chunks, like chalk. Hardened Insect spit held it together. It was smooth like ceramic, and sometimes with froth set hard as stone. Inside were chewed tree branches, furniture from ruined villages, armor from old battles. There were also the shells of dead Insects, pieces of tents and weaponry, and children who disappeared many years ago. Here and there a rotting arm or a horse's backbone protruded out, faces could be seen within it, unevenly preserved when the milky saliva set hard. Tawny's fyrd had moved aside the rolls of barbed wire and were hacking at the Wall with hammers. He saw me and waved. I tipped my wings to him.

"Can you see behind the Wall?" he bellowed as the battering ram came to another shuddering halt.

"Oh, yes," I said.

"How many Insects?" he yelled. Thousands of glossy brown bodies were gathering on the other side of the Wall. Each the size of a man, they clustered at its base, feelers touching. More and more gathered, running out of tunnel mouths, from underground.

"Thousands! They are—" And then they broke through.

Tawny's men drew together. "Guard!" he roared. A shield wall went up. As Insects began to pour through the breach in their Wall, they met, ricocheted off, crawled up the colored shields. Tawny's men were shoulder to shoulder and their arms were strong, but the gap between them and the Wall filled quickly with Insects. They rushed over each other, their sword's-length jaws scraping at the painted shields. I flapped upward for a better view.

The men on one ram were safe. They raised their square shields and retreated until the shield wall absorbed them.

The second team's ram was stuck on some rubble; they wasted a second heaving at it and the Insects went through them like living razors. I saw mandibles close on a forearm and sever it, the blood ceased as another Insect tore his throat open.

I saw two soldiers make a stand, back to back, but when the tide of creatures went over them they simply disappeared.

Tawny from the shield wall hacked off an Insect's antennae; confused, it turned to bite at other Insects.

An Insect nibbling at a fallen man got its jaws caught in the gap between breastplate and backplate. Another soldier severed

them with an ax, slicing his dead friend's body. He cut the
Insect's back legs off with another clean blow. He was a good
fighter, but he couldn't stand against the torrent that now
flowed between him and the shield wall. He went down chopping and screeching, Insect antennae flickering in his face and
claws sliding over his armor. Insects bit into his ankles to the
bone. They hauled him, still kicking, to the Wall, where Insects
crouched, repairing the breach. They built around the stranded
battering ram, which was being covered in fast-hardening froth.

The men felt the pressure on their shields, mouthparts and
antennae forced into gaps between them, and they shouted to
each other. The Insects made no noise. As it came up to me, the
sound of Insect bodies crawling over Insect bodies was a clicking, scratching, rasping. I watched, and flew so slowly I stalled.
Panicking, I climbed on a thermal so the shrinking battlefield
rotated below.

The men fell back in the center of their line. As they withdrew, a dent appeared in the shield wall; it grew bigger, curving
inward. Insects surged into the gap. Gradually, Tawny's division split in half, the men walked back and back, cramming
together. The maneuver created a conduit down which Insects
poured, men with shields controlling them on either side. I
marveled at the fyrd's bravery. On the ground men were
pressed together, crouching behind their shields, sweating,
shouting. Each soldier felt the strength of the man on his right,
the man on his left, and the wall held. An Insect antenna caught
briefly between one shield and the next. The soldier watched it
in terror, his arm in the shield bracket up in front of his face. All
his childhood fears were true. The Insect ripped its antenna free
and rushed on.

Some Plainslanders with ropes gathered around an over-
turned Insect; it was thrashing on its back, its soft abdomen
showing, compound eyes drab from grass stains. They roped its

middle pair of legs together and turned it right side up. The Insect tried to rush at them, but two men were braced with the end of the rope and it simply pulled itself over. It tried this a couple of times before giving up. Its mandibles gnashed and frothed. Confused that it had no freedom of movement, it twisted round and discovered the leash. It closed its jaws around the rope and the soldiers then wound another rope around its jaws, trussed up its back legs and dragged it off the field.

I heard the hollow sound of shell creatures rattling down the wooden tunnel, glancing off the shields. More Insects ran from behind the Wall and the flood went on. Insects, like water, flow downhill. They were directed to the mouth of a long corral.

The enclosure, built by Dunlin's men over the previous months, was made from sharpened wooden posts, set deeply into the ground. It was half a kilometer long, and archers on higher ground sped Insects along down the narrowing valley. I left Tawny's fyrd and flew over Lightning's, gaining height to be above the arrows. Awian archers were an azure splash on the parched yellow ground. They had quivers on their right hips, bare heads, and scarcely any armor. They drew only to their cheeks, because the distance to the corral was short, and they shot at a rate of ten flights a minute. Their mechanical repetition impressed me, and I circled above hearing Lightning's voice distorted by distance: "Notch. Stretch. Loose."

"Notch. Stretch. Loose."

Closer—"Notch! Stretch! Loose!"

Swarms of arrows flew up, reached their greatest height just beneath me, descended on the corral like hail.

Lightning shaded his eyes with a gloved hand and looked around the sky for me. I flew behind the archers' ranks.

"Messenger!" he yelled. "Comet? Are you there?"

"Yes!" I yelled back.

"Get out of the sun so I can see you!"

"Sorry."

"Is everything satisfactory?"

"They've nearly all gone past," I said, circling.

"Are you *sure*?"

"There are very few casualties."

Lightning looked pleased. He turned back to the two lines of archers. "Attention! Now to resume! There are arrows left. Notch! Stretch! Loose!"

When they reached the end of the corral, some of the Insects were so full of arrows they looked like leggy hedgehogs. Most were missing limbs or were wounded, dripping yellow liquid. A few had holes in their carapaces where arrows had passed straight through, sometimes catching and hanging in their transparent vestigial wings. Arrows do not kill Insects unless the creature's head is hit directly, with enough force to break the shell. Rather than points, the arrows that Lightning's team shot had broad heads, like blades; they tried to sever limbs and shatter shells. All along the valley enclosure I saw trails of yellow fluid, pieces of glossy carapace. Insects skittered on the ground, some with just one leg left, some with no legs; thoraxes with just the stems of legs attached, bulbous joints with holes where legs should be.

The end of the corral was a palisaded pen, and Insects ran round and round inside, filling it. Still they ran silently while the men howled with effort. Around the fence, the Awian infantry was waiting. Dunlin and his guard were on horseback some distance at the rear. His gray wings trembled.

Some more of the generals—Mist and Ata—were even farther back with a division of the Island Fyrd. They were under orders to ride following the soldiers and round up those who ran away in terror, and push them back into the fray. Mist peered at the corrugated wall of the rough corral rising in front of him; stared back toward the gleaming inhuman Wall behind. I saw Mist's stripy charcoal hair, and Ata's polished armor under a limp smalt-blue cloak that hung over her saddle's cantle and her horse's butt.

The Awian foot soldiers raised their sarissai to the top of the palisade. These spears were full seven meters long with crossbars behind the point. They used sarissai to thrust at the Insects that were running around inside the corral. Javelins thrown by another fyrd division reached the center of the corral. Insects hit by javelins died pinned to the ground.

Too many Insects were dying at one place. The mound of carcasses built up until—so fast I couldn't call out—it grew high enough for Insects climbing it to fall over the top of the palisade and escape. Five were free. Ten. Fifty. A hundred. The first skewered and writhed on the sarissai, then Insects went under the spears, and between them. The Awian spearmen turned and fled. They ran into the men behind, who also turned to run, but Insects cut a path through them, biting, clawing, throwing them aside. Spearmen at the edges who were smart enough to draw broadswords and maces lasted a little longer but two Insects together are more than a match for a man.

"Shit," I said. "Oh no. Shit!" I flew through a thermal and had to flutter furiously.

Dunlin from his vantage point saw what was taking place. I streamed down over his cavalry as soldiers lowered their lances, and a hundred spurs set to a hundred flanks at once.

I screamed, "Rachiswater—Dunlin! Can you hear me? Do what I tell you!" The wind whipped back my words and I got no answer from him at all.

We rarely ride horses against Insects. They normally fear them and will simply shy away. I've seen past battles where horses bolted over lines of infantry. But one of the advantages of having immortal leaders is that we live to learn from our mistakes. Hayl Eske had spent centuries breeding and training the Awian destriers that Dunlin's men now used.

The Insects were covered in human blood as well as their own. They moved fast, close to the ground, their six legs jointed above low bodies. Claws raked on the ground, lifted; the same ground flattened by Dunlin's lancers a second later.

I flew fast enough to overtake the Insects and saw that they were fleeing to the Wall. I wheeled back and tried to tell Dunlin. His helmet visor was down, the blue and argent mantle was tucked into the back of his belt but it billowed. I could see the blue sheen on his chain mail. His guard followed in a wave; on their saddles were fastened long feathers cut from leather, wide ribbons, metal lace.

They went round the side of the corral opposite the archers, and I saw Lightning and those at his side draw their bows and take out the leading Insects. Lightning's arrow went well home, the Insect died instantly and rolled, then the rest trampled it. The archers would have drawn again but Lightning stayed their hands as Dunlin thundered past.

The lancers crossed the clearing where the battering rams had been, littered with bodies, chewed edges of wounds drying like brown mouths. They went past Tawny's fyrd, who, axes in hand, were standing to seal the mouth of the corral. Tawny's barrier had by now broken up into amorphous groups of men, tan and wine colored. As Dunlin's lancers passed them shields were raised instinctively. Tawny stood openmouthed. I circled him; my wings were fucking killing me and this was all going wrong.

"Follow him!" I shouted at Tawny, but that was impossible. Tawny's broadax over his shoulder caught the sunlight. He started walking after them, and his soldiers gathered in a crowd around him. They looked so immovable from the air.

Dunlin charged on, over the dead grass.

And then he went through the Wall.

He went through the Wall where Tawny had breached it,

and onto the Insect plain. All the soldiers followed, heads bent over horses' necks, braids in horse tails streaming out behind. They knew it was forbidden to cross the Wall but curiosity spurred them. They'd follow Dunlin.

I know why he is doing this. It's bravery, not bravado. He really is determined to beat the Insects and he does want to show the Castle how much can be done. He may have reasons for disobeying my orders, but that's no less reprehensible. I decided all I could do was watch, witness the actions of the King, to relate to the Emperor later. I was shaking with tension.

The riders passed a paper archway half-sunk in the ground. It was the mouth of a tunnel, like a gray hood, standing without support and leading into a smooth passage. A few minutes later, they reached five identical archways in a line between gnawed tree stumps. The Insect group ran down the first of these without breaking pace, and disappeared. Dunlin reined his horse in so rapidly she lost her footing and stumbled to a halt in the tunnel mouth, her eyes showing white with fear. The soldiers stopped in a mass around him, listening to him curse. "We've damn well lost them after all that." He stripped off his gauntlets, slapped them on the saddle pommel. "I don't believe it. Damn it. Shit! Let's get these horses out of the tunnel; they hate the Insect stink."

One of the soldiers called, "Your Highness! Can we ride back to the other side of the Wall?"

"If you want, Merganser, you can." Dunlin stared at him and uncertain laughter stirred among the soldiers. They were glancing around, taking in a new landscape where half a kilometer away, an endless sea of paper roofs began. There were hundreds of thousands of identical Insect buildings. They were pointed pagodas and low halls, like angular fungi. No windows, no doors, just gray paper cells. I flew between them, seeing their laminated surface, rippled and unbroken. I swooped below the height of the Wall, and called again, "Dunlin, can you hear me? It's—"

"Yes. I can hear you."

"Come back to the camp. That's an order!"

He ignored me. Nobody had seen the tunnels so close before unless Insects were dragging them there. Dunlin seemed to be rapt. "I'm going down," he said. "Anyone to follow me?"

"No! Rachiswater!" I searched about for a safe place to land and stop him.

"Don't you want to know what's down there?" Dunlin asked his men. "Let's go!" He drew on his gauntlets, plated with tiny metal squares, and lowered his visor. More than half the men followed his lead and he gave them time to arrange themselves, muster their courage. Merganser backed off, turned around deliberately and began to canter back toward the Wall, which looked just the same on the Insect side.

Dunlin urged his horse forward until he was in the overhang's uneven shadow. A soldier, sword in hand, came to guard him. They looked down into a steep, circular passageway, cut into the brown earth, dark as night.

A cry came from behind them, sound of metal on shell. Swarms of Insects were running from the other tunnels. The Insects moved fast. There were hundreds, the ground was covered. Barbed claws gripped Dunlin's thigh, pulling him from the saddle. With a slash he severed them; they hung on, dripping, and then there were eight more as another two Insects grabbed hold.

No—please god, no! When I got control of myself again I called to Dunlin. With his guard he was fighting for his life, cutting Insects down left and right, a backhand with a long sword, sticking a stiletto knife through the shell heads that came up to the saddle. His heavy horse stepped sideways to crush the Insects gnawing at her hooves. Landing would not be wise. I leaned back on the air and, wheeling, left him.

Merganser had almost made it back to the Wall. His black mare swayed on the scorched grass. I unhooked my spurs from my belt and, legs dangling, glided round and landed in front of him. It knocked the breath out of me, but I ran on and he reined in his horse. I could see the creature's eyes beneath her scallop-edged armor. She may have been bred to deal with Insects, but she wasn't keen on Rhydanne and I thought she would rear.

"Merganser," I panted. "Get off your horse and give me it. Now. *Quickly!*" Merganser gaped at me and threescore emotions appeared on his face—fear was the first and reverence the last. It was easy to recognize me—who else can fly?—but he found it hard to believe that an Eszai would ever cross his path.

He wriggled from the armored faring and jumped down. Wordlessly he passed me the reins and stood aside as I scrambled into the high-backed saddle.

He was a slim young man, brown hair knotted at his neck, and he was tall so the stirrups were set at the right height. I waved my feet about until I found them. I plucked the lance from his grasp and held it over my shoulder.

"What should I do, Comet?" he begged.

"Advise you run like buggery." I jerked the mare's reins left, gave her a hefty kick in the ribs. The smell of Insect blood was strong in the air but she obeyed.

Dunlin pulled his horse round, slashing at brown carapaces and compound eyes. His soldiers were vanishing. They were in a tight group, facing outward, but they were too few. Insects bit at his horse's legs. She stumbled over them and fell. Jaws half a meter long, jagged and razor sharp, stripped the skin from her ribs immediately, the guts falling out. Dunlin rolled from the saddle, on top of a mashed Insect. Although only the head and thorax was left, it clung to him with two remaining arms, wet with yellow paste.

The time it took to reach him was agony for me. I had been flying so long I still wanted to yaw left, pitch right; and here I was on horseback, stuck with just two dimensions; a gallop is far too slow. Standing in the stirrups I let the horse run over Insects at the edge of the fray. They clung to her straps and I poked them with the lance. I'm no lancer, so I used the chromed weapon as a spear, jabbing at Insect thoraxes, rupturing abdomens, tearing their wings. I soon dropped it and drew my ice ax, which has a long haft and a strong serrated point. I hewed a path, swinging the ax and grunting with effort. The movement was familiar; it was like cutting ice steps in a glacier climb. Insect after Insect fell, headless and coiling.

Dunlin recognized me and moved nearer but there were too many Insects in the way. The fyrd gained strength from seeing me struggle toward them and they fought harder still.

"Get out!" I screamed, waving at the Wall. "Move!" Their way was blocked by the horde.

I could see Dunlin pressed between bulbous brown bodies. A mandible was in his leg, slicing to the bone. I saw him put his weight on that leg and the chitin tore out. He raised his visor, blinded by brightness, and stabbed ferociously at an Insect clutching his wing.

His sword skittered over its hard thorax plates. The Insect grasped it, losing a claw, put two other claws over the flat of the blade, and twitched it from his grasp. It snapped at his face. Antennae brushed the back of his neck. Insects behind and in front of him brought him down, kneeling, spidery arms pulling. Little cuts sank in, sawing, wherever the Insects could find a gap. Mandibles snipped. Not a man or horse was left standing; the Insects chewed live flesh.

Dunlin turned on his front, visor down, and covered the back of his neck with plated arms. The Insects stripped his wings and then left him. Some ran toward the Wall, and I hoped Tawny had readied his fyrd. Some picked over the carcasses, their heads inside horses' barrel-ribs.

By the King, a single Insect crouched on complex leg-joints. A blow had cracked its carapace across, pushed the shell into a dent from which cream-yellow liquid oozed, running down between black spines. Its snapped antennae hung down like bent wires—still, it sensed me. It opened its jaws and I saw mouth-parts whirling like fingers inside. I kicked it, and it struck at my foot. Its jaws gashed my boot open from toe to shin. The crack across its thorax opened wider, and beneath I saw a pale wrin-kled membrane, damp with the liquid that was crusting at the edges of the wound. I smashed the ice ax down into its back with so much force that it disappeared to halfway up its hilt. Then I shook it free, my hand dripping. "Next!" I shouted. "Who's next?"

Dunlin. The King. Heroically I thought of leaning from the saddle and lifting him onto the destrier's neck. In reality I am not that strong. I grabbed his belt and dragged his body on the ground while the horse shied sideways. I beat my wings but I still couldn't heave him up. Eventually I had to dismount and tie him to the saddlebow with his own sword belt. It seemed to take a long time, I glanced at the tunnel mouths every second. I became covered in feather fragments and his blood, which was soaking through and turning the chain mail into one big clot. The aftereffects of cat and adrenaline grew oppressive. I thought of what it means to die, which raised feelings I didn't understand. "You're a noble charger," I snif-fled at the mare. "Black is the proper color, don't you think? I think his tomb should be black marble. Come on, now let me return you." The death-scent didn't disturb her, but she was aware of the stickiness as rivers of blood drained down her sides. I talked her into a trot, but the movement jarred

Dunlin's corpse. The corpse stirred and murmured. He was alive!

"Rachiswater? My lord?" No answer. I ripped his cloak, bundled it under his head as a cushion. What should I do? Lowespass—the fortress! I wrapped the reins in my hand, pressed a filed spur to the mare's flank. She ran like a Rhydanne.

CHAPTER TWO

For fifty kilometers around Lowespass the land is as battle-scarred as Tawny's flesh. Lightning can remember when it was green undulating hills, seamed with darker hedges and patches of woodland; the only graze a pale gray promontory on which Lowespass fortress would later be built. Now the fortress is over a thousand years old, and its earthworks fill the valley. The moat is made from a redirected river, the outer walls take in the whole crag. The stables and arms depots are entire villages.

This is rampart warfare—Lowespass is sculpted, the ground churned up. There are six corrals, some with multiple entrances and holding pens; palisaded tracks, ditches, mounds, ashlar walls, some with iron spikes. All act to slow the Insect advance, and soldiers are constantly rebuilding them, changing them, as little by little, they are overthrown.

Lightning is familiar with every centimeter of ground. He remembers the construction of even the oldest embankments—five-meter-high ramparts now like lines of molehills, and trenches that are now shallow and grassy. The earth has been dug up and the valley remodeled, not once but again and again, so I think that in Lightning's memory the land itself seems to move—to throw up artificial banks and crease into hillforts, white scars soon sprouting green—to sink artificial pitfalls and flood-land of its own accord.

Fyrd train in the tortured landscape which one generation prepares for the battles of the next. They cull Insects and clear the Paperlands. We call Insect pulp "paper," but it doesn't have all the properties of paper; it is rigid, inflexible, and the Insect spit that holds the chewed paste together has a fire-retardant effect. Our wooden buildings are burned when abandoned to stop the Insects chewing them, but Insects use anything they can find; fabric and bone as well. The fyrd wield axes and set patches of pitch-fire to clear Paperlands, but it doesn't burn easily.

Lowespass terrain is like a board game—three-dimensional, in marble and green velvet. This land we've lost to the Insects, and won again, and lost—so many times. Dunlin knew that it was originally farmland, as tranquil and productive as the golden fields of Awia. But I could never make Dunlin appreciate how long ago that was. He was incapable of sensing the vastness of time that had passed since then, although he trod every day along roads that ran through the living rooms of deserted villages and over ramparts raised from the bones of the Fifthland fyrd. Dunlin was adamant that the land could be occupied peacefully again, if only it was reclaimed. We strive for that, of course, but perhaps if we won, the fyrd's screams and the clash of battle would stay in the Eszai's memories and Lowespass would seem unfamiliar without adversaries.

The Zascai soldiers' concept of the Lowespass front is even more limited than Dunlin's. This is a valley where terrible things happen. Every fable and every childhood threat hangs on the Insects' jaws and the way they move inspires every nightmare.

I see the Lowespass landscape in yet another way. There's bloodshed, sure, but I'm also grabbed by insane joy of freedom when I fly there. The valley alters dramatically for me, but by the hour. Clouds chase over it, cumulus spins into wave-clouds beyond the Wall, but at the moment the western sky is clear and warm. Every morning the sun rises out of a mass of peaks behind peaks stepped like shark's teeth but sharper.

In the Darkling mountains Oriole River starts as a torrent and widens as it flows east through Lowespass, to Midelspass then the coast. At the place where we use the river to undermine the Wall, the Oriole is so fast-flowing that the waterweed looks as if it has been combed. Crayfish live there and, like little Insects, they have fed on dead soldiers' flesh. Then it flows into an earthwork, and at the foot of Fortress Crag the river is channeled twenty meters deep. The Darkling foothills are tamer in Lowespass, the valley is lined with supply roads. Mass graves are covered by woodland but burned bone fragments rise to the plow. Farmsteads built on latrines of the eighteenth century fyrd are very fertile.

Ramparts and hollows, which make all the difference in a battle, are hard to see from the air because they are often evenly grassed over. I flew low and my shadow flicked over them, changing size. I wished I were not the only one who could see Lowespass from the air. I have tried to design machines that glide so that other people could fly, but I have not had much success. I guess that if god wanted us to design gliders, it wouldn't have given us wings.

The door burst open and Staniel paced into my room, Lightning behind him spreading his hands apologetically. Staniel was taken aback by me sitting cross-legged on my bedding, which was on the stone floor, not the bed. The aroma of sandalwood incense and the fact that I was halfway through writing an Imperial report also unnerved him.

He kept his head bowed, gaze fixed on one stone slab. His chest was almost tubular, very narrow, and he covered it with one hand on his breastbone in an act of supplication that was nearly a bow. He faltered, "Please. Dunlin—how is he?"

"Well . . ."

"I have to know how he is! Rayne won't give me any answers!"

"You've seen. He hasn't changed. He's still in the hospital. Rayne is still tending him, and he's still unconscious."

"He'll wake up, won't he?"

"I've been that wounded and survived."

"But for a mortal?"

Lightning raised his voice. "I don't think Jant wants to be disturbed at the moment."

"Apologies, Comet. But . . . Supposedly the Eszai assist us at times of tragedy."

"What do you want me to do?"

"Dunlin's going to die, isn't he?"

"I don't know. Yes."

Staniel's clothes were clean and pressed, as befitted his status at all times except after a battle, when he was expected to be as filthy as the rest of us. His long, corn-gold hair was still damp; he had been sitting in the river upstream of the overheated soldiers who crowded the river bank to bank. I had forded the river in a chaos of spray, blood, mane, and hooves, and behind me a whispering started that the King was dead.

I was grimy and had a few broken feathers, Lightning's mantle was stained with dust from his ride back, but already Staniel had managed to find black textured silk, the color of mourning. Buzzard feathers were tangled in his hair, from a thin silver crown set with lapis lazuli. His blue eyes were bloodshot from rubbing them; he looked more tearful than a teenager. Lightning laid a hand on his shoulder, said, "We don't have to discuss this until the morning, Your Majesty."

"Stop calling me that! Honestly, Archer." Staniel twisted the silk tassels of his long sleeves, leaving sweat stains. "To follow me is disagreeable enough, but then you say, 'Your Majesty,' 'my lord,' constantly! How can *you* call *me* 'lord'?"

Lightning didn't say anything, but I could sense the intensity of his disapproval directed at the Prince.

I repeated, "What do you want me to do?"

"Save him."

"Rayne is doing all she can; she doesn't need my help." Or respect it. "What in Darkling do you expect me to do?"

"I don't know . . . I just don't know." He rubbed his face with both hands, because to wake would be the best escape from grief.

The Archer tried again with a tone of complaint: "There's coffee in the Solar. Genya has laid out some bread and meat. The men have eaten, I don't see why we should fast."

Staniel started at the name of Genya, like a child who has been told there is a dragon in the drawing room. He was used to me, but had never encountered a female Rhydanne. I had sent couriers to her and had persuaded her to provide food for the exhausted, wounded fyrd.

"Genya . . ." he said, with mixed fascination and repulsion.

Anger flared—I was so weary. I have seen the same emotions on the faces of people meeting me. Often fear and aversion has made city people turn on me with insults at best, then arrows. I fought back in my own way, but I have thicker skin than Genya, and she was very violent. "Careful!" I told Staniel. "If you trouble her she will scratch your eyes out."

"We have to keep a vigil for my brother."

"We'll be more use as commanders if we eat and bloody sleep! My lord."

"I can't eat."

"It will help you feel better."

"Maybe I don't want to feel better."

Lightning took a deep breath. "I cannot believe the dynasty of Rachiswater has at its end produced someone as spineless as yourself! This is a terrible situation, of course I admit that, but are you going to stand up and confront it? You're grown from Avernwater, the lineage that held the throne and the walls strong for five hundred years since my line ended. The Rachiswater branch grew so powerful and prolific that it became another tree. I find it hard to accept that one of the leaves on the twigs of the branches of that tree can be so different from the rest. I am not having kin, no matter how distant, shunning the responsibility placed on him by means of birth and tutelage at a time when the whole of Awia needs him. I don't see anything I recognize as Rachiswater in you! Your grandfather Sarcelle would never have cowered in the pavilion the way you have since you came to the front."

Staniel glanced at me for help. He stood his ground, and I took pity on him because I do not agree with Lightning's notion that men should be compared to each other. Staniel was no warrior—a coward, in fact—but I had noticed his grandiloquence. With time I might turn him into a prosperous diplomat.

I said, "Calm down, Lightning."

"No. For example, Staniel has disturbed your rest to ask about His Majesty without bothering to thank you for bringing Dunlin back in the first place. He is so thoroughly—"

"Enough!" I saw that Staniel had begun to tremble with confusion. If his nerves had been frayed before they were ripped to shreds now. I wanted to give him a chance to speak, but stopping Lightning mid-rant is as difficult as halting a bolted destrier. I reached out to Staniel, and he gained composure as he shook my hand, although with another little shudder as my long fingers enclosed his hand completely.

"Yes. Certainly. Yes . . . Comet," he announced. "Awia commends you greatly for rescuing my brother; it was an act of great courage at no little risk. I have inscribed my profound gratitude in a missive to the Emperor, which unfortunately Lightning won't yet let me dispatch; perhaps you could convey it yourself. Thank you also for averting the casualties of those fyrd who would otherwise have been dispatched to retrieve my brother's body."

If words on paper could be transformed to a token of gratitude in cash I'd be more delighted.

"Where were you?" inquired Lightning.

"Um. Press conference."

"What?"

"And I also apologize on behalf of Dunlin, that he transgressed your unambiguous orders and rode into the Paperlands." Staniel stood nervously, his blond wings limp at his back, fading to white at the round ends of the feathers. He had thin gold bands on them, like the rings on his tapering fingers.

I shouldn't listen to Staniel's apologies, and I know the Emperor won't. Dunlin had no excuse; his plight is an example of what happens when Zascai no matter how blue-blooded disobey Eszai on the battlefield. On the other hand, I didn't want to complicate the situation. There was plenty of time to argue in the following months, rather than at the King's deathbed.

"I accept your apologies," I said. "But more of this later."

"Will you come to the Solar?" he asked, and there was a tiny noise out in the corridor.

Staniel froze, mouthed, "What's that?" I sensed the feeling of intensity caused by another presence.

Someone was listening very quietly, with a concentration that thickened the air. I caught the faintest odor of bracken and alcohol. I leaped across the room, flung the door wide. We ran out into the corridor but there was nobody there.

"Genya," I said.

Staniel repeated, "Genya Dara."

The first time our paths cross in ten years. It's all right, I told myself. Nobody knows.

A crescent moon became brighter as the surrounding sky dimmed. Soldiers' muted conversation drifted through the corridors and courts of square gray Lowespass. The akontistai-javelin men; lancers and archers, sarissai and cavalry alike were waiting for the latest news of Dunlin's progress to be announced.

If I hadn't been so busy, it would have been my duty to walk among the soldiers and talk to them in order to gauge their opinions. Tawny and Staniel were now set to this task, Tawny with the Plainslands fyrd, and Staniel in the Outer Ward. The Outer Ward was a walled grassy enclosure studded with limestone outcrops. The Awian infantry had raised their tents where the soil was deeper, by the thick curtain wall. Most were asleep, but some sat in groups talking in subdued voices about their companions who had been left out in the field.

Primroses grew down by the river, and after Slake Crossroads Battle ninety years ago, their yellow flowers had bloomed with pink petals. The soldiers picked these in remembrance of the fyrd who had gone before, because I once wrote it was our blood that stained the flowers, back in 1925. It was strange to see a strong man, weathered and bristly from an outdoor life, with a primrose bloom threaded through the links of his chain mail.

I walked around the keep, trying to dispel a vague feeling that something was missing. It was a sensation, not a conscious thought, but it was very familiar and I knew it was worsening. I would become more and more jumpy, until eventually I would have no other choice but to lock myself in my sparse room and take some more cat. Everywhere I went people asked me how Dunlin was, whether he was still alive, and how long the fyrd might be expected to stay in the cold fortress.

I passed a window left open, and I knew Genya had been here. I could smell her. Pacing along an austere colonnade, which turned sharp corners every hundred meters as it followed the curtain wall, I had the prickly feeling that someone was watching. I called her name and the feeling subsided. Silently, she had gone.

I didn't blame her for wanting to watch from a distance, and I was pleased that she should want to observe me at all. Possibly she was playing a game with her own emotions as well as mine. She was teasing her fear, creeping as close as she could to the edge of the abyss. She was also placing a strong trial on my desire. I kept walking, as she sped through concealed corridors. I imagined her climbing over the ridges of broken-tiled roofs, past cisterns, pantries, cluttered kitchens; running through halls where men looked up in surprise. The image made me growl: *I am an Eszai. This sort of lechery won't do.* But I knew that if I wanted to, I could catch her.

I came to the church, which was part of the main complex inside the imposing walls. As I walked past the glass-paneled door, Ata Dei emerged from the gloom inside. I immediately stopped thinking about Genya; Ata's hair was a beautiful distraction. There was hardly any light in the square church porch, but her hair still shone.

"Hello cat-eyes," she said, looking through me. I had thought her face to be shaded, but as she strode nearer I saw that the shadow was really a bruise. It covered the bridge of her nose and one eye, swollen from lower lid to cheekbone. The bruise was dark, and pinpoint red showed vivid where the skin had been broken.

"Did you get that in the battle?" I asked.

Her bloodless lips twisted. "Oh, aye. But it was nothing to do with the Insects. Mist hit me. I wish I didn't need him!"

"Why did he hit you?" I asked warily. I knew better than to get involved in a fight between husband and wife. Anyone caught in the crossfire between Ata and the Sailor fares worse than either of them. Long practice had made their sparring into an art form, and I didn't know the rules.

Ata spat. "Because Dunlin and his guard rode straight past us. I say, 'Let's follow,' because it looks to me like he needs backup, and you're telling Tawny the same thing. Mist says, 'No, stay here.' He's frankly fucking awkward. He's been alive too long. So I say, 'You stupid bastard, I'll do it then,' and I'm just about to call the Islanders when he flings out a fist and smacks me in the face."

"Ow."

"I tried to stab the dim git but he parried and then I realized the fyrd were watching. I thought you would intercept Dunlin; you were quicker than a curse in a courtroom."

"I couldn't stop a charge." Wingless humans, like Ata, and the Awians, who are winged but flightless, will never understand that while I can view the battlefield from the air, I can't control it.

"Aye," she breathed. "Well, I hope you're proud of yourself." I stayed mute until she added, "Dunlin requested eight thousand troops. If you'd mustered them from the Plainslands rather than the coast like he told you they'd have been here by now. We were short of at least a thousand men this morning, and I doubt the sanity of his plan if we had twice as many."

I was wary of Ata; her mind set us apart. I'm smart, but not so farsighted. My best strategy is to stay out of her vicinity. She has a mind like a steel trap—people are either in or out. Those caught in the middle when it springs shut are generally cut in half.

"If you had followed Dunlin, you would have lost the Island fyrd," I said.

"Well, I know that there were too few lancers, and Lightning may infer the same. Let us hope the Emperor doesn't guess."

"I hope you don't inform him."

She smirked and said, "What are you doing here, anyway?"

I waved my hands in the air vaguely. "Organizing things."

She indicated the church door. "If you're looking for a place to shoot up, this is not it."

"I'm clean," I lied automatically. When found out, I suffer intense remorse and indignation—a weird feeling of wanting to crawl and apologize as well as rebel and confront. The danger of being found guilty became a pleasure for me a long time ago, and now I can't quit.

"Aye, right. You're not even walking in a straight line." She folded her arms, which detracted from the impression of motherly authority it was intended to give because it also gave her an impressive cleavage. I told her she looked wonderful, but she diminished the compliment with a shrug. She put no effort into her appearance but her hair was still mesmerizing. She had pure white hair, almost translucent against her tanned skin. Her hair hung straight down her back and over it she wore a maline veil, twisted into a wreath.

"How's the King?" she asked.

"I don't know."

"For an official response, that is completely crap, Jant Shira. I thought you had more imagination."

"He's dying."

"Aye. Mmm. And without children, the royal fool. How will King Staniel repel the Insects? Death by sonnet?"

I giggled, wrapping my arms around my waist, a gesture which Ata scrutinized until I boiled with humiliation. I hopped from foot to foot, feeling slightly strung out.

Ata joined the Castle Circle by marrying the Sailor, becoming immortal four hundred years before me. Those who dislike Mist have said that he proposed to her because he was anxious she would Challenge him for his place in the Circle. By marrying Ata he sated her craving for eternal life, but the wedding also guaranteed that she would be nearby to quarrel with him for the rest of his existence. And like the other Eszai who have joined the Circle through marriage, Ata is dependent on her spouse's continued Circle membership for her immortality.

Ata's shirt was diaphanous, pale blue gauze with a layer of saffron yellow beneath it. What I took to be a skirt was really wide trousers; from her slack leather belt hung a rapier with a basket hilt so fine it was steel filigree. She had been frozen at age thirty-five for six hundred years.

"Watch out, Jant. The last thing the Emperor needs is a translator who's taken so many mind-expanding drugs that he can't fit it back in."

"Leave me alone."

Ata shrugged, and did so, saying, "Your Rhydanne mistress has seen you. She wants to know what you're doing."

"You've spoken to Genya?" I said, too hastily. She nodded, and walked away.

Rayne had a room on the far side of Lowespass keep, which she ordered to be built within the keep when it was constructed. She tried to keep the room supplied with medicines, gauze and water. When she worked at the front, she stayed in the fortress and the wounded were brought to her.

I thought about Dunlin, and I felt, rather than thought, about cat. It seemed that the best thing to do was pay Rayne a visit, for the sake of the kingdom of Awia and my own state of health.

In the Inner Ward I moved syncopated through sleeping snarls of people. I avoided them, feeling uneasy and empty inside. The hard muscles moved under my skin, my belt pulled across to the very last notch, the stringy flat arms of my wings hugging and rustling against my back.

Boots handmade in Morenzia clicked on the worn cobbles, the beads in my hair bounced off my backside. Jackdaws sped between the towers, sparks in negative. Good for them, I thought. This reminded me—what am I walking for? It only took a couple of seconds to struggle airborne and join them, and then I quietly let myself into Rayne's hospital.

Dunlin was lying on a plain bed against the gray wall of the first room, which had no windows and no decoration. Firelight glowed through a nearby doorway, the bustle of servants preparing food and medicines, and soldiers moaning, screaming. I closed the door and noiselessly watched over the King.

The signature of pain in Dunlin's face changed his whole appearance. Lines between his eyebrows and a furrowed forehead made him look fearsome; his body was braced against the pain. His short hair was matted with dried blood, and Rayne had cut it even shorter on one side, to sew up a gash along his neck from earlobe to collarbone. His lips were dry, with blood at the sides of his mouth. The rings had been stripped from his hands, which lay like dead leaves on the cover, and he wore the padded white shirt that lancers have for protection under their armor. Nobility was written in his face there with the pain.

The other thing I noticed was the scent, not of blood but of time. No matter how old people are when death is approaching, there is the smell of age. It clings to clothes and lingers in rooms, an earthy tang which made me whimper. The King's eyes flickered open, drugged and bloodshot.

"Don't move," I advised, in Awian. "We thought we lost you, and I'm not sure exactly what Rayne's done."

"Is . . . ?"

"Don't try to speak either," I added softly. "I can't tell if you can understand me, but you should know that Staniel's beside himself. He's so highly strung he could pass for a Rhydanne. I tried to calm him down. Lightning just intimidates him."

Dunlin croaked for a bit and then coughed. His square face was dead ashen under a leathery tan.

"I hope the Insects take years to recover," I said vaguely. "I'd like to think it was all worth it."

He coughed until he could speak, managed, "This is . . . *agony.*"

"Yeah," I said. "It'll stop soon. You're lucky."

I leaned closer to hear him as he said, "I wanted to be immortal," and a smile played across his face without touching his lips at all. There was a silence. What could I say? I felt a creeping guilt that he will die and I could not. But the world isn't fair; it was only in the Emperor's power to make a man immortal. I contemplated whether to tell him about the Shift. I couldn't stand the risk he might still be capable of ridicule or disbelief.

"This pain . . ." Dunlin whispered.

I thought about the trouble I would be in if anyone found out. But who would know? His crusted eyes were fading; he was outwardly oblivious. Blood seeping through the sheet sealed it to the cuts in his sturdy throat, which armor had left unprotected. His wings were fragments of bone with some muscle still clinging. They shocked me.

"There's the Shift . . ." I ventured.

"Mm . . . ?"

"It's another land. Another world, I mean. If you die here, you can stay there."

"Mm. Really?" There was the smile again, more sardonic than regal. "How?"

I clicked open my compass, took out the folded paper. "With

this," I said. Dunlin sighed. He didn't have enough energy left to try to understand. He didn't care.

"It's immortality, of a sort."

"Then do what you can."

Lightning might boast of a golden age under Teale Micawater, but I couldn't recall any time when Awia was as well treated and trusted, as under this King. I bit my nail to the quick, stood mournfully feeling like the last of the wine at a funeral. I spoke to Dunlin for a few more minutes and he dictated his will, which I copied word for word onto the sheet.

On a low table by the bedside was a pewter cup, a pitcher of water, and a plate with a sponge. Dunlin's ring was there, blue agate set into a silver bevel, engraved with the seal of Rachiswater.

I sniffed at the cup; it was half full of liquid that smelled of cinnamon. I tipped in the powder from the paper wrap, stirred it with a finger, and replaced the cup.

That was compassion, I think. I justified my action by recalling the ending of *The Complete Herbal*, which I owned when I lived in Hacilith: "It is our duty to correct illness, to alleviate suffering and ease pain; a noble duty." Rayne wrote that book hundreds of years before I was born.

I don't know whether it is correct to ease pain by hastening death, but at the time it seemed right. He was certain to die, and I wanted it to be with more dignity. I couldn't bear to see the King, who had always been my friend, so altered by agony that he seemed a different person. I told myself that had he been Eszai, he would have survived. If we could have taken him to Rayne's hospital in the Castle, then I could have done more for him, but recently in Lowespass there was a shortage of everything, and the dregs of medicines were god knows how old. I hope I never have to make the choice again, but if so, I would do the same, and I remember leaving him with a light conscience and a smile of goodbye.

Compassion? Regicide? The question is always in my mind and will only be resolved if I am found out. If that happened, I would have to resign my place in the Castle. I'll fall over that hurdle when I come to it.

Only two beds in the next room; on one I recognized an Awian lady who was paper-pale and only stirred when I kissed her hand. The other body was a shallow mess of mandible cuts criss-crossed with bandages. On the floor, lying full length or leaning against the wall, were roughly fifty soldiers. Two tried to stand, but I waved them down again as kindly as I could. I went through to Rayne's private room, slipped past her and she sighed. "Dunlin's asleep," I informed her cheerfully.

"At las'. It's good t'see you, snake-eyes." I hugged her, the soft covering of fat on an old body. She had a long, stained brown satin dress, and a bloodstained apron. Her wrinkled face just reached the level of my chest.

I glanced at the shelves cluttered with little bottles and vials, sticky cordials and spirits, powders and pillboxes. The light was too dim for me to read the browning ink on their ancient labels and as I peered over her shoulder Rayne realized what I was doing and pushed me away. "No!"

"Please. I really need some cat." My voice slipped into a hateful whine.

"How is Staniel?" She tried to change the subject.

"Put me together a fix and I'll tell you."

"Already? Damn i', Jant. I thought you had enough to las' you the res' of the century."

"What will you trade?" I asked.

Rayne gave me her *you're-not-human-are-you?* look. I dislike being stared at. With feeling I said, "The Circle is really going to need me tomorrow and I'll be no use by then if I don't have some soon." A familiar tension was settling around my eyes; my joints and back ached. Soon I would be able to add shivers and nausea, at which point I would probably panic and fly to Hacilith in an injudicious attempt to score some more. "Can I help you at all? What can I make for the hospital?"

"More birch bark ointmen'?"

"Done."

"Aqua·absynthii?" ·

"Done."

"Papaver?"

"Yes."

"Moly?"

"Ah—done."

"An' you can cross my palm wi' silver, as well." Rayne flashed her scrimshaw grin. I kissed her cheek, dashed across and picked a clear glass bottle from the shelf. The label said: *scolopendium, 10%*. That's Centipede Leaf Fern, which in Hacilith is called cat. I don't recommend that anyone try it. Behind me, Rayne made small talk but I was too preoccupied to reply. She watched me with professional concern. "Do y'think i'could be a good way t'die?" she asked dreamily.

"I don't know! I never have!"

"Do y'know there's a spli' second of peace when t'heart stops and before t'brain congeals? Tha's when you no'ice how noisy your body always was. Y'see a las' graying picture frozen through your eyes, and slowly lose comprehension of wha' i'is. Even fas' dying has got t'seem slow."

I sighed. "Rayne, this is becoming an obsession."

"Jant, don' you talk t'me about obsession."

"I'm an addict, not an obsessive. Please don't talk to me about death."

I searched through little velvet-lined drawers for a clean glass syringe. I pushed the needle through the seal of the phial and pulled clear liquid back into the barrel. My resistance broke down and the symptoms overwhelmed me. The muscles in my arms twitched, and shivers ran down my back, ruffling my feathers. I settled my wings and folded them in a fluid movement. My hands remained rock steady; I watched them making these precise actions, my mind elsewhere.

Rayne's assistants bustled back and forth outside the door to her room. I paused to calculate how much. Some. More. This is not an exact science.

If I double what I usually take, it should be enough.

I untied a black silk scarf from around my neck. It was fairly ragged, but I twisted it into a tourniquet and looped it round my arm. A vein swelled up underneath. Then I licked my arm and watched distantly as the point dented the skin and broke it. I loosened the makeshift tourniquet and pushed the plunger home. A bead of blood and cat welled up. The shot hit hard. I decided it would be a good idea to lie on the floor.

I smiled, I was happy with the floor. The worn carpet was warm and bits of me were merging into it. Rayne just looked worried. I tried to reassure her but I couldn't manage the shape of the words. Some. More. Way, way too much.

Now I am not my problem. I smiled faintly and fainted, smiling.

I was jolted into the Shift harder than ever before. I was so badly disoriented that I had to stand with my hands over my eyes, thinking: oh god. Oh god, oh god, Jant, you are really going to regret this.

As I lowered my hands the brightness of Epsilon came

through. I was standing in the marketplace. Sweet air was ravaged by the shouts of stallholders.

There were stalls with sacks of spices, jangling curtains of lazulite jewelry, brass and glass ornaments on striped rugs, pyramids of cloth rolls, incense; stalls with meats and vegetables, and some things which could have been meat or vegetables, half-rotten fruits, cages with live animals in, which flapped and pecked.

There was the sound of hooves as quandries rocketed past along narrow cobbled streets, pulled by teams of four whorses. Humans and some naked Equinnes sat at a round table outside a café, supping wine. Jeopards—leopards with square spots— purred on the City Hall steps or sat hunched beneath stalls waiting for tidbits. Jeopards ran sleek and fast, but only in straight lines, as they couldn't see curves, which meant that Epsilon citizens had to spend a fair amount of time rescuing them from the fountain.

Two men crouched against a stained white marble wall, behind a blanket spread with bronzes, strass, and tombac chains, rings, all cheap stuff. One of them was smoking, and I could smell his apple tobacco, which above all made me believe in the reality of the Shift. I was here, and still alive.

Living dirigibles floated and jostled low in the sky. A fiber-toothed tiger prowled embarrassed through the crowd, receiving gleeful pats and strokes down the length of its striped back. A couple of children looked scared, then pointed and laughed as they realized its teeth were made of string.

I waited for a long time, while people and Constant Shoppers milled about in the marketplace. Tine strolled up and down, wire baskets on their polished tortoise backs. I watched the archaic and spicy bazaar, where men thumbed dog-eared fortune cards and the edges of secondhand sabres. The market sprawled beneath a gleaming building, a complex of meteoric chromium, concrete, leafy restaurants, and elevators carrying shrieking kids.

I wait, I wait, I wait; and just as I was thinking my plan must have failed, I saw him. I sprinted across the square and took his arm. Dunlin was standing, spear-straight, with his hands over his face, where I had appeared at the edge of the market. At my touch, he jumped in panic. I had made myself more powerfully built, tanned, with a dark pinstripe suit and some bronze spines in auburn hair. It took a little rearrangement of these improvements before he recognized me. "Comet?"

"King Rachiswater."

"What happened?"

"You died. I think you'd better sit down." I led him across to the little fountain and propped him on its low wall. He was gaping at the noisy market like a fish in thin air. "Welcome to the Shift," I said.

He stopped gaping at the market and began to gape at me. "Remember Lowespass?" I prompted.

He flexed his arms, realizing that all the pain had ceased. "I didn't believe there was an afterlife," he murmured.

"There isn't." I smiled. It's a human story used to calm frightened children. "This is the Shift." I gestured at the market. "The Squantum Plaza, in the City of Epsilon." Dunlin, a paranoid gaze in his eyes, looked at me with an expression that said I had explained precisely nothing. I was afraid what his reaction might be, so I dropped my hand to the hilt of my dagger. "There's a drug called cat. It's a painkiller. If you take too much, it lets you come here. But I'm afraid that for mortals, it's a one-way trip."

"I see . . . I think. Shira! I'll *never* see Rachis again?"

I bowed my head. There will always be a time when mortals have to die and those left behind them suffer a sense of loss, although they lose only one person from their lives. Dunlin had forfeited everything, and I felt the inconsolable depth of his loss; it even muted the tumult of the market.

"You'll get used to it," I said. "Some things are the same. Good company. Food. Women. Insects. I know you'll have questions."

"That's the understatement of the century."

"Don't dwell on it. I'll introduce you to someone who can answer." I indicated some golden biotic buildings on the possibly north side of the Plaza and we began to walk toward them through the crowd and between the stalls. Although still stifling and savannah-bright, the shadows were lengthening to late evening, which seemed strange because when I arrived it was only midday. I couldn't tell the time from these dual suns; I had a watch but it melted.

"You look different," Dunlin said.

"Yes, well. If you were half Rhydanne, wouldn't you want to change your appearance?"

"Do you mean we can look like whatever we want?"

"No, no. I can because I'm not really here. I'm still in Lowespass and I'm afraid I'll have to return there shortly. You . . . . can't go back."

"There's nothing to go back to."

"My lord."

Dunlin led me aside into the shade of a paper lantern stall. God, he was strong. "Did I just hear you say there are Insects here too?" he demanded.

"There are Insects almost everywhere."

Dunlin ground his teeth, infuriated. "Who else is here? When do you come here? Why didn't we know?"

I shrugged. "The Fourlands has locked itself in a darkened room," I said, with melancholy so profound it could have been rehearsed.

He shook me. "I'm stranded here, you total bastard! You callous immortal bastard!"

"Let go! I don't have much time left!"

It was evident that Dunlin was stronger than me even here. Physically more powerful, and he was taking to the Shift like a goat to Scree. I had assumed practice would make me more proficient, until I saw the wild light glittering in his eyes. I had never seen anything approaching Dunlin's vitality, especially for a dead man. I began to be a little afraid of him.

At that time, Felicitia was working in Keziah's bar. After landing the King of Awia in the Shift, I thought it was hardly kind to leave him with Felicitia, but Felicitia had the advantage of coming from the same world. I mean, if Dunlin hasn't a life of his own yet, at least he can tag along with someone else's. I couldn't resist introducing them so I asked Dunlin to follow me, through the shopping mall and beyond the Tine's quarter, to the low thatched building of a bar called the Bullock's Bollocks. Dunlin cheered up when he saw the pub, since it looked superficially like a Fourlands inn, and inside I installed him on one of the wooden benches around a scarred table.

I found Felicitia propping up the bar. "Jant!" he exclaimed, raced across, and embraced me. The bar fell over. "Have a drink, on the house, on the rocks! What would you like?"

"Get off!" Bad memories made my pulse race. "If you do that again I'll rip you wing from wing!"

"A kiss, at least, for old times' sake."

"There never were any old times!"

"Oh, not just any old times, those precious hours we spent together in Hacilith, my negligent boy." He tried to pinch my bum but I was too fast for him.

Dunlin was staring with an expression of bleak despair, his powerful arms crossed over his chest. Before I could compose myself Felicitia was pulling pints of beer for us. He was making the most of his life in the Shift, had sequined stockings, layered hair, and moved like well-shagged smoke.

"Would you like pizza?" he said.

"No." I try to eat as little as possible in the Shift, at least since the Tine took over the burger chains.

"Automato sauce and monsterella cheese? Angstchovies?" I shook my head and he sighed dramatically. "You're so *thin* these days."

"You should see what I look like in the Fourlands now."

"Would that I could, my lascivious lad! And who is this?" he exclaimed, pretending to notice Dunlin for the first time.

"Dunlin Rachiswater. The King of Awia."

Felicitia smirked, realized I was serious. "Can't be. Tanager's the ruling family," he said in a stage whisper.

"In your time, but not now."

"Oh, Jant, my forgetful friend, you never keep me up to date." He dropped a neat curtsey to Dunlin, who put one hand over his eyes. "How did a Rachiswater get here?"

"Same way we did. My lord, this is Felicitia Aver-Falconet, from Hacilith. I . . . ah . . . That's Hacilith two hundred years ago." Dunlin said nothing, although he must have been aware of Felicitia's gaze on his biceps.

"Jant, is this someone you're setting on me to stop me having a good time? I'm dead and I intend to keep partying."

"I hoped you'd act as a tour guide," I admitted.

"Whatever you ask, my beneficent boy." Felicitia was wearing a white miniskirt and shiny boots which added ten centimeters to his tiny figure. He had a chemise of stretchy lacy material, which clung to his little muscled chest. "You can come with me *wherever*," he added to Dunlin.

"The Aver-Falconets are an Awian family," Dunlin stated.

Felicitia grinned. "So I am," he said. He spread little brown wings, stretching the blouse thin as it rode up over them. The feathers were highlighted with silver and cinnabar red.

Dunlin was shocked. "I wish to return home."

"Can't be done." Felicitia minced over and looked him up and down—although more up than down as Felicitia was so short. "Jant and I go back a long way," he said. "Two hundred years! Well, and I've been holding a candle for him all that time. Two hundred years and I never even got my fingers burned."

I said, "This is hardly important at the moment."

"He's so *shy*. But yes! We should drink! We should celebrate! Keziah—beer for his Kingness. Whiskey for the Rhydanne. Pour yourself a tomato juice."

"Don't mind if I do," said the lizard.

"Happy Demise-day, Your Highness."

"Jant. I should skin you alive."

The King found himself immersed in raucous camaraderie, while dusk gathered and snow began to build up against the bull's-eye–paned windows.

I was halfway through explaining the Shift to Dunlin, when the heat-blistered door shuddered open, the bar fell quiet, and my voice rang out loud in the sudden silence. A Tine lumbered in and walked to the bar, creaking the floorboards. Keziah handed him a liter-jug of red juice which he downed in one, received a refill, and seated himself on the table we were using, squashing the ashtray and levering the far end of the table high into the air.

The Tine had transparent plates like flexible glass sewn into his arms and legs, surrounded by thick seams of scar tissue, and at every movement his muscles' pink mass stretched and smeared against them. Blue tattooed dots, the size of pennies, ran in lines over his face; his silver-white hair streaked a wispy blue and purple, starched into long spines; and at least twenty thin silver rings pierced the edge of one ear.

He was easily the biggest creature in the bar, and his arms and legs were knotted muscle-columns, his only clothing a thin blue silk rag wound round his waist. His back was covered by the round, highly polished plates of his oval shell, like a tortoise shell. A crack across it had been badly riveted together, and the bronze studs were turning green with verdigris. Wires crusted with dried lymph, and bound into a bundle with yellow and red tape, ran from under it and disappeared into his spine at the small of his back.

His eyes were pale blue, no differentiation between pupil, iris and sclera. They were fixed on us, as with a deep, ursine voice he grunted, "More tourists."

"Let's go," I said.

"I'm not a tourist," Dunlin answered, his blood heated by the interruption. I pulled at his sleeve. First thing to learn in the Shift, Tine are dangerous.

"What the fuck're you then?" He squinted down, eyes like azure pebbles. Awia will mean as much to a Tine as the Cult of the Perforated Lung does to us.

"The Sovereign of Awia."

"Yeah. A tourist. Get lost before I spill your guts."

No one in the bar had made a sound since the Tine appeared. Silence deepened as every creature surreptitiously listened in on our show. The Tine snarled, showing myriad, laniary teeth.

"Dunlin," I put in quickly, raizing a hand as the Tine reached out. "Know when to back down or you won't last two minutes. Tine," I addressed him. "I'm an immortal. *Deathless*. And I'm protecting him. So just fucking try it, beast."

The creature lumbered down onto talons and knees. His bulk pushed the table aside as he gravely licked my boot toe with a tattooed tongue. "Lord. Am Pierce. Am Tine. Drink basilic vein blood, eat spleen, have your testicles for breakfast, tourist. Not that y'have any, hur hur."

"How did you do that?" said the Sovereign of Awia.

"Immortals don't fit into their creed. So I usually get worshiped—or attacked. Beliefs are stronger here than in the Fourlands, but don't ask what the Tine believe in; you don't want to know. What are you doing here?" I asked the brute.

"Got thrown out of the Aureate," he rasped. "The Cult of the Clotted Artery's a heretical sect. No good slaying here; can't make enough for a cut of meat."

"I'm sorry to hear that," Dunlin said calmly.

"Do you know you smell of streaky bacon?" said Pierce.

Now that trouble had passed, Felicitia reappeared and started dealing out drinks. I think Dunlin started to relax, although that may have been a bit much to ask. How could I help him further, now he was stranded here with a lizard, a Tine and a gay Awian? I decided to give him my palace, which I had built over many, many Shifts, a long and painful project.

"The least I can do is give you Sliverkey," I said. I unpinned my chart from the wall behind the bar and laid it over the table. My outline flickered. I began to feel the pull. With careful timing I said, "You can have this as well. It took me decades, it's a map of Epsilon. It's the only map of Epsilon." My outline began to flicker rapidly and started to dissolve. "Dunlin!" I shouted. "Goodbye!" We rushed to shake hands, but mine were like smoke and Dunlin reached straight through them.

I looked up with a half-smile and faded out halfway through a bow. Dunlin's last connection with the Fourlands, severed.

CHAPTER THREE

I figured that if I could move my little finger I would eventually be able to move my arm, then my whole body and
thus be able to stand up. I sent frantic mental messages
down my outstretched arm, but the hand—curled up, skeletal
and bluish—refused to move. The syringe was still hanging in
the crook of my arm, rooted in my bloodstream. I felt as if it had
poured another soul into me, an unreal one, leaching out my
quick colors, leaving me chemical.

The thought of this angered me so much that I twitched my
fucking little finger, then the rest of my hand, my aching arm,
and sat up in an unplanned movement that made the room
whirl.

Rayne was still sitting in her rocking chair, watching with
timeless patience. She called on god avidly on my behalf. I told
her to shut up.

She said, "Jant, that's not a habi', tha's a suicide attemp'."

"Actually I have much to live for."

She said, "Jant, wha' you used was practic'ly clear."

"Do you think impure is safer?"

"Perhaps eterni'y's a poor escape from immortali'y."

"I used to call overdose 'eternity,'" I agreed. "But these days it's simply oblivion."

"Dunlin died."

Her somber tone whipped my brittle mood up into fury. "I know, Rayne! I already bloody know!" I creaked to my feet, the effort making laden blood crash my mind. God's wings. "I have a job to do."

"Yes. Go deliver the will. They're meeting in t'Solar. Can y'make i'?"

"If I die will you bury me?"

"Comet?" she sounded concerned.

"Listen, Doctor, he died happy. When he rode behind the Wall he did what he wanted to do. He was in control of his own life. Let me know when you find even one immortal who can honestly say that."

Rayne spread her brown smile. "That's why we *don'* die," she said.

When I walked back through the hospital I saw that the King's bed was stripped. Now empty, the pewter cup was still on the side table. There are ways of testing for scolopendium. I dropped the cup out of the window, into the river.

So we are agreed?"

Mist's voice, "I back him."

Ata: "Aye."

I insinuated myself into the Solar Room as Staniel said, "No. I strongly disagree. With all due respect, Archer—"

"Oh, here he is!" Six pairs of eyes met mine, Staniel looked away again.

I said, "I'm sorry I'm late," realizing that I must look as sick as I felt.

"*At* last. Now we have to go through all this *again*. Where in god's Empire have you been?"

I answered the rhetorical question: "I've been ill. It was a hard day." I collapsed into a ladder-backed chair at the foot of the table, my wings tight against it. This furniture had certainly not been crafted in Awia. I looked down the long dining table—transformed into a forum of war.

Mist and Ata sat on my left, with Staniel opposite. Past them on the right were Tawny and Vireo. Candles had been lit to dispel the darkness; it was about one in the morning. A fire in a large stone hearth was reduced to red embers, which with the flickering candle flames cast an ever-changing pattern of shadows over their faces. Coats hung on chair backs; in the last hour Mist had filled a little ashtray to capacity with cigarette butts. I could see another packet in the bag under the table, with a knife, his blue cloak rolled up and a copy of *What Whore* magazine.

There was a carafe of water, which no one had touched, and Genya, presumably, had ordered there to be a whiskey jug as well. The night was hot and I could smell the spirit diffusing from the stoppered jar. I helped myself to water, with a very careful sip. It lessened the nausea and I started to feel a little healthier. I was strongly tempted to just put my head down and go to sleep, but I caught Lightning's look. I said, "Pray continue."

Lightning had taken control of the meeting, walking around the outside of the table and occasionally getting sullen responses. He said, "Comet, we will send you back to the Castle, to relate these events to the Emperor."

"Of course."

"I'll stay to disband the Plainslands fyrd, and then I'll follow on to the Castle, so I should meet you there next week."

"I have business at the coast," put in Ata. The bruise around her eye was yellowing, making her look even more frightening than usual.

"The Sailor and his wife will leave for Peregrine. But so we do not leave Lowespass undefended, I recommend that Tornado and Vireo, and Staniel remain here with the Awian fyrd."

I said, "That sounds fine to me. I can—"

"No. I do object." Staniel spoke up. He had been sitting with eyes closed, thin fists clenched in a mass of golden hair, drowning in self-pity. He said, "My brother . . ." His voice was so uneven that he stopped, but couldn't quite pull himself together again.

Vireo said, "We'll send a cortege tomorrow."

Staniel said, "I . . . I . . ."

"Yes?"

"I would like the Emperor's Messenger to announce the news. Every shop will be shuttered; every flag will be lowered. I would rather not sojourn here; I will depart for Rachiswater tomorrow to arrange the coronation."

Lightning cut in: "Patience, my lord. Awia is safe." He gave a smile that only I saw as condescending. Awia might well be a safe country to Lightning, who owns a little less than one third of it. "You shouldn't leave Lowespass under Insect threat. The more commanders here, the better. Follow in your brother's footsteps!"

"Comet once said I was no warrior," Staniel pointed out.

"Would you learn?"

"Need I learn when Tawny and Vireo guard Lowespass? I'll take charge from the Palace which my family built, and then conceivably I will live longer than Dunlin."

Staniel was suspicious of Lightning's motives. Uncertain of

what moves the other lords might make, he wanted to secure his kingdom. It seemed to me that such misgiving was part of Staniel's weakness—an overlord who fears those who answer to him will not be a sound ruler. I also knew that Lightning would rather not have him as King, but the Emperor has made it clear that Eszai should influence the affairs of mortals only lightly, if at all. Our purpose is to help them rather than rule or overawe them. It is a difficult balance for Lightning to maintain; his plans for his manor develop over centuries. He is always more comfortable when Awia has a wise overlord—one wise enough to know when to leave well alone.

My history is as far removed from the power play of Awia as the slums are from the Palace; it is my responsibility to remind them of the Castle's authority. I addressed Staniel: "Your Highness, if you wish to leave that is your decision as King, and we must agree to it."

"Is he, though?" said Lightning softly. "Castle will take charge if it isn't clear who rules."

"But it is clear."

"We don't know Dunlin's will."

"We do." I took the folded piece of bed linen from my back pocket and shook it out. "While you lot were sitting here and bickering, I was doing something useful. Shall I read it?

" 'I, Dunlin, leave the manor of Rachiswater and the Kingdom of Awia to my brother and heir Staniel. The fortune is entire for him, for no other and to be split with no other. Signed by my hand this night August 15, 2015. Witnessed by Comet Jant Shira and signed by him below.' "

I took the ring with its eagle close emblem, and passed it to Staniel, who sat with shoulders bowed. "You spoke to him?" he asked.

"Yes."

"What else did he say?"

I shrugged. "He barely had breath for that, let alone any more." The will was passed around the table and when it reached Staniel, he examined it carefully. He sat up straight, said, "Nothing will stop me leaving as soon as daybreak, with an escort of five hundred. Jant, do you agree?"

"As you wish."

"And Lightning, have you got anything to say?"

"Only that your authority will need practice before it ceases to sound like arrogance."

Hurriedly I said, "Lady Vireo, stay here. Tawny, stay with her. Defend Fortress Crag. Keep the Calamus Road clear so we can supply you with food and weapons from Awia."

Vireo was overjoyed; she had just gained a fortress. "Thank you! That's to my taste! Jant? Look! That's *her*."

Genya grasped the top lintel, swung herself through the window and ran a few paces, jumped onto the table and crouched like a spider in the center. Her arms and legs extended from a swath of pale green material which encircled her body, and she silently proceeded to unwrap herself, passing the material between her legs and over her shoulder, until it gathered on the table and she was left, a very thin peeled figure. I thought the green fabric was a curtain but she took an edge in each hand and opened it out. It was the Lowespass flag. She had taken the flag down. Genya stalked across the table and left it in a massive bundle in front of Staniel. "For the Featherback King!"

"Thank you," said Staniel.

I said, "Genya. Welcome . . ."

Mist kicked my ankle. I shook myself and wiped a couple of drops of drool off the tabletop with my shirt sleeve. I put out a hand to her, she strode over and buried her face in my palm, breathed deeply through her nose and mouth, taking my scent. She pushed her face against my palm, the way a cat does when it is urging you to stroke it.

"Genya. Genya. Mmm." I tried to kiss her but she jumped back. I shuffled in the seat, aware of an increasing pressure against the crotch of my leather jeans—thankfully hidden by the table. "Can you run?" I murmured.

"Rrrrrrrr." A purr or a growl?

"Excuse me, you two."

Genya stood up, traversed the table toward the Archer with a single stride, the Insect antennae in her hair waving. She flourished long bare arms at him; he looked rather uneasy.

"I want to know what is going on," she proclaimed. "I spit on Insects from the battlements. Insects bite at the walls. What you do is sit in dark halls and talk. What did Dunlin fight for?"

"Listen, Rhydanne—" snarled Lightning, and she was behind him in a flicker of movement, thin hands with nails like daggers caressing his neck.

"What say?" she asked.

"I'm not talking to you until you behave civilly."

"You talk, Featherback, or I rip you throat!"

"My lady."

Genya slid back onto the table and sat legs crossed, a wide grin splitting her face. She held her head on one side, a ponytail of frothy black hair cascaded down to her waist. She wore skimpy shorts; all her clothes were minimal because Rhydanne can't feel cold. She liked to make a point of showing this. Her pale, limber legs were wreathed in invisible designs, zigzag flashes and scrollwork. They were ikozemi tattoos, cut using white lead and still poisonous. They only become visible when the skin is flushed, for example by hot water, pleasure, or drunkenness—Genya only ever has the last of these.

Lightning sighed, attempting to mitigate her presence. "We were discussing—" he began.

"Help me."

"How?" I asked, nervously. How much would she tell? I

wondered if I would be able to stop her if she intended to reveal any secrets. I knew I couldn't hurt her.

Genya crawled across the table on hands and knees, and regarded me quizzically. "I want to go home," she said. "If I run the Insects chase me. So I am trapped here. Jant says he will help me, but how long have I been here? Jay is gone, so why stay? I want to know where is all the snow? This place is so bad. It is hot. The air is thick. It is full of Insects, and now it is full of Featherbacks."

Staniel removed one hand from a bloodshot eye, said, "Excuse me . . . ?"

Genya ignored him. "This is not like Darkling," she concluded flightily.

I caught her gaze and said warningly, "Sister—"

"I am not your sister! If I was your sister I would marry you!"

"This isn't Scree. Please be quiet."

"You are a pathetic, Shira. Insects gnaw us out from where we sit and you would not notice. In Scree this would not happen."

"That's because there aren't any Insects in Scree," I muttered, but she caught the comment.

"No," she agreed lightly. "There are just mistakes."

I hissed. It hurts to be reminded that I'm illegitimate, a Shira. Genya's surname was Dara, born within marriage, and in the mountain culture that meant that she could feel superior to me. My hopeless lust turned to anger. A Rhydanne born in wedlock wouldn't associate long with a mistake like me. My childhood of abuse flashed to mind—

"Fucking Dara slut! Slow-runner! Bitch! *Sgiunach!*"

"Goatherd!"

Lightning forced me back into my chair. I pointed a shaking hand at Genya. "Get this lone wolf bitch out of here or I'll kill her! Tawny, throw her out the window!"

"Don't," said Lightning, and the conflicting commands rendered Tornado too bewildered to move. I gave Genya a longing look, which wasn't requited.

She strutted on the table, stretching her lean legs, patting Staniel reassuringly on the head.

Staniel gave her the kind of look a child would give a hunting hawk. "I comprehend," he said softly, "that you have had no exemplification of our abilities in recent hostilities and also precious little toward you in the practice of chivalry. It occurs to me that, my lady, since your husband left you as Governor in Lowespass, we have been presumptuous in prevailing upon you. My jurisdiction extends only to *Featherback*-land, but I propose, with the good will of the Eszai, to serve you as we may."

I had to translate this for Genya, who clapped thin hands in delight. "I want to go home."

"Well, a Rhydanne would run away," remarked Vireo.

"None of that now!" Ata rebuked her.

"Jay shouldn't have gone out riding along the Wall by himself," Vireo taunted.

"Fishwife! He killed more Insects than you could count."

"Hush and hear what Jant says," said Mist. "Horse's mouth."

All eyes were again on me, as if they sensed there was something between Genya and me which it was my duty to end, and end peacefully. I thought for a while, knowing that to Genya, Lowespass was a foreign and frightening place. Vireo and Tawny would certainly not take her into consideration. From living in comfort with her kindly husband, she was alone and confused. From ruling the manor and its solid fortress, she suddenly had nothing at all. It was like being conquered.

Genya discovered the flask of whiskey on the table. She plucked out the cork, threw her head back and glugged noisily.

"Sister?" I said. Her green eyes blazed. "Come down to the stables tomorrow. I'll find a horse for you. Leave the fort to Vireo; I'll let you go home." I saw her pause, eyes narrowed. "No tricks, I promise. I'm sorry."

Ata practically slavered with the desire to know why I was so contrite.

Genya nodded. She unfastened the top button of a thin shirt and pulled out the Lowespass seal, on a dirty string. She bit through the string neatly, and dropped the fat gold ring in Vireo's outstretched hand.

Vireo clutched it, her face glowing with pleasure. After a while Tawny gave her a bear squeeze hug.

"Good horse?" asked Genya, peering up through fine fronds of black hair.

"Yes. And now I need to rest, my sister. We've been awake all night."

"What!" Staniel spluttered. "You were asleep for hours."

"I was awake all night. Just somewhere else." I pushed my chair back, and was nearly—nearly!—quick enough to catch Genya's hand.

She jumped from tabletop to windowsill, making Mist swear. She fastened her fists in the ivy growing outside, swung herself over the edge and swarmed effortlessly down the wall like a squirrel. At the foot she halted, wreathed in foliage. The courtyard was still so she ducked free, sprinted across, and disappeared under a portcullis at the far end.

She trailed a moon shadow rapidly over the tiles of the Inner Ward; muscled, bone-thin, and athletic. That's not just the thin of women who aren't fat; there's something essential in her, an animal's constant hunger. Genya is sex on a stick to me, just the stick to everybody else.

The stables of Lowespass Fortress were two long, low buildings. The walkway between them was cobbled and slimy, with a gutter running down the center into which my boots kept sliding. By the time I reached the stable entrance, a square black mouth in the dark hours before dawn, I was covered in mud and horse shit, and I wouldn't be surprised if it was human shit as well, since the latrines in the fortress are a hundred years out of date and have never worked properly.

The walls were whitewashed stone, roofed with slate. Behind the barn stood Lowespass' Outer Ward, its thick wall topped by a covered passageway. I have spent hours up there, walking along logs painted with pitch and sand to prevent them becoming slippery, looking out over the scenery.

I leaned against the doorpost and waited for Genya's arrival.

Each room of the fortress held a handful of men, and many were injured, but the only sound came from behind me, where tethered beasts huffed and coughed. Some sensed my presence and whinnied uneasily, stamping on the strewn floor. A straw fluttered down from the hayracks attached to the stable beams; it brushed my nose. I flicked it away and found that a few more straws had landed in my hair. I removed them swiftly, as my hair is one of my best features.

Soon I will be at the Castle, and I couldn't wait for all the comforts like hot water, clean clothes, customized drugs, my wife. A straw twirled down from the stable. The sky was cut by a long horizontal streak of purple. I watched it turn from dark blue, through violet to wine-red, and it healed as the sun rose, to a pencil line, leaving the sky a pale blue and the walls of the stable clear white.

I waited for Genya. I wanted Genya desperately and I was tormented by the thought I might never see her again. She could lose herself in the mountains, and even if I waited in Scree in a snowstorm she might not come back to the Filigree Spider. Even if I tracked her, above the snowline and in the corries—and I am a good tracker—I might never catch her.

What makes me great also isolates me. Had I been pure Rhydanne, and single, Genya would have married me. Then with the Emperor's consent she would be made part of the immortal Castle Circle. But no, my father was Awian, so with their wings, elongated to a thin Rhydanne build, I can fly, and Genya looks upon me as a freak. In Rhydanne culture early marriages are arranged and the husbands help to raise their children, while the narrow-waisted women recover from the trauma and regain their hunting speed. A newborn Rhydanne is put on the floor—he will be able to stand up. By the end of the day he will walk, and by the end of the week he will be running around uncontrollably.

I fuck my mind up for a little longer with an old, familiar agony: how the Awian trader, rapist, my father, could have managed to catch a Rhydanne girl.

Time does not heal all ills. Some actions can only be seen clearly and understood wholly when viewed through the glass of time. Sick, muddled memories don't fade away but weigh ever more heavily on us as time progresses. They are actions that nobody witnessed, and which I desperately need to confess, but to do so would ruin me. Acts which reappear in nightmares, and that's my punishment.

A stable hand, yawning, disturbed me from my memories. He wore a bright red suede waistcoat slit at the back for his wings. He scuttled by, looked startled when he recognized me, but managed a greeting: "Good morning, Messenger."

"It looks like a good morning for flying," I said. He looked to the meter-long primary feathers at my back. My wings were crossed under my coat, although the bumps at my waist showed the sinewy limbs. The servant had never seen anything like it. He nodded cautiously toward the doorway. "Want your race-horse ready?"

"No. I want the black mare I rode in yesterday. The charger with the chevronels on its chafron."

"That's Merganser's horse. From Rachis. Called Charabia."

"Bring her out and make sure she has excellent tack."

"Your wish, Comet."

"I don't care about ornament, but she has to go some distance, so make it sturdy. And let me alone now." Let me alone to sulk. Still I waited for Genya, scanning the rooftops where she often climbed, wishing for a glacier in the Outer Ward and icicles on the parapets. I waited, I waited, and flinched when a rustle came from just above me. I waited—a giggle—I looked up, and behind the bars of the hayrack were a pair of eyes, vertical pupils, gold as they reflected the sun. Genya was lying full-length in the hayrack. She plucked another straw from her bed and dropped it down on me, giggled, pushing long fingers through the slats. Quickly I grasped a beam and pulled myself up, hoping to lie there with her, but when I climbed in and floundered in the straw she jumped lightly down and paced, tip-toe swift between the stalls, speaking to the chargers.

"Are you good? No, I don't think so. Bad horse, good horse? What about you?" Her body comprised of coat hangers, hanging from thin straight shoulders like her face hung from cheek-bones. Paper-white and angular, an origami face, pencil-lead shadowed with lack of sleep.

"My lady! My lady!" I fluttered down. I threw myself at her feet, seized her long, long legs and buried my face in the lace-ups of her boots. She tried to kick me in the nose. I pulled at her leggings but she remained upright with vicious poise.

"I'm sorry about what happened," I begged. "Please forgive me. I want to help you."

She nipped my shoulder violently, the long nails cutting in. I imagined her running and bit my tongue. "Speak Scree!" she demanded. "I speak Awian...not very good." That would make a mess of my plea, as in Scree there were no words for "sorry" or "forgive." Never trust a language that has no future tense and twenty words for "drunk."

"You're safe with me now. What we did was wrong—the Awians would call it wrong anyway. I regret it, and I want to repay you, Genya. Come out to the yard; I help you go back to the mountains."

"All the horses are spoilt beasts; they bite!"

"I've found one that doesn't seem to mind being ridden by a Rhydanne."

"Ah—fuck that as well, did you?"

Don't make this hard for me. It's difficult being near you without you making me angry. The cursorial girl was close enough for me to grab, or I could draw my knife and force her to the wall. I was greatly tempted to take her. Damn it, who'd know or care? "I've seen you catch mice. Don't tempt me to play with you the same way."

She tossed her hair and stalked out of the stables, ducking under the hayracks.

Staniel's men were gathering in the courtyard and all around was the clink of tack, men fitting saddle straps into buckles, rolling up sleeping bags, rolling fags and chewing on dripping bacon sandwiches.

I saw one sword being examined, but most had left their cleaned weapons in their packs. They were tying little drums, painted gold, amethyst, and fuel-blue, to their saddles, plumes and Insect antennae in their hair. The lancers had rolled their colorful caparisons into long bundles and were using them as cushions. Lances had been transformed into pennants, ivory and light blue, embroidered with eagles, with white quills, towers, an appliqué dog with pearl eyes, and a sleeping falcon with florid feathers.

A lame man leaned on his lance; his friends heaved him into the saddle, his hair still streaked with the blue dye that the most flamboyant wear to fight. A few men chuckled covertly with pleasure at returning to Awia, but most were quiet, bearing Staniel's orders in mind. The black martlet volant was my wife's flag, and I recognized the thickset man who bore it as the warden of Wrought manor, but I couldn't speak to him with Genya treading like a puma at my side.

Genya poked her foot into a stirrup and was astride the horse before it knew what was happening. It kicked, it bucked, and walked round in a little circle, trying to throw her over its head. She clung on to two handfuls of black mane, her forearms like twists of rope, her eyes dancing. The Awian soldiers stopped their preparations and watched, eyes wide and drop-jawed.

I mimicked them. "Do you want to catch all the flies in Lowespass? Mind your own sodding business!" Genya brought Charabia under control by the simple means of letting it become so knackered it gave up trying to throw her.

"Promise not to eat the horse, Genya . . . Well, at least make sure you get back to Darkling first. Here's my compass."

I showed her the silver device and tried to explain but she just said, "Pretty!" and shook it to keep the painted disc revolving. I removed it from her talons.

"Keep the sunset at your back," I said. "Those hills become the mountains so if you keep going up, you find the trade road which takes you to Scree pueblo."

Genya grinned maniacally. I took the knife from my boot and passed it to her. If I can't give her my compass she might better understand a knife. "You could need this, for Insects or thieves. Remember, Insects are too hard to bite. Stab their heads."

"Yes, Shira."

I wanted to ask for a kiss but kissing isn't in Genya's repertoire. Instead I took her hand, her pale skin cold to the touch, seeing the even white half-moons on her pointed nails. I will always be able to remember the chill ghost of her skin like marble, and the contrast between it and my wife's warm feathers always makes me feel queasy. I thought, they're too different and yet I want them both, because I am a bit of both and as good as neither. "All you need is a decent patch of snow to lie in and be as right as Rayne," I told her.

The gates opened, and Genya urged her unwilling horse forward and through them at a canter. She never looked back, but I knew she was smiling.

Some things are not and can never be yours, no matter how deeply or for how long you know them. I knew I should allow Genya to leave because my lust for her was destructive—although I've never really understood what's wrong with wanting destructive things.

I paid the stable hand generously and went to my room, thinking. In order to be at peace you have to let go of the thing you cherish; you can't move on if you cling to it and even immortals have to develop. Lust for the Rhydanne girl had been holding me back, even as far as the time when I lived like her. I knew it was much better to let her go. So am I at peace? Am I fuck. I cooked up a heavy dose of cat and injected it, enough to Shift.

CHAPTER FOUR

In the Shift, Keziah was hiding in the Aureate with a hacksaw. We were standing in the shadow of a thick, reflective wall, which stretched up as far as I could see. I was handsome if rawboned, in black and white, which the wall threw back as different shades of yellow. Keziah never wore clothes. He was a man-sized lizard who walked on strong back legs, stunted forearms hanging down in front. His long snout was full of pointed teeth. The scaly plates of his skin were mottled moss-green and gray. I was desperately trying signs and whispers, to make Keziah come back to his pub.

I had started in Epsilon, looking for Dunlin Rachiswater where I left him in the Bullock's Bollocks bar. He was no longer there, and I heard from the punters that Felicitia had left as well. No one could tell me where they had gone, or why. I then tried my palace at Sliverkey, but it was uninhabited and untidy, as usual. Searching for Keziah, in order to ask him, had brought me to the Aureate.

Keziah was of the opinion that fly-by-night bar staff like Felicitia were worthless drifters. He was better off without them, and Awians in general regardless of how royal. "They split at daybreak, dude; who knows where they are? Join me and we'll both be rich."

"This is the Tine's quarter. If they catch us they'll kill us!"

"It's made of solid gold," Keziah hissed. He turned to see me since his eyes were at the sides of his head.

"I know that!"

"So if we cut a piece out we'd—"

"Cut it! Are you mad?"

"Ssh! We'd never have to work again."

"The pub—"

"Screw the pub; dude, look at this . . ." He gestured for me to crouch down and pointed at two jagged saw-marks that ran into the base of the gold wall, carving out a triangular ingot. The cut surfaces were bright, the wedge connected to the wall by half a centimeter thickness at its apex. "Nearly rich," whispered Keziah.

"Greedy bastard." I watched as the hacksaw bit into the wall. He grasped the handle with his hind leg and sawed rapidly. The slice of gold loosened and fell. Keziah caught it in a foreclaw and wrapped it in a piece of cloth. "Let's go." he said. We crept to the edge of the wall, and peered round. A group of big Tine were standing there calmly watching us.

Tattoos spotted their pale blue skin, scarred and tanned to indigo. Each Tine had a flat black shell on his back, pocked with designs and sprouting loops of gold wire. The most immense one had stubby horns grafted on his forehead. Gnarly claws curled into fists. A dozen pairs of pupil-less eyes blinked. A forest of needle-teeth appeared as they all slowly smiled.

Faster reactions than Keziah, I turned and ran. I looked back from the gold cobbled road to see him drop to a fighting stance. He roared.

"Come on!" I yelled.

"Run," he snarled, showing his terrible teeth. "You coward!"

The Tine clustered round him, the smallest taller than him, muscles crawling under their blue skin. Keziah kicked the nearest one. His claw opened its stomach. Pink guts spilled out over its belt. Another Tine finished it off and began chewing on its backside.

Keziah lashed out with his tail. He struck the cannibal across the back of the neck, killing it instantly. It slumped over its meal. The lizard evaded another carnivore, bit at it, driving it back. He kicked again, his talon sinking into a belly, where it was caught. Two Tine dashed forward and seized his leg. He teetered and fell over.

I saw the Tine simply pick Keziah up, clawed hands all over him, and twist him apart. Those at his head twisted left. His legs twisted right. There was a series of sounds like strings snapping, then I heard the wet crack as his spine fractured. Tine clamped their teeth in his scaly tail; another began to pick long fangs from his gums. He screamed and thrashed. Blue fingers pushed into his eye sockets, trying to fish one out. His tongue was ripped and Tine fought among themselves for it. They plucked his fingers with gristly sounds and chewed them like twigs.

A Tine took a length of intestine, and squeezed out the contents. Murky slime pattered onto the cobbles. He put one end of the gut to his lips and blew it full of air. He twisted it a few times, held it up. A balloon dog. Tine fell over each other laughing.

Helpless, I kept running; the monsters saw my movement and followed. The gold path shook with their footfalls. They smelled of rotting meat. They couldn't gain ground. They couldn't catch a Rhydanne as shit scared as I was. But they wouldn't give up the chase.

I pounded, slipped, and jumped down the gold road. The road narrowed, came to an abrupt bend. This was the knee.

Holy buildings with stepped gable ends crowded close on every side. Red gold, white gold. Stench of burned flesh in the air. Smell of lizard blood and excrement. I set off down the shin of their city.

Shin, calf, the Ankle Plaza. A rounded edifice stood in the center, full of Tine. They had blue loincloths and thongs round their legs. Their custom was to drop molten gold onto their legs and feet, which set in their skin. It seemed as if they had grown from the golden road, gradually changing to blue. I skidded to a halt in front of them. The Tine chasing me piled in behind. They reached out with transplanted fingers. They made a stinking wall of muscle.

I put a hand to my sword hilt and found that it had gone. I tried to spread my wings but was rooted to the spot. The Tine tensed to rush me.

A skein of voices on my left—"Shira!" I looked to where a woman was standing—a blond woman, wrapped in a cloak. There had been no girl there a second ago.

The Tine didn't like her one bit. Forgetting me, they closed in on her and I screamed because I thought they would rip her apart. She threw back the cloak; underneath she was completely naked, and very lovely. The Tine sniggered and licked their chops. As the cloth hit the cobbles her body followed it, disintegrating, flowing down and spreading like the twisted trunk of a tree, then like its roots, running out in thick strands over the floor. The broken facade of her face was last to go. And then silence.

Some Tine went down on one knee. Some backed off. I just kept screaming. Her body became a thick cable of flesh, made from smaller threads. It snaked across the plaza and over to a gold drain covering, where she reassembled into a beautiful girl, and beckoned to me. She raised the grating, although Tawny himself couldn't have budged it, and slipped through.

The Tine began to recover, and looked around for me. I

pelted across and followed her down the drain, grazing my
wings as I eased through. I retched at the stink.

We were in darkness. Blue arms wedged through the hole
and waved about, but they couldn't grab us. A scimitar was
poked down. The Tine began to howl. The girl took my arm
and we walked a little way along the edge of a deep gold trough,
running with blood and dirty water, a few fragments of splintered bone carried along, organs and knots of hair and Insect
shells; some other pieces I was glad I couldn't recognize.

"This is the main drain," said the girl sweetly. "I advise you
not to take a swim."

"What? Who? Who are you?" I panted.

"This is just a bad dream, Jant," she said.

"How do you know my fucking name?" I tried to shake free
of her grasp; it was impossible.

"You have to go back to the Castle and forget all this," she
said. She spoke Awian perfectly. She had a very mellow voice,
very high pitched, and as if lots of voices were speaking together.
A couple of gaps appeared in her cheek; with a shifting of flesh
they closed again and I suddenly saw that she wasn't solid at all.
I peered closer and recoiled with disgust. She was made up of
thousands of long, thin worms. Knotted together and constantly
moving, they gave the impression of skin. She smiled, or rather,
the worms that were her lips parted briefly, and I saw the worms
that were her teeth.

"It's a shame to see such a seasoned traveler so lost," she said.

"Who are you?" I repeated, terrified. I was stuck between
this creature and the blood-filled canal. Her faint smile reappeared, as if she had no need of a name, and I was being stupid.
She must have come from a very distant place, to be so alien. "If
you think I'm strange," she said, "you should see the rest of the
court." She put her hand through her chest and scratched the
back of her head.

"Court? What court? The only court is the Castle!"

"The Royal Court is concerned. I think the Tine are not very happy with you," she said, understanding in a studiedly feminine way. Her calm voice stroked me. If she was invisible I'd be in love. "Never come back to the Aureate. Never talk to the Saurian."

"Keziah's dead," I told her. Another faint smile.

I recovered what few shreds of courtesy I could. "Thank you . . . Thank you for saving my life. Maybe in the future I may have the honor of performing the same service for you, my lady. In the meantime, is there anything I can do to repay you, singular or plural?"

"You must go home and stay there."

"Apart from that!"

"How about a kiss?" she said, sticking out a tongue which unwound into a cluster of worms, and waved at me. The end of the tassel suddenly bloomed red, as all the worms opened their tiny mouths, and stuck their tongues out. I backed away.

The girl laughed and dissolved, writhing down as before and separating out into individual creatures, which squirmed between the cobbles and, clump by clump, plopped into the drain, where they swam away upstream. The last of them merged together to form a floating disembodied arm, which cheerfully waved farewell. I returned the gesture, wondering if she could see me.

I then sat down by the gory canal, and waited to be pulled back. I would have a hangover on my flight to the Castle. When perfectly sober, anticipating a hangover is a bitch. I hated the thought of my useless body lying on the chamber floor, back in cold Lowespass, where the Insects swarmed.

CHAPTER FIVE

If the Castle had been built in the shape of a sundial, it couldn't have been more accurate. Three o'clock in the afternoon exactly, on a late summer day, a shaft of sunlight pierces the slats in the shutter of the Northwest Tower and slides across my desk. It's done this reliably for hundreds of years; this time it woke me.

I woke with the sun in my eyes, sitting at my desk, my head resting on a stack of smudged papers, post-battle correspondence. That probably meant the wet ink had imprinted in negative across my face. I would have to spend another night writing it out again with the aid of a mirror. I sighed, stretched and yawned.

"You're burning yourself up," said a warm voice behind me. A cinnamon voice. A scent of vanilla. Tern.

Without looking round I said, "I didn't know you had come back."

"I took the coach from Wrought last night. Arrived midnight. You were already . . . asleep."

"And did you have a good time in Wrought, O piquant one?"

Tern was lying on the chocolate-brown velvet chaise longue, a honey-colored silk parasol over one shoulder and a paperback novel open on her breast. "We have to get that fixed," she said, indicating the broken shutter with a finger spiced with rings and nail varnish. "Then you can sleep all day."

This may sound strange but her voice is the main reason I love her. She breathes rounded words like the heady steam from mulled wine or cocoa, word fumes glazed with brandy and syrupy accents. I love languages, and my greatest wish is to be sugar-preserved in Tern's slow voice forever. I gazed at her fondly, warmed by the rogue beam of sunlight. She had a long-sleeved, faded cream dress, mostly lace. Chic, slight, and delicate, she looked like icing on the chocolate divan. This is the lady I chose to make immortal, the girl who, to me, is the best in the world. The sweetest in the world, ever. She started spinning the caramel parasol, proud of my attention, just like a child. Her hair was dark, her skin the color of demerara sugar, soft and warm. Her face was defined by subtle makeup, lips the shade of red that is nearly brown, like sherry; champagne, coffee, and licorice, her eyes. "My love," I said, "you look good enough to eat."

She glanced deliberately ceilingward. "You're still high," she accused.

"I'm not. I've given up."

"Nonsense," said Tern succinctly. "My dear, you have more holes in your arms than there are in the roof of Wrought."

I searched for a way to escape the conversation. Persistence wasn't one of my wife's strengths. I knew from experience that if I bluffed for a while her attention would wander to something else. "I'll be fine."

"I worry about you, Jant. Your habit hasn't been this bad since 2006."

Yes, that was the last time I saw Genya. "It's the memory of the battle, and Rachiswater's death that's made it so bad," I lied, feeling the pleasant warmth of Tern's sympathy—I know it does me no good, but I love to bask in her attention or concern. I contemplated which hiding places I could use should Tern decide to throw out my hoard of cat. It was rare for her to be so bothered about the fact I indulge occasionally. I thought I owed myself a little pleasure after all I had been through.

"Can I help you come off it?"

"Ah—I'm not ready to quit just yet."

Tern sighed, she had heard that one before. Prudently I offered, "I'll cut down. I really mean to. Really." Tern heard the strain in my voice and relented. The last overdose when I Shifted had truly frightened me, and I was taking less cat because I didn't want to risk accidentally tripping to Epsilon. The Worm-Girl's warning still haunted me—never come back to the Aureate. I didn't want to think about it any longer. Dwelling on the problem made me want more cat, and I was feeling shaky enough as it was.

"Please do, darling. You're skin and bone—" She would have continued but I threw myself on the divan, on top of her, and started trying to fit kisses down the front of her dress. She yelped, giggled. "Leave me alone! Mmm . . . Ow!" I bit her shoulder.

"Come to bed."

"Mmm. OK. No—there's a note for you."

I stared at her. More work? "From whom?"

Tern gestured toward a square of yellow card on the mantelpiece. "The Archer," she said.

I tried to stand but Tern wrapped her legs around my waist, a rather neat trick. I poked her belly with the parasol until she freed me. "Lightning can wait," she said sulkily.

"Well, if he wants me I should go," I replied. She tutted. I read Lightning's fastidious copperplate: *"Come and see me as soon as you can. Your reinforcements arrived last night: Governor Swallow Awndyn with her retinue, bound for Lowespass. Owing to Staniel's misfortune she decided to divert to the Castle, for which I am grateful."* I flipped the card over. *"Although I fully intend to wring your neck for calling Swallow to the Front. LSM."*

Tern regarded me quizzically. "You're in trouble." She had an expression of looking at me over the tops of her spectacles, although she never wears glasses.

"Do I care?" I began to lick her legs hungrily, my mouth full of dress hem. Tern stroked my feathers rhythmically, driving me mad with lust. "Will you do that thing with your legs again?"

"Like this? Why?"

"Because then I can do *this*." Tern gasped. Even her yelps were like helpings of cream gâteaux.

Tern tugged at my wing, which extended until she rolled off the bed. I pulled the strong muscles back with a snap.

"Come on, come on. You have to go!"

"Only mortals hurry. Give me another kiss."

"He's waiting for you!"

"Yes, love. No, wait . . ."

"Ready?"

"Wait a minute. I'm missing something here. What did Lightning mean 'Staniel's misfortune'? What the fuck is he talking about? What day is it anyway?"

"Friday."

"Can't be. It was Friday when I last went to court . . . Oh, shit. Not an entire week."

Tern sighed. She had definite opinions about drug binges that lasted a whole week. She rooted around on the untidy floor for a folded newspaper and passed it to me:

The Wrought Standard *is pleased to amend previous reports by bringing you the news that His Majesty King Staniel has reached Rachiswater Palace alive and well after yesterday's disaster. He has not been harmed and has just issued a statement praizing his bodyguard (printed in full, page two) who remained with him dutifully during the fast ride back although seven-eighths of the column behind them was killed. A survivor said, "We came upon the vanguard of our own host cut to pieces and returned with haste, so as to ensure the safety of His Majesty."*

The death toll reached five hundred when Insects beset Staniel's column of soldiers peaceably bringing the body of the previous King home. Insects outnumbering our troops two to one attacked at night while the soldiers were unarmored on the march and unprepared for such an onslaught. Their bodies have not been found and the casket containing Dunlin's remains has not been recovered, as Staniel has pronounced it is too dangerous to venture back into the area. He is, however, mindful of the opprobrium that this accident and loss has brought upon his family.

Many families in Rachiswater and Wrought are in mourning. The whole kingdom shares their grief, which will long endure.

Staniel has not dismissed the survivors, and has also summoned the rest of the Awian fyrd to protect him in Rachiswater, an unpopular decision as it leaves Calamus Road and the northwest of the country unguarded.

JANT SHIRA 9/9/15

Shit. No wonder Lightning wants to see me. "It's impressive," I said. "I wrote for the *Standard* without knowing about the fight."

Tern gave me an antique look. "You owe me one."

I looked in a couple of other broadsheets that were lying on the floor among gory Insect dissection textbooks and my chemistry notes. *The Moren Times* just listed what courtiers wore to the coronation, and had good tits on page three, but the *Moderate Intelligencer* had this to say:

> *Never before has a King raised a host solely to protect himself. We may ask why he has separated from the other manorships in Awia, and how will the smaller manors defend themselves against the Insects? It is the Castle's role to shield Awia but how is it to accomplish this without troops? Why has the Castle not made an official statement? Is the Emperor supporting Staniel, who seems prepared to forsake Lowespass and Tanager? With some notable exceptions, the smaller manors are coming round to the view that Staniel should be deposed and replaced. We look again to the Circle of unusually silent immortals for advice on this issue, while Insects roaming south of the Wall destroy what's left of our cattle and threaten our children.*
>
> KESTREL ALTERGATE 9/10/15

"I've got to go," I said to Tern. I had to find out what Staniel was trying to achieve.

Tern nodded. "One day we'll have more than a day together," she said ruefully.

"I'm sorry." I snorted some more cat, thinking of it as a medicine to stall the onset of my sickness, although it would leave me restless. It's a stupid delusion, I know, because what I call medicine is really the cause of my sickness.

The stifling world outside was hotter than I had thought possible. The sun was a silver coin burning through a white overcast sky, trapping heat beneath the clouds and suffocating the Castle. I stripped off extra clothes as I walked, and by the time I reached Lightning's rooms I was carrying my crowskin coat, a long-sleeved T-shirt, and was verging on indecency.

I have had two hundred years to become familiar with this wing of the Castle, but its grandeur would make anybody feel uncomfortable. I feel I shouldn't be here, but the building also seems gracious—as if the people who do belong here will smile and allow me a little time. In a corridor deep inside the Palace interior of the Castle, black and white tiles were laid to appear three-dimensional. The sides of the Neo-Tealean corridor were open white arches, and I go through one, across an immaculate lawn, into a white building with long, many-paned sash windows.

The brickwork on the lower stories was emphasized, with plain walls above. The windows were set so closely together that the wall was mostly glass, with dark blue velvet drapes. From inside one can see every centimeter of the formal gardens, the square lawns and conical cypress.

Music wandered out onto the lawns. I followed it like a stream to its source, thinking that it was a very pretty harpsichord duet, but when I got to Lightning's rooms I discovered that it was just Swallow, who had found a way of playing both parts of the duet at once.

Lightning was sitting in a chair as near to her as etiquette allowed, with a distant smile on his face, pleased because Swallow was now not only in the same room as him, but she was thrilled with his latest present, a gilt and blue cloisonné harpsichord, with scroll legs, keys of gold, and lapis lazuli.

The furniture matched, but with a few modern New Art pieces of enamel and silver. Lightning has always been a collector, and refused to stop although he bemoaned the fact that no artist in the last few hundred years has had any taste. The room's furniture was a record of exclusive trends, from the turn of the first millennium. It was mostly baroque and tortoiseshell but a polished shield with a blue mascle on argent hung on the far wall, with arrows splayed behind. On either side there were ancient oil-painted portraits. Below, a variegated marble fireplace took up most of the wall, winged statues supporting an inlaid mantelpiece. An elegant glass wine decanter stood on a table with a pedestal of polished Carniss granite. Smoked salmon was arranged on a silver tray. Other seafood had legs and shells and looked too much like Insects for comfort. I skirted round it and touched Swallow's green devoré shoulder to wake her from her reverie. The last chord hung in the air for a long, sweet time before dying.

"Hello, Jant," she said. "Great makeup."

I could grow to love some people. "Governor Awndyn, it's good to see you and I wish the situation was different. Do either of you know what the fuck is happening in Rachis?"

"No," said Swallow cheerfully. She folded her sheet music, pulled a pencil from behind her ear, and began to write more music on the back. In a drunken conversation I once heard Lightning admit it was a shame Swallow keeps her hair short; it was a coppery red like sparks, like strands of silk. She also had thick eyebrows, and freckles all over her face and even down her arms.

Swallow preferred to spend her days practicing the piano rather than going riding, and as a result was plump but unfortunately without having big breasts which many well-built women are blessed with. She sat cross-legged on the harpsichord stool, wearing a jacket made of different-colored squares of velvet. She also wore a dark green beret, which sat at a dapper angle on her ginger hair—such a jaunty angle, in fact, that I found myself braced to catch it, starting forward nervously every time she moved. She wore other stuff as well but it was the motley coat I really noticed, because it was so outrageous.

Lightning stretched his muscular arms and sighed. "Take a

seat," he advised. I sank into an armchair which all but smoth-
ered me. "The Emperor asked for you this morning. I don't
know how you dare stretch his patience. I received a letter from
Harrier, my steward, who attended the crowning ceremony.
Staniel was so anxious to get into the throne that he couldn't
wait for any Eszai to be present, damn him—it's the first coronation I've missed in fifteen hundred years!

"Anyway, naturally Harrier was frightened for Micawater. If
Rachis is surrounded by troops to protect it against Insects, what
about my house which is only fifty kilometers away? Harrier
wanted to know whether an invasion is likely. I have reassured
him. I have sent everyone I can find to the front, and further
arms to the fortress."

"You don't want to follow the trend and protect
Micawater?" Swallow asked.

"Of course not! If we can't hold the front then the whole
thing will fall apart."

"Staniel wants Rachiswater to be a safe haven," she added.

"It will be safe all right. It will be a starving island in a sea of
Insects. How long will even the best troops hold out with Staniel
in command?" Lightning sighed. "Swallow, I wish I could keep
my fyrd for myself but you know we have to work together to
save northern Awia from being overrun."

"I came with two thousand men as reinforcements, I don't
see why you can't let me go to the front."

"No. Not until you become Eszai."

I took a glass that had evidently been laid out for me, and
poured some refreshing white wine. "The Insects will stay
behind their Wall, Saker. There can't be so many."

"Yes, and they'll push the Wall out and build new Walls and
more Walls until we will have lost all Awia. I remember how
quickly they used to expand, at the beginning."

Better change the subject before Lightning starts telling us again about the old heroic days of the founding of the Circle. "It looks like Staniel's close escape has unsettled him."

Lightning picked up a letter with a *Top Secret* seal. "From the tone of this, he is terrified."

"He spends summers lying in a haystack writing poetry, while Dunlin practiced jousting," said Swallow, citing the popular opinion of Staniel's military prowess without looking up from her sheaves of paper opera.

It may have had something to do with the wine, but I was feeling optimistic. "Don't worry. He can't keep soldiers at Rachis for long, they've got homes and lovers and a harvest to bring in next month."

Lightning sounded grim: "Well, let us hope they would rather cut wheat and bake us bread than sit on their arses in Rachis Park for five pounds a day."

"He's *paying* them?"

"It seems so, if I don't misread this letter. And as time goes on, and if the crops start dying for lack of attention he'll have to start paying them more and more. The treasury will run dry. If Dunlin was still alive he would die a thousand times to know how his brother is misusing their fortune."

"Let me go and speak to him."

"Yes, and we also want to know how Tornado is faring in Lowespass; at least one of us is out there. I should go back . . . But San thinks what I'm doing here is more useful for the moment."

I could not say much in front of Swallow, but I itched to know, "What *are* you doing here?"

"Simply writing letters and talking to people."

Swallow put her manuscript down. "If you're going to court, can I come?"

Our predicament had nothing to do with Awndyn and I told her so, but Lightning said, "It would help Swallow's petition if she could see the Emperor again. You compered her concert in the Hall, now I would be grateful if you could accompany her into the courtroom."

I suspected that this whole visit was just a plot so that Swallow could see the Emperor San again. "Why don't you take her?" I moaned.

"I would hardly be viewed as impartial."

Swallow had said that if she was accepted into the Circle, she would consider marrying the Archer and not before. It was a clever move, because Lightning now arranges as many audiences with the Emperor as possible. I know that once San's mind is made up on an issue it rarely changes; in fact his opinion defines the issue and in pressing her case Swallow is denying him. San owes his Eszai nothing because he pays us in lifetime, a currency so valuable it leaves no favors outstanding.

Lightning asked me to take Swallow because it meant that he would not lose face if her application should be rejected. I don't fear loss of reputation as much as he does because my reputation has been singed with scandal for a very long time. If I helped Swallow toward success then Lightning might look kindly on me. He might agree to another loan, or at least waive the interest on the two hundred thousand pounds I borrowed in nineteen-thirty.

Lightning first looked after me when I joined the Circle, fresh from Hacilith, knowing nothing about Insects or sword-play, wary but eager to please. He gave me lessons on horse riding and etiquette, as well as letting me run riot in Micawater until I learned the Awian language thoroughly. During that time I became his closest friend and, like Tern, he keeps me on the straight and narrow. I could return the favor by taking Swallow under my wing. I beckoned to her. "Come on then. Saker, what are your plans?"

"I'm going up to the gallery to watch."

"I bet you are."

Swallow said, "Perhaps I should sing in court. I would be able to melt even the Emperor's heart. He would agree to making me immortal so he could hear perfect concertos forever."

She didn't say it boastfully, she said it as fact, and I thought she was probably right but for all I knew the Emperor hated music, or couldn't tell the Eclipse Sonata from a football chant.

"It's harder for me, because there is no Circle Musician for me to Challenge and so displace. Don't the opinions of the other Eszai hold any weight?" she asked.

"None," said Lightning sadly. He had seen Swallow change over the last year: with each disappointment her desire to join the Circle grew, till now there was a determination hard as diamond and brittle as old glass in her, which could exhaust her maiden's spirit, leaving her resentful and still aging.

"Shall we go?" Lightning finished his heart-stoppingly expensive wine in one gulp. Pale with anxiety, Swallow nodded. Lightning once told me that growing wan was as sure an indication of love as blushing was an indication of modesty. As far as I could see Swallow was a frightened girl backed into complicated situations by the rabid dog of her own ambition. I wanted to free her. I could tell she was worried because she wasn't looking directly at me; she was too busy looking inward, at imagined court scenes. Aware of Lightning's jealous gaze, I hugged her chastely and told her to have courage.

Lightning had told Swallow many times that the struggle to become Eszai could be over immediately, if only she would consent to marry him. A year later she still refused. I needed to find out exactly why she wouldn't marry the Archer, so I could convince her that she was wrong. I can't feel as profoundly as the Archer, thank god, but I did want Swallow to join us. Even with the little I know about music I could tell she was the most talented composer the Fourlands had ever produced, and she was an excellent drinking companion, who could play the guitar so well.

I walked automatically avoiding the uneven floorboards, but Swallow had not been this way before, and she found herself trotting along in an unbecoming fashion in order to keep up. The Archer strode beside her, arrows crackling together in a quiver at his hip.

I wanted to put the cantatrice at her ease. "Spent all your life in Awndyn?" I asked chattily.

"Apart from last year in Hacilith."

"Your mother must have been from Diw."

"Yes. How did you—? Oh. You can pick up my accent. That's amazing!"

I shrugged to show it was no more impressive than her ability to remember every note in every symphony. She wrote two before she was twelve.

The flight feathers of her wings were barred. They were a dark, rust red and had red-brown lines across them, which was very rare. Her wings looked sumptuous, and the rest of her body looked so soft and tender that I wanted to touch her. I quelled the urge and lengthened my stride to put the temptation behind me.

A colonnaded narthex runs around the outside of the courtroom, which is the very center of the Palace, itself the center of the Castle, which is the center of the world. I led Swallow down through carved arches and spiraled columns, to a staircase where Lightning left us, ran up the stairs and vanished through a door leading to the arcade. Stone Insect heads were carved in deep relief on the walls; their obsidian compound eyes polished to hungry black mirrors. Swallow shuddered when she saw them. The stone antennae of these heads were knotted together intricately so that the triangular heads hung in a column like bunches of onions. I once heard that the carvings substituted real trophies brought back by the first Eszai. I expect they were replaced because of the smell, or because courtiers got sick of maggots wriggling out and dropping on them.

Busts and escutcheons were set into the walls, which Swallow examined to see if she could recognize any emblems. "You won't," I said. "This part of the Castle hasn't changed since its founding, and the manorships are different now."

"Yes. Is Micawater here?"

"No. This was built two thousand years ago."

Swallow fell silent; she glanced furtively at the faded heraldic paintings on the ceiling—dark gules like old blood, raw umber and green earth. I have researched their delitescent meanings for a hundred years and I am still really none the wiser.

I fretted about the entrance to the courtroom, a huge door of oak so old it is petrified, set with black iron studs. It took all one's weight to move it, and all my weight is not much.

A guard stood by the door, simply and immaculately dressed but dark around the jowls. He held a finely honed spear and had a broadsword buckled at his hip. He saw me and stood to attention, then relaxed when I waved at him.

"Comet."

"Hello, Lanner. I haven't seen you for ages."

"Lanner was my father," said the guard.

"Oh."

"I am the little lad you used to give sweets to and say, 'He'll make a fine soldier one day.'"

I nodded, fazed. Mistakes of this kind were happening with increasing frequency.

"My lady?"

"This is Swallow, Lightning's love. She wants to be immortal. She wants another title to replace her unfortunate name."

He looked Swallow up and down before addressing her. "You must give up your weapons here."

Swallow glanced at me. "I don't have any weapons," she said plaintively.

"Not even a knife?"

"No!"

The guard grinned at me over the top of Swallow's head. "You have to leave your jewelry too," he said.

I explained: "Zascai aren't allowed to wear gold in the Circle court." Swallow nodded, thinking it was another rule designed to make people feel small and unimportant.

I said, "Everybody feels insignificant in front of the Emperor, even Eszai. It is always unwise to hide behind gold trinkets rather than your own solid achievements."

"And your watch."

"Why?"

"Because time doesn't exist in the Emperor's presence," the guard announced.

"Because it's bad manners to look at your watch in court," I said.

Swallow dug out her pocket watch and handed it over. The sentry walked backward with his back against the door, to open it. Swallow started forward but I put a hand on her shoulder. "A word of advice, sister. Don't look up."

The first thing Swallow did when she stepped inside was look up. She stopped, wide-eyed, entranced, spellbound, and her mouth open. I gave her a firm push and she tore herself away, her shoulders rounded in defense.

"Breathe in and go," I muttered.

"Shira. It's *massive*." Her voice was solid awe.

I glanced up, and farther up, and the ceiling sucked my gaze into the heights of its arches until I was completely disoriented, feeling as if I was falling upward. The ceiling was gold and mosaic; huge bosses with churning ships and gyring eagles hung from the pinnacles. There were figures ten times life-size with their cloaks swirling around them like pleated clouds. Oil lamps lighted the ceiling, and candles in gold candelabra illuminated the aisle, on torchères like graceful statues. But once swallowed by the size of the vaulted ceiling, it was difficult to tear my gaze away. I am used to distance but my eyes ached to focus across the vast hall. I looked at the narrow arcade, so dizzyingly distant I had to fight the urge not to spread my wings for safety, and I saw Lightning there, leaning over. I could feel the strength of his apprehension; his will that she *must do well* shone down like a beam.

Swallow swore cautiously. "By god. Oh, god. How many times could Awndyn fit into this hall?"

"At least you didn't come from a Scree sheiling, sister."

"Did *god* build this?"

"In a way. I think it asked the Emperor to."

She began to walk, and as she walked down the scarlet carpet between the thin brass railings I saw her gather gracefulness into herself. Her shoulders went back, her head proudly upright; from somewhere she found an impassive expression and her hands, which had been tapping pizzicato, became still, at her sides. She paced without pause all the way down the Throne Room, past the screen, which Zascai are not allowed beyond.

We walked past beautiful Eszai in stunning clothes, who were sitting in pews along the walls. They whispered to each other as Swallow passed.

We walked past ebony eagles at the ends of the benches; they had opalescent eyes.

Her shadow jumped, grew, jumped, and shrank as we walked past the torchères. I wished I had had chance to look in a mirror before coming in here.

We walked to the steps of the dais where the Emperor sits beneath a sunburst of silk and burnished gold.

Swallow was sensible enough not to look at the Emperor. She knelt, on one knee, and then on both knees, and then her hands touched the floor as well. Her head was bowed. I stood behind her, a hand on her broad shoulder, and proclaimed, "My lord Emperor, I bring Governor Swallow Awndyn from the coast, a mortal who has a message for your attention."

"Have I heard this claim before?"

"This time last year she was sent away from the court. But since then she's done much, traveled throughout Awia, built an opera house at Awndyn and sung at the Moren Grand." I recounted a list of Eszai and mortals alike who supported Swallow, a verbal petition that stopped abruptly when I realized the Emperor wasn't in the slightest impressed.

"Awndyn," said San, and at his voice she tensed. "What is the purpose of my Circle?"

"The most talented person of each occupation is made immortal so that the Fourlands can have a repository of wisdom and expertise, which it needs since god has left us and we are at war."

"Castle's aim is to protect the Fourlands from the Insects, is it not?"

She nodded and the Emperor continued: "So how can a musician help us? Your melody turns Insects to stone, is that it?"

I said, "She can rally the fyrd and I have heard her play marches—"

The Emperor laughed, gratingly. "Messenger, enough. Next you will have me believing that brave speeches can rouse the rank and file. I think Swallow's presence might even act as a distraction to Eszai who should be fighting. Governor Awndyn, if we were at peace your art might find a place here, but like all arts it is the pastime of mortals, I fear . . . If I was to make you immortal, on what grounds would another Musician be able to Challenge you? It would be impossible to judge the best."

Her soft body pressed against my leg. She shook with restlessness; she had nothing to lose and wished to make the best of the incident in which she was trapped. But I was angry—how could we decide if one activity is more worthwhile than another? I've seen Lightning's tricks with arrows and my flying often verges on acrobatics. For a start, it's impossible to separate the creative arts and the arts of war; they influence each other continually. Creativity is the humanity we're trying to save. If Eszai are war machines we're no better than Insects.

"Even in war, there's space to compose," Swallow said softly, but the Emperor chose not to hear her.

"I don't wish to endow people with immortality on the strength of their hobbies," he mused.

"My lord, she is the best of all time."

The Emperor smiled like a wolf in a children's story. "Governor Awndyn, I think you have made yourself immortal already. Your music will not die easily."

"My lord Emperor, I could do much more—I could create forever! If I die the Fourlands would lose my gift."

"Would your creativity survive becoming immortal? People create in order to leave something of themselves in the world when they die. Immortals do not have that pressure."

"My lord, only with an immortal lifetime can I express all the music I have inside me."

"Everyone in the Empire can witness the martial skills of my Circle, but not everyone can appreciate music, and they would criticize your membership."

Swallow's courage failed her; it was impossible for her to argue with the Emperor and she fell silent out of fear that she had said too much already. I thought the virtuoso had a different kind of strength, distinct from mine but equal; those who understood her musical feats would be convinced of her stamina. Many Eszai are jaded and love innovation; some of us, like myself, invent to make our lives easier and to prove we are the best specialists in our various professions. The more confident immortals embrace novelty and would welcome Swallow's continual creation.

San said, "Do you think music requires an eternal guardian, as Lightning controls the skill of archery? Would it be better if music was left to change and develop as future people wish? I think that your dedication to join the Castle has little to do with music. You confront me with a very selfish determination. Comet asked how he could serve me, but instead you seem to demand eternity."

"My lord, I'm sorry if I seem hasty. It's the nature of mortals to believe that their time is running out and death is imminent."

The Emperor's agate eyes softened and he sighed. "Ah yes," he said. "I remember . . . Messenger, do you think Awndyn's music would be better loved if she were one day to die?"

I thought of the shields outside the Throne Room, which used to be so important they were fixed in the center of the Castle, but now nobody knows which divisions of land they represent. I said, "It isn't the same music if Swallow isn't there to defend and interpret it. When she dies, her work dies too."

I braced myself, straightened and met his gaze. The Emperor was vulpine, thin-faced, white-haired, his arms in an ivory and gold cloak out over stone armrests. One candle-strength of humor lit his immeasurable eyes.

"How old is she now?"

"Nineteen, my lord."

"How old have you been for two hundred years, Comet?"

"Twenty-three. But I've grown wiser!"

"Have you? I think it would be a shame to deny the Fourlands the music she would make if she were to grow more mature. When she gains more experience her music will be so improved that the rest of the world will learn from it. We will consider." San finished, "I will see you again. This evening I will hear you play."

Swallow stood and walked backward a few steps, then turned and left the Hall. In the still space I heard a clatter from the gallery as Lightning raced out to meet her. A couple of Eszai close on the balcony chuckled.

San limited the numbers of people in the Circle. There are fifty immortals, not including the Emperor, or husbands and wives, and there are rarely positions free. It looked like Swallow would have to wait a long time.

"And what shall we do with you?" San asked. It was my turn to drop to one knee, watching the red carpet. "Take yourself over to Rachiswater and speak with the King. I want to know what he wants, how he plans, and how he feels. The last is most important."

"Yes, my lord."

"You may remind him that the Circle is still at his disposal."

There was a weird inflection in the word "still" which prompted me to ask, "Would it be better if there was a new King?"

"Comet, you know better than that. The Castle does not have its own fyrd. We have no authority over the King of Awia, nor the Governor of Hacilith, nor any of the governors or lord governors of the manors. We help when they decide to ask us, and we provide advice when they desire it. Otherwise, how will we last for the millennia before god returns?"

"Yes, my lord."

"If we are seen to be forceful, we would be questioned. It falls to the governors of Awia to decide between them if Staniel should be replaced. Lightning is the only one of them who has made his opinion clear to me. He is concerned that the manors will start fighting between themselves. That would be a disaster."

"Yes it would."

"Make sure you bring any news to me first. Not to Lightning; he can be a little overconfident sometimes. And it has been a contretemps for the Castle to be so slow in understanding the situation. Which is your obligation, Comet. I've heard nothing from you, except that which your wife has sent with your name on it."

"Ah, yes. I—"

"I gather that you needed a rest. I'm interested in knowing how often and for how long you need *to rest* . . ." The Emperor left a gap in which I was presumably expected to say something, but even if I had anything to say, I was too scared to speak. "If this happens again we will remove your title."

Feigning flippancy I managed, "I don't have a title."

"I mean people will stop calling you Comet."

I dropped a loose hand to my sword hilt and looked up, grazed with worry. The Emperor continued, "You are only immortal for a while, Comet. I suggest you try to remember why you are lucky enough to have a place here, and imagine what would happen if I called for Challengers against you."

"My lord. I'm sorry."

"Remember when you speak to Rachiswater that you address him on our behalf. The Castle's representative. He's afraid of you. Yes. Of course he is. I know you find that amusing but please don't exploit it. Frightened kings are dangerous."

CHAPTER SIX

The cool smoothness of Rachiswater was calming after the bright autumn morning. The whole Palace was designed to be airy; it was open plan, invaded by its own gardens. Arches and sweeping white walls had elegant, linear decoration, flowing like script.

The Palace was composed of curves, in a garden that featured only circles and spirals. From the air it looked like a long cluster of giant bleached bones in lush downland; even the hills had been sculpted. It was a very modern building, and the hall outside which I waited was completely circular. Every surface was white, the far wall was distant; it was like looking into a vast drum. A balcony hooped the hall, five meters up from floor level, its plain plasterwork picked out in cream. There were no steps inside; one enters from a grand outside staircase.

It was fascinating to fly to Rachiswater from the Castle. I had become lulled by random patterns of the forest canopy. But as I approached the Palace the woodland changed, becoming a little more preened, more cared for. Hunting lodges took the place of villages. The natural forest became neater and neater until it stopped abruptly in a clean-cut border and I was over the geometrical gardens. The Palace rose in front of me, five-story wings open in a stone embrace. A sudden current played havoc with my steering. I kept head on into it, twisted, stooped. I flew down the curved avenue of trees, so low as to go through the top of the fountain. Straight up and over the roof. Dropped down into a courtyard.

How can I describe flying? You try to describe what it is like to walk.

I jumped up onto a second-floor sill and peered inside, clinging to the masonry tendrils around the window. Some soldiers saw me soaring in; my shadow on the pitch stopped their game of football and sent them running about like guilty children. I had a few minutes before the news reached Staniel and I wanted to watch him.

Staniel sat alone, on the spindly silver throne, which was polished to brilliance. His corn-gold hair was tied back with a taffeta bow; a white shirt with buttons along the tight sleeves showed the gauntness of his arms. His keen pale face was bowed over a tall card table. I watched him move the cards about rapidly: a red five under a black six, a red ace of swords under a black deuce, a black ten under a red soldier. The red soldier went under a black governor, under a red king.

He's playing patience.

Ten minutes later: god, this is boring.

A black five and a red six under a black seven.

I seem to spend a ridiculous amount of time standing on windowsills.

I bet whoever built this window never thought that Comet would use it to spy on the King of Awia. At this point, aren't I supposed to learn some vital and intriguing piece of information?

Swallow once told me that patience allows us to achieve our goals. Unlike her I don't believe that "talent will out." The only thing you achieve with patience is a damn long wait.

Exasperated, I hopped through the window and glided down across the panopticon, landing neatly in front of the King. I bowed low, flicking my long hair back and folding my wings. "My lord, I congratulate you and bring the Emperor's best wishes."

Staniel jumped, slapped a hand over his heart. "Don't you ever come in by the bloody door?"

"The Emperor sent me to ask whether the new King of Awia has any requests for the Circle or plans to be made known."

"I have everything under control," he said airily.

"Yes, apart from occasional lapses of etiquette."

Staniel huffed, leaned back in the fragile-looking throne and clicked his fingers. A servant appeared almost immediately with a glass of white wine for me on a salver. This country has its good points. "Tell me about your adventure," I suggested.

"I barely escaped with my life! So now there are Insects in my province. We encountered a thousand or more; it was a cloudless night and I cannot be in error. They ran along parallel with us, close to the ground like big ants . . . Ugh. I hailed my escort; we had no other thought but to flee. They are everywhere! Comet—"

"Jant."

"Jant, where do they come from?"

I shrugged, hands wrapped around the cold crystal. "Do you know that once Insects appeared in the slums in Hacilith? Dead

Insects have been found on islands far out in the sea. Nobody knows, Your Highness."

"Perhaps underground." He shuddered at the thought of caverns festering with Insects below us, waiting to break forth.

"I'm sure Insects are one of the threats that god expected the Fourlands would have to face. That's why it asked the Emperor to be its steward for the lands until it returns. So you should let us deal with them, which I'm afraid we can't do until you grant us troops. Then we will cleanse Rachis of Insects and push them back behind the Wall."

"If the Castle had been fulfilling its function we wouldn't be in this situation to begin with!"

"I beg to differ."

"Jant, hear me out. You couldn't save my brother, could you? Castle didn't protect him then, in that battle. I . . . Oh, *damn*. No matter how . . . how strong he was, Eszai-strong, it didn't avail him against those . . . little *butchers*. So what chance have I?"

"I'm sorry I couldn't save Dunlin."

"He disobeyed your orders, didn't he?"

"That's right."

"So I must apologize on his behalf as well as mourn him."

"In the heat of battle, any man might do the same," I baited.

"Not I, Jant. I aim to benefit from experience. Having clashed with Insects after dark, I know enough never to go beyond Rachis Town again."

Staniel would be shocked to see the network of scars I carry. I waved the glass around and the frowning servant refilled it. Staniel continued: "Let the other manors raise more troops. Let Lightning use Micawater, which I have noticed is often spared. Get Hacilith to work for once. I am staying here because if the worst comes to the worst, then the capital will be safe."

"Is that the answer I must take back to San?"

"Unequivocally. I will dismiss my guard when I am satisfied

Rachiswater is safe. Let you immortals prove your worth to me. There is a space in the mausoleum where my brother should lie and I will never forgive the Castle for that. At least you tried, Comet, but where were the others? Mist and Tornado have boasted of slaying that many Insects between them."

"They were too far away."

"Then I blame Lightning's inefficient planning."

"Is there anything else you would like the Emperor to know?"

He thought for a while. "I am as secure in this Palace as Vireo is in Lowespass."

"Yes, I am impressed with your defense."

"The soldiers are one thing, but we also have sufficient supplies."

"And funds?"

"Not so good, but manageable. I'm the last of my family. The end of the dynasty has come upon us. My family saved and hoarded in case of such an impasse. I am determined to use their accumulated wealth to the best advantage so their endeavors are not in vain . . . What are you smirking at?"

"Rachiswater was the smallest manorship when I was born," I said.

The Awian thought my comment less than useful. "Try to understand us mortals," he sneered. "Time has distorted your viewpoint so much it's useless! For you, Jant, every day is the beginning of a golden age; chance to be playboy of the entire world. To Lightning, the world is broken; the best times ended in eleven-fifty. Even Mist looks like he's been left behind in the last millennium. What is the point of Eszai helping Zascai when they have seen so many of us die that we might as well be ants! How do you *really* think of us? As ants? For god's sake, Jant, I'm just trying to stay alive!"

"I promise you will."

"Ha! I'd be a sacrifice like my brother in the blink of an eye. While you're assured of eternity! Have you noticed that the Castle walls are even thicker than those of Lowespass Fortress?"

"You have a thousand times more soldiers than there are Eszai," I said, reassuringly.

I realized I would get no sense out of him while he was so worked up. I only risked making it worse and I certainly didn't want to raise his resentment against the Circle. It would be best to leave for a while and tell the Emperor what I had learned. Staniel's arrogance was like an addict's, which stems from fear and from the fact one is forced into a more and more extreme position without being able to admit it. I know well the deceit of trying to clothe pain and confusion in mystery and romanticism.

"Let San know I mean no threat to the Circle."

"Not directly," I muttered. "Do I have your permission to return with news at any time?"

"Of course."

I bowed again and took my leave with a word of farewell. Staniel summoned his glowering servant to accompany me across the circular mosaic and through white passageways to the main gate.

I asked the servant what she thought of the new regime. She kept her head bowed and didn't reply. She was beautiful, slim, and brisk. I plucked at her sleeve and when she glanced up I tapped the scarification on my upper arm to show her the wheel that Felicitia had carved there.

"See this? It's the insignia of a Hacilith street gang. I was nothing once, just a homeless stray. Now I'm an Eszai I never get the chance to chat to people, and I really miss it, you don't know how much. Please don't be shy to speak to me, just tell me the truth."

"We're beat," she said. "We really can't feed all these men. I heard His Majesty say he will pay them what he can. Lord Eszai—I don't think I should be telling you this."

"It's all right."

"Every hour Staniel demands the town wall be built faster and faster. I don't know why. Some say the Emperor is angry with us; we'll have to fight the Circle and that will be the end of us."

"That won't happen," I said uncertainly.

"And some say an Insect swarm is massing worse than the year two thousand and four, that will overrun Lakeland Awia and devour us all."

I returned via Hacilith, where I collected a letter from the Governor addressed to San. I stopped off at every Plainslands manor on the way back—Shivel, Eske and Fescue—in order to reassure them and gather correspondence for the Emperor.

The missive from Hacilith said:

My lord Emperor,

We are gravely concerned about the actions of the Sovereign of Awia who has withheld his men from the Circle's command and is no longer raizing troops nor sending them to the front. With deep regret we must inform you that the city of Hacilith and Moren will also no longer raise troops. The far country of Awia is unwilling to guard its lands, so we do not believe that fyrd raised in Moren should be sent to protect it. If the Insect threat is as imminent as King Rachiswater believes then Hacilith, your Holy City, requires all its divisions to defend its walls and the other human towns within the borders of Morenzia.

We will reverse our decision when the Sovereign of Awia releases his fyrd, either to be wholly disbanded or placed under the wise dominion of the Circle. We trust he will not be long in making such a decision, and we implore you to send your Messenger to direct his judgment. We humbly and fervently await your answer.

K. AVER-FALCONET,
LORD GOVERNOR OF HACILITH AND MOREN

The missive from Eske said:

My lord Emperor,

Communication over the Plains is rapid; it's quickly come to my ears that Awia and Hacilith are amassing their own hosts. I find it hard to accept it's because Staniel and Aver-Falconet fear the Insects, when the Castle has always been able to control them. Eske shares one border with Rachiswater, and is only three days' ride from Hacilith so I feel that it's important for our security to keep Eske fyrd available. Lowespass, the Plainslands, and Morenzia are all human countries and are on excellent terms, but we fear the same is not the case between the Plainslands and Awia. You will remember past instances when Awia expanded its realm forcibly, into the Darkling Mountains, and we would not wish the same to happen to the Plainslands. I beg you impress your authority on Rachiswater and the city for the sake of our safety and cooperation.

C. ESKE, LADY GOVERNOR

From Fescue:

My lord Emperor,

Your thrice-great Messenger has just explained the situation and has urged me to raise more fyrd. It grieves me to say there are no more. The meritorious campaign of Dunlin

Rachiswater has depleted our manor and I risk an uprizing if I continue to ruin homes and tear men and young women from their families' embrace. Your loyal subject, I await further counsel from the distinguished Circle court, but circumstance forces my hand to add that if Comet does not bring your response within forty-eight hours I will join Eske in reserving my fyrd for this manor alone.

L. L. F., GOVERNOR

When I returned to my Castle room, I scraped off the wax and resealed the letters with care. I used different types of wax and fake seals of the manors which I had crafted over the last hundred years, and which I keep in a locked cabinet. Then I took the letters down to court and presented them to the Emperor, with my report.

An hour later, I found myself leaning against the wall outside the Throne Room, gasping for breath and shivering head to foot, like a burning puppet hanging from hot wires. My legs and wings trembled from extreme exhaustion, and when I rubbed my inflamed eyes I smeared the eyeliner everywhere. Dropping altitude too quickly had given me a nosebleed. Blood. Mascara. Fucking wonderful.

Home, I thought. Sleep, I thought, but I simply stood there trying to work out which way was up so I could attempt to walk.

When I need a fix I get flashes of past. Darkling, Hacilith, Wrought. Bleeding on the battlefield, running from the gangs in the city. I fear I will shake myself apart. May leave sweat stain on the wall like a shadow. Need rest. Need chocolate. Want a solid gold hypodermic and Tern to massage my wings with warm oil.

Shearwater Mist swaggered down from the gallery. "The Emperor certainly took it out on you," he observed.

"Uh . . . Yeah. Only stopped because he could see I was . . . knackered."

"If I flew seven hundred kilometers I'd be knackered too. Rest. Wicked. We're only bloody human. Flesh. Bone. Rhydanne, in your case."

"Yeah." I slid down the wall until I was sitting with my knees bent up in front. Mist's lined face loomed over me, above a rough cloak wound like a chrysalis around his barrel chest. "No offense," I slurred, "but I'm going to be sick."

"So tired?"

"Need cat . . ."

The Sailor plucked me upright and allowed me to lean on him. The most bizarre sight in the Castle—like a rotund crow trying to support a heron—I was so much taller than him I ended up draped over his broad shoulders. He trod on my pinions, I stumbled on the flagstones and eventually we made it to the Hall where he poured rum down me—and into my mouth—and averted his gaze while I shot up some scolopendium.

"God. Oh, god-and-the-long-wait. Ow. Fuck. *Why is the Empire fucking falling apart?*"

"Are you all right now?"

"Oh. Yes." I giggled abruptly, realized I was being hysterical and stopped.

"The Emperor shouldn't put you through that."

"Hey, we're immortal. We have a duty to work hard."

"Hard, yes. To death, no. Candle. Both ends."

"If San wants a scapegoat it will be me! I'm the most dispensable, Mist. He'll blame it all on me and throw me out of the Circle!"

"That's drug talk. I've heard such from the sailors in Hacilith Dock. Clear conscience?"

"Not really."

"Nor have any. Comes from living so long." He sat hunched over his tankard, a well-rolled cigarette in one three-fingered hand.

"Don't tell anyone you saw me in that state, *please*," I urged. My problem must not become widely known. Mist shook his leonine head, with an "it's all right" smile.

"There's been so much happening here lately to distract us that nobody'd notice you. Drop. Ocean. Swallow Awndyn's louder, for instance."

"Huh?"

Mist drew on his cigarette. "She threw the biggest tantrum of all time. She was even louder than Ata." I realized that I had broken my golden rule: preoccupied with my own news I had not asked for the most recent happenings here.

"She destroyed Lightning's harpsi-thingy, you know. Gift horse. Mouth. That thing was worth a ship and a half. Why? Well, waif, you missed a real treat. Swallow had the harpsi-thingy set up right here in the Hall and she sang her heart out for two hours solid. Pounded the keys till I thought they would break."

"What did she sing?"

"Opera, mainly. Some blues. Without accompaniment. The reprise from 'Lynnet's Song.' Over my head, it was. The Emperor was here. All here; your wife looked gorgeous." He rolled a cigarette deftly and passed it to me. I declined because smoking is a bad habit.

"Ha! Pot. Kettle. The Emperor listened to Swallow an' he seemed to enjoy it . . . It's only the second time I've seen San out of the Courtroom . . . He spoke to her afterward. He said her performance was excellent, but he said she couldn't join us. Cat. Pigeons. She was exhausted—she didn't look as foxy as usual. It was after that she went completely crazy. A woman and a ship ever want mending. We could have done with you there to help calm her down. I think she fancies you. Birds. Feather. So now she says she's going to the front—"

"What!"

" 'S right. She won't listen to Lightning. He's pissed off as you might imagine but he brought it on himself. Heart. Sleeve. He's a fool for love, always has been. The Circle is no stronger than its weakest link."

"Lightning is not a fool!"

"You never had a father, did you?" Mist asked.

"No . . . What's that got to do with it?"

"Grow up, waif. You hang around Lightning like one of his hounds. You'd lick his hand if he let you."

Nonsense. "I want to know about Swallow; when is she leaving?"

"Oh, I guess tomorrow—or rather, later today because it's half midnight. Strike. Iron's hot, she tells me, but I think she just wants to be out of the Castle to escape embarrassment. I've noticed all Lightning's loves look the same. It's because—"

"She'll take her fyrd?"

"Sure. They're getting in the way here. I'm off to Peregrine because Ata has something to discuss with me about our daughter. Absence. Fonder."

I gave him a look that I expect was mostly green because my pupils were contracted to fine lines. I floated on the drug. "It's like when Staniel left Lowespass."

"Yes. Frying pan. Fire. But the foxy redhead is too smart to get in trouble, like the rich sissy did. Chalk. Cheese. No offense but I want the sissy to be King because he won't dare interrupt my trade in Peregrine. It's an ill wind. Bloody Dunlin kept taxing tobacco." I thought Mist was wrong; Staniel was stupid enough to meddle in anything.

The Emperor and I were the only ones who knew how desperate the situation was. Reading other people's letters brings with it a terrible responsibility.

"Did the Emperor order Swallow not to go?"

"On the contrary, he said it was her choice."

"Damn it!" I tested my weight on my shaking legs. Result: not good. I had to go to Swallow and stop her riding out. She wouldn't last a minute at the front.

"Where are you going?" asked Mist.

"Have to see her."

"Don't be daft, waif. Haste. Speed. You're in no fit state to—"

"Don't care. Have to go." I wobbled to my feet and Mist turned his attention to beer. "I'm telling you, Jant, rest first. You've been run ragged."

"Cat keeps me going."

"No fit state . . ."

I made it across the Hall and almost to the door before I passed out. I woke up in bed two days later.

CHAPTER SEVEN

It wasn't difficult to intercept Swallow's Band although I had to landfall a couple of times to be sick. They followed the Eske Road north, toward Awia, and the twin columns of horsemen, infantry, and baggage train were seven kilometers long. While Swallow and Lightning, riding proudly in the vanguard, passed the half-timbered Eske manor, the tail of her fyrd were still entering the manorship. Those in the middle helped each other traverse the river. When Swallow passed the Quadrivium Cemetery, the middle of the column was bunching together in order to get a long look at the manor, and those at the end were still crossing the river. When Swallow crossed the border into Awia the middle of her column crept past the Cemetery and those at the end straggled to glimpse Eske. She rode past Silk Mill and Donaise, Foin, Slaughterbridge, and the Place de la Première Attaque. They passed through Rachiswater, and held up all the traffic in the town. Lightning craned his neck to catch sight of the Micawater estate wall.

Lightning rode straight-backed on his white horse, red-caparisoned, by Swallow, his armor gleaming like the sun. Often he hung back, reluctant as a dog that's sensed danger. But he had given up arguing with her a long time ago and was now following her for her own protection because he knew she wouldn't see reason. I thought that if he had strength enough to stop following Swallow and let her go alone, after ten kilometers she might have suffered self-doubt, and turned back to join him. But each kept the other going, and they radiated a dangerous courage that rose like warm air. Swallow's hair was copper; she held a guitar on her lap. Her dolphin standard leaped and twined. The fyrd moved with a rustle along the road deep in infinite colors of autumn leaves, sepia brown, russet, rust, and gold.

And all the time I hung above them, as high as a kite.

There was nothing I could really do to influence their strange dilemma—Lightning's unrequited love for the musician. Although I had been a confidant to both, I was not intimate enough to break the seal of such a private problem.

Unintentionally attention-seeking, I have taken too much cat on occasion, but I couldn't raise Lightning's wrath when he was obsessed with Swallow. Swallow hasn't noticed me even though I have cheekbones to die for. Adamantine Awndyn has eyes for no man.

I can't divert you with observations and epigrams on the nature of love, because I know so little about it. I decided my disinterest in love was lucky. I've had lots of relationships, starting with Serin in "The Wheel," and ending with Tern, but none have been as intense as Lightning's agony. I have noticed that lovers can be nostalgic for places where they lingered, even gray tram platforms on freezing nights, which makes me think that love is not just blind but blindingly stupid. I do love Tern, but I love within reason and within the bounds of comfort. Lightning's old-fashioned way of loving shakes the roots of his very being.

Lightning first saw her in the opera house in Hacilith. She caused a sensation, a standing ovation, and he heard the news while he was practicing archery in the Long Field at Micawater. Immediately, he took his coach to see what all the fuss was about a "new talent." The Moren Grand was sold out, but he owned a box so close to the stage he could look directly down on her. When she walked forward into the spotlight and began an aria he was overcome and, leaning out, dropped his program, which fluttered down slowly, slowly and noisily in the complete silence onto the stage at her feet. He spent the rest of the performance in the dark recesses of the box, head in hands, overwhelmed because her voice was so perfect. He decided to send her red roses, and the floral carnage was such that roses have been rare in Awia since.

Lightning paid me to carry the first letter to her, and I found Swallow backstage in stripy tights and a green velvet shawl. A visit from the Emperor's Messenger frightened her; then when she read the letter she fainted and I had to bring her round with sal volatile.

I flew their correspondence all year. Lightning pressed a letter into my right hand, dropped fifty pounds into my left hand. I stepped over the ledge and off I went. Swallow dropped a note in my right hand, pressed five pounds in my left hand, and off I went. Lightning sipping coffee on the archery field in Mica, Swallow tapping two-four time on the podium in Awndyn. Lightning in a long brocade coat, Swallow in a tuxedo and tails. Between them, I made a killing on the travel expenses.

Micawater Palace Mews
Saturday 20 June
The Year of Our War 2014

Dearest Swallow,
In your last brief letter you were kind enough to thank me

for the gift I sent. It was nothing, a mere trifle. I beg you not to worry about the value of such things when you yourself are so precious to me. You say the difference between Awndyn and Micawater is too great, but I assure you that material wealth matters little. Gold and banknotes are only valuable because we—every one of us—accedes every day in allowing it. We acquiesce in the illusion, but money is simply shaped pieces of metal and paper that we can wisely use to serve us. A small amount can be used as wisely as a fortune when it is the use to which it is put that matters. In terms of your musical prowess you are far richer than I.

Know that I will wait for you and that I can be relied upon. It is good that you want to become immortal on your own worth. As I have said before and you urge me to say again I believe wholeheartedly in your ability, your music is live haunting to me and I speak to the Emperor on your behalf at every available opportunity. I can wait, even, as you say, until you grow old. Eszai who are old forever are more grateful for immortality than the young impudent ones, but they miss their youth and wish they were eternally young.

I can never receive a straight answer from you, you twist and turn like a swallow in flight, but although it pains me to wait, I will. Do you know, heartwood is used on the inside of longbows because it is older and more resilient. As it is hard, it springs back to shape quickly and so can throw an arrow farther. Micawater is the heartwood of Awia, a resilient family with flawless honor. But good bows need sapwood bound to heartwood, to make them more pliable and so shoot true.

I am tormented by wondering how I can prove myself worthy of you. Tell me what you will. Love balances the weights unequally, always forcing a man to love a woman whom no amount of sedulous courtship can win, since she does not entertain reciprocal feelings, not having been fired by love's arrows. Marriage is eternal, and it is mortals who fail it. Only immortals can be truly married, and an immortal can only be truly complete when married.

Don't worry about my Messenger. The first Rhydanne I ever met disturbed me too. She told my brother how he was to die. For a long time I thought it was a power they all had, but it was simply a coincidence. My brother Shryke was an accomplished hunter; he went riding every day and returned with deer and boar. He enjoyed the amphitheater where we had bullfighting, and we brought in Insects and whole packs of famished wolves.

A fair would converge every summer on the meadow by the river. My brothers always clamored to go visit, but Mother always withheld her permission. On this occasion, there were archery tournaments as part of the fair. Mother was both proud of my skill, and keen to remind Awia that our family was worthy of the throne. So I went under the protection of Shryke, my second eldest brother. I remember toffee apples, fire-eaters, iced wine, jugglers, and horses racing on a grass track.

The Rhydanne was telling fortunes, using cards like the ones Jant has. She was sitting on the damp grass among all the patched, bright tents and banners. She had a long black skirt, spread out on the grass, and the cards were placed on it. I was uncertain, because she looked so strange, but Shryke was very interested—he lingered near her until people had drifted away, and I wanted to leave too. He gave her a coin, and she looked at it fiercely, in the flat palm of her long hand. He took it back from her, went and bought a bar of chocolate with it, and presented her with that. She smiled. I expected her teeth to be sharp, like a cat's, but they were quite normal. Then she cut the cards and arranged them, while Shryke stood and watched. She said he would die within the year. She said that an animal would cause his death.

I watched the Rhydanne girl. She knew she was telling the truth. Shryke laughed and dismissed it, boasting that everybody had to die sometime. All the way back he told me that fortune cards didn't work, it was nothing but a game, and anyway only mountain people believed those things. The next day he went to fight leopards in the amphitheater. Nothing could discourage him from hunting, fishing and falconry; in fact he grew more ambitious, careless, trying to prove that cards are foolish. Celebrations resulting from the archery tournament eclipsed my fears, and soon I forgot all about it.

Mica River cuts through a narrow gorge in the forest near Donaise. Shryke was fond of walking down there with his favorite dog on a lead, and often I went too. It was a great challenge to jump the gorge, it could be done in summer when the river was low. He left one morning and I was in my room, when my cousin came in, tears streaming down her face. I tried to console Martyn but I could not, and she bade me come to court. There we found Shryke's body laid out on a catafalque, and Mother sitting on the throne room floor, wailing and beating her fists in the air with grief.

The gamekeeper found him in Peregrine, which is twenty kilometers downstream. His limbs were broken, and his skin vivid with bruises from being in the whirlpools. Nothing can survive the rapids there, they even carve holes in rock. Mother said that brigands had killed him but when the faithful dog came back wearing its lead I knew that Shryke had simply tried to jump the gorge. The little dog refused, and so pulled him in.

I never spoke to another Rhydanne after that, until Jant arrived. He has done much since which convinces me that they can't see the future.

My love, while I write it has grown dark and the stars are reflected in the lake. Stars, like people, do not change but very rarely I have seen a bright star bloom among them—like you,

Swallow. Write to me, don't deny me a letter; it is deceitful to deny what has been pledged. Your reluctance to love is good because you will be more willing to keep secret what I confide. There have been many women in the past seeking to prey upon Micawater's wealth and the promise of immortality, but I have shunned them because their love is not genuine. Your reluctance marks you as worthy. If I could only succeed in winning your hand, and if just a little of the ardor you show for music could be set aside for love, then I would at last be content.

Yours,
SAKER

On receiving this, Swallow wrote to me:

MEMO
FROM: SWALLOW, THE BEACH, 8/2/14
TO: COMET, FILIGREE SPIDER, SCREE

Jant—Help me! Help me! The Archer asked me to marry him!! You said I could treat you like a brother so please help—should I say yes? Can I say no without insulting him?? He isn't someone I should insult! I want to be immortal on my own worth, and this sounds more like a demand than a proposal! I know what my father would have wanted me to say, but I never took any notice of him when he was alive, so why now? Send your reply to Awndyn. And, Jant, I know you have the biggest mouth in the Fourlands but please don't gossip about this. Or else.

Lightning offered her the most fantastic opportunity in the world. In fifteen hundred years, she was the one. Proud and principled, she was turning it down. Maybe she didn't understand how untouchable an Archer Lightning was—his immortality seemed the most secure of us all. She must know more about what she had done to him. And as Lightning's bride, Swallow would have plenty of time to convince the Emperor to make her the Circle's Musician, immortal in her own right. I sent a hasty reply:

The Filigree Spider inn
Turbary Track
Scree
September 27, 2014

Dear Governor Awndyn,

In answer to your question: say yes. Micawater has held out this long before asking because he doesn't realize how long a year can seem. Tern has made me think of things I would never have otherwise considered; so I suggest that if you do consider yourself to be an adventurer in this life, the very best thing you can do is accept his belated proposal. In fact, if you want my advice, I'd like to invite you to Wrought so we can discuss it face to face and over a glass of whiskey.

The Archer is a hunter and a fighter, he is not a successful lover albeit he has spent centuries practicing. He usually keeps his business private but in the last few days I have seen him shattered with apprehension, which cannot be assuaged even by vintage port. I thought he had forsaken romance, that time had made him indurate. I wondered on whom you had set your sights instead . . . But now I write to say please accept Lightning's offer; if you do not you may end him completely. Even in my worst moments I doubt I have looked so unwell.

If you make your way north on the Coast Road after Cobalt and Peregrine you will reach Wrought manor; wait there. I will come down to meet you. Then we can speak face to face and out of the Archer's way.

I can think of many anecdotes which would sway your appreciation of him one way or the other. If you had seen him with Savory in Morenzia, you would not doubt his tenderness. Unfortunately Savory did not survive. He was blood brother with her, take a look at the scar across his palm. He used to say that he was married to her. I used to say that she was the fifth race, that there were Awians, Insects, humans, Rhydanne, and Lady Savory. He was in an adolescent storm of passion; I was like a chess player, touching pieces he did not wish to move.

On the other hand, and not to put it lightly, Lightning can be an arrogant and nasty piece of work. He has refused to lend me money when I have been most in need of it, and in dealings of real estate can be absolutely mercenary. Your relationship with him must be all or nothing, clear-cut black and white. I am aware so far that it has been "nothing" rather than "all," but now I beg you to reconsider. Surely you should be pleased that he can be bad.

For example, I still haven't forgiven him for what he and Tawny did to me on my stag night. We're talking late December 1892. I held it a week before Tern and I got hitched—it should be the night before but I didn't think that would be particularly wise. Lightning lent me the folly at Micawater to stage it and, since I was famous for giving parties, everybody was there. Everybody male, that is, from four lands, and we had been drinking for two days solid by the time this happened . . .

I'd had syllabub for supper, actually I was covered in it, and a bottle of whiskey. Well, let us say I was a little intoxicated. Lightning had been planning for this, and said with that scornful smirk we all know so well, "Do you still think you're the fastest thing in the Fourlands?"

I stutteringly asseverated that indeed I was. He prompted that I didn't sound convinced. It's essential to be convincing because otherwise the next day brings a flood of Challenges from idiots thinking they can outpace me. I climbed onto a *table and announced it to all and sundry. Sarcelle Rachiswater smacked his hand on the table gleefully and said, "Right! Grab him!"*

The next thing I know I'm in Tawny's vast grasp, with my face pressed against the table and my wings belted up behind my back. They stripped me, wound a deerskin around my waist, and with a strap under my chin, placed a pair of antlers on my head. They were heavy, twelve-tined, gilded. In exploring them with my hands I dropped the deerskin, to much wild hilarity from those not unconscious or preoccupied with the call girls.

Lightning stood, gauntleted hands on hips, and said, "Now you are the king of the forest."

The best I could manage was: "Look guys, this isn't amusing." Sarcelle whimsically slipped a butter knife into my hand. Tawny picked me up over one shoulder and carried me outside, in a ribald procession, into the frosted gardens. The tower clock was striking one, a hunter's moon jaundiced the snow. I stood there, they stepped back and regarded me silently. I said, "What am I supposed to do now? Piss against trees and eat berries?"

Then from round the stables, came a barking and a baying, the sound of frost being crushed under a hundred scabby paws. They had released the dogs. And you know what Micawater hounds are like: purebred and well-trained, evil little killers. Lightning gave me an experimental push, and said, "I think you'd better run."

How I ran! I ran deep into the forest, in the semi-darkness, with the pack behind me. I ran till my feet left blood in the prints. I ran wide-eyed and bruised with cold. The antlers kept catching on low branches and jerking my head back—I lost valuable seconds crouching down and struggling with the strap. I went over fences and stiles rapid as prey, heart match-

ing my strides, salt taste in my mouth, every decision the same: run. At the back of my mind, although reduced to instinct, becoming stag, I knew I could do it. I believed with a chance I could outrun twenty dogs. Then I just ran.

Until at length I reached the summit of a rise and looked down on a shallow valley strung with hammock fields. I realized this was Bitterdale; at the far end were the lights of Wrought. Stopping for breath, I heard the snuffling of hounds closing in. They began to howl in excitement. I backed up against a tree which I had no strength to climb. On the edge of Tern's manorship, at the brink of safety, my spirit gave out. I was too exhausted to care anymore. I would make a stand.

The dogs were pouring through a gap in the hedge, blurred by the darkness. The first ran toward me, gathering itself to spring. I wondered whether it was possible to shove the butter knife down its throat before I would be teeth and fingernails with the others.

I hissed in a breath. I knew the beast's exultation; I've run down so many deer myself. It closed in, canines, spit, and dirty fur.

The dog leaped, and an arrow caught it in midair, slamming it down into the snow, where it curled, whimpering, skewered through the shoulder.

The muscled bulk of a white horse galloped between us, and Lightning's hands, one on my wing the other on my backside, lifted me fluidly over the cantle. In the same easy gesture he swung the quiver onto his shoulder, wheeled round and rode through the pack, which scattered. The hunt master, on a scarred charger and with a whip, was following. He made a tight bundle of the dogs and we returned in silence. I don't remember the details of that, except for a bumping, jarring, the world being upside down. I was still drunk; my loose hands brushed the top of every hedge we jumped.

I remember Lightning prizing the knife from my grasp, placing a firm hand on my neck for my heartbeat which was calm and cold. He murmured "Rhydanne . . ." with an awestruck tone.

Lightning fed us with mulled wine and venison until I recovered. They figured that I had run forty kilometers, across Donaise to the outskirts of Wrought, just out of Lightning's manorship. Forty kilometers may not seem impressive when you know I have done a hundred in a day, and three hundred when flying, but under the circumstances . . .

Swallow, when I last saw Lightning he was splitting arrows at two hundred paces on the archery field, with lifeless repetition. He's hooked on you: obsessed. Don't say, "But he doesn't even know me"; he has been alive so long he knows the type of person you are. He can predict all your decisions from his own experience. Perhaps every second century he'll find a strong-willed woman who is worthy enough, otherwise they are a disappointment to him, and those with fewer morals shock him entirely.

So, sister, when the Governor Lord Micawater goes down on bended knee, you say yes. I shouldn't have to tell you this; it isn't as if you're Rhydanne. You want to be immortal, don't you? By all the blood of Lowespass, what does it take to get through to you?

Never think that you are young and have plenty of time; you cannot know how soon the end will be. I will gradually let you into secrets that will make your acceptance into the Circle much easier. There are things which the Emperor does not want Zascai to know, and assumes that Eszai are less likely to tell.

The first room in the pueblo has been whitewashed. It is white only from ground level to head height, because the owner couldn't be bothered to equip himself with a ladder. God, I love this village.

Now I should go. Judging from the way clouds are form-
ing and eagles wheeling over Mhadaidh there is some lift to
be had there. I am tempted to join them, but I will meet you
on the ground, in Wrought in a week's time. Don't forget to
bring your guitar.
    Failte bhâchna.

Yours with the will of god and the protection of the Circle,
COMET JANT SHIRA,
MESSENGER AND INTERPRETER FOR
THE SOVEREIGN EMPEROR SAN

Twenty letters later we are here, in the Rachiswater manorship on the edge of Lowespass. Weather: bracing, even for me.
Swallow's fyrd marched until nightfall and then she gave the
command to make camp. They had reached the southernmost
trenches, and the soldiers set about clearing them out, a very
nasty task. While the daylight lasted, they dug around the camp
making a square ditch and rampart. Some soldiers were posted
along the trenches to keep watch. From the air I could see their
round steel helmets in a line as they patrolled the edge.

Broken Insect limbs jutted into the air like machinery; there
was a jumble of dirt-colored skeletons unearthed by the trench-
diggers, waiting to be thrown in a mass grave. The trench earth
was fetid; sleet pooled in the clay, becoming freezing mud. It
stank of sulphur.

I had the feeling I was just keeping pace with the day, only
managing the bare essentials until the tiredness wears off and I
could tackle the real questions at last. I flew over the encamp-
ment, bleary-eyed, incapable of thought, observing the altered
landscape that unfolded below. Rachiswater was wreckage. I
saw a ruined barn where the fyrd had trapped Insects and
burned them. I saw Insects themselves, tiny in the distance, run-

ning across the pale green fields. The perspective was strange—
at a distance they looked as small as ants, but they tried to cross
a barbed wire fence which I knew to be two meters high, so they
must be as large as deer. My first coherent thought of the day—
this can't be true. We were at the front with fewer soldiers than
ever before, and there were more Insects than ever before.

I focused all attention on the spot where I had to land, and
swung in over earthwork and barbed wire, over canvas roofs to the
Castle's pavilion. Lightning and Swallow were standing outside,
trading opinions. She had a guitar slung over her shoulder, inlaid
with mother-of-pearl plaques. I bounded to a halt in front of them.

"Good evening, Jant. Nice flying."

I struggled to get my breath. "Ah . . . Swallow! Turn round
and go back. What do you think you're doing? Saker, you
should know better! How many fyrd do you have?"

"Six thousand."

"How many sodding Insects do you think there are?"

"Is it the Emperor's command?"

"No. Mine."

Lightning said, "Swallow, I told you. Listen to Jant."

"You go if you wish, Eszai. I stay."

"For a start this isn't the best time of year," Lightning said.

"So you're scared of a little snow, as well?"

"It's hard to keep a bowstring dry in this bloody weather."

I shook my wings to dislodge shards of ice, and attempted a
conciliatory tone. "Let's go back to the Palace. The soldiers can
camp in the park, and I can talk to Staniel and hopefully convince him to help us. Then we can march into Lowespass and
reach the fortress. It's foolhardy to try it with just six thousand."

"There isn't enough time. I've already sent messengers to
Eske and the Plainslands manors asking for assistance,"
Swallow informed me.

"You have. Good. The Plainslands manors have all refused

to send fyrd to Awia, as they don't agree with Staniel's tactics. That's Eske and Hacilith Moren; Swallow, you're on your own."

Palely, she asked, "And Tanager?"

"You know what happened to Tanager? She took her fyrd to find the casket of Dunlin's remains which his brother dropped so unceremoniously. She didn't get farther than the Lowespass trenches before the Insects ripped into them and they turned back. Half her men were killed there. Eleonora's a brave lady, but she's licking her wounds in Tanager now and gathering new troops."

The Archer let out an exasperated breath. "We're an Empire. The Empire isn't fragile! It's the most fundamental collaboration! Why are they not working together anymore?"

I sighed. If this was outside Lightning's experience what hope did we have? "Swallow, let's leave . . . ?"

"No. Let us make an effective contribution."

"I can tell you're getting older." Swallow was starting to use those callous efficient words which allow one to deal with the world without thinking about it. She knows how to say "I'm sorry" when hearing news of a death. In that context, what the fuck does "I'm sorry" *mean*? She knows how to say "hard luck," "good day," "I'm fine," "see you next year"—how daring it is for a mortal to anticipate that! The shell is growing, and it hides her. In a few years she won't be thinking or feeling deeply at all, and I am afraid that then her music will cease.

Lightning said, "I am willing to try to gain the next line of trenches. That is twenty-seven kilometers of land we can ensure is free from dispersed, straggling Insects. It's a small strip of land but it will prove that Castle is still attempting to protect the Empire, regardless of what help is sent. Then we can move, and wait to see if our statement merits any response."

"That's great, Saker. I knew you were with me."

"Would that I could always be with you."

"And I have to prove myself to the Emperor. He said that

Eszai are good warriors, well, it is his recurrent theme *a crescendo*. If it will help my cause, I'll show him I can fight."

I looked at her insouciant body carefully—her wide, freckled face, tip-tilted nose, and delicate lips, though she had bitten nails, and muscular legs. "If your claim to be Eszai is that you are the best musician in the world—"

"And I am."

"What good does it do you to fight?"

Swallow shrugged. "Ask the Emperor. It's beyond me."

I turned away from her and peered into the stripy gloom of the pavilion, palms up, saying, "No offense, but you are not a warrior. Your father kept you from the field. How arrogant it is! You think you can command where Eleonora failed, and Rachiswater. Eleonora is a skilled swordsman, you are a pear-shaped pianist."

"Jant, watch your mouth."

"Saker. Give me my orders for I'm away. I'm not watching your cold, hungry troops turn to pillaging their own country, and fed like tidbits to the Insects for the vainglorious lust of some ginger hussy."

"Jant!"

"He's just frightened," she said.

"If the Insects kill you, San will have a fat problem taken off his hands. Is the myth of your short life fame enough? I'll put up a statue—maiden armed with guitar against the hordes! Inscription: *More ambition than sense*." I whipped my sword from its scabbard which was tied upside down between my wings, and prodded the grass between her feet with the point. "Come, and leave the hard work to the Eszai. One day you'll thank me for saving your life."

Swallow put out a hand to the Archer, who understood the gesture. He unbuckled the sword belt from round his waist and handed the Wrought sword to her, hilt first. She grasped the hilt and pulled the blade from its jeweled sheath. A few soldiers nearby looked up, interested. "Guard," she said.

"Don't be bloody stupid."

She was furious that I didn't consider her worth fighting. As I turned away she lunged, the blade catching the inside of my leg, slicing through the leather. Bitch! I batted it down; it slid up my sword to the hilt. I parried her next blow easily, and then we were at it in earnest. I was faster than her. I had longer reach. I thrust, the heavier blade turned it. She swung up to my throat, I jumped back. I hacked at her legs three times and she checked each stroke, wincing. She feinted left, left again, and then I lost sight of her sword completely. Where is she? Right? Right. Oh, down there. I dropped the blade low, like a scythe.

I was off-balanced, reaching out for nothing. My arms flailed wildly and then I landed on my side in the mud. The breath was knocked out of me as Swallow stamped her flat foot heavily onto my kidneys.

Her sword pressed into my back. "Is it here?" she asked.

Lightning's voice: "No. Lower."

"Here?"

"Ow!" The point cut through my leather jacket.

"Jant? I can push this point though your backbone here. It separates two vertebrae. It doesn't hurt very much but you won't be able to run anywhere ever again."

"Eeep!"

"Do you fancy that?"

"No! No! Please!"

"Let him go," said Lightning. Swallow ruffled my scapular feathers, withdrew her sword and I got up with alacrity. She handed it back to Lightning who said, "Not bad. With practice you'll learn not to look at the blade at all. It's an extension of you. Watch your opponent's reaction."

"He's been giving me lessons," Swallow explained, while I pulled bits of mud out of my hair.

I glared at Lightning. "Why didn't you teach me that trick?"

"I had a feeling that one day a lady would need it to get the better of you."

"Swallow, I'm sorry."

"Glad to hear it. Are you with us now?"

"If I must."

That night a fire was lit in the middle of the compound and the soldiers roasted deer and warmed bread brought in from the villages around Rachiswater. Swallow asked for the venison fat and ate it sloppily with her dagger. I appreciated her appetite, wondered if she was as voracious in bed.

Flying made me hungry, but I was sulking at having underestimated Swallow. Many women are excellent fighters and could beat me; I respect their ability. But Zascai soldiers saw Swallow win; I knew that the story would spread fast and far.

I left while Harrier was handing round cups of wine, and I concealed my supply of cat. I couldn't resist taking a little. Handling it helped me relax, and the ritual focused my mind. Powder lined in the folds of paper, mesmeric candle flame, hiss of liquid, satisfying resistance of solution in the syringe. I was taught about herbs in Hacilith when I was young, and my knowledge can be relied upon when everything else is so vexatious. I am good at it, and it makes me feel safe, but I'd like to be able to stop.

My feeling of inadequacy grew as I dwelt on the Castle's immense depth of time. I thought about all the immortal Messengers before me; the title lives on although the individual might not. Archer, Swordsman, Messenger; the title is important but the person is dispensable. I'm immortal, and the other immortals before me have died, so I shouldn't feel inferior to them, but by my actions I feel I'm letting those worthy people down. I feel I'm letting down the first Comet who joined the Circle at its founding, and at least twenty others that came after him in progression; the last Comet being a cheerful blond Morenzian woman I beat in a distance race in eighteen-eighteen. There's only ever been one Archer, and he remembers all my predecessors. Indulgently I speculated about who they all were, and how they might have died—displaced by better runners, or injured by the Insects beyond repair.

I had just taken the needle out of my wrist and was dabbing at a spot of blood when Swallow fought her way in through the canvas entrance. I checked that everything was hidden, hoping that she wouldn't notice my drooping eyelids and white lips.

"Jant, I'm sorry about earlier."

"Why? You did well."

"I showed you up. It was cruel. Everyone could see you were tired."

Being offered sympathy by a Zascai was worse than being beaten! "You'll never make an Eszai if you worry about such things," I said softly.

"If immortals aren't fair, the world will cease to love them," she answered.

I flapped my hands at her. No one on a rush can bear to sit and suffer truisms. "Know what the Circle is, sister? Just a way of taking powerful people out of society and herding them all together in the Emperor's care where they can't do any harm . . . Of throwing the world's best at the Insects so the world never changes . . . Swallow, be clever. Stay and rule Awndyn where San can't clip your wings and command all your potential. We're going to need you free and carefree in twenty years' time."

"I have no freedom now that I'd lose in the Circle."

"Mmm." I lay back on the bearskin and looked up at her. "You're trying so hard to entrap yourself forever. Mortals are free of the responsibility of . . . this . . ." I waved floppily at Lightning's stacked sheaves of arrows, bowstaves and armor. "In many ways I was happier when career-less and clueless in Darkling."

"I don't want to be forty."

"Well, I have no answer to that."

She passed the mother-of-pearl guitar to me. I caressed the beautiful instrument; the pegs were ivory, the strap blue and gold, and Awndyn's insignia was painted on the back. She smiled when she saw how lovingly I held it, not knowing that the clarity of cat made it breathe under my hands. "Please look after it for me," she said.

"Why?"

"I won't play another note until I've killed Insects in battle."

"Oh, Swallow. Why are you doing this?"

"The Empire is forcing me. I'll do whatever it takes to be Eszai."

"Marry Lightning."

"You know he'd wear me down. I'm not a river, or a butterfly, or a star, or anything else he says in his letters. I'm not as pure and perfect as any of them, but still more varied than any of them together."

"Yes, you are." I tapped my nails on the scratchplate, lay with the guitar on my stomach and played a riff.

Swallow yelped. "It's never made a sound like that before!"

"I'm sorry."

"No, go on." She urged me to play the rest of the melody. Although she was surprised that I knew the headstock from the bridge she didn't look down on me. She aimed to learn from everyone. I felt the frets and then played, eyes closed for a while before embarrassment stopped me. She was grinning.

"I made money that way in Hacilith," I said.

"In the concert hall?"

"Hardly. Busking. One of the Wheel's members taught me. He was called Babitt."

"Come out and play for me by the fireside."

"No! Leave me alone."

Using scolopendium is a very solitary activity and I wouldn't want to appear in public for at least an hour afterward. But Swallow is persuasive. She simply attributed my condition to exhaustion and said I needed fresh air. She dragged me out to stand by the fire, where soldiers were drinking, cutting roast meat, talking boisterously, laughing more often as Swallow raised their spirits with a song. I played reels and wild czardas while she danced, gleaming and beaming, in front of the fire, and Lightning looked on.

Two hundred years ago in Hacilith the air was dreadful. I remember that I was coughing so badly I dropped my guitar and doubled up, trying to spit. Babitt the dwarf perched up on the black iron railings.

"Put it this way, Shira," he said eventually. "I wouldn't give up your night job." I remember the stench of the seagull oil which he used to set his hair.

I spluttered, "I can play it! But it would be nice if I could breathe."

"Felicitia says you've made more money dealing and so you should stick to that. He says he can't feed us. He says there's no money left in our gang." Babitt scratched at a hairy backside, which his patchwork trousers scarcely covered. I picked up the guitar, began to retune it.

Babitt was pudgy, hairy, short, and smug, I was tall and usually bemused; I'm sure we looked well together. We hated each other but Felicitia's word was law. Once I remember he ripped off a pet shop and Babitt called me up one night and said, "Look, I have two thousand goldfish, what can you do?"

I said, "Didn't you get the money?"

Patiently he answered, "Felicitia got the money. I got the goldfish."

So, anyway, I explained to him that I'd given up dealing, because Peterglass had a contract out for me, and I was sick of having my clientele trail around after me everywhere like the undead. Babitt gave up scratching his arse and started scratching his mustache.

"Felicitia will be angry with you."

"He could be pretentious at me, is that it?"

I crouched down and began gathering our coins before Babitt could get his hairy hands on them.

"You might not know this, but even Felicitia goes under if I stop dealing," I added.

Babitt grinned, which was not a pretty sight. "Shira, I know it. You'll never stop pushing cat in Hacilith. You're hooked on the power, which is *worse* than being undead."

"That's all you know. The whole world will kiss my spurs." I slammed my hands in deep pockets and slouched off toward Cinder Street. Babitt followed, his eyes at the same level as the guitar across my back. A smell of beer paused us on the steps of the Kentledge pub. We looked at each other, tempted, and eventually gave in. I held the door back while Babitt rolled inside, and dug in my pocket for the handful of grubby coins we'd collected that morning, offered them down in a languid hand for Babitt to translate.

"What are the little round ones with holes?"

"Buttons," he said.

CHAPTER EIGHT

HACILITH 1818, HOW FELICITIA DIED

Thunder in the morning seemed misplaced, storms should only happen at night. Five in the morning, bruise-brown clouds drifted in from the sea and collected over Hacilith, obscuring the dawn. I had been awake all night watching the person who was watching my house.

I don't think she's seen me, but I knew she had a crossbow because she had been practicing on all the cats of the neighborhood. I was out of the shop by the back door, and reached the street corner in the cover of a flaking brick wall. Crouching in litter and broken glass I glanced back to where the girl was waiting. She turned round and looked straight at me. I ran—

—Along a pavement spotted with chewing gum, over a narrow iron bridge, past the Shackle Sheds. The girl loosed her first bolt and it went far wide. I ducked. It hummed past me and lodged in the slats of a high green fence. I scrabbled over and paused for breath on the other side. The fence was covered in graffiti. The best graffiti was mine.

I ran on through dirty puddles and pigeon shit. She lost me at a block corner. I skidded and swore. She heard and put on speed. Hacilith's thick air caught in my throat, early sunlight reflected on the filthy river. You can't outrun a Rhydanne, I thought, as her second arrow missed my heel by millimeters. Who the fuck are you, anyway? The Bowyers' bitch.

I cut across a rubbish tip. The passageways through the refuse were clear to me but the girl's experience was of the other side of the river and she was wary. Half a kilometer out of her territory and she might as well have been in Scree.

I reached a warehouse by the dockside. Here, rings and iron mushrooms were set into concrete, which narrow boats used to moor and unload. The dock was silted up, derelict; it smelled of salt and decay. The warehouse was the size of three town houses, built of wooden planks now rotten and supported by sandbags. I hammered the fastest-ever secret knock on a smaller door set within the huge sliding gate at the top of a slipway, as the girl emerged, grease in her golden hair.

I slipped inside the warehouse, slammed the door, leaned against it, panting. The head of a crossbow bolt splintered wood by my shoulder. I flung open the door and found her five meters away. She hesitated in fumbling a new bolt into the breech. I unfastened the buttons on my shirt and held it open, giving her an excellent view of an excellent naked chest, then slammed the door again and barred it top and bottom.

Thin laughter trickled from the darkness behind me. My arrival had brought something back to life. A weak voice wheezed, "You're late, goat-shagger."

In Darkling, things were straightforward. Life in the mountains was simple—I went to bed early, and I was always hungry. Every day was the same; only some days we had more storms, and less food. But Hacilith city draws complication round itself like a cloak. I have a little of the city like pollution in me now. The city supports people who would never have survived in Darkling, for example, Felicitia.

"I had to wait till dawn." I sighed, picking my way into the bleak space of the warehouse. Torrential rain thrashed on the corrugated roof.

"Thought you could see in the dark?"

"No."

Felicitia Aver-Falconet lay on a moldering sofa by the side of a low table, the only furniture, in the middle of the pressed earth floor. He was reading by the light of candle stubs, fixed by their own wax to the tabletop.

Aver-Falconet ruled our gang. We were awed by his talk of expensive parties and fashionable society, boastful and offhand. But then, he was the grandson of Hayl Eske who lived at the Castle, and to us the Eszai in his ancestry put him on a par with god. Aver-Falconet had hurt me before, so I hated him. The Wheel he carved into my shoulder has lasted like a brand all my life.

Felicitia devoured my flesh with his eyes. The whites of his eyes were yellowish, and the pupils too high on them, as if they wanted to rise and hide under his eyelids.

"Have you got the drugs?" he asked, anxiously.

"Yeah."

"Come here and make love to me, oh macilent boy."

"No!"

"That Wheel on your arm means you belong to me."

Felicitia wriggled to change position, but couldn't sit up. He had lingered in the gin-shop with me, in the casino with Layce the cardsharp, and eventually malingered in our dockyard base, shooting up every few hours and reading melodramas. I pinched them when he had finished dog-earing the pages, because I had a vague idea that such knowledge might help me if I ever got to the Castle.

"You're lucky, my bagnio boy," he croaked. I continued to appraise him, his only clothes a stained leather skirt wrapped around well-shaved legs, and an ankle chain with a charm in the shape of a wheel. I knew it would be pure gold. I tingled with avarice.

"Oh, and why's that?"

"That girl is an Eszai-good archer, my ophidian-eyed boy."

"You know I can fly," I replied, not without pride. "And I'm an Eszai-good runner. Layce told me so." The concept that my ability to run, or fly, or fight could be as good as the Eszai was recurring in my mind with infuriating rapidity. I wanted to join them.

Felicitia hummed affirmatively. "I suppose you have to run fast to catch the goats," he mused.

"I have to run fast to get this madness over and done with before my master wakes up. Are you better now?" I asked, with a mildly professional air. Felicitia was a wisp of flesh, a skeleton in makeup. I could see eye sockets, cheekbones, skin colored blue by innumerable puncture marks. His skin was pale, his mouth slashed with lipstick and a peroxide streak in dark brown hair. The fire in a makeshift hearth was down to smoldering ash scabs. It was becoming cold, but Felicitia wasn't shivering. He was past shivering; his skin was as cold as the dock water.

"Now? What's 'now'?"

"Don't start that again. Either you're better, or you're not. And if you're not, then I don't want to know."

"Nothing matters but cat, my sweet miscegenation. Not even your indescribable beauty."

"You're going to die, you know," I said softly.

"That doesn't matter, my sweet itinerant," Aver-Falconet assured me. "I'll live in the Shift. I've been there for days . . ."

So you keep telling me. "It's been *months*," I said.

"I'm in love with the Shift," he said simply. Informing me of a luscious secret, his cracked voice dropped to a whisper: "You can be anything there. Even female."

I was disgusted. "What the fuck do you want to be a woman for?"

"For fucking," said Felicitia, and sighed.

I was unnerved by his power, to break rules I did not know existed. Not regular rules, that were authorized by the Castle or by the Governor; I broke those every day. Felicitia played havoc with the rules of nature.

"There's a marketplace with jugulars and ferret-eaters and buskers playing pangolins . . ."

I giggled. "That's a scaly kind of animal."

"No, you're thinking of a peccadillo, my boy."

Having no fixed point he thought free-form, and came up with plans that shocked us. "Layce loves you," I said, biting my lip.

"Huh. You can have her, my avid lad."

If only I could. She was under my power only because Felicitia was dependent on me. I stayed with him because I knew he wanted more than sensation—he legitimately needed escape; it was the way he was formed. I understood because I was a mountain creature stranded in the city, I despaired of fitting in. He was woman in the body of a man, and had taken to scolopendium as a prescription for frustration. I knew he shouldn't have gone into East Bank with a grain-a-day habit. I would never get him back to the shop.

"I've brought your drugs, but I need the money first."

"Hooked on it, aren't you?" Felicitia rasped.

"What?"

"Hard cash."

Oh, yes. Definitely. He offered me a key and I swiftly

removed his week's pocket money from a little strongbox under the table. I counted the notes three or four times, while Felicitia pursed his painted lips like a bar-room bitch. "That's a hundred quid," he snapped. "What do you spend it on, sexless?"

"Is it less of a crime if I spend it on books?" I was learning to read Awian, with the notion that it was a Castle language. I was weekly adding to Dotterel's library back at the shop. Felicitia tutted; he thought that spending money on books was the biggest crime of all.

I touched a white square of paper in the left pocket of my fringed leather trousers. "What if I take the money and run?" I asked, half-jokingly.

Felicitia smoothed his skirt. "My angelic archer outside is waiting for you. At a word from me, she'll finish you off."

I didn't understand. "It's Peterglass of The Bowyers..." I said. I had assumed Peterglass was sending the assassins because he was a dealer and I was poaching his clientele.

"Yes, but none of them actually hit you," Felicitia mused. I took an angry step and he gave me a pleading look. He would have loved me to touch him, so I didn't. "I have been paying Peterglass's archers to ensure they are poor shots. Peterglass doesn't suspect their treachery; he still wants you dead."

I couldn't believe this. "Why protect me?"

"Because you make the best cat, my amatory boy. *Obviously*."

This isn't what I wanted to be! Felicitia and I weren't keeping each other alive; we were keeping each other half-dead. I had become his personal dealer. I wanted to serve Dotterel, run marathons and read books. I wanted Layce, money, freedom, and thought I could gain them by mountain-boy meekness. Cold fury condensed in my mind; there was a faster way.

I bowed and thanked him. I am a great believer in getting my arse-licking over and done with. Then I put my hand into the other pocket, where there was a folded packet identical to the first, which I used when I wanted to rid myself of debtors and freeloaders. I passed it to Aver-Falconet with all due ceremony.

"Cook it for me, would you?" he asked.

"That isn't in the contract!" I didn't want to touch the stuff more than was absolutely necessary. "It's enough for a week," I added sweetly.

"Enough for a week. One week! There's enough for a month in me now."

I loved the chemist's shop, and every morning, when opening the shutters, would gape up at the green and gold lettering above the windows—Dotterel Homais. I hoped one day it would be my name up there—ambitions all confused with those of joining the Castle Circle, which I thought were unrealistic. Perhaps I would keep my master's name up as an honor: Dotterel and Shira.

Thin shelves of glass bottles in the window were filled with colored water. They gave a riotous display with each rare beam of sunlight. The dispensary smelled of spirits of wine and dusty paper. Some labels on the sprays of plants hanging from the ceiling to dry were in my writing. For the first time I had a feeling of belonging.

As well as my love of niche, I was awed by the novelty of authority. I respected my master. I regarded him as a genius and (because he could speak Scree) as a savior. The terms of my apprenticeship, which would be complete in a year, were framed in ebony and behind glass, hung in the gallery of my memory. As Felicitia, now lying on his side in order to reach the table, dissolved an alarming quantity of the poison I had sold him, I ran through those rules. Felicitia gave me a wry glance; he didn't understand that words written on paper were sacrosanct.

Word for word my indenture was, to learn the art and

mystery of my master's craft for the term of seven years. To neither buy nor sell without the said master's license. Taverns, inns, or alehouses I shall not haunt. At cards, dice, or any other unlawful game I shall not play, nor from the service of my said master day or night absent myself but in all things as an honest and faithful apprentice shall and will demean myself toward my said master and all his during the said term.

That's six of seven years of living a double life, Lord Aver-Falconet. You don't need me to tell you the tension. I've infringed each and every one of those rules even though the contract was written on paper. I knew that if Dotterel had the slightest suspicion of what I was doing I would be homeless again, and a Rhydanne wouldn't survive a week in a workhouse.

"I hope this is good stuff," Felicitia said, his voice juicy with anticipation. I inclined my head for shame, which he took to be honor. "The last one Shifted me for a day and a half," he chuckled. He pushed a needle, still hot from the candle flame, in through his Wheel tattoo. I flinched, and looked away.

He knew something was wrong, and started cursing. Pain turned the curses to screams. Rigid, his back arched, the tendons in his neck standing out, blind eyes bulging.

That's the effect of scolopendium mixed with strychnine. I watched in horror. I could have given him a faster death, but I'd planned a slow reaction to give me time to escape. But I was transfixed, and stared at his clawed convulsions, listened to gasps of agony. Eventually he slid off the divan. I gazed at the blank wall and waited till his varnished fingernails had stopped scraping at the floor. I glanced at him and looked away disgusted. His face was black.

"Felicitia?" I murmured. "My love?" If it were at all possible for him to return from death to hear that, he would have. I therefore reckoned I was safe. Drenched in Rhydanne superstition, I thought his animated corpse would grab my ankle.

I tried in vain to close his vacant eyes, and my fingers got sticky with mascara.

Closing a dead boy's eyes is supposed to be easy. It was impossible to close his mouth. I stripped off his jewelry. The objects on the table I threw on the fire, getting a little comfort from the brief heat. The novel and the anklet I pocketed.

Jant, you killed one of your own gang. But he wasn't really living anyway. Neither are you. You're Peterglass's prey now. Shit. I have to get out of here.

Wind shaking the walls reminded me of the world outside. Let's go; there's nothing besides remains here. Leaving Felicitia's minute and twisted corpse I ran to the door and risked a glance outside. The crossbow-girl had gone. Another training then kicked in—all that Layce had taught me. The sparse furnishings went on the fire. A tin of paraffin stood by the door; I doused it on the walls, walking round the vast empty building, splashing enough to overcome the rain. Then I stood back and threw what remained onto the pile of furniture. Starved yellow flames sprang up and crackled; within seconds the whole building was alight.

Through a gathering cloud of black smoke I choked my way out, shut the door and touched the Wheel insignia daubed across it. I ran back a safe distance and with juvenile jubilation watched our base rise in flames. My life in Hacilith was ending, the same feeling I experienced when leaving my valley. I was on a knife-edge a hundred times sharper than the icebound cliffs. These are children, by god, and highly dangerous. But how could I explain to my master? Take everything and leave without explaining? Forget him—how in Darkling could I explain it to the *gang*?

Watching the smoke I decided it would be easy to climb on that thermal and fly back to Galt, rather than risk running all the way through East Bank again. I stripped off my shirt and stretched my long wings strung with muscle. The fourth and fifth fingers were joined together, the thumb rigid and unopposable, the bones swept back into aerodynamic curves, shaped by the stresses of airflow throughout their growth. Right, let's ride Felicitia's funeral pyre home.

"You do and you're dead, darling," said a voice behind me. I started and looked round. The angelic archer was sitting on a mooring, leveling her little bow at my face. "How distressing," she commented. I had to agree, folded my wings to show I wasn't going anywhere, but also to keep them out of harm's way.

"Felicitia?" she asked. She had a shrill voice, which with her pipe-cleaner legs and broomstick arms was that of a child prodigy in the music hall. She was half my height.

"I'm unarmed."

"Parently you don't have to be armed to leave a trail of fucking destruction. You're coming *with me*." She spoke loudly, over the fire's roar and hissing molten lead dripping from the warehouse roof. Yellow flame reflected on stagnant green water all along the docks.

"My lady," I said, images of glory and fortune dissolving before my eyes into a vision firstly of Dotterel shouting for me to bring his breakfast, and secondly of me being nailed to a waterwheel, unable to brew coffee let alone cat. "Would you let me go for a hundred pounds, which I have right here?" I tapped one pocket hopefully; she giggled.

"No, but I'll have the money as well." She walked toward me keeping the crossbow bolt pointed sometimes at my eyes, then at my chest, and efficiently relieved me of Aver-Falconet's cash. "What did you do to him?" she asked.

"Drugs," I said glumly.

She was unable to keep the excitement from her voice. "There's another hundred waiting for me at Peterglass's base when I bring you in. Kindly accompany me." I ignored her terse gesture with the bow. It was delicate enough to be held in one hand and although the point was sharp it didn't look powerful. "No!" I shouted, feeling the intense heat feed my fury as it was scorching my wings. "I am going back to Galt. So sod off, flat-lander!"

"These are poisoned," she informed me.

"My master knows the antidote to every poison!"

"There's a grown-up involved?" she shouted, shocked.

"He will be if you don't let me go!"

"An *adult*?"

"My master could end all our games for good." Winning an award for bravery I took the hand not engaged in stroking the crossbow's hair trigger and patted it soothingly. "I can almost hear him calling," I added.

"You're my prisoner!" she shrieked. Rain was bouncing off the shoulders of her leather jacket. Sudden tears of confusion turned her soft-fruit face bright red; strands of wet hair stuck to her round cheeks. The arrow point wavered as her hands shook and I watched it carefully. This girl knew The Bowyers, I knew The Wheel. If we could work together, Hacilith would be ours.

I shrugged, saying, "By the way, I bet this is worth a million in blackmail."

"What?"

"The Governor's son, Lord Aver-Falconet—vanished some-where in the East Bank slums. Murders, drugs, sex. The list is long! I think the gossip column would pay well, but his father would pay better."

"I'm warning you, cat-eyes . . . Um . . ."

"Come with me and we'll make a million." I ventured a smile. "We'll leave Hacilith. Travel the world. See the Castle, even. That's better than The Bowyers' gang, isn't it?"

"Blackmail . . . ?" The blond girl removed the bolt from her crossbow and stuck it in her wide leather belt. She sniffed and tentatively offered me her hand. "I'm Serin. Apart from being a wily assassin, I dance at the Campion Vaudeville. You are *still my prisoner*."

I took this with a pinch of salt. "I'm Jant," I said. "And I can fly."

Suspicion flickered in her eyes. "If you trick me I'll hunt you down through all Hacilith. I'd enjoy it——" She jumped, startled as a section of the warehouse collapsed behind us. She threw one arm up to shield her eyes as a tidal wave of glassy heat rolled over us. "Meet me at the Kentledge at six tonight," she yelled. "It has to be six because curtain-up is nine."

"At six o'clock, my lady," I said. She executed a perfect curtsey, with a supple chorus girl's grace, and then watched with amazement little short of adoration as I tested the rizing air and took off for home.

That's all I'm going to say about my past for the moment, because I keep receiving unhappy letters from the Hacilith Tourist Board.

CHAPTER NINE

Lightning was listening to a hasty report from a tired soldier who had plunged over the frosty fields to reach us. I was kneeling to buckle Swallow's hauberk because her fingers were too cold to manage. The time before battle is known as the "drinking hour," and the men were washing down their breakfast with mouthfuls of rum. There would be no more venison—the deer had been disturbed by our presence, and we were reduced to eating half-cooked salt beef and bread. I saw a cask of wine being hacked open; the frozen wine was broken with an ax, and carried away in baskets and helmets. Planks were laid as pathways through the mud.

The scout's face was reflected in the bracer on Lightning's arm. I addressed him: "You were with Tanager's fyrd?"

"Yes, Messenger. I've been as far as Lowespass and the villages are empty." He had a heavy eastern Awian accent and a splendid beard.

"Have you seen the fortress?"

He paused. "The Insects are building a wall round it."

"Can't Tawny stop them?"

Lightning related the beginning of the report. "Vireo and Tawny haven't enough troops to face so many Insects. I think they might run before the wall closes, and come south to meet us. If not they'll be trapped, San help them."

I knew they had some food supplies, and remove a half a million arrows in the armory, so if we could reach them we would be able to replenish our own stocks.

The scout bowed his head. "The valley is full of Insects. They were roused by some men from Rachis who chipped the Wall trying to pull their friend out."

"It's forbidden to touch the Wall," I remarked. The scout shrugged as if to say that Castle's rule meant little in Rachiswater now. He said, "Insects are moving south. They're on their way. They're coming."

"How many?" I asked, fiddling with Swallow's buckles.

"Many, many Insects."

"Can't you be a bit more specific than that?"

"Hundreds of thousands."

I looked up in disbelief.

Three trumpet calls were sounded; at the first every soldier had to pack his gear. Most of the tents were left standing since they were stiff with ice. At the second, the fyrd were to join with their manors, which did not take long as there were only the manors of Awndyn and Micawater. At the third trumpet call the troops took their designated positions, with the banners, and the host began to march.

The fyrd were organized to advance open order, the lines of men being spread out and keeping a good space between them. The scout and a number of archers stayed behind to guard the camp, wagons, and trenches. Those who remained behind were mainly soldiers who had seen the Insects recently and I did not want to mix them in with the fresh, spirited troops.

Swallow's horse left hoof prints in the thin sprinkling of snow on the ground; she rode biting chapped bits of skin from her lips and blowing on her frozen fingers. The morning sky was a mixture of pallid colors like the mother-of-pearl guitar. Passing metal-gray clouds dropped wet sleet on us. At the cloud edges a lemon-yellow light came through occasionally in bright patches—then we sighed and stretched and tried to dry off in the sparse sunlight, but the sky was gradually filling with the color of steel.

10 A.M.: Swallow rode away from an argument with Lightning and myself. She vowed to lead her men into battle and was determined to ride at the head of the rectangle of troops. I explained that if the men had to form a shield square she would simply not be strong enough to survive in the tight crowd. She hated the thought of being a weak link physically, but as she was not built like Vireo, she had to accept it.

Lightning told me that the war had killed Swallow's father, and she believed that he couldn't possibly have died for an unjust cause. So Swallow rode, resolute, behind the first division of infantry, with the cavalry following. The marching lines snaked and contorted as they broke the ice on the frozen fields.

10:30: Lightning took me aside and asked me to watch over Swallow. Misgiving was written clearly on his face. "Stay with her," he said. "Please."

I clapped his shoulder. "Yeah, don't worry."

"Jant, I'm serious. It's agony for me being on the flank; I can't see her half the time."

I was irritated. Lightning didn't believe in me. "I swear I'll guard her as closely as you would yourself! From the Insects and the men, should they rebel against wet feet and Insect bites."

"I'm afraid for her," he admitted. It wasn't exactly what I wanted to hear. "When fighting begins you must try to move her out of the way."

I thought how Swallow had bested me in the duel; her big shoulders seemed more muscular by the minute. "If fighting happens I'm going to get behind her and plead for protection."

"I *am* serious." Strained, Lightning sounded as if he was holding a breaking heart together. I swore strongly I would protect her—surely he knew I was capable? He nodded, placated, and went back to his division.

10:45: Lightning changed the structure of his entire division so he could ride slightly closer to Swallow.

11:00: The men grew more cheery as the marching warmed them. They had permission to speak so bursts of conversation—about swords, axes, and how best to maim Insects—drifted back to us. Some shared tobacco and sips from their hip flasks. They were allowed to change position in an open order march, since men walking in close formation in harsh conditions suffer low morale. We marched into driving flurries of snow, our fronts white as it stuck to us. The soldiers' waxed cloaks flapped; they wore felt scarves wrapped around their faces and carried their shields edge on to the wind. They leaned into the wind and walked, starbursts of flakes driving into their eyes, legs aching from marching against the intermittent gale.

Midday: Marching is repetitive and I, who have studied movement for so long, found the ride soothing, not boring but hypnotic, so that I was calmed, my fear-knotted muscles relaxed and I actually began to enjoy it. Each kilometer we rode was recaptured land, which formed a secure strip behind us. It was not too far now to the Lowespass trenches.

Swallow and I sped up at the foot of each field, forcing our horses to jump the hedge, which the men climbed over or slashed through, before reforming their lines. Swallow kept glancing at her pocket watch. She looked around with a sighing expression, bowed her head and bit her lip. I thought she was missing her guitar, but when I offered it to her she refused: "Jant, you know what I said. Not until we reach the trenches. Not until I drive the Insects back behind the Wall."

Eleven thousand feet, two thousand hooves smashed through the ice. Cracked it to shards. Splattered grassy water. Squelched in freezing mud, as we rode on.

2:00: After midday we entered a more hilly landscape, crags and limestone pavements at the tops of the hills. We're nearly there, I told Swallow. At one point Lightning took the lead and Harrier's division moved behind us because the ravine was too narrow for the archers to ride on the flanks.

Several times we saw single Insects running along the road or small groups in the scrubby woodland. None escaped; our men rounded them up and slew them all. The land we left behind was free from man-eaters.

I watched my shadow lengthen as the day progressed and still we marched north.

3:00: The Archer came over and said, "We're losing the light already. We should camp here."

Swallow disagreed instinctively: "I would like to reach the end of the ravine. Jant says it opens into Lowespass. We can see the fortress from there. It would give the men a good feeling of achievement."

"Jant says, Jant says." Saker flicked his reins angrily. "The Rhydanne may be happy to blunder around in the dark but I'm not."

"It's true there's only two hours till nightfall," I said to Swallow.

"Could we reach Lowespass in half an hour?"

"Yes, but that doesn't leave us much time!"

"We should at least try. How can we camp in this tiny ravine anyway? How could we maneuver?"

"You're right," Lightning conceded. It would be easy to make a shield wall across the gorge, which would prevent the Insects passing, but then we would not be able to use our numbers to defeat them. Lightning knew the archers needed space, and we thought of the massacre that would happen at night if we were caught without room to move. "We should try to secure the end of the valley. Swallow's quite correct," he said. After that nothing I could say would convince him that his sweetheart might in any way be wrong.

3:30: We came out of the valley under the last throes of a fantastic sunset, and there before us lay all Lowespass. Seeing the Fortress Crag, the men gave a triumphant yell. Then just as suddenly, they fell silent.

"What *is* that?" Swallow trembled.

"I don't know," I said. "It wasn't here before."

"Saker?"

Lightning was shouting at the men to remain calm. A swath of infantry sat down in a spiky mass, staring at the view. "My god, I don't know. *I've* never seen anything like it."

Next to the fortress, and taller than it, there was a bridge. Half a bridge. It looked unfinished but it dwarfed the crag, arching up into the clear sky. The last rays of sunlight shone between its struts.

"How does it stay up?" breathed Swallow.

"*I don't know*." Lightning whirled. "Make camp here! Harrier—I want trenches on each side of the ravine and pavilions up right here." The men moved obediently, muttering.

"It's Insects," I said.

"Well it bloody well isn't human hand," said Harrier.

"*Move!*" Lightning yelled at him.

The ground under the colossal bridge was covered in gray-white Insect buildings. Low, pointed roofs of their cells looked like frozen waves. From the foot of the bridge to the pale horizon was gray paper, with long sections of Insect walls emerging from the mass; walls the Insects had passed that were now redundant, and walls at the edge of their sprawling complex, which they were still constructing. I looked to where the friendly smoke plumes of Whittorn should be, and saw nothing but Insect buildings. The village had gone. The burned framework of Pasquin's Tower stuck up from a cluster of walls. Lowespass Fortress itself was ringed with walls.

"Summerday?" I said aloud.

"Who?"

"I hope the Insects haven't made it as far as the coast," I explained. "There's thousands of people in Summerday town."

"How does the bridge stay up?" Swallow repeated.

"It can't be a bridge. It's not leading anywhere!"

It was gray-white like the cells, with thin, twisted struts. They must have been much stronger than they looked. They supported a walkway which curved up for perhaps a kilometer. At a height of two hundred meters the bridge ended abruptly. At that end there were no legs to hold the walkway up. "It's beautiful," she said.

Lightning was shaking his head. "Insects are coming down it." I squinted into the twilight. He had great eyesight; I couldn't see too well in the jester dusk. I could just make out the familiar low bodies scurrying down the walkway, which was truly vast. Insects were running down the bridge, into their city, but no Insects were moving the other way, toward the apex. My eyes hurt as I tried to spot the point at which they appeared out of the air.

"You could fit four coaches next to each other up there," he said.

"Shall I go closer?" I spread my wings and my horse reared.

"In the dark? No, Jant, stay here and we'll investigate tomorrow."

3:50: We had just set camp when the Insects attacked.

3:55: Insects, one and two, cast about them like the lead hounds of the hunt. Then there were suddenly thousands, pouring down the valley, from ruined houses, tunnel openings, the paper cells.

Swallow swore. "They go on, and on, into the distance."

"So do we."

3:57: I screamed at Swallow, "Put that fucking watch away!" Lightning was quick: "Out! Fan out, Select! Full draw! Donaise, central; Bitterdale, wings!"

No time to lose, I ordered the infantry, "Go forward!"

Shield-bearers ran out, dropped to their knees. Their great shields crashed into position, a sixty-meter interlinking line.

The archers darted past, moving forward. Two hundred archers ran off into the darkness on either side to form the wings. The first line shot straight out over the shield-bearers' heads. Two lines behind sent volleys up into the air. Arrows hissed, rained down hard on the Insects' backs three hundred meters away.

Stench of Insect blood began to fill the air, coppery, like old coins. Dim shapes grew clearer as they ran up against the hail of arrows. The stampede moved like a single creature; mandibles dripping septic spit, claws rasping on rock. Their legs razor-tipped, rake-edged, saw-toothed; the shape of every weapon there, adapted for slaughtering. Their antennae were flattened to their heads. They can smell us. Taste us! But I only saw ant heads emerging from the festering night. Paler gray, taking form and color as they got nearer.

Lightning's voice on the left: "Slower, Donaise division. Six per minute is all I want." He appeared next to me. "I'm saving arrows," he gasped. "Half an hour at that rate and we'll have none left."

Insects battered at the shield wall. The ringing of blows, metal on shell, metal on metal, sounded like a foundry. "I don't like this," said Lightning. "The men haven't eaten. They've been walking all day."

I ordered a fire to be built at the back. The men passed fire-brands from hand to hand until weak points of wavering light lit the mayhem. We held against the Insects, and still more Insects came. We passed water bottles to the shield wall so that the human fortification could drink. They were crouched with all their strength against the shields. The archers were barefoot for grip in the mud. Lightning sent those on the outside to join the brawl and kept the Donaise division shooting. None of us could see where their arrows were going. He sent an order for our horses to be brought close behind us. Our breath hung in the air; it was freezing cold.

"I can't see Harrier's horsemen," said Swallow. "I just bloody hope he's still there."

"He's trustworthy," said Lightning.

"Yes, but where the fuck is he?"

There was little to see. I raised my lantern to glimpse the chain mail and leather-strap backs of the foot soldiers directly in front. They stood shoulder-to-shoulder five men deep before merging into darkness. I couldn't see the ends of the line either. I heard grunts, shrieks, and steady chopping from the shield wall. A scout told me it was crushed and breaking.

"Comet?" Another anxious pale face.

"Yes, Scaup. What's it like down there?"

He pointed. "That side is breached and Harrier is advancing."

"I didn't hear anything," I said to Lightning.

"Comet," Scaup blinked, "there's but a handful left."

I'm the Messenger so I should be down there, among them, to pass on Lightning's orders, but I had promised to protect Swallow.

The shield wall fell in on both sides before I saw it fall in front of me. Lightning and Harrier had already pressed ahead. Insects went over the wall in a wave, crashed into the fyrd behind. Men raised their swords and shields. Some raised their hands instinctively and the Insects sliced their fingers off. Insects continued pouring in. How many were out there? They mangled the shield men, their weight crushing, jaws lacerating those trapped beneath.

I nodded and Scaup shouted, "At them," on my left. "At them!" echoed on my right. A woman's voice: Swallow.

Bloodthirsty bitch! Just like Vireo. Why do battles have this ruthless effect on women?

We drove the horses forward all of ten meters before coming up against the crush. Insects clambered toward us over corpses; their shells were wet with melted snow. Guiding my horse with my knees, I tangled with the first Insects. Swallow hewed them with her sword. She smiled. She hacked down at an Insect on her right side, severing its antennae, and then up in a flat arc that cut a compound eye in two. Twenty Insects later her arm was aching and she wasn't smiling so much. I fended off twenty more, before it became clear they would never stop. Scaup's horse stumbled; Insects slashed its belly and dragged it down.

Lightning's armored white trampled the warm carcass. "We must go," he said grimly.

"Then we'd leave the foot soldiers behind!" Swallow protested. Her gauntlet was stained with blood from a gash over the wrist but she appeared not to care. That made Lightning's decision: "We're leaving, right now. You first—get to Rachis."

"No."

"Jant is going. Harrier is going. Swallow—put that shield at your back and follow them."

"This is my stand—!" She seemed determined to die with the men. Her shout ended in a gasp because I grabbed the reins from her hand, whipped her horse with the end of them, and we lunged away together.

We skittered down the hill into the ravine, scattering stones. We rode blind, the Awndyn cavalry following us. I glanced back to see how many there were; perhaps seven, eight hundred. Had we lost a hundred horse?

Behind them chased the chitin tide of Insects. Lightning was following; I saw him pulling sheaves of arrows from his saddle-bag and stuffing them into the quiver.

Cries and thuds reverberated in the ravine as the abandoned

infantry fought to the death. The voices thinned quickly, though
the noise they made grew in desperation, and then abruptly
there was silence.

Scaup had gone. Harrier was missing. I couldn't see any hoof
prints on the path. My legs were shaking. I leaned over the
horse's neck till her mane brushed my cheek. She was spitting
foam, running with sweat. Ice had lacerated the skin on her
forelegs. Swallow's bay was in worse condition, foam mixed
with blood. But Swallow kept a smile on her face that fired my
heart. I understood why Lightning loved her.

We fled in the direction we had come. I looked back, calling the men to follow me. We left many Insects
behind—our soldiers' corpses distracted them.

"Slower, Jant," Swallow pleaded.

"Not yet. Soon."

"You're going to kill this horse."

I wanted to ride to Awia. We could regroup then; hopefully
we would be near Rachis.

At 6 A.M. we passed the border. An hour later we slackened
our pace. Swallow's bay was mad with pain. With Lightning
between us and the trailing Insects, and the smooth cobbles of
Rachiswater road under our hooves. I thought the crisis had
passed.

"We left the infantry," Swallow said. Her face was a mask of
guilt.

"Don't think about it. We're not safe ourselves yet."

"They were in agony. They all died. It's my fault."

I remembered Lightning saying that all Zascai die, it's just a
question of when. I could not comfort her. I was watching a
dark shape just left of the road resolve into a mass of Insects.
They ran alongside us, and attacked immediately.

Swallow copied my line of sight, and screamed, "Where the *fuck* are they all coming from? So close to town!"

"This way! The Palace for shelter!"

Swallow urged her dying horse. I led them at a gallop off the road and across leveled grass. We sped along a plantation path and into the gardens of white Rachiswater Palace. We splashed through the edge of the lake.

Mad confusion as we rode. We had no formation. I had no way of making my orders known save yelling. But everybody was shouting. The horses were protesting, the wounded soldiers screaming. The women soldiers howled. Men called to their companions. The air was a cacophony. Swallow gathered a tight group of riders—her rich voice carried well, she commanded attention through sheer volume. But it was terrible—Insects ran among the riders, biting at horses' legs. Men seemed to rush from all directions to the light, toward the Palace walls.

Flickering torchlight shone by the foot of the wall. Yellow torches glowed on the top, reflecting in the lake. The stench of smoke was so strong that I thought the Palace was burning. Then I saw reinforcements marching out, a welcoming party for us. They held long pikes and stood along the foot of the walls. Men crowded into the torchlight, eager to get through the gate, and for the first time I clearly saw their rictus faces. The gate was shut.

"Swallow," I shouted. "Stay close!"

"What's happening?" she begged.

I didn't know but I dreaded it. The men held their long spears at rest. The others carried a quickly collected array of torches, candle lanterns, and oil lamps. Shadows from the pikes striped the wet grass. A word from the gatehouse—I didn't hear through the tumult—and the pikemen stepped forward. As one, they leveled their staves. Uproar from the Awndyn cavalry, suddenly on the wrong end of the pikes.

I pulled my horse in and she stopped less than a meter from the closest pike.

"No," screamed Swallow. "No! This is all wrong!" She shook her sword and shouted at a pikeman, "You there! What are your orders? What has the King said?"

He stayed impassive.

"Why won't you let us in?" She bit back a sob of frustration.

The soldier made not a sound.

I approached the cylindrical gatehouse. "Don't worry," I said. It was a strange misunderstanding, but I could sort it out. I called, "Comet calls on you in the name of San Emperor, for the will of god and the protection of the Circle." That was my phrase of command which Messengers present and for immemorial decades before me have used and it has never failed to work before. "Open these gates!" Nothing happened. I tried again. Nothing happened. "Staniel?" I called. "Rachiswater? Come to the parapet and speak to me!"

"You bastard," said Swallow, but I couldn't tell whether she meant Staniel or me. Where the light was poor, two horses had run onto the spears. That heralded the arrival of Lightning's men. Lightning's archers were hopelessly mixed in with more Insects. More and more Insects arrived. They covered the ground. The Insects got to work biting horses, pulling down men. The horses forced away from the Insects, between the pikes. Unhorsed men found themselves on the ground where they were trampled or gashed. A crowd of unhorsed men grew; they pushed back from the pikes, squeezing the cavalry closer to the Insects.

Lightning saw Swallow's leaf-green livery and forced through the crush to our side. "I had dire trouble following you," he said. "Harrier got bitten."

"Is Harrier here?" I asked.

"He's somewhere in that mess. Why all the halberds?"

"I don't know." I watched in horror as an unhorsed man cap-à-pie in white armor grappled against Insects.

"We'll soon put a stop to this," said Lightning and raised his voice. "In the name of San Emperor, for god's—"

"I tried that," I said.

"Open up! Open up *now*! Do you know who I am? Lightning *Micawater*! Comet is here! Governor Awndyn is here! In the name of the *Emperor* let us in!"

"Maybe they think we're attacking them," I suggested.

"I bloody am now." Lightning fitted an arrow to bowstring. "I'm going to shoot them one by one."

"What good will that do?"

"It'll give us some space."

"No! They still won't open the gate!"

"Have they forgotten who we *are*?"

"It's because we're mixed with Insects," Swallow said.

I glanced at her dirty face. "You're right." Staniel's fear of Insects was so great he wouldn't risk allowing even one into the Palace courtyard. If that meant men would struggle and die outside his very walls then so be it.

Every second we stayed it became more difficult to leave because we were hemmed in by our own dead and the dead Insects. My horse was treading among the fallen men. Our cavalry pushed into those on the ground, knocking them over and trampling them. The shaggy hooves as big as dinner plates came down on heads and smashed through shields.

Two of our captains were still alive. I waved at them and yelled, "Go to the edges! That way! No! *That* way! Get Donaise to follow you and head toward the town. Go *slowly*!" I told them to be slow because they would need time to regroup and any fast movement might lead to panic.

There was attrition at the edges of the mass, as well as loud screams from the wounded at the center. Men at the edges were running away. Men were so terrified they would chance fleeing into the infested park. They threw off their helmets the better to see, flung down swords and they ran like madmen. One ran at full tilt, legs pumping, fisted hands ripping off armor as he went. When one ran, the men on either side gave up and ran as well. Then the ones next to them ran, and within seconds a whole section of the crowd had bolted. They had blank, honest faces without any shame or fear of reprisal.

"Shit." I realized that those who risked the darkness were certainly doomed. There was no way of stopping them. We would have to pick up the bodies later. But what chance for "later" if we don't save ourselves?

The captains did their best to move men down the bulwark, easing the crush. Harrier had shouted his division into some sort of order and they seemed to perceive the correct direction for the town. I looked down on this mass of struggling people. Those on foot were at head level with the horses' backs and they were suffocating. The Castle's badge drew them to me, but I could do nothing to protect them. I felt the incredible pressure of bodies on bodies. Men positioned their shields to stop their ribs being crushed.

I moved my horse outward, but that just pushed the horses behind me more tightly against the Insects. Swallow used her spur against a man's cheek, then kicked his neck as he reeled back. She sobbed uncontrollably. Harrier pointed to Rachis Town, raised both hands questioningly, clenching the reins. I wanted the unhorsed men to escape in front of us before the horses followed, but I had to get Swallow out of there.

I felt so powerless that callous indifference took hold, and I was thinking: he must be dead, god, she can't survive, as people fell, wounded, around me.

The Insects were ripping through immobile horses and men. I heard them crackling. I heard the sound of flesh tearing and the horses' screams, louder as Insects chewed their way closer.

My face got spattered with blood when an Insect bit into a horse's heart. Swallow screamed as she was sprayed with blood head to foot. It looked black in the torchlight. She stared in my direction with blind panic, trying to pull her leg up onto her mare's back away from a grasping claw. Then she was gone. Aghast, I saw her foot caught in the stirrup. It flailed in the air. It vanished completely as the Insects pulled her down. The horse stumbled over her.

I heard Lightning bellow through the tumult, yelling something to Harrier. My horse's foreleg gave way as an Insect bit through the tendons. She fell forward and collapsed, spilling me from the saddle. I hit the ground in a burst of pain. I clutched my shoulder, thinking it broken. I saw the underside of a thorax as an Insect jumped and just had time to shield my face. It wrapped four legs round the shield and wouldn't let go. I struggled with its crushing weight and then had to cast the shield aside. I scrabbled for my ice ax in the mud and dispatched the next five Insects with flair.

But behind me, left and right, were Insects, scissoring mandibles, raking spines. It was impossible. Every time I raised my arm one would grab it. They were pulling at my back plate and belt.

I fought my way between close mounds of dead looking for Swallow. The hooves of riderless horses pounded down around me. Swallow. Where's Swallow? Where the fuck is she?

I saw her and called, lost concentration for a second and was knocked flat by an Insect the size of a pony. Its antennae swept my face. I shielded my face with one arm and its mandibles scratched my armor. Inside the serrated jaws another set of mouthparts churned in thick slime. I brought the ax down heavily. It crunched into the thing's top shoulder and embedded in the shell—I couldn't free it.

The Insect's integument was dotted with spiracle holes. I reached down and shoved my fingers in one, tearing the membrane. The Insect kept biting. I was pinned down. I choked. I struggled to hold its face away from mine. Its jointed antennae were swept back out of my reach. Black palps hanging below its jaws slopped across my mouth and neck, tasting my skin. Its hard thorax pressed against my chest, its bulbous abdomen held high.

My face reflected over and over in compound eyes and in three ocelli like buttons on its forehead. Its triangular face pushed into mine, suture lines between the brown plates.

Stiff fringes on sharp forelegs, tarsus feet clawed my neck. A centimeter closer, its mandibles opened to cut my throat. I looked straight into the cogwheel maxillae. My arms shook, screaming pain. This is how it ends, I thought. I braced myself for agony. I let go.

The Insect collapsed onto me, its heavy head smacked into the mud. I yelled, no longer trapped, and slithered from underneath. The Insect lay still. Was it dead? I kicked it, and saw an arrow shaft projecting from the back of its head. The steel point emerged from between its eyes.

Lightning was a hundred meters away, nocking another arrow to string. I cheered him and he frowned. Two deep breaths, then he held his breath. The bodkin point came up from earth to target with precision. He loosed the string and an Insect fell some distance behind me.

It thrilled me to watch the greatest archer ever. As I watched, my confidence returned. I was Eszai, I was powerful, I would fight.

Lightning's horse stood still while he aimed and loosed again, sniping the Insects down in one tight area. Where a ragged shape lay—a red and green shape. Then I realized he was stopping Insects from eating Swallow. I drew my dagger and ran to her. I sliced between sclerites, stabbed through the pedicel waist of an Insect on top of her, kicked it aside and picked her up. Her mail was wet with a shocking amount of blood. Swallow's face was very, very pale.

"Damn you, Jant!" Lightning arrived. "Don't do that again!"

"This is the mother of all routs—" I stopped because Harrier appeared. He was on a different horse and had a ripped shirt wrapped around his bleeding leg.

Swallow began to wail, her eyes tightly shut and her teeth stained red. "Harrier?" Lightning asked.

His servant took the hint. "Pass her up to me."

I lifted her carefully onto the saddle in front of him; she lolled back against his chest and nearly slid off but I showed him how to hold her.

Lightning put arrows neatly through two more approaching Insects. "Is she badly hurt?" he asked. "Will she live? Can she stand a long ride?"

"Yes. Perhaps. To where?"

"My house."

"We can't ride all the way to Micawater!"

Swallow kicked feebly. I saw a deep wound in her hip, its walls glistening. "Follow me to the town."

"Micawater is better . . ." Lightning stared.

"I don't want to ride into any more Insects," said Harrier, who had his hands full.

I said, "Staniel has fortified Rachis. If they let us in it should be safe."

Too bruised and exhausted to run, I took charge of a riderless Carniss roan and cantered with them until we reached the main road. Then I urged my horse on and galloped faster. The forest flew by on either side. I tied the reins back. I stood up on the saddle, balancing, and the distressed horse ran even faster. I tilted my wings to get the correct airflow under them, and spread. Three beats and I was up, looking down on Lightning's white and Harrier's sorrel mare.

We traveled without pause and arrived just before daybreak. The half-finished walls were thick, rugged stone not yet faced. The sight was worrying, I thought—Zascai don't trust us anymore. The wooden gates stood ajar and a stream of men poured through. I looked down to the disheveled, silent soldiers already crowding the marketplace to capacity. The town had an air of unreality, so many people here at dawn. I knew I must find residence for all of them or the situation would become volatile, but I had to help Swallow first.

I flew along the streets at first-floor height with Lightning and Harrier following. I got lost twice; the roads had changed since my last visit, only thirty years ago. With a plan view I found the Grand Place, and led them to the magnificent Spread Eagle Hotel. I settled on the stuccoed balcony and watched Lightning and Harrier dismount.

A cold, chalk-blue quiet, an expectation of the sunrise, made Lightning and his servant talk with muted voices. They took care, as if a sound could cause Swallow to slip away. I glided down as Harrier carried her up elegant steps into the entrance hall.

CHAPTER TEN

The hotelier was a short, vigorous man with a paunch, and a duster in his back pocket. He recognized Lightning and me, fixed on the sunburst insignia. We marched into his hotel. Behind us he saw a battle-stained warrior with an injured girl in his arms, dripping blood on the pale pink marble. He was speechless.

It'll be something to tell the children, I thought. "Give us a room."

He put a hand over his open mouth.

"You'll be paid," added Lightning.

The hotelier saw our urgency, and found his tongue. "Immediately, my lord." He ran up a New Art staircase—a confection of metalwork swirls and glass petals. Lightning followed grimly as he threw the door open onto a sumptuous cream suite.

"I'll clear the guests from this floor," said the hotelier. "The whole building is at my lords' disposal."

"That's not necessary." I smiled at him.

"Thank you," said Lightning. "We'll call you when we need—"

I looked back but the hotelier had vanished.

I tipped the cream sheets onto the floor so that Harrier could lay Swallow down. I tore the curtains open on their brass rails to let a little of the bruise-blue light into the room.

Lightning threw himself on his knees at the bedside. "You would tear my heart out," he murmured. "It looks bad, doesn't it?" he asked, voice catching. I nodded, checking her over the way Rayne had taught me.

"You can help her?"

"I'm not a surgeon."

"Please . . ."

"I'll do what I can."

"No . . . Another one. Not again. I hope you can do more for my love than Rayne could with Dunlin!"

"Mm, yes. Swallow? Swallow, can you hear me?" She made no response. There were deep gashes in her thighs and belly. They were covered in blood clots, and it took a long time to peel off the torn cloth so I could see how deep they were. One foot was a chewed mess, bones splayed out. I had often seen wounds like that caused by Insects slashing cavalrymen's legs. Harrier was limping from a shallower cut over his knee.

I touched Swallow's forehead and wondered if she had a fever coming on. "I'm going to need all sorts of things."

Lightning beckoned to Harrier. "Anything you want, don't count the cost."

"I don't think bandages will be enough; I need some clean sheets to tear up. Need gauze, boiling water, liniment from powdered oak bark, tormentil, comfrey—that'll stop the bleeding. For internal bleeding—shepherd's purse and horsetails. Tincture of yarrow and arnica to clean the skin. For painkillers I'll need aconite, to calm her I need papaver and if she gets a fever I'll need elder in decoction. I also need thread and a knife . . ."

Harrier bowed with quick assertion.

"And some scolopendium."

"Messenger, I won't be able to find that. It's been illegal in this country for years."

"I know where to find it," I said.

Rayne's thesis advocates careful observation when treating patients. Over centuries of observation she has discovered that illnesses and infections are caused by dust. I studied her treatise every day when I was an apprentice in Hacilith, and it impressed upon me the fact that even a tiny amount of dirt can induce sickness. Dust is present over everything and very often is invisible, so it is important to be rigorous. To clean instruments, Rayne urged the use of hot water, salt water, alcohol and flame.

Lightning lingered until he realized I was stripping Swallow and when I got down to skin level he made a hasty excuse and left me to it. I made sure the room was dust-free and emptied of antiques, and that Swallow's wounds were sewn and dressed before I called him back. There was another problem to deal with.

"Will she live?" he implored.

"This must be our headquarters for a few days until her condition stabilizes," I said.

"Needs must, if we have to rough it," he replied stoically, kneeling beside the cream satin four-poster.

"During that time, Lightning, we have to gather any surviving Awndyn fyrd, reward them and send them home. You realize they will hate the Rachiswater pikemen now, and the longer they stay, the more chance they have for retaliation."

"Leave it to me," he murmured, peering at Swallow's closed eyes. "She looks like she's sleeping."

"She is sleeping. I want a reliable courier to carry my report to the Emperor, another to go to the Governor of Hacilith; and I want fifty horsemen to scout the north of the manorship to see how much damage the Insects caused last night, and where they are now."

"The Insects trounced us. It is a disaster for her," said the Archer, venturing to stroke Swallow's hand on the coagulating sheets.

"I'll face the Emperor on her behalf. And I want the tags of all the men who died in Staniel's Palace grounds because I'm going to present him with a list of names."

"You will look after her, please?" He glanced up.

"I won't move from her side."

"Then I will do the rest." He kissed her hand and stalked out, calling for Harrier.

I wrote to Rayne, who sent me instructions that I followed to the letter, but I sighed six times an hour with despair. What the fuck is a metatarsal and where has it gone? The responsibility was overwhelming, the job was gory. But I kept my doubts to myself, for Lightning's sake.

The hotelier brought my meals to the suite. Nothing could induce him to exchange more than a few words each time. My shape and the musician's blood under my fingernails awed him, and he only told me what he thought I wanted to hear. Harrier kept us informed of the events in the town.

Swallow had not regained consciousness after two weeks at the Spread Eagle. I reluctantly allowed a day's journey to move her to Lightning's Palace in the neighboring manorship. A white coach with two chestnut horses appeared one morning. God knows what day it was—I was hollowed out and hyper from nights awake watching over her.

Harrier and the hotelier maneuvered Swallow on a stretcher

down wide rose-marble stairs and installed her in the carriage. I knelt beside her to prevent her from moving as the horses walked.

As we entered the portico of Micawater Palace, Lightning visibly began to recover his shattered optimism. Old Eszai are not accustomed to losing, and I could tell it would take him time to recover from the outrage. We placed Swallow on the bed in a dark blue room which overlooked the lake. Checking that the room was clean, I noticed constellations of gold stars painted on the ceiling.

Lightning held the musician's warm, limp hand for hours, kissing each finger individually. I found him still there in the evening; he had not moved at all.

"What will we do about your King?" I asked.

"First Dunlin, now this . . . Oh, beloved. Did you think you were immortal already?"

"Hello? Lightning?"

"Is she going to wake up soon?" He was definitely happier with the bold and adventurous Swallow than with the girl who lay prostrate and had to be nursed.

"Saker," I tried again with a sympathetic tone. "We must gain control of the capital. Go and visit Staniel; don't take a large retinue, but make sure you bring him a gift."

"That waste of time should be apologizing to me for the ruin he's caused!"

I bit my tongue on "I told you so." "Praise Staniel highly. Tell him he chose the correct course of action."

"But—"

"Saker, just imagine how terrified he must be by now, although he may not admit it. I want you to give him all the reassurance you can—as sincerely as you can. If he is convinced of our good will it may be easier to influence his next moves."

"Or stop him making any."

"No!" I checked that Swallow was still asleep. "The war has come to Rachiswater. I want Staniel's fyrd to hold the front and stop Insects moving any farther south. Offer to join him. Be a loyal subject rather than an immortal adviser, understand? Offer a division of your fyrd for his direct control. Keeping his host together requires money, which I know he lacks. You must seem so satisfied of his claim to the throne that you will offer to lend him funds."

"Never," Lightning said, clasping Swallow's hand.

"It's only temporary. I'll put Wrought at his disposal as well."

"Now I know you're joking. Wrought has no money, and that which you do have is pledged to feed the refugees."

"We'll supply arms. Your troops might need arrows too? If we give Staniel sound and kind advice now he might be more willing to take it in the future."

"Never."

I had had a wholesome meal, a hot relaxing shower, and was free from my leathers that I had worn so long they were practically welded to me. I had taken a welcome injection of quite high quality cat and felt wonderful. I was comfortable telling Saker to be the legate for once. "I'd do it myself but I have to treat her."

"I don't want to leave her."

"Harrier will find you if there's any news."

"Jant, I wish you had been more harmless."

"Huh?"

"San is now wary of ambitious youth. I knew you came from East Bank Hacilith but your malfeasance became more obvious with time. Your ambition was as strong as Swallow's although it's long since grown decadent. San realized that such zeal could agitate the Circle. He needs no more felons nor makebates, idealists or drug dealers. He can't take the chance that she will turn out the same way—if it wasn't for your misdemeanors San would have made Swallow immortal by now."

"Hardly fair!"

"Look after her well. And if you take drugs in my Palace again I'll have you locked in this room."

"I'll try not to."

"I can't risk the servants finding out. *Please* act like an Eszai."

If you are an Eszai, then to act like you do is to act like an Eszai. I thought this loudly, but didn't dare say it.

"I shall talk to His Majesty. I didn't spend fifteen centuries preserving Micawater to have it destroyed by Insects now." He kissed Swallow's hand and replaced it on the sheet.

At the end of the third week Swallow's fever turned to shivering and I knew the crisis was over. I altered her medicine from vulnerary plants to rubifacients and kept the healing stitches clean. Harrier was a great help, as he was far from squeamish and very willing to learn. I had to treat his wounds as well, which he had not bothered to look after.

Harrier was a likable man, far more relaxed whenever his lord wasn't around. He was private but not secretive, polite but not obsequious, a servant who stood with shoulders squared. He had a house in Donaise, but he lived with his family as wardens in the Palace, and he was clearly proud that Lightning had so favored them.

King Staniel offered no apology, and kept his guards close at hand. Lightning worked with him to plan trenches and bastions in Rachis Park. The soldiers' imposition caused riots in the town; we had to send them food and wine in order to ease the pressure. The villages of Slake Cross and Tambrine were destroyed in an Insect attack. A new prohibited zone was created, east to west, from the coast to the foothills of Darkling, which followed Rachis River and the manor estate boundary. The Insects responded by building their own wall, which terrified the civilians. It took a month of fighting for us to slow the Insect advance.

Swallow slept on, unconscious, all that time. At the end of the second month she woke.

W ill she ever walk again?" Lightning pestered me, as we walked through the water gardens to the impromptu infirmary. The gardens were dim and vacant, cut back for the winter; only a few red maples around the lake still gripped leaves.

I said, "Insects stripped the muscles from her leg. I don't think she'll walk unaided. But she's intent on trying—determined as a human. I don't know if she can bear offspring now; it's unlikely. I haven't told her yet—"

The Archer stopped and stared. "Swallow can't have children?"

"She was sliced from rib to hip, Lightning, I *haven't* Rayne's expertise. Come on!" Usually unhurried, now Lightning found it hard to walk and be dramatic at the same time.

"Swallow can't have children. Are you sure?"

"I can't tell for certain. But it's far too great a risk."

"That's terrible! I . . . She was. We were . . . The way I see it, she still hasn't got long to live. No Zascai has. What will happen to Awndyn manor?"

I shrugged. "Swallow's lucky to be alive. She's in a lot of pain, and I'm amazed at her progress. She's happy to still have eight fingers, two thumbs, and a guitar. She can sort out the succession of Awndyn later."

Swallow was propped up on plump white cushions; she gave us a brilliant smile as we entered the golden and sapphirine suite. I loved her courage, and it wasn't lost on Lightning. Dunes of manuscript paper covered the four-poster; slipping off onto the floor, scribble of semi-quavers marching like Insects. She held a jotter, full of torn pages and crossing-out.

Lightning eagerly gathered some of the papers and examined them. He began to laugh sincerely. It's impossible to begrudge or be jealous of genius; you must wish such extreme talent well. Genius sees past the separate circles of darkness in which we live, to the light beyond. Even without words Swallow's music can make the listener laugh; it's because she sees through to the great hilarity on the other side of everything. After her concerts people feel they have been touched by an almighty truth which they yearn to keep forever.

The composer was smiling too. "Wait till you hear the darkness, the basso continuo power of the battle. You won't laugh then."

"You must stay here and write it," Lightning said.

"I kept my vow. Fought the Insects, didn't I? Although it didn't turn out exactly like I'd hoped."

"Don't fret about Lowespass. Don't dwell on it." Lightning and I knew that Insects were nightmarish creatures and, after an encounter, they find their way into nightmares permanently. Neither of us wished the terror of Insect dreams on innocent Awndyn. "You're welcome to stay here as long as you want, until your strength returns. See how lovely the Palace is in spring. When you are ready, I'll ask the Emperor to grant another audience and we can pursue your claim to the Circle again."

I had been creeping toward the door, thinking it would be kind to leave the couple to their conversation. Swallow said, "No!" and started laughing. I hastily returned to the bedside.

"What?"

"Forget the claim, Archer."

"What?"

Swallow paused, glancing at the blue damask canopy, dividing her agony into separate streaks of pain. She was much thinner, from sweating with fever and being unable to eat. In the vast bed, she even appeared dainty, with her millefleurs shawl over a faded print-silk blouse. "I have a new perspective now. I'm not afraid of death anymore. In that battle, and especially after it when I nearly died, I learned something I can't express. I can't even play it, and if I can't express it in music what chance have I in words?"

I suggested that she might at least try.

"I could try, and I might even manage to say something worthwhile, but there's no point in telling you, because you're immortal, and you could never conceive—" She broke off, mirthfully. She was managing to laugh at her experience. She laughed for a long time, with a clear happiness. Her eyes danced with happiness as weightless as it was profound. "Immortality's pointless compared to what I can do."

"Die?" said Lightning, with a voice like slate.

"Change. It's important for me not to forget this lesson—I'll bear it in mind always until it becomes a part of me . . . All my life I've been knocking at the door, calling to be let in. San's refusal makes him ridiculous. Well, forget it."

I looked from one to the other—Swallow was far more comfortable than Lightning. If there had been a year-long battle between them, she had won.

"But I still love you."

Swallow just threw her head back and laughed harder than ever. He stared at her, not knowing what to do, then turned and walked out, slamming the door. I heard doors slamming—bang, bang, bang—all the way down the Long

Corridor, which runs the entire length of the front of the Palace.

"Oh dear," she said. "I think that's an ending."

I n all, Swallow spent fourteen weeks in bed, in coma, in fever and in recovery. She spent a further week practicing hobbling about on two crutches in the confines of the Palace and gardens. She played music and sang, to the limpid lake and empty flowerbeds in which she saw great beauty. Her eyes were bright with tears of wonder; she began trying to put her secret into music. Swallow was right that I didn't understand her, but I knew that no immortal could make music that magnificent.

At the end of November she took the coach back to Awndyn, unescorted. Unfortunately I missed the festivities of her departure, which Lightning insisted on holding. I didn't even see her leave, as throughout the celebrations I was locked in the sapphirine room.

CHAPTER ELEVEN

To: Comet, for petition to the Emperor

From: Lady Vireo Summerday

11/12/15

Lowespass Fortress

I write to report that my town of Summerday has been evacuated. Families have moved south into Rachiswater. The warriors of Summerday and the entire regions of Lowespass, Midelspass and Miroir have come to Lowespass Fortress.

We do not have enough food. I have already begun to ration. None of us will survive over two weeks in these conditions.

Tornado has groups of fyrd working day and night to stop the Insects completing their wall around the fortress. We are being sealed in. Our efforts continue in vain; yesterday the wall grew fifty meters. While we demolish it on one side Insects build it on the other side of the keep. Their numbers

*are vast; in half an hour I counted three thousand. We are
confined to Fortress Crag as Insects flood the valley. They
make no sound except for their shells scraping as they clam-
ber over one another.*

Addendum:

*Jant, if we could understand the way Insects work we
would be much closer to defeating them. They place Walls at
the extent of their captured land. It is as if the Walls are not
to keep invaders out of the Paperlands but to keep the Insects
in. They wall themselves in because they know we are dangerous.*

*I sent my ideas in this letter because it might be my last. I
fight every day. Please present my plea to Staniel
Rachiswater. We need reinforcements now; I think soldiers
from Rachiswater have the best chance of reaching us.*

VIREO, GOVERNOR OF SUMMERDAY AND LOWESPASS
TORNADO, HIS MARK: T

I spent the flight home and much of the night when I arrived
at the Castle bitterly resenting how I'd been treated in
Micawater. I can pick most locks, but the one on the door of the
sapphirine room had been crafted by human hand in Hacilith
and it was far too difficult to crack.

I had nursed Swallow, the singer who dabbled in warfare. I
sent letters to King Staniel via Awian emissaries who were less
likely to daunt him. I flew over Insect territory to carry Vireo's
despairing letters from Lowespass Fortress. And all the thanks I
received was to be locked up like a criminal.

Mist says that when he joined the Circle he was drunk for a
decade, so it's possible that mainlining scolopendium may be just
a phase of adjustment I have to endure, as I now wake every

morning realizing I'm two hundred years old and shouldn't be alive. When I'm hooked even Lightning's Palace isn't sacrosanct, and indeed nowhere is special except the warmth of cat, or the Shift hallucinations. I suppose I'm always going to seem like an outsider. When in Scree, I act like an Awian. In Awia, I behave like a Rhydanne, and when I'm in the Palace, I behave badly.

I started using scolopendium when courting Tern—it gave me confidence and energy so I could fly all night to Wrought and vie with her other suitors. Before that, when mortal, I was a dealer. I quickly saw the dirty side of the business and longed to stop trafficking but I couldn't, by then—Felicitia forced me.

HACILITH 1812

I was young when I first encountered The Wheel in Hacilith. Apprentice in Dotterel's pharmacy, I applied my knowledge from the dispensary to the streets. I had been working all night, for several nights, and was on my way to the market to pick up some crisps for breakfast. I took a paddle tram along the main street of Hacilith; they trundle slower than walking pace. From the front of each battered carriage a twisted cable runs, the length of several streets, ending in a hook. Where the trams terminate, all these cables run together, a greasy black web of tensed wire, at about head height. Boys were employed to shunt empty trams up and down the cobbled courtyards of the terminus. They played tightrope on the cables. They fastened the hooks, polished by the wear of a thousand grimy hands, onto the mechanism that pulled them—huge waterwheels standing in mesh cages and spinning slowly under the turbid assault of the Moren River. Many have lost limbs in the Shackle Sheds, but the trams remained more popular than the dreaded eventuality of having to walk into town.

The tram's slow movement was relaxing, a steady pull as the

cable wound onto a reel. Soon, I fell asleep. The familiar land-marks of the narrow area I knew peeled away, and stranger sights gathered in the tram's dirty Insect wing windows. We passed the market, most passengers left, and I, oblivious, remained taking up most of the backseat. I often found places in Morenzia to be a little too small, but I had grown used to sleep-ing on a shelf in the shop's cellar. A tram's backseat was luxury in comparison.

A sudden halt jarred me awake. I rolled from the seat and pressed my nose against the window. Air drenched with the stench of oil, a rattle from the front of the tram as it was unhitched, and then a team of boys laid hands to the brackets on its sides and hauled it under a lintel and into darkness. I listened to the chanting: "One, two, three—heave!" as the baroque brass carcass slid along the rails. "One, two, three—heave!" Grubby lads ran up the steps and started looking under seats for lost property to claim. They stopped in front of me, astonished, all crowding round.

"Who's that?"

"*What's* that?"

"What're you doin' here?"

"You're not supposed t'be here!"

"Kids that ride to the End of the Line *never leave*!"

"Shut up, Sam."

I said, "Please let me go now. I will reward any friend who can show me the way to Galt." They grinned at my accent, and taut words—although proficient I wasn't familiar enough yet with the language to be sloppy. Smeared faces bobbed like bal-loons, but they didn't rush to offer help. Instead, the largest one leaned over, forcing me back into the seat. He had red hair pok-ing through his string vest. I could smell oil and onions on his breath. I could hear his brain clicking as it freewheeled. "I know you," he said.

Oh no. Please. Not now. "I don't think so."

"You're the one Peterglass is looking for. The Bowyers offered twenty quid for the whereabouts of your den." The crowd froze at the mention of such a healthy sum. "Fifty quid for your dead body." They regarded me inquisitively. "A hundred pounds for you to be brought in, live and whole, so you can be tortured."

Well, at least I was going to get out of the depot in one piece. "No. I am afraid you are wrong. I do not know Peterglass. I have never heard of The Bowyers. You must be looking for someone else."

"Oh yeah. Hundreds of people look like you round here, cat-eyes."

"Well then it must be one of them." I stood up and they grabbed me.

I've heard it said that crowds have a fine sense of right and wrong. Crowds made only of children have a fine sense of how many packets of sweets can be bought with a hundred pounds. I was pulled out of the tram, shoved, dragged, and kicked over the cobbles while Hairy Shoulders and the older boys went into a huddle. They were all strong; I couldn't push between them, I couldn't see over their sweaty heads. Fists clung to every centimeter of my clothes like weights. In the midst of this gang I was tram-handled out into bright sunlight where they squashed me flat on the ground and sat on my wings.

Hairy Shoulders emerged from the huddle and declared, "We'll take it to Felicitia. He'll be madder than an Insect if we sell it without showin' him."

"My name is Jant," I said indignantly from floor level.

He hauled me up by my T-shirt front. "You just confessed."

All the time, curious boys had been peering out from behind trams, slipping between the greasy wires, skipping over the brass rails as they dashed to join the throng. Untended trams were backing up in every direction; a dangerous squealing came from unhooked wires that pulled tighter and tighter. Hairy Shoulders didn't want to attract the attention of anyone over twenty, so he ordered most of the children back inside. Some ran to fetch their bicycles; others kept a firm grasp on me. Their leader hefted his finely carved bike onto his shoulder, encircled my upper arm with his other hand and led me, walking, what seemed like kilometers through the streets of Hacilith, junctions and alleys too many to remember, while a phalanx of orphans marched tightly alongside. Hooting kids on wooden bicycles swooped and raced ahead, and paraded along behind like a comet's tail.

A bicycle propped against the wall of a gin-and-cordial shop suggested much more wealth. The belt strap that drove its wheels was leather, not canvas, and it looked very well kept. It was upright and ebony. The boys poked their admiring fingers into the ornate carvings—horses, falcons, and snakes. The seat was a wolf's head. A pink feather boa and satin streamers were tied to the handlebars. The bike was leaning under a sign which read, "Drunk for a penny. Dead drunk for two pence. Floor space for nothing."

Twin teenage guards in fyrd-surplus chain mail let us into the pub. We all squeezed through, then the crowd dissipated, leaving Hairy Shoulders and me alone. The room was quite small, with six round tables cluttered with debris of card games, smoking and drinking. The people there were all young, mostly in leather and denim, watching quietly. A fan snapped open and a voice behind it oozed, "Vance, darling boy, what have you brought us?"

"I am Jant Shira and—"

Vance twisted my arm. "This is the kid who's been dealing cat in Galt. Lord Aver-Falconet, as you know Peterglass of The

Bowyers has offered money for him. I found him . . ." The voice trailed off into uncertain defiance. Aver-Falconet? That was the Governor's family name. I started to wonder why a backstreet kid would take a pseudonym from the family who must hate us so much.

The fan lowered, revealing a little, heavily made-up face. Lipstick mouthed, "Really? A Rhydanne, no less! Isn't that totally behind the Wall! I can see why you haven't been caught all this time, unruly child."

I simply gaped, mind blank and uncomprehending. It was a boy, I could tell that much. But he wore a green gown, and only girls wore dresses. Boys wore trousers. Girls could wear trousers or dresses. But boys never wore dresses. Did that mean he was a girl? Yes? Maybe he was a girl who looked like a boy. Or maybe it was a fancy dress party. I'd read about masquerades, but I thought they were usually more fun than this. Again Hacilith had thrown up something new; every time I regain my poise the city disorients me. Trams, the sea, money. The crowds, crime, hierarchy. I thought I had grown so used to culture shock I could take these novelties in my stride. But he was the most confusing thing I had seen so far. I couldn't ask my master about this!

"Rhydanne . . . ?"

I half-spread my disproportionate wings. I knew Morenzians were sluggish people; that's why they needed bikes. I used to go everywhere at a flat sprint, and humans didn't do that. "Only partly," I said. "I can run, and I can fly."

The boy laughed delicately, then the rest of the room laughed too. "Fly? No really? I don't believe that!"

Let them not believe it. With a little luck they would throw me off the roof.

"Shira," he mused. "By that name you must have been born out of wedlock. Rhydanne are very strict about that. I guess you're an orphan." I nodded. "And not married. Oh dear, oh dear, left on the shelf, my vigorous hybrid. I can see why you chose to come to the City."

"Last year I ran away from Darkling because a landslide crushed my house," I informed him. My voice had power even then; so factual it made them glance at each other. "And Eilean Dara within it. She had thrown me out into the storm, so it was her cruelty that saved me. When the storm cleared I flew east until I fell from exhaustion."

"And now you deal cat?" Smiling redly. "I find it hard to believe. You must have been here for many years to speak Morenzian so well. Sweet darling, you certainly have Peterglass hopping mad, dealing drugs on his patch. Better quality, much cheaper, and much more prolific than he. Why do you sell such pain and suffering under the guise of pleasure?"

"Junkies would buy cat if I were here or not." And my merchandise was the safest.

Dotterel had explained finance to me and once I had mastered the bizarre concept, I clung to it and pursued the gain of money with obsessive fervor—my new faith, a very reliable faith. Apprentices were not paid, but night by night I was gleaning what I could from the streets and quays. Surprizingly I had a talent for it. I could talk to anyone; they craved what I gave. I hoarded the crinkled notes in a little tin box. I would stop when the box was full. My aim was to have enough money to escape from Hacilith, or be able to set up my own shop, and marry, be accepted and loved. I was working to improve my life, who can blame me? I was dangerous because although I was good with coins, notes and white powder, life in Darkling had taught me bitter survival rather than affection or remorse.

The busty lady on Aver-Falconet's left took a sip of her gin and rose-hip syrup. "We have to go soon," she grumbled. "Just kill him."

"Tut, tut, Layce! Have you lost the scent of cash?"

I declared that I only worked for myself and alone. It was a stupid thing to say. Aver-Falconet rose with a rustle, and gestured to Vance. Vance and his lads rushed over and beat the shit out of me. A blow in the stomach and I doubled over. Back of the neck, chin, and kneecaps. I managed to gouge the cheek of one of them; he kicked me in the balls. I dropped to the sawdust, curled up. Fuzzy black formed round the edge of my sight. I swallowed bile—please god don't let me be sick in front of all these boys. My lower half vanished in a sea of white flame.

A pair of green high heels minced into my field of vision. "Oh, my milk-and-water miscreant. What a shame."

"Piss on it," called Vance.

"As if wrecking his chances isn't enough." Aver-Falconet arranged me into a position where I could see the table. He swept the white cloth back, spilling bottles and lanterns. Under the table was a cage. The girl in the cage huddled away from the bars; she was so dirty that the terrified whites of her eyes were shocking as Insect eyes.

"This is the deal," Aver-Falconet announced. "Jant Shira, please join us. The Wheel is the ruling gang of Hacilith's East Bank. We offer you protection against Peterglass in return for only three-quarters of the profit you make."

Still nauseous, I shrugged, shaking my head. I didn't need refuge, usually. Usually I could outrun a coach-and-four.

"If you do not agree with me I will let Serin here go free. She belongs to Peterglass's Bowyers and she will carry a message for us. Peterglass can come here and we will hand you over for an adequate price. I do not think they will let you live very long."

The blond girl in the cage soaked in his words. She realized I was an outsider, and was looking at me as curiously as I was at her.

There was a lull in the storm that seethed inside me. I was

beaten already, or rather, beaten again. I couldn't fight these boys. Slum children were out of control, people said. They were right. "Yes . . ." I said. "I know poisons, and the cures to them. Cat is only one of the medicines I make. I can earn two hundred pounds a week for The Wheel if you keep Peterglass off my back."

"Who'll keep Felicitia off *your* back?" muttered Vance.

Felicitia? This *was* Felicitia Aver-Falconet? I stood up, painfully, and the older boy offered his hand. The fingernails were painted sea-green, with little rhinestones glued to them. A stroke of inspiration—I took his hand, and kissed it. There was a line of pinpoint scars on the back of his hand, reddened and bruised. I began to recognize the signs; he had his own reasons for recruiting me.

The fan flicked open like a peacock's tail to hide his blush.

"If I'd known who you were I would have sworn loyalty at first," I said. He was the Governor's youngest son, estranged from the family and standing to inherit precisely nothing, but he still had the name. I knew it was important to feign interest in titles.

The room held its breath but Felicitia smiled. "Don't mention it again."

"Have you finished?" Layce's rough voice wilted his fan. "Have we finished with the goat-shagger?"

"Yeah. Ah, yes. Ahem."

"We have tickets to see Fevvers on the trapeze at the Campion. Like now. Let's move." Layce's gang set down their glasses, gathered their coats and headed for the door. From outside came the sound of whirring bikes.

Layce took Felicitia's arm but he twisted away and addressed me again: "Do you want to come with us?"

I stuttered. I'd never been to anything like the Campion before. I was afraid of the bright lights and the sheer number of vibrant people. If you could add together every sound over ten years' time in Darkling it would never make a din as loud as one night's performance in Hacilith. No doubt this would be the first trial of initiation. "Yes . . . Oh, yes—I would love to."

"Can you ride a bike?"

"I'll meet you there."

Layce had feathers on the back of her dress, fashionably aping the mainly Awian aristocracy. Her fake feathers were looking a bit worse for wear. Felicitia walked close by, one and a half meters of emerald chiffon sewn with glittering Insect eye facets. Should I be frightened? What does he want? Grown used to accepting, I accepted his hand on my arse.

All this self-pity was making me hungry, which curtailed my introspection. I set to work on Castle correspondence until the quadrangle clock began to chime midnight. By then I was so ravenous I couldn't concentrate on anything so I left for the Great Hall where meals are continuously laid out for the Eszai, visitors and servants.

The Castle was so quiet it seemed unoccupied, which suited me fine. I'm happy on my own until I hear other people enjoying themselves, and have to compare myself to them. If there were no other people I wouldn't feel alone.

CHAPTER TWELVE

The Great Hall was tiled dark red at the servants' end, the color of dried blood. Rows of pillars down the center supported a vaulted ceiling. The Hall seemed larger at night as most of the tables had been cleared away. I glimpsed my frosted breath in the moonlight from a tall arched window. A sudden noise stopped me and I listened hard, heart racing.

I stood in the shadow of a red pillar and tried to make out the indistinct voices. Two men at the other end of the Hall were shouting in anger. I edged closer. There was a crash, a chair screeched on the tiling, a metal plate dropped to the floor. Still closer, it resolved into words.

"Well, I thought I would find you here, you bastard." Petulant and deep, round Awian vowels like overripe fruit. Lightning. The other voice said something with a low sneer.

"Touch Ata again and you're dead," said Lightning.

"I should have *known* she'd run to you. Port. Storm. When I catch her I'll—"

"You will have to pass me first," the Archer pointed out. "Everyone knows she is better than you." There was a scuffle and another crash. Then nothing.

I couldn't think whether to stay and listen, or make my presence known. Blankness comes when I have to do something, when it's best not to think. For example when facing Insect swarms, or cooking a fix. That's it, I'm leaving. The part of me that charges the Insects or shoots an overdose took control. I dropped my hands to my sides and stepped out into oil lamp glare, stood there blinking.

"Boys," I said. "Let's not fight."

Shearwater Mist was sitting on the edge of the table, leaned back, his thick arms among plates of food. Blood was running down his leg from a shallow cut, pooling on the floor. Lightning stood over him with a sword; he had just taken Mist's own rapier from him. He had a quiver of arrows on his back, the embossed strap hanging down, and his flickering shadow on the ocher wall looked like a porcupine. I turned my attention from the suckling roast to Mist's lined face. "What is this about?" I asked.

"Get lost, waif," said Shearwater Mist. Lightning thumped him on the shoulder with the sword pommel. An Insect had once bitten through that shoulder, and the Sailor winced.

I edged forward but Lightning pointed the sword at me and sighted down the flat of its blade. "Mind your own business," he said.

He's right, it's not my business, and he doesn't want me to make it my business, and I shouldn't be creeping around in the dark anyway.

I closed the space in a couple of strides and grabbed Lightning's free arm. He flicked me away. Mist snarled, looking like a wolfhound. I felt like an alley cat watching lions fight.

"Stop that!" Lightning yelled at Mist.

"You have so much explaining to do, Mica," Mist shouted back.

"You would be nothing if not for me!"

"Trying to steal it back? Pigs. Fly." The sneer rolled up one side of Mist's face like paralysis. Lightning seemed itching to hit it.

I sneaked a bottle of plum wine from the table and sat down on a pillar plinth, watching them. Mist hooked the remaining fingers of his left hand under the quiver strap that ran diagonally over Lightning's chest, against his shirt. He tried to drag him closer. I thought the strap would break, and arrows would be all over the floor like pick-up sticks.

Lightning dropped the rapier, drew his own short archer's sword. He pressed it against Mist's neck so the blade ran behind his ear. "You'll regret this," he said. Mist tried to kick his knee.

Mist hadn't altered his twisted smile; he looked like a wry shark. Gray hair straggled on his collar, a broad white streak in his hair, which I thought couldn't be natural until I decided that nobody could keep it dyed for so long. His stony eyes were on the Archer.

"I'll tell San," I declared.

"There are many things I could inform the Emperor about Jant," Lightning called back. Extortion, our instinct.

"Go ahead," I muttered.

"Just because you have all the money you think you can do what you like!"

"This concerns honor, not wealth!" Lightning bawled in his face.

"Money is honor," I remarked irrelevantly, and Mist gave me a genuine smile for a second. Then the sneer was back firmly in place. He grasped Lightning's wrist holding the sword hilt, with his right hand, and squeezed. Lightning flicked the blade and a little trickle of blood ran down from behind Mist's ear. There was a battle of wills, Lightning's brawny arm tensing, the veins standing out on Mist's thick hand. The Archer dropped his sword, and Mist slid off the table with a foot on both blades. He picked the rapier up. I could see white fingerprints around Lightning's wrist; he narrowed his eyes as Mist squared up to him with the weapon.

"Shearwater . . . ?" My voice sounded small.

"Get out of here, you inky-fingered waif," he said menacingly. So I did.

I ran out to the courtyard, icy cobbles sliding under my boots. In the center of the dark square I spread darker wings and struggled up to my window, where I had left the shutters ajar. I kicked them open and stepped down into a deserted untidy room. The only sound was a steady drip of candle wax onto the floor, where blue stalagmites were growing. "Tern?" I called. "Tern! *Tern!*—Governor Wrought! You skinny horse." A scribbled note by the dead fireplace informed me she had gone to Hacilith. She was asking the Governor to accept the refugees swarming her manorship, with the idea that she could do more for them farther south, in the city.

I took a swig of sickly wine, realized I was holding a bottle. A potential weapon. Down in the Hall, I had a weapon all the time without realizing. Not a very worthy one, to use against these Awian lords. I giggled.

I only cut someone with broken glass once—that was a rich lord too, back in Hacilith. I left the gin shop in the dark, walking through Galt's stained streets. Eventually I became aware of someone following me. I was so naïve; I had come as far as Cinder Street before the idea crossed my mind. The shop was nearby, the wings of its canopy folded back for the night. I couldn't risk a dash to safety; Felicitia would learn where I lived. Instead, I took a detour, ran round a corner. Outside the Kentledge pub, drunkards had vomited so often the pavement was starting to dissolve. I picked an empty bottle from an over-flowing bin, smashed it and lay in wait.

A figure came round the corner, and I jumped for his throat. I pressed the glass to his mouth. If I had twisted it, it would have sliced out his mouth, and the skin around it, like a circle from a pastry cutter.

"Who are you?" I yelled. Fury is the main passion I remember from that age.

"Mmm mm mm!"

"Oh. Bugger."

I removed the bottle tentatively, my fingers tight enough to break it and Felicitia regarded me calmly. Blood was running into his mouth from a mustache of little cuts. He smeared his lips together like women do with lipstick, gave a broad red grin. "Well, my belligerent boy," he said. "The East Bank gangs really do need you."

These are memories of which Lightning and Mist couldn't conceive, and I can't imagine the sort of memories they might have. I crossed to the only clean table and lit the burner under my still, made sure there was enough water and fern in the hopper. This is something I do automatically every time I come into the room. I couldn't calm the older Eszai, I was truly useless. Lightning had always used Mist as a case in point when training me in combat, calling up examples of his foolishness. "Protect your eyes, fingers, teeth. These things don't grow back. You don't want to live without them, like Mist who caught his hand in an anchor chain, back when he was a *common sailor*."

I sat down at a writing desk and started transcribing orders, sealing them with the Castle's sunburst crest.

Several letters later—my subconscious had been counting the drops—the tone of their falling into a little glass beaker

changed, and I knew I had enough cat to fill a syringe. The needle scratched against the glass as I sucked it up, still warm. I
wound a leather bootlace round my arm, and after some mess-
ing about, sank it in a major vein.

Tiredness vanished. I went to sit back down at the desk.
Cat's a work drug. Sometimes cat is a work drug. With a steady
hand, I went back to scripting the commands that San wanted
me to send out. After a quarter hour, the peak began to fade, but
I resisted taking more. Then I went and topped it up with
another shot. Wish I had veins like the Sailor's. I concentrated
completely on the letters for a while. I have a theory that everybody in their lifetime gets fifteen minutes of ecstasy. Except me,
'cause I do it every night.

I crashed out of the second high too quickly to manage the
distance between my desk and the still. Instead, I sat and stared
into space, at the forested windows. Tiredness began to grow on
me, unbearably. The glass was iced up in thin fern patterns, like
fronds of scolopendium. They swirled around each other, curving, moving. They curled like girls' downy feathers. I wish Tern
were here. The frost plants changed color slowly, becoming
murky gray, then a sharp light blue. I was puzzled. Ice is white.
Blue is not white . . . Blue things are things like the sky . . .
During the day . . . Daytime. Of course. I had better go to bed.

A hand on my shoulder shook me gently. I realized it had
been there for some time. I gathered what little strength I had
left and looked round. I found myself eye-to-eye with
Lightning's belt buckle. My gaze traveled up to his square face,
short hair the color of burned sand. He was losing his tan in the
Plainslands winter. "Good morning," I said, in Scree by accident, then repeated it in Awian. I rubbed at my stubble; I need a
wash.

"The door was open. I knocked but you gave no reply. It's
cold in here," he observed. He used my books as stepping stones

through the chaos of papers, from *Posteventualism* to *Pharmacopoeia, Darkling Linguistics* and *Solution Chemistry* in three apologetic steps.

"Is it? I wouldn't know."

A glance toward the still, which was dripping away, filling the air with a scent of hot oil and cut grass. "Oh. Jant? Are you all right?"

A streak of the old fury flickered through me. The idiot was still carrying a quiver over his shoulder. He also wore a circlet, which hid in his hair like a gold worm in hay. "I'm nothing. It's not fair. This is no time to pursue your fifteenth-century quarrels, Micawater!" I glared at the arrow tops until he swung the quiver from his shoulder and laid it, with a crackle of sticks, on the carpet. The arrow fledgings were dyed bright red, which is the Castle color, but it also makes them easier to find in the snow, like little drops of blood.

Lightning makes a nervous gesture with his right hand sometimes, subconsciously. The frequency of that gesture shows how worried he is. He makes a fist with his hand, and then slides the tips of his fingers back over his palm, straightening the hand out. I know he does this to feel the deep ridges of a scar. When he was blood-brother to Savory, he grasped a sword and drew his hand along it, a quick motion cutting twice to the bone, from each edge of the blade. He loved her and the pale hollow of that scar must be very reassuring to him. It was because of the wound that he lost her, though. Couldn't shoot straight with a hand cut to shreds.

I pushed myself out of the chair, stumbled across to the divan, where I lay curled up, my head on a cool satin cushion. Lightning said, "I wish to make reparation for what happened last night. You deserve an explanation."

Did I? I didn't care, really. I wanted a hit. But still I was grateful that he had thought of me. "I want an apology from

Shearwater," I declared, spreading a wing to form a bony blanket.

"Him? Ha!" Lightning passed a broad hand over his eyes, settled himself in the chair I had just vacated. He looked shattered, actually. "I hate Shearwater Mist," he said. "San help me, I despise him and I always have. Ever since he joined the Circle. Violence is no way to treat a lady. Women are . . . Ata is . . . The way I feel about her is . . . One should never strike a woman." Yes. They hit you back.

I thought I had made a mess of my life with drugs, but that is nothing to some people's disaster with love. I offered him a broad smile of encouragement. "Talk," I said.

"Ata has an idea, to deliver Tornado from Lowespass. She can sail great ships, with fyrd on board, up the river, as close as possible to the base of the crag. We can fight to the Fortress from there, with much lower attrition than if we march by land. You know that Insects don't go into the river. If Mist's caravels could manage it, and I had archers on them . . ." Lightning hesitated as he remembered how little I like ships.

"So you back this plan?" I asked.

"I don't know. It is a new way of fighting. I would prefer to rely on our proven strengths . . . But I can think of no better way to reach Tornado."

"Does the Emperor approve?"

"He thought it a great innovation!"

I said, "Then I don't understand. Why doesn't he order Mist to sail upriver?"

"Mist won't do it. He advises San that the venture is impossible, Oriole River too shallow. They gave San conflicting information. Mist completely refuses to give her authority to try it. Then, right there in the Throne Room, Ata Challenged him! She said: 'Look to your title, Shearwater Mist!' They left the court and he turned on her.

"Ata sought me, for safety. She is still hiding in my room now; she locked the door. She is covered in bruises, Mist beat her; he is a coward and a miser. Ata wants to prove herself a better seafarer than him—and I think she is," Lightning added loyally.

"What did San say?"

"That Ata has a legitimate Challenge."

"Yes, but now, of all times!" I picked up a handful of letters. "Summerday town, gone. Rachis, Tanager, under attack. Insects sighted in Wrought. In Carniss. Insects on the Alula Road. Avernwater wants aid, Sheldrake won't send any. We need Eszai in Awia; she is mad to make a Challenge now." Mad or brave, I thought; and Mist is equally wrong to force her into it. "It's a rash act; Mist will divorce her and San will throw her back into the flow of time, and I won't miss her."

"To hit a distant target one must aim high. I do support her, if she really means to relieve Tornado and the Lowespass fyrd."

I was silent as what he said sank in. I examined the letters I had been writing to organize our operations; now everything had changed. I raised an eyebrow. "The Emperor needs Mist, because with Staniel on the throne, only Peregrine manor will keep you from taking over Awia." Probably females have nothing to do with it, I thought.

"No! Since Mist owns Peregrine? No! How *dare* you? I suppose you don't know. Listen. There is much you don't know, Jant. Peregrine is my land, as well; the manorship was mine. Mist is no more Awian than you are. His family are lying thieves, they only aspire to what they cannot be." He sighed, gave me a shrewd look. "It is hard to talk about the past," he said. "So spare me. I had to sell Peregrine manorship in the Bad Years. I didn't want my people to go hungry, and the coast was doing well. Shearwater had ships that brought us supplies. I lost Tambrine, and Donaise was completely deserted. I put vineyards there, where there had been houses, which is how I managed to buy Tambrine back. The Insects destroyed it last month . . .

"Shearwater kept Peregrine, although I pleaded for him to return it . . . *If you stick that needle in your arm again I'll thrash you!*"

"I, uh, wasn't going to. Would you like a coffee?"

"Please. And light the bloody fire; it's cold as an Insect's backside in here. What I am trying to convey is that the Shearwaters have always been opportunistic parasites without an ounce of morality between them. Thank you. Peregrine Micawater was my eldest brother. There were eight of us, and I had one sister. Peregrine was a traveler, he was a little like you in that way. He was a brilliant archer also. He visited Hacilith, and saw the Emperor's birthplace. He spent most of his time at the coast, where he built a mansion that we called Peregrine. It was under his orders that ships were first built, in order for him to sail between the islands. Previously Awia had no fleet. My brother wished for Awian ships to be the best in the world. Hence we have Awndyn, and the Aver-Falconets, and Shearwater, all owing to the power of ships.

"When Mother died Micawater was willed to Peregrine. I was in the Circle by then but to give the Palace directly to me would have caused some unrest. Besides, I was slightly out of favor with my mother's side of the family. He kept the lands well, although I realize his heart was sold to the ocean. Just like Ata. He added to the Palace as much as he could, because he knew that before he died, he would give it to me. And I could preserve it forever. I saw them all grow old and die or slain by Insects; Shira, you have not had that agony.

"My second eldest brother was still alive. He believed that he was next in line, and he wanted the Palace. Peregrine declined to give it to him. He did not respect Peregrine's wishes, and asked me for it. I refused and we had a terrible row. I said he was responsible for killing my sister. I regret that. His family changed their name.

"Shearwater Mist refused to bring his betrothed with him when he came to the Circle, believing he could have an eternity of young lovers, the selfish bastard. Now he goes through life with none at all, and serve him right!"

Lightning stopped, and gazed at me. He had been on a rush; the past's a drug for him. He did the weird gesture with his arrow hand again, the scar showing like a white ribbon.

I shrugged. "We should be fighting Insects, and not each other."

"God, I like you, Jant. So deep and meaningful. Fighting for Ata's cause might be the only way to beat them."

"You love her, don't you?" I was rolling the sleeve back on my other arm.

"Not properly. It's all right, go ahead. Do it."

"What?"

"Oh well. You treated Swallow, and you need a rest. Can I stop you?"

"It's more relief than reward," I said, but Lightning had removed the thrill of guilt. I put the syringe down, still loaded.

He was digging in a pocket of his embroidered red coat. "I have here a letter from Ata to her husband," he said, offering me a square envelope addressed with very feminine script. "I hardly wish to speak to him, so I would be grateful if you would deliver it."

"Where do I find him? Harcourt?"

"In the Hospital. Rayne is mending his broken ribs."

"Oh, *Saker*!"

"Nobody draws a sword to me, Comet. You should know that by now."

Lightning seemed more lighthearted now that he had

unburdened himself of a piece of history. He left, full of thanks, asking to see me soon. He thought he had an ally in support of Ata. He strode down the spiral stairs, and away in the direction of the stables. I shut the door, barred it, and began to fill the hopper of my still with fresh water. I had to figure out a way to steam this letter open.

I nsects were advancing into Tanager and Wrought manors. Tern told me that the Wrought people were packing and moving out along the coast to Hacilith. I directed ten fyrd divisions to Eleonora Tanager, and sent a letter from the Emperor advizing her to move west, and telling her how best to protect the people.

Next, I wondered how I could stop all this talk of caravels and fortunes. I wanted to stop Mist and Ata destroying each other when the Empire needed them both. And I would rather have a blow job from an Insect than go anywhere near a ship.

I sorted out clothes, soap, and a massive meal of inoffensive things that I would hopefully be able to keep down, and then went to court, where I discovered that San had no inclination to stop Ata's Challenge. Then I flew to the Simurgh Passage and, hanging on a convenient breeze to the entertainment of quadrangle people, I figured out which windows were Lightning's, and which one of those had the curtains drawn. I landed on its windowsill, and tapped on the glass.

Ata's face appeared disembodied between the curtains. She swept them open and wrestled with the catch. One cheek was swollen and purple; her lower lip was split in the center, a wide red gash. The face that launched a thousand ships. She was pallid and looked ghostly, but the fire of resentment in her eyes would have fueled hundreds of phantoms. "Queen of Ships," I said, looking with horror at the bruises her makeup could not conceal. "Did Mist do this to you? I'll kill him myself!"

"Yes, he did, but there's nothing you can do."

Not face to face, perhaps, but I can put him and his fyrd in a bad position when we next fight Insects. I can talk Rayne into giving him some really nasty potions.

I produced the letter. "I'm just checking that you still want me to deliver this."

"Aye," she said, her mouth twisting.

"I just have a slight feeling—call it a hunch—that you might have been very angry when you wrote it."

"How—?"

"In fact, never since you were a fledgling in gingham have you written such a furious letter."

"I—"

"A letter so sharp you could gut fish with it. A note, succinct, but boiling with such execration and castigation that it would mean conflict between husband and wife, all-out civil war as well as Insect war in Peregrine, havoc and carnage and a fight to the death."

"Come back when the drugs wear off," she said.

"So you don't regret it?" I asked. "You know him well, and you understand the effect that words such as might be contained in this letter would have on him. You're calling his bluff, or mine; that's fine, I only live here—" The platinum blonde reached out and pushed me off the ledge. My spread wings caught like hooks on the steady wind and I hung there, on a level with her teary eyes, slipping the note into my jacket.

"Give him it!" she spat. "You're afraid of everything! Jant, the Emperor encouraged me. Why is Shearwater being so obstructive? Because it proves I'm a better Sailor! He's a sea trader, doesn't consider the opportunities that being a river rat might bring—I can do both! Frost says it's possible, theoretically on a spring tide. She's the best architectural engineer there is; she uses the river to control Insects, her maps are very reliable."

"Ata, that means we only have ten days. It'll be hard to mobilize enough fyrd, but I'll try."

"Nothing will stop me."

I nodded. "Lady Dei, I beg you to give me one more command. Would you like me to fly to Grass Isle and ensure the Sute Towers are yours? I can ask Bittern Diw to lay in supplies."

The ghost gleam in her eyes became searchlight strong. "Aye." She beamed. "I'll never trust you, though. Come back tonight and there'll be letters ready."

"Can't wait," I said, angling my wings so I was flung straight up, like a kite. The wall sped away, shrank, and soon I was looking at the moss-green Castle roofs. Now I knew something that the Archer didn't; how dare he say, "You deserve an explanation"! I had to know more than him about what was going on; it was a heavy habit to feed.

Shearwater Mist was the only man in the Hospital, so he was receiving Rayne's attention in full. I think she was inventing things to do to him. I had been the subject of her experimentation before, with my Rhydanne need for eight-thousand-meter-altitude air and my heart rate that goes down below fifty. I knew how thorough Rayne could be. She showed me where he was, sitting up in a starched white-sheeted bed. Gray eyes watched me woefully; he breathed through a dry, open mouth, little sips like a dying animal. Gray chest hairs like wires poked over the bandages. The bandages were wound around his muscular chest under his white shirt and pale yellow cravat. Rayne must have stood on him to pull them that tight. "Hello, waif," he gasped. "You're looking smart. I should have dressed up. Beggars. Choosers."

"I'm not staying long," I said. "I am here to give you a letter from Ata. She requires no immediate answer." I handed him the envelope, checked my exits and stood well back. It lay on Mist's injured leg, looking tiny. "Aren't you going to open it?"

"Jant," he sighed, "I'm sorry about last night."

"Never—"

"That this happened to me. Pride. Fall. Lightning is a quite excellent swordsman. When Rayne lets me leave here I'll confront him again. This time without such an audience. Flies. Shite."

I was nettled but kept calm. "On the other hand if you want a neutral go-between, I'd be happy to oblige," I offered, dodging his sundial nose as he shook his head.

"Horse. Water. You're known for disobedience, and I should think that Lightning has told you his side of the story by now."

"He has."

"I hate him. Him and his bloody hunger to call all Awia 'Micawater' and leave none for the rest of us. Dog. Manger. The problem is people believe the richer side to every argument. I know I have no support. He's greedy and loud; though I keep stating my case no one listens. Head. Wall."

"I would preferably describe him as acquisitive not esurient."

"What?"

"I understand your side to the story. It's far more reasonable than Lightning's."

"Really?"

"I looked it up. He sold Peregrine to your father in the drought of the 1580s. It seems a fair deal to me. In fact it's despicable to bear a grudge for so long; it's affecting his judgment. Everybody knows how fiercely Lightning conserves Micawater, believing he owes it to his family. I had no family, so I don't understand his need. The other issue doesn't concern me. I'm Rhydanne. We're not fond of prying. What you and Ata do is between yourselves."

"Yes." The wedding ring on his index finger, a battered stripe of gold. "At least I *had* a wife. Bird. Hand."

I gave him the thin benefit of a cat-eyed stare. He couldn't meet it. When I was in Hacilith I always avoided eye contact. I dropped my gaze to the floor when passing men in the street. I craved obscurity, knowing that they would gape in amazement, or throw names and stones after me. Now, difference seems to be a source of power.

"Can I rely on you to join me against the Insects?"

"Of course, waif. By land, out of Rachiswater. Safety. Numbers."

I said, "Now you sound like Staniel."

"He's a fool but he's a King," Mist said, regret in his veteran smoker's voice. "Who's to say he won't be a fool with Eszai behind him? It's our best base to strike north; he has over fifty thousand men in Rachis town. I have the future of my manor in mind. I don't want it to suffer Staniel's displeasure. One hand for yourself and one for the ship, as they say in Diw."

Mist coughed, and winced. "Jant, why won't San trust me? Live longest. See most. I told him, about seven meters' depth is what you need, and you don't get such margin in a river. An unloaded caravel draws five meters in salt water; loaded, and in fresh water they displace more, of course. San listened to Ata because she's loud, not because she's right. Squeaky wheel. Grease. The Oriole bay's all tide races and sand bars. Ships above five hundred tonnes don't enter, they discharge at Summerday. These are ocean-going caravels, not bloody barges. Book. Cover. They're fouled with weed and all kind of dross; they'll drag in a river current like they had sail underwater. If Ata tries it she'll be beached, drowned or torn to bits by Insects. But, desperate diseases. Desperate remedies; no one will dare Challenge me again."

I told Mist that was why I was here. Ata seemed very angry with you, I said. I seem to remember she has fyrd in Diw, as well as on Grass Isle at the moment. I finished these musings with a suggestion: "Should I order her fyrd to Awndyn? I'm sure you would rather not face three thousand Islanders if things get rough."

Shearwater thought for a while. "Do it," he said.

"At your word. Is there anything else?"

"Er. No. Not yet, waif. Thank you."

I made my way out of the Hospital as his nicotine-stained fingers began tearing at Ata's envelope. I resisted an urge to dash, but found myself walking faster and faster, with ever-longer strides until I reached the relative safety of the bleached white corridor. I paused there, head on one side, and a scream then a stream of abuse and cursing in Plainslands ricocheted down the corridor and burst around me like flame. Sailor's swearing could melt lead.

Shit. Fan. Life is certainly becoming more interesting these days.

CHAPTER THIRTEEN

Ata left the Castle on horseback. I made sure her journey was fast; she reached the coast two days before her husband. I left her on the quayside at Diw, before a brilliant pink sunset, which melted the massive sky and still ocean together in waxen rose. A boat was prepared for her, five men to row. She stepped down and rested a sixth oar in the lock, saying that she would row with the rest. They splashed out of the harbor and toward a caravel's sharp baroque hulk.

Diw manor belongs to Ata's daughter. She has another two sons who are jewelers, and two who build ships. Originally Ata had five daughters, all of whom married. The five daughters had twenty-five children, of whom ten married. The twenty-five grandchildren had a hundred and twenty-five great-grandchildren. The hundred and twenty-five great-grandchildren had six hundred and twenty-five great-great-grandchildren. After that I stopped counting. Ata put word out that she needed help, gossip ran round her network like a rat in a treadmill, and money started pouring in to Diw.

Some of Mist's children supported him, but he usually paid them little attention. Ata kept in touch with the intricacies of all her generations, and they defended her keenly.

Pink became crimson, then dark and darker purple. I rode failing thermals from Diw to Grass Isle, a black cutout clustered with lights. Ata built a flock of twelve towers there, around the coast, before the Emperor forced her to stop. They were known as the Sute Towers, and each looks out over a separate expanse of ocean. No ship could put in at the Island without falling under the silent watch of those squat sentinels. In this way Ata made the entire island her stronghold, while Mist had simply embellished the port. I soared around the island's circumference, twenty minutes from Towers January to December, sound of breaking surf and stink of burning sea coal. When lights came on in the meeting hall of July Tower I cut short my circuit and landed on a red-tiled roof. From the ridge to the eaves, in through an open window, and I was suddenly in the midst of crowds: servants and sailors knocking each other over in their haste to obey Ata's orders.

At length the sparse hall was empty. Sute was abandoned to a garrison only. Lights were extinguished across Grass Isle, keys turning in locks, doors were being barred. The air of finality was terrifying; Ata was clearing her island for troops. Motionless, I had waited at the window, and now Cyan and her nursemaid were the only civilians left. Ata sighed and slid into a chair behind her candlelit desk. She suddenly looked old. The bruises on her face were brown and yellow, like a frieze of autumn leaves. Her hair was a white silk shawl, paler than her bronzed skin. She crossed legs in tight blue leather trousers, folded azure slashed sleeves over a waistcoat embroidered with cobalt-blue and ivory plumes. Her shirt pulled tightly over shoulders rounded and upper arms flattened with muscle. She stared into space.

I eyed Cyan's maid, who was sitting on the floor trying to interest the reticent child in an ugly doll. I had always assumed nursemaids to be stern old women, but this one was thin and under thirty, and very attractive.

Ata sighed and leaned back in her winged chair. A little bulge of fat showed over the top of her belt. Fat softened the line of her jaw and candlelight accentuated crow's feet around her eyes. The rest of her body was still youthful steel. She could easily beat me in a fair sword-fight. "You know, Comet," she said. "I just can't figure you at all."

I waited. I use silence as my main defense; flatlanders drown in silence, they find it unbearable. They will say anything, no matter how stupid or recriminating, in order to break it.

"I mean, why are you here anyway?"

Creating debts. "Awaiting my lady's command."

"Don't take me for a fool! You're watching the show. Well, I swear you this, the show will be worth watching." She stood up and walked across the room to Cyan, past the girl, to the window and back. She paced back and forth, saying, "I've had all I can stand. I'm doing what I should have done five hundred years ago. This is what I was born for! But no—I thought he was right and I was wrong, and in a moment of self-doubt I followed him. Now things will change! My stupid husband waits for instruction from Rachiswater—Staniel is killing Awia with cowardice!

"I should have Challenged Shearwater; by god I *did,* then lost heart. So I married him and sailed with him for five hundred years. Five hundred fucking years! Blood and sand! Sorry, Cyan. Come here, child. I thought joining the Circle by marriage would be as good as having the title myself, but it isn't, of course. Shearwater takes the credit for everything I do and I never had the fucking guts to complain! Those ships still fly the Awian ensign. Not anymore! No fucking longer! There will be no pennants on the Castle fleet. My flag will have no emblem. I'll nail his balls to the mast!" She paused. "I need you, Rhydanne, but I don't know how to play you. You're too damned smart. No loyalty."

I sat down cross-legged on the window seat. Behind me, a sheer drop to the sea-washed rocks. "I do admire independence. You say it took five hundred years to realize what I realized at the age of five. But then, I was put through a harder mill than you."

"Oh, you were?"

"Yes."

She crouched down behind the desk, leather creaking, her sword-hanger's gilded chain clinking against the basket hilt. She slid the bottom drawer open and took out a stack of banknotes tied with ribbon. "Your loyalty is to money?" She gave the ribbon to Cyan for her hair. The sheaf of notes was split in half and counted. "This is all I have left," she said, which I didn't believe. "Take two hundred pounds. It will come in useful next time you go to Hacilith."

"Ata, I'm not asking for money."

"I've heard tell you need all you can get."

I took the battered gray notes from her, riffled through them and shoved them in a frayed coat pocket.

Ata continued, "Mist is the Castle's Sailor; it's your duty to do what he asks, no matter how much I pay you. You're a wild card. Well, we're all wild cards; every card in the fucking pack is a joker.

"Take Cyan down to the harbor. A boat is waiting. Make sure she is safe at all times, cross from September Tower to

Peregrine Quay, where there is a coach. A closed carriage, please—watch for Insects! Deliver her to the nearest place where she will be absolutely safe . . ."

"Which is?"

"Micawater Palace."

I giggled. "Lightning will never agree to—"

"He already has. If you wish to return you must fly because there will be no sailing between the coast and the island after you leave. Cyan will have the last boat out. Also, there will be no access past the island, Awia will have to manage its affairs and affrays by land."

I stared at her. She shrugged, hands down on Cyan's checkered shoulders. "It isn't as bad as all that," she said. "There'll be a fee to escort ships taking fyrd to the front."

"You mean a toll?"

"I mean a fair price for the pilot. The *Ortolan* and another five caravels will enforce it in the south. The sound will be patrolled by four caravels, which will be fast enough to cut down Mist's ship."

I hadn't been aware she had such resources under her control. Then I realized she had everything that Mist left in Diw—sixty caravels—the *Stormy Petrel* and the *Ortolan* with the greatest weight of sail.

She continued, "I am afraid that you will take my child to the manor rather than through Peregrine and leave her with Mist. You will not do that, of course, because Lightning expects to receive her—and you want to keep your creditor content."

"I'm not a bloody nursemaid, Ata."

"No." She shrugged. "You can always refuse."

"Oh, I'll do it. But San will hear of this." I slid off the windowsill and offered the girl my hand. Cyan clung to her mother's leather knees. She patted the child's shiny hair—candlelight reflecting in a halo around her head—and whispered something in her ear. Cyan grabbed two bundles of blue skirt, ran to me, stopped just short, and raised a hand solemnly.

"Cyan Dei of Peregrine," she said, timidly.

Ata winced. "Of Sute, darling."

"Of Sute. Pleased-to-meet-you, sir."

"Jant. At your service and that of Sute."

"Right," said Ata briskly, turning away and sitting at the olive leather-topped desk. "You leave with the tide, so you have five hours. Until then, Rhydanne, make yourself useful—do what you do best. Take yourself down to the Night Jar, and buy all the sailors drinks on my behalf." She split the sheaf of notes again and handed me roughly a hundred pounds. "Listen to the gossip; I want to know all their thoughts and fears. I want you to play your fortune cards for them when they ask, and you will predict that every skirmish between my *husband* and myself will end in my favor. Can you do that convincingly?"

"Easily." I smiled. I bowed to her, shook out my wings, watching Cyan's astonished eyes. I climbed out of the window, and welcomed a waking rush of air. The girl clattered to the window, hands on the sill, and gazed out on my slow glide down to the dark quay.

I can tell by the way the road is becoming smoother that we have almost reached Peregrine. Anxiety grows on me. I say anxiety when I mean fear. The coach stopped briefly to change horses, but I kept the blind down. It is between two and three in the morning and we have been shaken like dice in this tiny black lacquer box all night. My coach has no insignia, the dirty windows are made of veined Insect wings, the flat springs squeal at each corner, every bump in the road. The landscape outside will turn pale gray soon, and we will rush screaming and foam-flecked into another dawn. There will be myths of ghost coaches on this highway.

The ceiling is a canopy of rusty taffeta; the walls are dented plywood. I sit on an uncomfortable leather-covered bench and gaze at the little girl opposite. I find myself wishing she had twenty more years, and that this was Hacilith, not the Awian border. She is lying on the bench, knees pulled up under a long dress, her head resting on my coat. She has a copper ring on her tiny finger, and a wide lace ribbon loosening on a flaxen pony-tail. That is all; no coat, no luggage, no spare clothes. I carried her on my shoulders over the fetid beach at midnight, and I am plastered in gritty mud, and sweat from having been in a boat, but at least her white socks are still clean.

"Not a word from you," I had said, lifting her into the coach. She shrugged, unbuttoned her ankle boots and curled up. "Aren't you scared?"

"No."

"Well, you should be."

The ring was a minute dolphin, which looped her little fin-ger, its tail welded to its snout. She was more interested in it than in the real world. "Do you know what's happening?" I asked her.

"Yes."

"Mummy and Daddy are fighting again. Only this time it's for real. This is serious. Cyan Dei, look at me when I'm talking." I pushed my sunglasses down my nose and glared at her over the tops.

"You're one of them," she said, "aren't you?"

"One of who?"

"People who don't die."

"That's right."

She gave a contented sigh and put her head down on my coat, evidently deciding she was perfectly safe. She was asleep in minutes. Her trust was touching, which is why I have been watching over her all night.

We sped through Peregrine manorship with the coach blinds anchored tight. I remembered how the gang used to tip coaches over in Hacilith, with a rope strung across the cobbled street. Wheels spun helplessly in the air, we slit open black beetle cara-paces with cleavers and swords, pulled out spluttering riches and spilled the horses' hot blood.

A single Insect could scare horses into bolting, and then we would be out of control. On guard, I waited for all this to hap-pen in confused darkness, but we were lucky; no roadblocks, no starving Insect packs, and then we were through.

Cyan woke with the first rays of sun, and stretched along the bench. Splinters caught at her skirt. "Have we got any food?" she said.

"No." I pulled a silver hip flask from the top of my boot. "If you want, you can have some of this."

Her fingers traced embossed knot-work around the bottle. She seemed to love beautiful things, shiny things. She unscrewed the lid, sniffed. "What is it?"

"Sloe gin. From the Night Jar."

Cyan took a sip, seemed to like it. She sipped again and rolled the sticky liquid around her tongue. Definitely Ata's child, I thought. "Steady, steady. It'll make you sick!"

She pulled the dolphin ring from her finger and offered it to me. "My father gave me this," she said, and started coughing. I slapped her on the back. When the girl could breathe again she continued, "Could you please give it to him? To say that I'm safe and I still love him. Very, very much."

"Of course I will, Cyan." I am taking orders from an eight-year-old now.

The smooth, shortbread-colored stone of Micawater Palace glowed in blue daybreak light. Harrier stood on the steps, between fluted columns, in a striped gray waistcoat and narrow trousers, long peach lace cuffs hiding his hands. Ornate gates clanged shut behind us. I lifted the blind so Cyan could see as the aching horses slackened and we scrunched along a long, curved driveway and rocked to a halt in front of the main entrance. I unfastened the coach door, kicked down the folding steps and emerged at last stretching thankfully and measuring the sky; this was a fine morning.

Tackle jangled as two boys rushed to steady the ebony horses and a third to help down the weary driver. A cup of steaming coffee pressed into his hands, he was accompanied into the house. I lifted Cyan from the coach and placed her on the ground. She fell over. The coach drew away promptly. I removed my hip flask from a ruddy hand and stuffed it hurriedly into the top of my boot as Lightning's steward approached.

"Good morning, Comet," Harrier announced.

"Jant," I corrected him. "I trust you're well? How's the Insect bite? No, we've had an awful journey. This is Ata's daughter, please take care of her. I have to be going now." I rescued my coat as Cyan tried to stand up, hiccuped and sat down again in the gravel. Even her hiccups were slurred.

"Comet, are you sure you will not stay? We have breakfast laid out especially."

"I don't eat breakfast. In fact, I don't eat. Give Saker my regards. Bye."

Harrier hauled Cyan to her white sock-feet; she dangled in a bundle from his hand. Puzzled, he tried to walk, but she kept straying out too far to one side, then swaying back and banging against his elegant legs.

I swept my wings through the air in a full beat, realizing hopelessly I was too hungry and exhausted to fly back to the Castle immediately. Harrier must have noticed because he foisted the hospitality of his lord's palace on me once again. "If you wish to rest and wash, the guest rooms are prepared."

A place to sleep. A place to lie down. Somewhere to shoot up, even. That was an unfortunate thought; a shiver ran through me, pooling the tension unbearably in the joints of my limbs. I gave Harrier a look of helpless pride. "Please . . ." I said.

"Our pleasure." He took a handful of the back of Cyan's dress and hoisted her effortlessly onto one shoulder, strode under the pediment toward a gleaming entrance hall, the reflection on his polished shoes miniaturizing the architecture.

CHAPTER FOURTEEN

When I arrived back at the Castle I found a note pinned to my door. It was sealed with light blue wax, six numbers only, a map reference. I followed it to where the ocean slides ugly up against the land—Sheldrake harbor, at night and without a breath of wind. It was eerily calm and warm.

Two towns—a real one and a bright reflection in the bay. I saw the reflection first and thought I was upside down. What the fuck is going on? What are all those clouds?

The harbor was burning, the fleet, ablaze. Flames pulsed yellow—smoke plumes were thickening, drifting out to sea.

One of the piers was burning through. I could see figures trapped at the seaward end. They were crushing together, yelling above the roar.

I circled the quayside, saw floating blackened planks and pale corpses jostling in steaming water. Ships' ribs clutched like fingers in the yellow light. Smoke stank of pitch. Mist's flagship was anchored in the center of the bay, well away from the fire ships, over its own rippled image. I flapped across to it, and a series of pennants went up which read, "Ata has done this."

I landed on the raised deck at the stern, unsure whether to cling to the railings and risk going down with the ship if she sinks, or to stand on my own two feet and risk falling over the side and drowning. In reality the *Honeybuzzard* was solid and perfectly safe. How could something so vast and ornate sit on the water, or steer round rocks and evade sea-monsters? How could people build ships this big? How can vessels so huge actually move? The flagship waited at anchor like a thoroughbred.

I gazed at the planks and fidgeted; sweat ran down my wings. Flame from all along the coast glowed orange on the deck.

I recounted, "Mist, there are four caravels in the Sound. If you sail in the lee of the island you would have to contend with six more. That's all I know. Can I go now?"

"Sail *how*? With the fleet in *ashes*? Look at all my ships! Where has that bitch hidden my daughter?"

". . . Micawater Palace. May I leave?"

"How did she get there? Fly? Where is Lightning?"

"Shooting Insects in Rachiswater. Can I please get off this ship?"

Mist had reverted to the Plainslands language, giving the impression he was feeling hunted. He had an expressionless brunette perched on his knee. She wore velvet shorts, and the dimpled flesh of her thigh overhung his leg. Half a cigarette festered in a scallop shell.

The shell ashtray held down one of my maps, which was scrolled out on the deck, paper cracking with age. I caught myself thinking that one tiny error, a miscalculation or omission, would lead to these ships stove in by serried rocks, hundreds drowned and the knowledge never reaching me.

Lord Governor Shearwater was wrapped in a long heavy

blue cloak with gold trim, although it wasn't cold. His thick arms knotted around the woman's little waist, his backside on the railings, chin on her shoulder, the gold chain from his stiff cloak collar straining across his broad chest. "Tell this to San," he said, pointing at the wrecked harbor. "See what Ata's done—trying to force me to Lowespass? I've lost forty ships, and who knows how many men! Bad to worse. How could the Emperor let Ata be immortal when she's capable of this destruction? At such a time! She can sit and starve on her paltry island. I'll return to Peregrine and find a way of stopping her for good."

Speaking of Cyan led me to remember her ring, which had fitted easily on my finger and was presently turning it green. I gave the copper dolphin to Mist. "The girl asked me to return this." He looked at it with no recognition in his leathery face, rather scathingly as the ring was a cheap little token.

"Well," he growled, nipping the fleshy lass's mottled thigh, "I don't know. There's been so many. Drop. Ocean." She giggled, lifting her head back to kiss air that smelled of burned meat.

"No, not a girl. A *little* girl." I held my hand, palm down, at the level of my knee.

"None of them have ever been that small," he said defensively. I was obviously wasting my time, but Cyan deserved persistence.

"You don't recognize it?"

"Jant, I've never seen it before. You must be mistaken—one fix too many."

A powerful arm wound back; he hurled the ring across the deck and over the railing. It dropped into darkness.

As it left his hand I moved. I dived from the rail. Two strong flicks of half-folded wings drove me down faster than falling. I couldn't see the ring. Hull sped up. The water came up, rippled bronze. The ring, a speck. I shot out a hand, snatched it as it hit the water.

I spread my wings, flattened my fall. I skimmed out over the surface of the sea. Tips of flight feathers touched, flicking drops into an arc. Pain flamed in the small of my back. I calmed it by breathing in time with quick wing beats. I kept going and built up speed to gain height and turn steeply.

The ship's hull was metal-clad. The figurehead had pink tits. A red lamp marked the stern. I slipped into a glide between rigging and masts. I came in fast. No wind to land into, so I backed with massive wings streaming the pennants out. The deck came up hard under my feet, jarring both ankles. I ran a few steps with a springy gait to slow down.

I started shaking, the ring tightly clenched in one hand. "You bastard! Arsehole. Mist, you know I can't swim! Shit."

The girl had detached herself from his grasp and was gaping at the railings, the paintings on my wings, my Rhydanne eyes, and giving me a look I've come to expect: "What the fuck *are* you?"

Mist pulled a gold case of cigarettes from a back pocket. He plucked one out and offered it to me. He leaned back, the smoke from his cigarette staggering into the air whilst smoke from the burning fleet and the Sheldrake breakwater billowed into cumulus above. I scraped a match and drew hot, constricting air into my lungs thankfully.

Cyan, I thought, you clever girl. I had underestimated her. "Give the ring to my father," she had said. Now I have to find out who he is.

CHAPTER FIFTEEN

The Throne Room carpet was a bright crimson tapestry, a vibrant purple-red. Gold threads formed a swirling design of gold leaves or feathers or waves, which appeared to move. There was also a network of little blue dots but these were actually hallucinations caused by the exertion of flying too fast, and from doing backflips on the wet roof ridge in order to impress Tern.

The edge of the carpet had a long gold fringe, like girl's hair. I followed it up as it angled over one marble step, a second, a third, but I couldn't follow its shining ascent any longer because the Emperor's throne was on top of the dais and he was watching me intently. It was not good manners to return his gaze. I couldn't because a recent dose of cat was singing in every capillary and if I looked at him, I would get the Fear. Not that the animated carpet was any better, I kept my head bowed and wished that the blue dots would go away.

"I don't think that's all you have to say," San remarked.

Somewhere above me, in a cradle of marble lace and folded samite, he sighed and stretched. I concentrated on a slightly more threadbare patch of carpet where I have knelt thousands of times before. "Because," San prompted, "I have been reading your letters from the coast. Thank you for your commentary, keeping the Circle so well informed of this unique situation."

Was that sarcasm? I couldn't decide, so I gave him the same sort of silence as I would any flatlander. Time was nothing to the Emperor; he simply out-silenced me. This could go on for hours.

"My lord?"

"Letter the first, Diw is burning. Second, Sheldrake quay is razed by fire. Third, Awndyn fights a skirmish to protect the ships in her harbor. Additionally a letter from Carmine Dei asking for soldiers to protect Moren port because she doesn't want that to go up in flames as well. Tell me, Comet, does the fleet have any harbors left?"

"My lord, it's more like there is no fleet left." More silence. "Ata stole sixty ships from Diw. Those she could not crew she burned. She sailed them all to join her caravels at Grass Isle. From there, she sent ships to burn the docks and everything at anchor in the rest of Mist's harbors. Awndyn harbor was spared, as Swallow's fyrd defended it. Throughout, Ata suffered no losses. Her ships returned to the island, where she now stays. She moves from tower to tower on the island, which is inviolable. I dispatched her infantry to Awndyn manor; I intend to use them against Insects in Rachiswater until Ata's Challenge is resolved."

"How is Mist?"

"The last time I saw him, he was preparing to race to Peregrine before Ata could catch him."

"No. I mean what does Mist have left?"

"Only what was at sea two days ago and escaped. The *Honeybuzzard*, with a loyal crew."

"That is all?"

"One square-rigger, my lord. Ata has eighty ships—I counted."

"So Ata is trying to make it impossible for Mist to proceed, or to move anything by sea at all." The Emperor smiled wolfishly.

"Not trying to, my lord; she has."

"What does Ata ask of us?"

I searched my memory through a haze of cat which unpleasantly seemed to be hauling me upward. "She sends this message, 'I wish to replace Shearwater Mist and I will return to the Castle only to become immortal, or I will harry the coast and every ship afloat until the end of my days.'"

I paused as the Emperor huffed angrily, and his liver-spotted hand clenched into a fist.

"Ata asked me to report that she regrets people have been killed, but says that would have been avoided if Mist had not been King Staniel's follower. She regrets that Mist lacks the flexibility of thinking, or is not brave enough to seize the opportunity we have to use caravels, the excellent service she is offering to the Castle, my lord."

His pearl brocade cloak folded awkwardly as the Emperor leaned toward me, lamplight reflecting on the white-gold spired crown. "And the tone?"

Exhilaration. The frustration has forced her to chance things for herself. Now she's free and all the possibilities are crying out at her. "She's awestruck by her own determination," I said.

"Did Mist send a message?"

"I left Mist when the *Honeybuzzard* got under way. His cheerfulness holds together like broken glass which a touch will shatter. He says this: Taking tolls is against the law, not to mention Ata's terrible piracy of coast towns. He begs you and the Circle to agree that she has gone too far. He asks that she be divorced and expelled from the Circle. He said any additional punishment ... Any additional punishment is the Emperor's prerogative. He never asked for help in regaining his ships or his daughter, or his standing." Eszai never ask for assistance. It would leave the world in doubt that they really are the best.

The hall behind and the space above me to an ornately painted ceiling was vast, boundless space as well to either side. I could easily fly in such a massive hall, between the slender engraved collections of pillars, through the circuits of galleries lining the turret. All this space concentrated on the Emperor's throne, under a tasseled portico, draped with cloth of gold. The cloth was deeply embroidered, the lavishly intricate Awian crest on one side, on the other the arms of Hacilith Moren. The Plainslands emblem was a white horse rampant, the size of a man, and its cleft silver hooves could just be seen projecting from behind the Emperor's bony shoulder. San asked me, a gnarled finger to pale dry lips, what I thought of Ata's behavior. I told him it was unthinkable that Eszai should fight each other and not Insects, and he knew I really believed it. I would not support Mist or Ata. I wouldn't say who was less to blame. When I felt brave enough I asked, "What will the Castle do?"

"Do?" he said, making me feel tiny. "Why, Comet, we let it run, of course."

"Yes, my lord," I said meekly.

"Go and watch them. This is Ata's Challenge to Mist, is it not? How else can we decide who is the superior master mariner? By now she has learned all his knowledge. Now let us see who has the greater skill. Return often, and tell me everything."

"Yes, my lord." I surprised myself by being steady enough to stand, reasonably gracefully. I turned to go.

"Comet, why are there Insects in Awia?"

My silence this time was not on purpose. I simply didn't know what to say—Insects are taking over because we are not slaying them. There are too many to deal with.

"I don't know," I mumbled.

San put on a show of fury. He slammed his fist on the marble armrest, making the tasseled baldachin tremble.

"*Why* do you not know?" he demanded. As if Insects were anything to do with me. I froze.

He shuffled forward on white cushions, doggedly glaring down. "Why so many Insects? Tell me! What are they doing that is different from before? What are we doing that is different? Or what are we not doing? Comet . . . *Think* about this. Come here tomorrow, first thing. Give me an answer. *I want answers!*"

"I don't—" I began like a boy to say, "It's not fair," but San silenced me.

"Think about it. What are you here for? You have an excellent mind. *Use it!* Do you deserve to be immortal? I begin to doubt. Tomorrow, come here and tell me why Lowespass is overrun. Now leave."

I bowed hastily, eager to escape. This was an impossible request. How was I to know what drove Insects? And how could I watch over Mist and Ata at the same time? I couldn't do it, but Eszai don't admit the impossible.

The Emperor summoned me back and asked me to write a supportive letter to Carmine in Hacilith. I agreed—"Yes, yes certainly"—in rizing confusion. The room started to spin about me. A couple of long braids in my hair had slipped out of my belt and were dragging on the floor. A few of them had even tangled through the bangles on my wings.

Like a white hound baiting a frail feline, San gave me my leave and again called me back. "You said Ata had enough men to crew ten ships," he asked innocently. "Where did she find two thousand sailors? Did she steal them, as well?"

He waited while I deliberated what to recount. There was no way I could avoid the truth, but this was suddenly a question of my own allegiance. I didn't want to involve Saker Micawater in any trouble. That's the mentality I've kept from gangland Hacilith. Anything goes but this—you don't lie, don't cheat, and don't grass on your mates.

"Tell me, Comet," the Emperor said gently, in complete contrast to yelling about Insects. I was right; he was giving me the Fear.

"Lightning," I muttered, "lent her sailors, and archers to protect her island . . ."

San gave a loud stage sigh. "Thought as much," he admitted.

I had my arms crossed over my stomach, for protection and because cramp was beginning to gather.

"Go and tell Lightning I want to see him," the Emperor added. "Immediately, please."

I walked down the worn length of crimson carpet, at any second expecting to be recalled, and striding faster and faster as I passed the screen. My throat prickled, saliva gushed into my mouth. Two guards held the crested doors back for me and I went through them in a flurry of silk and feathers. I managed to make it out to the terrace before I was sick.

An Insect, well polished and with a faded wreath of flowers round its neck, guarded the door in my tower room. It stood propped against the wall; a couple of chips in red-brown chitin gave it the patina of ancient furniture. Its name was Butterfly, and it was suffering a severe interrogation. I walked round and poked at its hind legs' translucent brown casing. I twiddled an antenna in a ball-and-socket joint, giving it a rakish angle. Butterfly wore a crested rusty breastplate and a sword-hanger with a daisy in it. It had been dressed in various ways over the years and I had even received costumes tailor-made for the creature.

"Butterfly, I have to know where you came from. I'd like to know where you thought you were going. Intended destination, route of journey, length of voyage, time of arrival, and by which maps . . . and under whose command. I swear it's more than my life's worth, which is worth a lot, to me at least." Awians say Insects aren't even sentient, but how can we really know?

"You're living in the Castle, under the rule of an enemy, the supreme Emperor San, god's Governor of the Fourlands, and you have to obey his every word, like the rest of us poor immortals."

The statue didn't say anything. I gave it a hug, and went to sit down at my writing desk. Butterfly tipped back against the rough wall. It was a hollow exoskeleton, like a suit of armor. The shell of the first Insect I had ever killed—the first of hundreds—I had cleaned and preserved with varnish. Its barbed abdomen was a hardened, paper-thin bulb, supported by a seam of thorns like vertebrae along the upper side. Serrulate mandible scythes reached to its chest. There were hinges so its thorax could be opened to see the ridged inside surface, like a crab's carapace.

I took the kettle off the fire and poured hot water into two cups of coffee. Tern emerged on cue from behind the curtain, which with a flight of steps separates our round room into semicircles. She rubbed the sleep out of her eyes, saying, "Jant—Jant, will you please stop the fucking dramatics?"

"Coffee?"

"Hugging Butterfly, how could you?" Tern put out a little hand for it, the fingernails painted bronze. Her white lace negligee, which wound up into a halter round her neck, accentuated rather than hid her pale body. Waves of glossy dark hair prowled round her shoulders, her folded wings made an inviting cleavage at her back.

"I have to find out how to stop the Insects, Kitten," I said.

"Snogging them won't help."

"You're gorgeous." I could smell her musk beneath the peach perfume; she still had traces of cream lipstick and glitter in her hair.

"You are *not* gorgeous," she said, a trace of anger flirting in her honey voice. "Staying awake all night!"

"Sorry, my love."

"Come to bed now," she said, the anger melting into lasciviousness.

"No time. I need some cat."

She came and put slender arms round my waist, head on my shoulder, and I held her gently. Her skin was soft.

Tern was very disappointed in me. We didn't really need to speak anymore, I felt her emotions forcing mine, like drafts of air when flying. I felt her sadness twist me into hardheartedness, the only way I could safely go. "And then I have to return to court, where the Emperor waits for any excuse to be rid of his wayward Messenger, perhaps you too, because kittens like you are too playful for the Circle. I should fly to Rachiswater and see if all your kinsmen have been devoured. Then I must go to the coast and see if Mist and Ata have killed each other yet."

I won't describe her tears, pleas, or tantrums. What use is Tern's whim against the Emperor's command? But now that I was home she wanted to make me stay.

"I'll leave you," she threatened. "I'll go back to Wrought and live there."

"If you leave me," I said, "you have three score years and ten."

CHAPTER SIXTEEN

The sea is only noisy when it meets the land. I hated the endless crunch and hiss of little waves curling and spitting at the foot of the cliff. A flapping of banners on the *'Buzzard* mimicked it. I could hear the remote sound of sail, whipping the calm air far out to sea. There was no other sound but the slap of water on wood. There wasn't a cloud in the cold sky; I soared above the cliffs being bothered by choughs. With long lazy wing-beats I flew out swiftly, away from the foam and over the foil-blue. The cliff sound receded; movement made a cold flurry on my face. The sun was so bright I had a headache from squinting. A cormorant arrowed along beneath me, its black neck stretched out. I dived and the bird veered away in panic. Then I gained altitude, eager to be away from the surface of the water, the gleaming specks of light. I hate the changefulness of sea.

This was Ata's message to Mist: "If you surrender *Honeybuzzard* I will see you safely to land in Peregrine. We need never meet again. If you pass my island in that or any other ship she will be lost with all hands." I wrote it on paper and dropped it in my satchel onto the deck of the *Honeybuzzard* from a great height. I won't land to give a message that dangerous.

Mist read it, sneered and waved a three-fingered hand. "Tell the Emperor," he yelled, "her time's up. Overstepped the line!" I tipped my wings to him and sailed up on a seaward breeze.

I listened to Shearwater addressing his men. He spoke directly to the whole crew. They packed in close to the stern deck's rails to hear him. They were scared and pessimistic but the Eszai's wild cheer was infectious. He punched the air, saying,"This is the fastest ship built and you are the best crew ever! If you work for me now, then soon you will captain your own ships." He praised them higher than any immortal ever praised Zascai, and they started grinning and nudging each other. He told them the chain of command and what positions to man. Then he pointed to where I was circling. Grubby faces peered up like stripy fungi in a window box. Mist yelled, "See? Jant seconds us! The best lookout the *Honeybuzzard* can hope for! Now, all hands. I want speed!"

The sky was clean; a good current blew off the land. I watched from a height. Able crew swarmed on the deck, tending the massive ship. She stirred. She sucked in a dripping anchor on a long wet hawser. She shrugged up a mainsail. The sail descended, flapping, dazzling white. Wind filled it and it swelled, three more unfurled simultaneously. The blue pennant of Peregrine streamed out ahead. The ship dragged in the water, gathered speed and began to slice the waves. Mist was a figure at the stern, shouting something down to the main deck. Men clustered together and hauled on tarred ropes. Sail wound down over the prow. It bellied up in a startling rush of red and yellow, emblazoned with the Castle sun. The ship lurched forward, smoothly gathering speed. Mist poured all his strength onto the

wheel, spinning it. I dropped back in the slipstream and watched
the rudder turn. He brought the *Honeybuzzard* round in a great
arc to get the wind behind her. She lifted. Suddenly she began to
race.

I flew round the ship watching from high above. I criss-
crossed in front of them, fast and free, damp with the spray from
their bow wave. I hovered in the slipstream of cool air escaping
from the sail's edge; it was very turbulent but I managed to find
a clear space where it was almost effortless to hang, being
dragged along by the ship. Cold air bubbled and gushed under
my wings, bearing me up. The pain in my stomach muscles that
comes from the exertion of beating gradually died away. It was
a wonderful ride.

The Zascai on deck sent up a few curious looks, but soon lost
interest as I hardly stirred, and besides Mist was keeping them
busy. They worked as a well picked team; Mist spoke to them all
by name. He struck a match on the compass at the helm. He
stood braced, and grinned at his second-in-command. When the
weasly Awian went belowdecks, Mist returned to looking
slightly distant and thoughtful. He gazed at the notched horizon. The breeze made his blue cloak flap. The cloak billowed
up; I realized he was wearing it to hide the bandages around his
cracked ribs.

The wheel on deck was the guide wheel, positioned next to
the compass. One man alone did not have the strength to keep
such a large ship on course, not even Mist. Below deck, there was
a system of gears, to assist the wheel above and hold a direction
in even the worst conditions.

The *Honeybuzzard* made good time from its offshore hiding
place, in sight of the Cobalt Coast and north past the cliffs at
Vertigo and the long strand of beach at Awndyn. An iron cloud
hung above Grass Isle, as if the island was reflected in the sky.
From my vantage point above the mainsail, I saw the island first.

To begin with it looked squashed, but it gradually grew from the ocean and I could see the south-facing Sute Towers of March and April on the coastline before Mist's lookout shrilled, "Grass Isle!"

There was a commotion on deck as sailors hissed in anxious breaths and scowled at the gray shape. Mist yelled at them. Then he yelled at me. I dropped a little height and hung in the air at the level of the railings. Any lower and I risked getting sucked under and squeezed out in the ship's wake. Mist stalked to the railings and grabbed at the air, as if to pluck me down. I did a quick circuit of the ship and returned. "Comet," he said. "Please help us. You're useless as a fucking figurehead up there."

"What can I do?" I'm not setting foot on deck.

"You know how hopeless this is. Flogging. Dead horse. We haven't had sight of her yet. The bitch is planning something. Look. Leap. Fly on a few kilometers and tell us what you see."

I nodded to him, gained height and held my breath for a few strong beats. I sped down a slight descent. Wind roared over my wings. To the crew I must have just disappeared. I looked back and the ship was a toy on immense water.

Behind the island, Ata's fleet was waiting; evenly spaced, lingering with a hunter's silence. Ata had made a net of fifty caravels, anchored facing in the wind's direction. Their sterns faced me, and prows pointed toward the Peregrine coast.

I flew at masthead height along the line and found Ata on the deck of the ship in the center of her trap. Two comely men were with her. The tassels of her white silk shawl floated on the gusts; she waved brightly, smiling broadly. The vessels were anchored with the width of a ship between them. I glided down the gaps, close to the hollows of the waves, and faces peered over railings and poked over sterns to watch. The ships were clean and scoured; their hulls were smooth. I flew the length of the line, seeing how Ata had made use of shallow water at the coastal side.

A larger carrack, the *Ortolan*, was patrolling the reef on the seaward end of the island. It stood a good chance of catching *Honeybuzzard* if Mist chose to go that way. He would have to sail all around the island, and in its lee, under the blank gaze of April and May, into Ata's net. I didn't see that Mist had any chance at all.

I flew back to Mist and said, "You don't have any chance at all."

"What has she done?"

I told him what I had seen and said, "I'm sorry I can't help. If I were you I would surrender."

He laughed. "Skinny waif."

I said, "Forget Peregrine. Go to Moren harbor or Ghallain Point, you can provision there; you could prepare properly."

Mist said, "There's no time like the present." He kicked a map lying on the deck to unroll it. "Come down and have a look at this," he ordered.

I couldn't land; it was too much for me being this close to a ship. "No," I whined.

"Come down! Bloody waif. Bull. Horns." He lost concentration squinting up at me, swore and glanced back at the compass.

"Ata will sink us if she catches us!" It was my worst fear.

"She won't board us. I can handle this craft better than anyone in the world. Tricks. Trade. I have for decades."

"Yes, but she has eighty such ships," I pointed out.

"Cooks. Broth. Come down, Jant, I'm going to prove I'm the fucking best."

"I'm sorry. I can't."

"It's beyond me how a nancy boy like you can land such a hot lady as Tern."

"I've never hit Tern."

Mist sneered. He never understood how to deal with Ata. Ata's assurance forced him to treat her like a man—I suppose if she was one of his sailors he would have had her flogged around the fleet.

Our argument was beginning to unsettle the Zascai, who were watching me superstitiously. Mist saw this and bellowed curses, ending the argument by sheer power of voice. He clutched his hand to his mouth and bent over the wheel, coughing horrendously. Embarrassed, I watched him cough for more than a minute. He coughed, hacked, spat, wiped his mouth on his cloak. He moaned slightly, hugging bandaged ribs. "Ah—I should've killed Saker when I had the chance," he said.

I pulled my wings in and dropped onto the deck. I scrabbled for the hip flask and poured the last of the sloe gin down my throat: Rhydanne courage.

"You know she has some of Lightning's fyrd?" I said.

Mist raised bushy eyebrows; he evidently hadn't known. He shook himself. "Well, doesn't matter. I'm going to Rachis, via Peregrine, and they can't stop me. Tournament archers, all of them. Micawater shoots at targets; damn it, he shoots at *fruit*."

One hand on the wheel, he ripped his rapier from its scabbard and stabbed at the map. "Those caravels, can they chase us? Anchored? Sails lashed? Sticks. Mud."

Mist's brunette was sitting on the steps between the upper deck and the main deck, sunning herself in the icy air. She regarded me for a while with the Zascai "I want to look, not buy" expression, gazing intently when she thought I wasn't looking.

I was feeling sick already. I knelt down beside the helm, careful to be facing into the wind, in case I had to take off in a hurry. The folded tops of Mist's leather boots, rough blue trousers tucked into them, and the gilded scrollwork of the helm took up my field of vision. My eyes were watering. I crawled forward and gazed at the crinkled map, dotted with rapier holes. Grass Isle was almond-shaped; it lay close to the mainland, along the coast of Awia. The island was just thirty kilometers long, with a cruel and rocky shoreline. The northern end gave onto unpredictable water and a reef, marked by a lighthouse. To avoid the *Ortolan* we decided to sail around the south side, between the island and the mainland, a very shallow pass at such low tide. Ata's fleet was strung out across the strait.

"They're from here . . . to here," I muttered, tracing a line from September Tower bay to the coast of Peregrine.

Mist peered over his shoulder. "Good," he said.

I whimpered, sitting against the baroque carved helm, I preened my wings out and tried to hide my face in the feathers.

I was sitting on the deck of a ship. Shit.

"There's no point in worrying," he said. "I know this coast well. Back. Hand." He kept on in this mode whilst people ran about on the main deck and the plump girl gazed at the swelling waves, and I sat looking into possible death. The cold waves were so smooth and sluggish they looked gelid, practically solidified. One shock could cause the whole sea to freeze. "I've been sailing this coast since the fifteenth century. My grandfather was a trader too. So don't be so damn scared. Born. Bred. From packing casks and rowing to commanding the Castle's fleet. There's always been caravels on the route from Moren to Peregrine, ever since we bought it off the Archer. That's what made Awia great, and I don't want it to change, but Ata does. Goose. Golden egg. Why couldn't she be happy? She had the best of both worlds. Cake. Eat it." This wasn't exactly true; Ata wanted all the cakes in the world and to keep them. "How can she think she's better than me, Jant? How can she Challenge me after all this time?"

A real fucking ship. How did this happen?

His deep voice rattled on: "I know she wanted to. I'm not stupid. But swept. Carpet; it's not the kind of thing you want to think about."

Honeybuzzard slowed slightly as we entered the lee of Grass

Isle. High cliffs reared up, yellow with lichen and etched with cracks, parading by as Mist steered into a deep channel running parallel to the coast. Peregrine could be seen on the other side, a sweep of pebble beach running down into crystal water. Where the rocks began, the water became dark blue; where we were, it was nearly black. Black and white seabirds swirled and bickered on the cliffs, in shallow caves scooped into the rock and on jagged outposts of stone, splashed white with bird shit and dead fish and strewn with foam and flotsam.

Suddenly the deck tilted viciously. I slid, grabbed at the helm, clinging for life. Waves on the port side came up as far as the railing, our keel ploughed air. I cried in panic, "What are you doing?"

"Tacking," Mist said. He had been chain-smoking and giving out orders which I had been too wrapped in fear to hear. I looked up to see the result of one command. The sailors had brought all sorts of objects from below deck, mainly bedding rolls and hammocks, netting and bundles of clothes hastily knotted together. There were planks and buckets, boat hooks and shields. They had piled them along the sides of the ship, wedging them between the railings and lashing them in place to form a thick screen.

"We need some protection from her archers," Mist explained. Impressed by his ingenuity, I saw him in a new light. He had been swinging the *Honeybuzzard* in full canvas and at its full speed between flat submersed rocks and tiny islets.

"Ahoy. There she is!"

From the air, Ata's ships had looked formidable. Now I was at sea level and facing them, our situation seemed much, much worse. They were invulnerable, solid and secure. Four hulks faced us, their sharp wood breastbones paring the waves. On either side the string of identical vessels stretched out, becoming smaller with distance.

The center ship hoisted a series of flags, which made Mist

laugh. "That's the *Petrel*," he said. "She's asking me to surrender. The cheek of that woman! Brazen bloody cheek."

The brunette squealed. She looked over her shoulder to Mist, who said, "Starling, darling, why don't you go below for a while and wait in the skylight cabin? *Not* the stern rooms—do you hear? I'll join you when this is over." She planted her feet in her sandals and scampered away. "And hang on tight," Mist added. "If Ata's body had her mind ... Damn. This ship isn't taut enough! Lengthen the topsail! Don't look at me like I'm crazy—do it! Method. Madness. And I want archers fit for action."

I could see archers in readiness on every deck. Only the ships directly on either side of us could use them, or they would be shooting over their own decks. We advanced toward the line at a shocking pace. I began to think surely we should be slowing now? Nausea paused me, undecided, then we were too close and I couldn't take off for fear of the bowmen.

"This is suicide!" I shouted.

"Isn't it?" He ignored the *Stormy Petrel* and steered for clear water between two smaller ships. Faces clustered along their lengths became progressively more agitated. There was a hasty argument on one and it began winding its anchor up, drifting slightly sideways and ruining the pattern of the blockade.

I could hear Ata's anger borne on the wind. "*Curlew*! Hold the line. *Hold* the line! *Stay* there!"

"That's it," breathed Mist. "Get out of my way."

We came at them, unwavering, faster and faster with the wind straight behind. "Have to trim the mainsail." His fingers were white on the wheel. "It'll never fit. Damn! I'd like to have some sail left." All eyes were on him. "Take it up!" he yelled. "Take it up, take it up! Lose it!" Sturdy men on the main deck leaped at his word. They hauled on lines that ran up to distant heights in the rigging. The vast white sail flapped for a second, furled, revealing blue sky. The third mast was trimmed, the spritsail went down and we covered clear water in a second before—

The impact slammed me against the railings so hard I was nearly over them. My wings spread reflexively. Mist threw himself against the wheel to steady it. The terrible sound continued. *Honeybuzzard* pushed between the two ships, forcing them apart. The sound was deafening; snapping, rending, scream of planks running against planks. I saw astonished faces at their railings sliding past us. Archers bent bows and loosed straight across our decks. Arrows in a hard flat rain embedded in the *Honeybuzzard*'s side, in our masts, in flesh like thirsty flies. I curled up behind the helm as they cut across the prow.

Our sailors ducked behind their improvised fortification. Arrows thumped into the screen. Two or three men who were not fast enough were thrown back with arrows in their faces.

Mist waved at his archers. "Shoot at the rigging! The sail!" They had arrows with broad white flights and their points rolled in cloth. They touched the cloth to fire in a brazier and bent their bows, letting fly volley after volley up into the rigging of the ship on our left. The flights caught in the rigging and dripped burning pitch. Ata's rain of arrows ceased abruptly, as all hands were called to quench the sudden flame.

Our momentum carried us through, wood squealing and moldings snapping, then we were stern to the prow of the starboard ship.

"Watch this," Mist declared. I clutched the railings. He spun the wheel, holding it at full lock. *Honeybuzzard* slewed round and we slammed against their prow, crushing it. The glass windows and ornate carving at our stern splintered and broke, shining fragments of sculptures and gingerbreads falling twelve meters into black water.

The smaller ship's narrow prow was sheared through. Her bowsprit snapped and she began to tilt forward, yawing away from us as water flooded into the lower decks. Our bowmen let out hoots and catcalls at *Curlew*'s crew not an arm's length away.

The *Curlew*'s deck slid into the waves, spilling people off into our wake. It bellied up and its hull surged skyward, copper-coated, slick and dripping. As it rolled its high mast crashed onto the deck of the ship to its right, bringing all the rigging down. Ropes trailing over the side caught at floating planks. Mist started yelling again at his dazed men.

I swore, and kept swearing for fucking ages.

"It'll stop her following me," said Mist grimly. "I was fond of that boat. Jant, for god's sake get off the floor." We had run out of momentum and were sitting there, on the landward side of her net.

My worst fears realized, I couldn't stand. I couldn't watch, was crouched against the helm with hands over my eyes and didn't stop shaking when Mist poked me in the neck with the square toe of his boot. He was exultant, scornful of my fear. He stalked to the top of the steps and looked down at the sailors who were stirring and returning to their stations. "Get the mainsail up, and let's get out of here!"

Before any of Ata's caravels could break free of the line and chase us, we set the sail and gathered speed for the clear run to Peregrine harbor. Ata must have been standing at the bow of the *Stormy Petrel* because her high voice carried through the roar of the sinking ship. Mist heard her and shuddered, drawing the blue cloak over his bandages.

"After them! No—forget *Curlew*!" A dark-haired man laid his hand on her shoulder to calm her. He asked for boats and ropes to be lowered to men in the water. "Forget *Curlew*! Raise the foresail!" She screamed at the archers to resume, but her Micawater fyrd was not accustomed to ships. The situation was too strange, Eszai against each other.

I took a peek through the balustrade to see her leaning over, white silk strands of her shawl sticking to the ship's side. The two men accompanying her now had longbows. She urged them to shoot. She raved like a selfish child. The burly one with bronze-scale armor stepped behind her, shaking his head. This drove Ata into complete fury. "Are you trying to get in my back-side?" she spat. "Where you came from? Give me that!" She landed a punch on his broad chest, grabbed the bow from him and flexed it, sending an arrow across to us. It lost height and stuck in the *Honeybuzzard*'s belly just above the waterline.

Mist moaned.

"Are you hurt?"

"They're my sons," he said slowly. "They both are. Flesh. Blood. It can't be right that she turns my own boys against me. It can't be right, Jant . . ."

"None of this is right," I said.

"They do what she says. Wrapped. Little finger. She's mad, waif. Hasn't she got to be bloody mad? Insult. Injury." Mist gave control of the wheel to his second-in-command. He coughed stickily for a while, grimacing. "I'm going below," he declared. To "Starling, darling," probably. "To check the damage."

"I don't think she'll be damaged," I said.

"Wha'?"

"Never mind."

The sailors dragged their comrades' bodies over the deck and down into the hold, knowing that they would be on dry land by the end of the day. I looked behind to see Ata's fleet clustered around heaving water as the *Curlew* sank. I was amazed at how fast it went down. One caravel from the farthest horn of the trap attempted to give chase, but we left it far behind. Mist returned, helped the sailors on the main deck clear up, and then joined me. I was sitting with my legs dangling over the side, feeling the effects of the sloe gin. "What are you going to do now?"

"Put in at Peregrine quay. Reinforce the harbor. Do repairs."

He shrugged. "If I can find anyone to help me. If not I'll do it myself. Where there's a will there's a way. I'll pay the crew. I doubt any of them will come back. Bitten. Shy." He handed me an envelope sealed with pale blue wax and addressed with his unsteady writing. "Take this to Awndyn," he ordered.

"What is it?"

"Curiosity killed. It looks like a letter. You're the Messenger. So just deliver it, will you?"

I stood up on the railings and unfolded my wings. Awndyn manor was on my way to the Castle. Uppermost in my mind was the fact I had to get back to court and relate these events to the Emperor.

"Shake?" He pressed my hand in a powerful grip. His arms were stocky as well, covered in wiry hair and thick gold chains. I liked Mist; no other Eszai would leave the courtroom for a quick smoke, go out on the terrace and bellow with laughter at my double entendres. I shook his hand with a bizarre feeling of melancholy. Mist must have felt it too, but he bit it back.

"I'd like to know what Ata thinks of me now," he said, and smiled. "Bet that took the wind from her sails." Gray eyes merry in a sea-sand–hard lined face, white twist of hair in a long charcoal frizz, compact wings on his broad back reached like folded gray fans to his belt.

"Shearwater," I said, "thanks for letting me through the Castle gate back in eighteen-eighteen." He knows I owe him that.

"You deserve it, waif. Don't mention it." But help me now, his tone implored. Trouble was, I didn't know how. I wouldn't be in Ata's confidence after this. All I could do was deliver the letter. I took it from him, said farewell and kicked off. I was seized by the breeze immediately and cast thankfully toward the shore.

CHAPTER SEVENTEEN

To: Comet, for petition to the Emperor
From: King Staniel Rachiswater
Stateroom
Rachiswater Palace
November 25, 2015

Emperor eternal,

I wish to present my most fervent apologies for the conflict that occurred outside my gates between the Awndyn cavalry and the Insects, in which six hundred men were killed or fatally wounded. I propose to compensate their families from my treasury, and I will do all in my capacity to mitigate the consequences of this terrible accident.

I am holding my two guard captains at fault for their negligence; their orders were to "let nothing through." The Palace gates are too wide for people and Insects to be segregated as they enter, and so my guards resolved to allow neither man nor

Insect past, lest the brutes overwhelm the interior of the Palace.

If I had heard the immortals hail us in the Emperor's name, I would undoubtedly have rescinded the captains' decision. But none of my guards heard the call above the clamor. At the time, I was within the deepest part of my Palace, monitoring the situation from the throne room as is proper. I now appreciate that the reports I received were erroneous. In the poor light my watchmen did not identify the Awndyn insignia, nor did they comprehend that immortals were involved. My guard have the notion that there will be repercussions in future but I have assured them that their fears are unfounded; the Castle does not castigate mortals.

Insects continue to wreak havoc in Rachiswater, from my window I observe many in the paths of the parterre, the ha-ha is overflowing with them. No animals survive—only a few cattle were brought in from the fields in time.

Governor Lady Eleonora Tanager has arrived from her manorship in the north of the country, which has been destroyed. It is the worst loss of life and the worst damage yet done to Awia; Tanager Hall has long been one of the jewels of this country. Lady Tanager arrived at the head of a sixteen thousand–strong fyrd guarding a wagon train con-catenation of eight thousand non-fighters who escaped with meagre belongings. They are being lodged with families in my town, as Insects commence to construct Paperlands in their fields.

Lady Tanager is guest in my Palace. She continues to pursue Insects in Rachiswater, wearing her silver 1910 heir-loom armor and surrounded by her lancers. She is a flamboy-ant individual, to say the least.

I venture to advocate that your travails should focus on the manorship of Tanager so that we may restore her to her

rightful place. "We are loved best where longest known," as
the poet said.

STANIEL RACHISWATER, KING OF AWIA
HIS MAJESTY'S SIGNATURE AND SEAL

To: COMET, FOR PETITION TO THE EMPEROR
FROM: LADY VIREO SUMMERDAY
LOWESPASS FORTRESS
11/25/15

How is it that, although I have called for reinforcements
and supplies, there are none on the way? We are reduced to
four thousand men and the rations are running out. We need
supplies now.

The Castle has betrayed Lowespass. Tornado is the only
man here who does not think the Empire has forsaken us. In
my fyrd rumors are rife that the Castle is prepared to let them
die, by Insects or worse, of starvation and winter snows. Why
are you unable to protect us?

We are completely enclosed. My lord Emperor, I entreat
you haste.

VIREO, GOVERNOR OF SUMMERDAY AND LOWESPASS
TORNADO, HIS MARK: T

"Where are the Insects coming from?" The Emperor began
to question me again immediately I knelt before him, as if no
time had passed at all since my report two days ago. I had spent
hours preparing for this audience, but my resolve vanished like
straw in San's furnace wrath.

"You don't *know*? But I asked you to *find out*!"

"My lord, I tried. I'm sorry." No one in the Fourlands knows
where the Insects come from. I have asked Eszai, governors, and

fyrd, and I heard only tales. Rayne said that two thousand years ago the Insects appeared in northern Awia, in an enclave the size of the Throne Room, with a Wall around it, which expanded like flood water.

We all knew this story, but nobody spoke of it in court. When the Insects appeared, the Queen of Pentadrica went to observe their paper enclave. The Insects killed everyone in her cortège. Only a couple of fragmentary documents survive to describe what ensued: half of Pentadrica was settled by Awian refugees fleeing the north, their beautiful towns buried under the Paperlands. Morenzia and the Plainslands fought over the remaining half in the first civil war. San united the countries against the Insects, and was proclaimed Emperor. He was given Pentadrica Palace on which to build the Castle and guard the remaining Fourlands.

"Tell me what you've learned," San demanded.

"If I may speak candidly, if anyone in the Fourlands has a chance of knowing where Insects come from, it is my lord Emperor." The Emperor smiled. I sighed and continued: "Most people say that Insects live underground. If I was to crawl down one of their tunnels I might see warrens and caverns alive with them, passages kilometers long, and chambers large as manor halls where they hide when conquered."

"And none can substantiate this story?" San said, in an unreadable tone.

"My lord—of course not!"

"I sometimes wonder whether the current members of my Circle work hard enough to justify their immortality."

Could the Emperor, who spends every day of eternity within the inner sanctum of the Castle, understand the carnage taking place right now throughout the Fourlands? Vexed, I said, "There are so many Insects that to set foot near the mouth of a tunnel would be suicide. That's how Dunlin died. If I tried it I wouldn't survive long enough to give a report."

"Yes, Comet."

"You can tell as much from Vireo's letter."

"Comet, I am disappointed that the Castle's integrity has split between Mist and Ata, and now you disappoint me as well. How will I recompense our failure to save Lowespass and Awia?" The Emperor left his throne and walked toward the edge of the dais. I looked past him, unable to face the glare in his sky-gray eyes.

I concentrated on the red-gold sunburst behind the Emperor's chair. Four thick columns supported the mosaic ceiling of the alcove behind the throne; one each of porphyry, azurite, hematite and jade. It was less awesome to look at these than at the Emperor himself. If my gaze could wear them away the columns would be thin as matchsticks. "Mist is on his way to the front. My lord, with a letter Castle-sealed I can force Ata to come to Rachiswater too and save her quarrel until later."

"Leave Mist and Ata to finish what they've begun. Here is a letter for you to give to Ata. After reading this, she will cease her raids on our harbors. Tell the coastal manors that the Castle has safeguarded them. Then send all the troops they have to Rachiswater. I want the front to be solid; I want everyone to appreciate that we will protect Rachis Town."

"Yes, my lord."

"Did Vireo Summerday give you letters to deliver to other governors?"

"No."

"Good. It will be difficult to save the coast, but there must be not one Insect on the Eske road. They would have access to these very walls.

"Send Hayl and his fyrd, the Armorer and all the fyrd he can muster, to Rachiswater. We will concentrate our forces there; I think Staniel will make no objection. Go to all the manors, negotiate with them, I want every mortal who can bear arms out there, every immortal in the Castle to lead them."

"Shall I stay in Rachiswater as well, my lord?"

"You? I have thought further about you. Recapitulate your account of the Lowespass 'bridge.'"

Shakily, I described the white bridge, its smooth construction of Insect spit which was so strong it held the weight of the walkway on wire-thin strands, etiolated like a snake's skeleton, stretching from the ground into the sky—where the Insects emerge—

"These creatures destroying the Empire come out of thin air!"

"It's true. Lightning can verify it."

"Comet. Find a way to stop them."

I looked at my hands on the floor, in supplication, the long fingerless gloves covering my needle tracks. Bangles were pushed far up on my arms, and there was the rich embroidery of tiny vines on my shirtsleeves. My sword's silver hilt was tight against my hip. How can one man solve the problem that has occupied the whole Castle for millennia? What is San talking about?

"You cracked the language of the Deirn Manuscripts in less than a year. You helped in the Carniss diplomacy. You should enjoy such a task, Comet."

I didn't answer. None of the Messengers before me would have been given this responsibility. San must want a reason to get rid of me, but of all times why now? Sure, I've been out of my face a lot recently, but that's nothing new. None of the other immortals are treated so badly.

"If you cannot help . . ."

I caught my breath. I won't be thrown out of the Circle. San must need me; no one else can fly over the Paperlands to the besieged fortress, and bring letters back. No one else can speak to Zascai so easily.

". . . you will be expelled from the Castle. I asked you to think about this! You have not given the question a moment of your time. If the mortals believe the situation is out of the Castle's control, they will band together against us, and then how long will god's Empire last? A matter of months? Weeks? Insects spread through the world and engulf it. You have been irresponsible!"

"My lord."

"Find out more about the Insects for me, Comet."

"I'll do all I can."

"Everyone in the Fourlands talks to each other through you. The Castle depends on it. Your life depends on it."

I bit at a perfect nail and ruined it.

"You can go now," said the Emperor. "I *said*, you can go now."

Wiping sweat from the cords of my neck, I left the court and walked slowly back to my tower. The clock in Great Court was striking midnight. I have had seventy-five thousand midnights, and I looked into a life outside the Castle Circle. What would it be like? Short. There was only fifty years left of my natural life to run. I had grown used to a fast flow of time, the way immortals see it. Fifty years would speed past, and I would watch myself aging. No, the Emperor couldn't give me age and death back; it was the cruelest threat. I rubbed my hands over my eyes, massaging a withdrawal headache. I would rather die than watch myself aging, I thought. I ran up the spiral stairs in a dissonance of silver, kicked open the door to our chamber but my overwrought wife wasn't there.

San can't throw me out of the Circle unless the crisis passes, because then he will be missing a Messenger as well as a Sailor. But there was no way to second-guess the Emperor. He had been alive so long, he might already have a plan that doesn't involve me. Facing uncertainty, I felt like a street kid again. I need some cat.

I got down on hands and knees, felt around under the four-poster for my needle case, which I had stuck to the bed slats with tape. Tern hasn't looked here yet; it's too dusty for her, and she can never bend down when fully dressed in whalebone hoops and skirts.

There is a pair of silver candlesticks on the cabinet, elegant and wispy. I unscrew the cold base of one candlestick; it is hollow inside, a glass phial slides out onto the palm of my hand. I sit and watch myself in the dressing-table mirror as I fill the syringe.

I strip off my suit jacket and light an oil lamp the better to see my familiar reflection. I'm used to this fox-face, ebony-black hair, deepset eyes; I couldn't envisage how I will look if I age. I sketch on my image with imagination, adding lines under green eyes, around my lips, which smile twistedly on one side. I try to picture my pale skin wrinkled, not so tight. I might put on weight like an old Zascai soldier. The thought repulsed me. Please, no, I thought, feeling sick. I spread my wings for the mirror's benefit, ripping my shirt neatly up the back.

If I am dismissed, I'll take the future into my own hands: suicide. I hold up the syringe and tap an air bubble out. Live fast, die young. I made a very strong shot. San is going to expel me from the Circle. The ground under my feet started slipping away and in an avalanche of emotion I turned from the mirror and crawled onto the bed. The Castle towers' moonshadows striped the bedroom like emaciated giants. I do what San says, whatever he asks. San trafficks time; I've been secure for so long I can't leave now. All the successes I've piled up to bring me fame will be nothing; I'll be nothing. My position in the Circle is all I have—to leave is to die, and condemn Tern too.

San knows when I lie. I'll have to face him again and admit I don't know how to defeat the fucking Insects, and that will be my death sentence. I craved Tern's encouragement. Where is she when she's needed?

I deliberated for hours on the Insect threat, as blue-gray silhouettes moved across the room, doubling when bright Tiercel, the morning star, rose.

Asking where Insects come from is not the same as asking how people were made, because at the beginning of the world god didn't create Insects; they appeared later. Unlike Awians or humans, they're present in lots of worlds, as I knew from the times I Shifted . . . I looked at the needle and thought, I want to Shift. I want to go under and not wake up for a very long time. This world that causes me so much distress could just fuck off.

I hesitated, realizing that I am not welcome in Epsilon either at the moment. Owing to Keziah, the Tine would still be out for my blood. I dwelled guiltily on Keziah's fate. The worm-girl had hinted he might still be alive—Tine prolong their victims in agony, making flesh sculptures till their organs are needed for rituals. Could I help him? Could I save him?

I struggled out of my torn shirt, took the band from my ponytail and used it as a tourniquet. My reflection in the mirror opposite was hunched and strained. Then, as my expression slipped into relaxation, I lay down.

Epsilon, like I'd never left; the marketplace was as strange as ever. I began to walk through the Constant Shopper's shanty town of stalls, bright striped rugs flapping and racks of crystal beads clattering. The worm-girl's voice was haunting me: "Never come back to the Aureate." Why not? Because the Tine will eat me alive. I wandered round Epsilon's market in painful indecision. "Never come back to the Aureate. Never come back to the Aureate." My curiosity will be the death of me. I settled feathers that were prickling in the heat.

Cobbled roads ran around the market square's edge, from which farther streets led to the quarters of the city. Coaches, rickshaws, and single whorses jogged up and down, sometimes scraping street corners, and bringing down the occasional stall. I walked until the cobbles became gold. Here and there scuff marks showed where people had tried to prize them up. There were scattered bloodstains, and withered hands bitten off at the wrist—people soon learn not to steal Tine gold. Tall buildings slid into Aureate glow around me as I walked on, into the Tine's quarter.

The Transgressor's Forest is the hair of the Tine's quarter. It is especially difficult to reach because the head is a large walled enclosure. Hundreds of creatures were promenading gold dust tracks between the twin Cathedrals of the Eyes, down to the Most Hallowed Nazel Grottoes, whereas the Mouth forms an Endless Chasm surrounded by gold teeth and the Ears are convoluted dishes the true names of which are not revealed to the faithless. I ran, dodged, and sometimes flew through this complex, and eventually made it to the high spiked fence of the Transgressor's Forest. Hiding, waiting, in the edge of a bushy gold eyebrow, I watched.

A Tine wandered into view. His saggy blue arms were pouring a flask of thick red-brown liquid into a watering can. I risked a closer look—he was alone, and seemed quite elderly. His clawed feet drew parallel lines in the glittering dust. He had frayed denim shorts, over which a floppy belly bulged. Thin wisps of white hair hung down a massive muscled back, over the vestigial shell that crawled with violet tattoo knot work. As a belt for his shorts, he wore braided optic nerves—the Cult of the Multiple Fracture. At his waist hung a big key ring, on which, instead of keys, were a bunch of ragged fingers. There were slender ladies' fingers, soldiers' thick knuckles, and children's bitten nails. I saw the turquoise digits of other Tine, and the podgy hairy fingers of lardvaarks, all pierced onto the ring. And they were moving, bending, tapping, stroking . . . All still alive! The Tine hefted his green watering can, and I stepped out from behind the wall.

Shoulders up and hackles up, the beast growled.

I coughed. "Excuse me? Perhaps you can help. I'm looking for Keziah the Saurian. He's a gray lizard, about . . . so tall, long snout with lots of teeth. Have you seen him at all?"

"Grrrr?"

"You know, I left him four months ago, but I think if he's still alive, he must be here."

"GRRRRR!"

"Well, if you feel that way, I'll just be going—"

"How *dare* you set foot in the Aureate!" The creature choked in fury. He took a step toward me and I backed off.

"I'm an immortal," I said, playing the only card fortune dealt me. The Tine gardener was too enraged to be impressed. Dry lips stuck to sharp canines as he snarled.

"What's it worth to let me have a look in there?" I gestured at the gate and blue pebble eyes focused on my hand. "Oh yes," I continued, bringing both long hands up with a flourish. "I was admiring your . . . finger collection, and I wondered what it's worth to let me search for my friend in your forest . . . ?"

The bristly beast pulled a razor-sharp knife from its belt. I held my hand out. "After you show me," I said, teeth gritted, "Keziah the Saurian."

The Tine's heavy head nodded. "He's impaled."

"What, on a spike?"

"No. In a bucket."

When I saw them, I was sick. The Tine marched me on, determined not to let me out of his sight among the rows of stinking bodies, the forests of flesh. After all, I owed him a finger. I kept my eyes on the lymph-soaked ground, shuddering. There were rows and rows of canes, irregular against the hot sky. Rows and rows and rows of planted things tied to the canes. Some screamed. The ones that were beyond screaming were worse, because they sighed. And then there were the ones that were beyond sighing, the ones with wet streamers of guts like runners from which new limbs grew. The gardener doused them all with red-brown liquid from his watering can.

We walked underneath a roller coaster made of bone. There were real creatures embalmed on a merry-go-round, and they called out to me through sewn mouths as they spun by.

Still we went deeper, where the smell of rot was salty, too overpowering, and re-formed things with eyes on finger stalks begged to be put out of their agony. Some looked like skinned muscle trees, lumpen and misshapen, and some were skeletal trees in winter, their off-white arms wired to carved wooden posts. Insects kill everything in their path, but Tine are into creative mutilation. The gardener directed me around a clotted bush of digestive organs, bile green and dark purple, and an arterial ornamental garden where sunken things bubbled.

"Keziah?" I called. Why does that tree have so many sets of teeth? "Keziah! Keziah!"

Eventually, "You are one *bad* cat." A voice softened with mortal pain.

"Shit, Keziah, I'm sorry." I stopped in front of a tall scaly sapling.

"What you doing back here, dude?" the sapling seethed. "You said you'd stay off the powder."

"I came to find you."

"Stunning. Come join the greenery, catch my drift?"

"There are some things I want to know."

Keziah's peeling face blinked down from a three-meter-high

trellis. Cables, ropes and gory tubes held his backbone in place, all covered with strands of dry slime. Keziah's guts were in a bucket, which the Tine drenched liberally with his watering can. The Saurian gasped; a membrane-eyelid flicked over his remaining amber eye. Just suspiring, "They'll never let you go, now. Not for all the meat in Pangea." He lisped, because he was missing his bottom jaw, which had been replaced by someone else's.

"Keziah. What is the Royal Court? There was a blond girl, made of worms. She saved me. When you were . . ."

"Ripped apart. Hurt, that did." His top lip curved up in a grimace.

"Who is she?"

"I can't t—"

"Who is she?"

"Bad news, dude. She's a Vermiform. Captain of the Guard . . . She works for the King."

A King in Epsilon, how bizarre. "Who's that? A Tine?"

Keziah paused and gasped again, looking to the Tine gardener for a little more red water. The gardener was transfixed on me, and didn't move. "The man you brought here yourself. Dunlin."

"Dunlin. *Rachiswater?* How?"

"He said we should all pull together . . . He hates Insects. Oh no. Oh *shit*. Here she comes."

"Wha—" I broke off as the ground began to tremble. I looked down and pebbles were shaking and jumping about on the ground. A long thin worm scurried between my feet. I jumped. Then all around me were worms, rushing together. Worms came out of the ground, disturbing the pebbles. In a five-meter radius they appeared, running in toward the center, where they met in a writhing pile. Up sprouted a twisting column of worms, taller than me, it consolidated and re-formed into the beautiful girl. She swayed, stood still, her hair was alive.

The gardener fled.

Keziah whined, "Oh for Cretaceous' sake. We're doomed."

"Jant," the Vermiform said, her voice like harp chords, "we told you not to return."

"Yes, I know. It was an accident," I said. "I thought I'd try to save my friend, but as you see, there's very little left of—"

"You told him about His Majesty," she accused Keziah.

"Not at all. He—"

"We're everywhere. We know."

She held out her arms, and they elongated—worms ran down her shoulders and neck, adding to the ends. Her hair shortened and vanished. Her head shrank, melted like candle wax as worms left it, adding to her arms. The arms were like tapering roots; they came to points instead of hands and the points laid hold of Keziah. He roared in anguish. I took a step forward to help but he shook his scaly head, a sly gleam in his eye. He had an end to his protracted agony. I watched, wanting to run, but I wasn't going to leave him a second time.

The girl's shape thinned, her height decreased as worms poured down her writhing arms onto Keziah, where they crawled quickly all over him. She was just a thin column, then the column shrank; she was just arms, then the arms dwindled, shoulder, elbow, wrist, and all her worms were wrapped round Keziah.

Keziah couldn't shake them off. A moving net of worms surrounded his snout. They crept into his mouth, between his massive teeth, and down his throat. They emerged from his ragged-cut neck onto the trellis, red and sticky. Worms crawled into his eye socket and forced the eyeball out. They pushed between vertebrae and dropped in the bucket.

I had my hand over my mouth to stop screaming as I saw rivulets streaming into his nostrils, eyes and earholes. Keziah's head hung down. He stopped breathing, and the membrane flashed across his eye socket one last time. I guess enough of the worms had reached his brain and mashed it up. They gushed from his open mouth, and in midair re-formed into the beautiful woman whose shape took a little adjustment as her feet hit the floor. She picked a lone bloodied worm from the bucket tenderly and stuck it back on herself.

She said, "Never come back to the Shift, Jant."

I said, "No, my lady."

If she approached me I would run, but I had seen that her worms moved like quicksilver.

"Then goodbye." Worms at her feet began to dissociate.

"My lady! Wait! I want to meet Dunlin again."

"He said he doesn't want to see you. Epsilon is at war."

"Why?"

"You stupid creature! If I see you again I'll eat you from the inside out." The Vermiform raked one hand across her chest, taking a fistful of worms. She molded them like a snowball, mouthed, "Catch!" and threw it. Worms splattered against my face. I squealed and spat, brushing them off—they ran down the folds in my clothes to the floor. When I could see again she was gone, the slightest tremble of gold soil showing her path underground.

There was a reorientation, and I woke. I woke in a familiar room, feeling a familiar feeling. I felt like death. I'd passed out with my eyes open, and they were so desiccated the lids got stuck when I tried to blink. I groaned, remembering the thornstick pain, metal through flesh.

Tern appeared, being comforting, holding my hand. I leaned over the bed and threw up. Then I started crying.

"What's the matter? What's the matter?" she asked.

"It's nothing. It's just the reaction of the drug. I'm a useless, stupid Rhydanne," I explained. Tern climbed in bed with me. Her legs were so smooth.

"Sh! Jant, it's about time you quit."

"I can't," I said, before I could stop myself. But Tern didn't see any hidden meaning behind my words. We listened to the sound of heavy rain drumming on the shutters. She stroked my wing for a while and then stopped, a typical woman—they don't expend any effort to help you if there's nothing in it for them. I ran my hand up under her skirt and got lost somewhere between crinolines, petticoats and unidentifiable lacy straps. I was a foiled lover, completely at the mercy of too many layers of clothes. Slowly I gained control and stopped sobbing. Tern doesn't believe in the Shift; nobody does. Poor Tern, she can't understand why her pathetic husband is killing himself. I hugged her, saying, "I just need to Shift once more and then I'll quit."

"Why?"

"I'll quit forever, I swear it."

"You've said that before."

"I mean it. Aches to move. Don't want to do it again." I rubbed my eyes and only succeeded in making the burning sensation worse.

"Then *why* bloody do it again?"

"I have to. Honestly, Tern. Trust me. Help me. Please?"

She shook her head, gazing in disbelief. I rubbed a hand over her stocking tops, hooked a finger under the suspender and ran it up to the belt at her waist, swept my other hand down her back, undoing hooks and eyes. Tern made an impatient noise and wriggled out of my grasp. "You're taking me for granted," she said.

"That's not the case. I . . ."

"You simply don't care that Insects have reached Wrought! It's under attack!"

She slid from the bed and stormed out of the room, the open back of her dress flapping, her little black wings and narrow shoulder blades sticking out. Her footsteps diminished down the spiral stairs.

I lay back, pressed on purple-shadowed eyelids and said "fuck" in every language I could think of. I used to find Tern's selfishness attractive, and I used to believe that with immortality she would learn patience. I'm losing her again, I thought; if she complains about my conduct to the Emperor that will be the end of both of us.

I started to shiver, hearing the rain and the low moan of the wind cutting around the tower. At length I got up and pulled myself across the tilting floor to the dressing table, which was a mess of perfume bottles, makeup and paper flowers, feather scissors and pens and one slim ornate syringe. I clutched it. Safe now. I fixed myself and lost consciousness lying on a bearskin rug, in front of the fireplace. I went looking for Dunlin again.

I felt much healthier in the Shift, which proved how sick I must be in the Fourlands. I'm sorry, Tern, I thought. When the Fourlands needs me, when Tern wants me, I'm lying, twitching, dying of overdose, alone in my room in the Castle. I knew I was treading the edge of death to take so much cat twice in close succession. Older Eszai would be feeling the Circle strain to keep me alive.

How much poison would break the Circle? How deeply damaged was too fucked to save? What would fail first? Respiratory depression, suffocation, heart failure, permanently Shifted; with maggot-girl trailing me.

With the Vermiform in mind, I began my search for His Majesty in places where I knew the floor was solid, where I would presumably be able to see her coming from a distance, rather than suddenly feeling worm-strands wrap around my legs and pull me down through the soil.

In the marketplace there seemed to be fewer Tine. After questioning people in bars and coffee shops I found that Dunlin was giving them good positions in his guard.

I raised a toast to Dunlin Rachiswater in the Bullock's Bollocks bar, and everyone there responded. Either they were loyal, or they were too afraid to differ. I learned from them that he had taken up residence in Sliverkey Palace; that I would find him there if the flag was flying, and if not, on any battleground with all the inhabitants of Epsilon pitted against the Insects. The punters toasted him again. Shift creatures had never united before; usually they gruffly ignored each other, or were cheery but vague. Only the Equinnes seemed capable of battle, but they had discovered athletics instead. Now they were so fanatically patriotic and bloodthirsty they seemed to be becoming Awian.

I left the bar intending to walk to Sliverkey, but I had not gone farther than the market when I was sidetracked by a stall selling maps. Another amazing development—I had never seen maps in Epsilon before. The Shift changes so rapidly it's difficult to plan. Enchanted, I realized that each was a hand-drawn copy of the chart I had given Dunlin four months ago in Keziah's pub. And now they were available to everyone! I bent over for a closer look and got both buttocks pinched at once. I whirled round, drawing my sword fluidly—found myself face to face with Felicitia Aver-Falconet.

Felicitia froze with a squeak, both hands over his face. He lowered them tentatively. "Lose the bleached hair and white jeans, my chimerical boy. They make you look like a ghost."

"Felicitia! Just the man I need!"

"Oh, my tardy lad! I've waited so long to hear you say that."

"I mean, I need you to come to the Palace at Sliverkey . . . God, what happened to you?" His arm was bandaged elbow to shoulder, hanging in a sling of lined magnolia satin. The sling matched the rest of his tight suit, which left none of his small toned body to the imagination. He was leaning on a crutch, which pushed his other shoulder up to his ears, from which marcasite rings dangled. His skin shone like soap, and ingenuous eyes brimmed like ink blots. He swung on the crutch, blushing terribly. "I was—"

"Oi, what're you doing talking to a tourist in the middle of the market?" At an angry shout I put a hand to my sword hilt again, but Felicitia slapped me.

"*Will* you stop doing that? It's not diplomatic. Over here, love," he added, raizing his voice, and a well muscled man with long red hair slipped to his side. The man was tall, tanned, and completely naked apart from a furry headband.

"This," said Felicitia proudly, "is an Equinne gunner. My guess is he could even fight Tornado and win."

I ignored the friendly hand, bulging with health, which was offered me. "I'm not a tourist," I said.

"Leigh, this is Comet Jant Shira. Less pigment than spaghetti at the moment but don't underestimate him. He can outrun racehorses, he's a Deathless—"

"Looks already dead," the muscled man observed with cheerful carelessness.

"Jant, this is Lieutenant Leigh Delamere from Osseous, who's come to help us fight Insects."

"At yer service, Immortal."

Questions buzzed in my mind. I couldn't believe that Felicitia—camp as a row of tents—would want to fight at all. Perhaps it was testimony to Dunlin's charisma. I couldn't believe that the Horse People would join Dunlin either. If their Shift land of Osseous had been in the Fourlands, rivalry between Awians and Equinnes would far surpass the Insect War.

"Pleased to meet you. The Castle Circle is at your service and that of Osseous." Which was safe to say because no Eszai apart from me would ever visit Osseous. "I would be glad to offer assistance against the Insects in any world."

"He's the Castle Messenger," Felicitia said.

Delamere grinned with a chummy politeness that left me quite cold. "I must ask," I said. "Why are Equinnes always naked?"

Delamere looked aghast, ran big hands over his groin and thighs. "I'm not naked."

"Excuse me," I said, "but I can see your—"

"This is one-hundred-percent impossum fur. Invisible marsupials. It took tons of them to make this suit." He offered me a brawny arm. I stretched out a hand, aware of Felicitia giggling, and stopped a centimeter from Delamere's skin, my hand sinking into warm invisible fur.

"That's amazing," I breathed.

"Cheers. They're bastards to hunt, though. Have to walk around until you fall over them."

Felicitia tottered on his carved crutch, wincing in agony. He asked if we could start toward Sliverkey straight away, as his broken leg was too much to bear in the heat and market crowds. "Those Insects are tough," he said.

Delamere took him under one arm, where he fitted perfectly. He clicked his fingers at a passing quandry, which slewed to a halt beside us. "Can you take us to the mansion at Sliverkey?"

"Well, I dunno, darling," said the leading whorse, licking lipstick smooth around its muzzle. "Is the price right?"

"I have money," I said, making Felicitia giggle again.

"God save us, a rich Rhydanne; nothing's changed at all, has it? Has it, my affluent lad?"

Delamere shoved Felicitia up into the open carriage where he sat swaying in girlish laughter. The lieutenant said a few short words to the leading whorse, in a different language; the beast pawed the ground and tossed her head. "If you please, love," she whinnied. "If you promise to give Dunlin our regards, this ride is free."

"All your rides are free," nagged the whorse shackled behind it.

"Oh, listen to the girl, she's such a bitch!"

"Mare!"

The quandry set off at a brisk canter, scattering shoppers and Jeopards, and a couple of stalls. We turned right at the City Hall and, as town thinned, increased in speed until we were racing at a gallop along country lanes, all the signs pointing to Dunlin's Palace.

E very time the colorful coach zigged or zagged or jarred Felicitia was thrown against me on the amber leather seat, and I was pushed uncomfortably up against Delamere's fur. First we passed the Aureate, vast twin gilded domes of the Breasts on the skyline. Then we rushed through open country, over a vivid green plain where manila antelopes took fright and jumped away from the coach, white tails showing. Groups of giraffiti stretched their long necks to watch us, their bodies and lengthy legs a crisscross of brown lettering on yellow hair. Herds grazed in the calm middle-distance. The quandry dodged away from snorting terribulls, which attacked to protect their herds, lowering their heads and gouging with gigantic horns.

After an hour the plain gave way to a bright blue lake, covered with lily pads, where fiery flocks of pink flameingos stalked on their matchstick legs. The air was crystal clear and sweet as melt-water; Delamere's hair streamed back like crimson silk.

In the distance I saw a gray line, like a low cliff, threatening as a bank of fog, which I recognized as we ricocheted toward it in the heat-haze—an Insect Wall. It loomed, silent; seemed to leach color from the vibrant plains.

"Did Insects come from here to attack Epsilon?" I asked.

Felicitia said, "Yes. Do you remember we used to call them Paperlands?"

"Back home we still do."

"That Insect city is empty now," Felicitia said. "Dunlin and I cleaned them all out. Didn't we, Leigh?"

"Yeh."

"That was how I got my arm broken. I was right in the middle of the fight! Just like Hacilith! Well, maybe not. We drove all the Insects back behind that Wall and there were so many they were stacked up on top of one another, running around."

"So there are no Insects left in Epsilon at all?"

"There's a few pockets of Insects left. There's quite a few behind the Wall at Osseous. Dunlin wants to attack next week and destroy them all, my sweet tatterdemalion. We're positive of success."

"There are too many Insects to hold in the Fourlands now."

"You Eszai are always saying that. You don't fool me, my pretty propagandist."

"It's true. Rachiswater's overrun, Lowespass is ten meters under paper, Wrought manor's infested. Insects have been seen in Micawater."

"Even! You need Dunlin back. See, here's where we camped; the Equinnes had such good fun."

"Yeh." Delamere smirked. "Bit slow, though. Prime your muskets and bide your time, the Captain of the Guard said."

"I could tell the Insects didn't like being all squashed up together because they built a bridge to escape. It's there—do you see?"

I did see. Half a bridge reared into the brilliant sky and stopped abruptly at the zenith of its arch. The bridge was identical to the one in Lowespass.

"They built tunnels too," Felicitia chattered. "Then they ran down the tunnels or up the bridge and disappeared. Can you believe? Dunlin was hopping mad because he said they were escaping."

"That half," I said slowly, "is the same bridge as our half."

Felicitia didn't understand. "There are lots of bridges."

"You don't know where they go to?"

"Well, no, my outré one. Do they have to go anywhere? Dunlin climbed it, you know. He is *so brave*. He threw things off the end but they didn't vanish like the Insects did. They just fell down. Didn't they, Leigh?"

"Yeh."

I started to feel strange. Invisible hands were pulling me back to my body in the Castle. Typical. Damn it, damn it, damn it. I fought hard, towing the line, pulling against the pull, a supple hook in my guts. My longest Shift yet was wearing off rapidly. I grabbed Felicitia, who simpered. "The Palace," I shouted. "It's important! I'll come back as soon as I can!"

"We'll be there," Felicitia assured me.

"Tell Dunlin not to ride against the Insects again! Not until I talk to him! I—ah . . ."

"But why?" Felicitia's hand went straight through me, to the amber leather. The bright plain was dimming, a fast dusk to a monochrome gray.

I looked imploringly at the now ghostly Equinne. He said, "You know where those bridges go to, don't you?"

"Yeh." And I was gone.

CHAPTER EIGHTEEN

I'm surprised I'm still alive. Awake and alive! The rush that knocked me out had faded, but the high remained, and it felt wonderful. I grinned, unstuck myself from the carpet, and bounced over to the washstand where I drank a whole pitcher of water. From the burned-down candles I supposed that I had been unconscious for four or five hours. I rubbed at the bruise in the crook of my arm. "Don't do it again, Jant," I told myself. "You'll get hooked."

Rain still whipped against the shutters, storm clouds were moving in herds across the sky. The land outside was dark and soaking. I took off my shirt because I'd vomited all over it, rolled it up in the rug and dumped them both in the bedroom.

I was descending the steps when I heard a hurried knock at the door. I was still utterly wired on cat and didn't stop to think who could be visiting in the middle of the night, during a hurricane. I bounded across the room and flung the door wide.

The figure dripping there gazed at me in horror. "Messenger?"

"Mm?" I blinked. "You're wet."

"Yes. It's raining."

"Yes. Well, I suppose you'd better come in then." The tall man pushed past me and it was only then I realized who it was. "Harrier?"

"Comet, this is terrible. I—"

"What the shining fuck are you doing here? What are you wearing?" The custodian of Micawater unbuttoned his saturated coat, wrung the rain from his ponytail. He carried a mighty bow, which I took from him and propped against the wall. He looked too upset to be bearing arms. I sat him down in a chair by the fire.

"Comet," he said palely, "I rode from Awia. I lived there all my life. I'm never going back. This is terrible." He seemed ready to collapse.

I had not seen this aspect of Harrier for twenty years. Gone were the elegant suits and polished boots; the woodsman was dressed as he was the first time I saw him, I observed as I poured a heavy measure of whiskey. His green coat and hood lay in a pool on the floor. Under his belt, peacock-feathered arrows were still bright and keen. He had a bracer on his arm and a sword and buckler at his side. On the other side hung a well mounted dagger. A horn with a green strap at his back and a silver medallion on his chest completed the ensemble. Harrier looked like this when he shot against Lightning in a Micawater tournament twenty years ago. Lightning won effortlessly but Harrier's skillful archery and impeccable conduct impressed him so much he offered the loyal young man the next stewardship of his estate.

Long time pining—through novels, librettos, and benefactions, with visionary masquerades and testing tournaments, Lightning created a golden age of the time of his youth which modern Awians desperately want to defend. Harrier and his family had subscribed to the fantasy and sunk without trace.

"I can never go back," Harrier repeated in dismay.

"Shut up." I gave him the whiskey; he slugged it down and then spluttered it all over the long-suffering carpet. He grimaced like someone weaned on expensive wine. "I have to see Lightning. The Castle's like a tomb."

He buried his head in his hands, and his shoulders shook. No, it couldn't wait till morning. Yes, it was urgent. No, he couldn't tell me. Yes, he could only tell Lightning. Yes, he was terrified. I took a deep breath. "We're all Eszai! I can help! Now stop sniveling and tell me what's going on!"

"I rode without rest. I left my horse in Great Court, half dead. Night before last during the storms, at the Palace, there was a fight. I'm so sorry. Fifty men forced the Lake Gate and rode into the gardens. A child could force those gates. There were no lights. Torrential rain, clouds were down to the ground. We couldn't see in the gardens at all. My family hid. The guards are useless—it was mayhem. Call them guards? Decoration, more like! We were expecting Insects, not men to attack Micawater! Men rode right into the entrance hall. I was on the balcony. I shot at them. I shot at *people*. I can't believe it. I took ten of them down with the arrows that were on the walls, but I only had ten arrows. Lightning will be devastated. Maybe I should kill myself."

Harrier appeared quite willing to do so; I tried to reassure him.

"I couldn't stop them! The men broke everything. The first floor is in pieces. Ceramics, glass. It will break his heart. They ran up the stairs. They knew the way. They took . . . They took Cyan from her bedroom and they took her away. I'm sorry. She wasn't crying; she was white with shock."

"You've lost Ata's kid?"

"Yes. I'm so sorry. We tried to give chase but the storm was too fierce. The entrance hall flooded, because the doors were smashed. At daybreak I sent out search parties but there was no sign. The roads are all churned up. And Insects! Insects all over the place! They ate everything in the gardens, including the gardeners. I had to deal with the townspeople, I told them to leave for Rachiswater."

"Do you know who's taken the girl?"

"Yes. He had the Castle's crest on a shield on his back. I had chance of a shot, but I didn't dare. I didn't want to hit Cyan. Lightning could have done it. But I couldn't shoot an Eszai."

"Mist?"

"Yes."

"He's more stupid than I thought!"

"I think they took her to Peregrine. I went there yesterday morning. The manor is like a war camp. There's a thousand fyrd there. They have the Grass Island badge, but they look very shabby. They told me to piss off," he added, in a hurt tone.

Where did Mist get a thousand soldiers? Oh. No. I know. It was my turn to founder; I sat down. I had thought that I'd tied up every loose end. Now I wished the world to swallow me whole. The Emperor and the Archer would be furious with me. I swore miserably in Scree while Harrier watched me shrewdly. "You don't know anything about this, do you?"

"Of course I do. I'm an Eszai. I know everything," I said. The immortal line. Appear to lose control and Challengers pop out of the woodwork like Vermiforms. I couldn't tell Harrier that I had relocated Ata's fyrd to Awndyn manor, to send them out of the way.

It could never be known that I delivered a letter from Shearwater Mist to Awndyn manor. And Awndyn was not far from Peregrine. That letter must have recalled them—Mist used Ata's men to abduct her child. "I'm going to knock their heads together," I muttered.

"I think we'd better let Lightning do that," Harrier said. "Comet, I don't understand. Why would the Sailor want to steal his child back? Does he want ransom for her? Is Ata so fond of her?" Just because Ata has had many children over the centuries doesn't mean she isn't fiercely protective of each one. "Perhaps he's going to use her to force Ata to drop her Challenge for his place in the Circle. Don't look at me like that. Everybody at the coast knows now."

"If that's his aim," I said, "he'll lose his place anyway because extortion is certainly against the law."

Harrier seemed to have mostly dried out now, and was warmed by the unfamiliar drink. He was patting his chestnut hair flat and examining my eccentric apartment with complete distaste.

"We'll go tell the Archer," I said. "He will not be in a good temper—he's feeling guilty. He had to answer to the Emperor for lending Micawater fyrd to Ata. He hasn't broken the rules, but they're bent completely out of shape."

"The lady deserves to be supported. She's suffered so much!"

I was of the opinion that the lady should be bound and gagged and dumped in the deep blue sea.

I led Harrier down my muraled spiral staircase, along one of the wide corridors that connects the Castle's thick outer walls to the Palace inside. He scuttled along behind me, one hand on his sword hilt, blunt head down as if he was still moving against the storm. There was a sheen to his pale skin that was not rainwater. He looked like a dying man, more gray than pale; flashes of lightning from the glassless windows lit his face in angles, light gray left, dark gray right—the timeless gray of the Castle stone. "Calm down!" I shouted over the sound of the storm.

"Slower!" he gasped.

"Don't die on me, Harrier," I said nervously. I have never found it easy to judge how much pain Zascai can take. He stum-

bled at a left-hand turn, sharp change of direction, into the corridors of the Palace itself.

"Not yet, Comet," he muttered.

It is a long run from my tower across the Castle to Lightning's
rooms. We paused in an unlit doorway, the engraved portal open
wide onto a little cobbled courtyard six centimeters deep in
pocked water. Sheets of water were running off the roof and
falling in a transparent wall in front of us. I pushed Harrier
through it, ducked after him, and sprinted across the sudden lake
to a gateway at the other side. Harrier gasped as freezing water
doused down his back. His shirt clung between the bumps of
wings.

Now we were leaving wet footprints on a dove-gray carpet.
Blue glass lamps had been depleted hours ago and the
narrow hallway was slick with the warm smell of oil smoke. A
midnight-blue embroidered hanging ran along the wall, thin
white hounds chasing like a pack of crescent moons after a
brimstone-yellow stag with a crown around its neck. I ripped
the hanging back on its brass rail and there was a double door
behind it.

"Are you going to knock or shall I?" I asked. Harrier tried
to hide behind me. I sighed and hammered on the blue doors.
Nothing. I knocked again, again nothing.

"Let's go." Harrier shivered. He could barely speak. From
experience I knew this would take a while.

Lightning, unusually crumpled and haggard, opened the
door and stuck his foot against it, leaning on the frame, his face
just visible in the gap, said, "What have the Insects done now?"

"Not Insects."

"Then could you go away, please?"

"This is important!"

"Comet, do you know what time it is?"

"Yes. It's—"

"I don't care what you're high on or what you have to whine about. Leave it till morning when I have enough energy to kick you back to Scree for waking me up!"

Harrier surfaced in front of me, and smiled like a ghost at his master. Lightning's demeanor changed completely. He ran a hand through tousled hair.

"What is it?" he said. "No. Wait, don't tell me, come in."

He dashed back into the room and started lighting candles in a candelabra on a low walnut table, fumbling with a tinderbox until I threw him a box of matches. Harrier walked into the room like a man into a new country, taking everything in. Polished floorboards reflected candlelight at the edges of the room, emerging from under a rug, iodine purple and potash gray. An albino bearskin stretched in front of the cold fireplace. Invisible rain battered the sash windows.

I closed the tall double doors, brass handles with copper-blue enameling, and waited there like a guard watching immortalized raindrops glitter near the stucco ceiling—the chandelier.

Harrier knelt at the edge of the carpet. I found myself looking at the top of his head. "You don't need to do that," I said, confused. He ignored me.

Lightning picked up a bow that was leaning against a bookshelf. He braced it against his bare foot and strung it expertly, then sank onto a gray velvet chaise longue with the bow across his knee. He thought: nobody can hurt me while I have this. An unlaced white shirt fell down over one shoulder; he had struggled into black trousers that were part of a dress suit. The first thing that had come to hand. "Comet. The harbinger of disaster," he said. "What is it?"

I motioned for Harrier to give the news. He did so, with an apology every second word. When he finished there should have been silence, hopelessly routed by the storm outside. Waves of rain tore against the windows, gales howled past around the corner of the building. The Archer was staring into a private world a meter in front of his face. "I see," he said, in a quiet voice. "I don't believe you."

"My lord." The woodsman hung his head, overcome with shame.

"This . . . doesn't happen to me. To the Palace. My home. What am I going to do?"

"Steady, Saker," I said.

"What am I going to do? I'll kill him. I'm going to kill him!" Muscles bulged in both arms as he clenched his fists. "We're leaving, right now." He took a gulping breath.

"Steady!"

"Nobody. Has. *Ever* touched Micawater. For fifteen *hundred* years. One *thousand* five *hundred* years . . . What am I going to do? What about Cyan? Is she hurt? Is she dead?" Lightning looked around wildly for something to break. Harrier had shrunk so deeply into himself that he was taking up no space at all.

He said nothing. He said, "I have to do something." Then, "What will the Emperor do?"

"Saker, sit down and calm down. To San it's just another manorship." I said it again in sixth-century Awian and he stopped, perplexed, the big hand went over his eyes like a visor.

"Please don't," he said.

"That is no way to comport oneself," I continued. "Would your father have acted thus? Would Peregrine?"

He struggled with his reverences. "Yes, they may well have," he said.

"Is this what they taught you? Or do you betray Awia by behaving like a Plainslander? What would Teale Micawater say if she witnessed this?"

It seemed to work. Lightning placed the bow on his chair and pulled Harrier to his feet, taking his hand. Ashen-white, Harrier was totally bewildered at the fact we were suddenly speaking a dead language. "I am so sorry," he kept repeating. "So sorry, my lord."

"No. No, Harrier, you did well. Your name will be remembered and your family will be rewarded for this service. I wish you to remain as steward in the Palace, if you feel you possibly could."

"It would be a great pleasure, Lord Governor, but I'm hardly worthy."

"On the contrary; you are the most loyal servant I have ever had, and a very talented archer."

I coughed. "Do I have to listen to this all night?"

The Archer turned to me. "How long will it take us to ride to the coast?"

"In this weather? A coach would take forty-eight hours; I could ride there in twenty-six hours if there are no floods. But I'm not going to Peregrine. None of us are." I drew the knife that I carry, Hacilith-style, in my boot, shaking with cat-comedown. "We should leave Mist and Ata to fight their battle. The Emperor's word. You have to stop the Insects in Awia."

"Insects! What about Cyan?"

"San's word!"

"I don't care . . ." He was intent on rescuing the girl, a casualty of Ata's Challenge and not really our business at all.

"Oh, for god's sake, leave her. How can we help the kid now?"

Lightning eyed me brandishing the knife. "I am going to the coast," he said coolly. "You cannot stop me."

"I can't stop you," I agreed, "but I could slow you down a bit." I flattened myself against the door, the paneling pressing between my shoulder blades. We gazed at each other, animals of different species in the same cage. "It's for your own good! What will San say?"

Lightning shrugged, retreated to the bedroom for a few minutes, leaving me alone with Harrier. The woodsman was too exhausted to stand, but too respectful to touch any of the furniture without permission. He drew strength from the fact that Lightning was satisfied with him, and maintained his sagging poise with gritted teeth.

"The moon had a golden ring last night; tonight there's no moon at all," I said. "A tremendous storm is coming. I've lived and flown in Darkling so I know."

"Worse than this?"

"Yes."

Lightning returned with the shirt laced and tucked in, his red embroidered riding coat, boots, a shield slung over his left shoulder and an arrow at string on a longbow.

"Jant, put the knife down. Thank you. Please write a letter to the Emperor, tell him that we have gone to find Shearwater—"

"Spare me the bullshit, Your Majesty. He'll dismiss you from the Circle."

"And ready my carriage? I know you don't understand . . . You probably *can't* understand . . . But this is something I should do."

I went to the servants' quarters and woke them all up, half past two A.M. I chose the best of them to be the driver for the first leg of the journey, and sent riders ahead. I left a letter for San explaining everything, and then went out to the courtyard.

The rain fell through lines of torchlight. Six horses struck sparks from wet cobbles with their hooves as they stirred uneasily, water running in streams down their broad necks. The coach had gleaming trim and the Castle's sun yellow and red on the back. Micawater's crest was on both doors, and in miniature on the horse brasses and the hubs of the wheels.

MEMO
To: Kitten
From: Me

Tern, darling, sorry I missed you. I have to go to Peregrine. Someone has to keep an eye on Lightning. He might be the best archer of all time but he's also a bloody idiot. Love you, Jant

We drove throughout the rest of the night, and the following day, changing horses at Eske, the Cygnet Inn in the dense forest, Laburnum House on the escarpment. There were no lights in Shivel; the town had fallen to the Insects. Altergate town was empty, and the people of Sheldrake had long gone. We pressed on through torrential rain, that at least would slow the Insects down. We changed horses at Salter's Stable, forded the flood-land at dusk where Dace River had broken its banks, and then we were on the coast road.

Before the first stop our coachman got hypothermia, so guess who had to drive the rest of the way? After nightfall we arrived at Awndyn-on-the-Strand; the sandy track pulled at the wheels. I halted the coach in front of a little stable, a thatched outhouse with half-timber and brickwork.

The manor looked as if its buildings had clustered together for comfort. Wet ivy scaled the pairs of tall chimneys, which were dark red, slick with rain blowing between them. A yellow glow backlit the lead-glazed windows; they were grouped in fours and eights, and beaded with rain. Awndyn's small archway opened under a coat of arms in deep relief, and an iron-caged lamp shone there, invitingly.

CHAPTER NINETEEN

Creased and aching, Harrier, Lightning and I hurried through the archway as if pushed by the storm. They were damp from their dash from coach to porch, and I was drenched to the skin. Swallow's aged servant kept us waiting in an oak-paneled corridor. Lightning sent me a worried glance. He was still seething with fury, he was as powerful as I felt sickly.

I had no time to dwell on my sickness, couldn't think of an explanation or excuse.

"Why the delay?" he inquired petulantly.

"I imagine she wasn't expecting company."

"Swallow has never been known to dress for visitors."

Eventually the servant returned and we were shown through to the little hall. Swallow was there.

Swallow wore a green silk skirt. She was playing the violin. Her head was tilted away from us and a shadow hid under her jaw; she was thinner than last time I had seen her. She lowered the instrument and smiled. "It is you! At last! I thought Pipit had been at the brandy. Did you get my letter? Have you come to hold the Insects off?"

Lightning simply stared, but fortunately I had more presence of mind. I bowed. "Governor Awndyn, I'm sorry, but no—at least, not yet. We need a change of horses on the way to Peregrine." I explained all, while Lightning's clenched fists dug fingernails into his palms in fury, and Harrier just stood behind him and looked peaky.

"Have you seen my town?" she asked.

"We came in along the coast."

"That was inadvisable, Jant. The waves will be over the sea-wall tonight and up on the main road. I closed the road because of Insects. Did you see the lights of the town? No? That's because I've had to evacuate it! The *disgusting* Insects have eaten everything in the warehouses and in all the shops on the quay. I have the harbor-men crowded in their friends' houses at the top of the cliff. Thank god for the cliff houses—that's all I have left! Those men put their lives on the line defending the canal basin against Ata. She's a traitor, Jant; I hope her daughter drowns."

"No, Swallow . . ."

Swallow picked up her stick from where it was leaning against a slender music stand, and leaning on it, limped toward me, her skirt flowing. "I'll help you, Eszai," she said, "because I owe you a thousand favors, and because of this fool here." She stretched up on tiptoe and gave Lightning a light kiss on the cheek.

Lightning asked for permission, seized her agile hands and covered them in kisses.

"You can have my ships," she said. "I can't spare any Awndyn men. I'll cooperate on one condition, that you make your plans here in this hall. Awndyn is the most powerful manor on the coast, if we can hold out, because now only Awndyn and Moren have harbors intact."

"Yes," Lightning said quietly.

Harrier gave a great sigh. She looked at him shrewdly. "You need food. Pipit! Fetch brandy! Bring bread and salmon, and stoke up the fire here."

Once into the refuge Lightning forgot the storm completely. Our coats were left on the hot tiles surrounding the central fire where they slowly steamed dry. We ate at a trestle in the warm dim hall, Harrier and Pipit at the same table, dipping into the same platters of roast chestnuts and baked potatoes. I couldn't be soothed; I was overwhelmed by sea-terror. I did my best to hide it, but I hated the salt wind howling down the vent, under the manor annex thatch. Thunder pounded with the waves on the long beach.

The cozy hall muted most of the noise; outside we would be deafened by the tremendous waves slamming into the harbor wall and hissing back, rain pelting into the ocean, blurring the sea's surface with the sky. I flinched with the impact of every wave, thinking that the ocean was eating its way closer over the dunes to the manor house. Waves will rear up and crash down on the roof like a wall of black water. How could the house keep standing against that weight of water? Any minute now we would be washed away!

"It's good brandy," said Lightning.

"Jant?" said Swallow. "Jant, are you all right? I've been offering you some for ten minutes and—"

"He's—"

"I don't like the sea," I explained.

Swallow experimented with a version of the first smile. "If you want to go upstairs please feel free. You need rest as well as repast; the storm will make it a hard ride to Peregrine tomorrow."

Swallow didn't know half the problem. I needed rest and I craved cat. I had to know more about Dunlin.

And Swallow was confusing me as well. What was she doing? From where had she suddenly found femininity? Why was she acting like a beautiful woman instead of a spoiled brat? Clearly Lightning loved it; he couldn't relate to the wounded girl, but Swallow in calm command of her manor was more to his taste and she seemed to reciprocate. Was she simply recovering her spirit, or had she realized how wrong she had been to turn him down? "Will you repeat your claim to the Circle?" I asked.

"I may," she said. "Now every morning I ride to town and we clear out the Insect carcasses, and we break down their walls, and we spend all the daylight hours killing as many as we can. And still we're losing ground! I'm not leaving my town to them!"

Lightning readily agreed, and I left them. Harrier took his cue from me and also left, treading lightly up the stairs to one of the linenfold-paneled rooms above the hall, hung with Awian tapestries and antler trophies.

I dawdled at the foot of the drafty stairs, where a little window with leaded diamond panes looked out over the strand. I could see only blackness, but sensed turmoil and movement, the roar of surf and flicker of lightning on flat cloud bases far out to sea. Violet flashes displayed the beach. In an instant I saw Insect carcasses jumbled above the tide line, spiny and angular.

By the stairs, a door led to the manor's church, which I knew was a calm, safe place to think and compose myself. Inside, the room was less than three meters square, and unadorned. Churches were more or less the same throughout the Fourlands.

An arrow of lightning illuminated a table set against the far wall, the only furniture. It was covered with a cloth embroidered with script that read: *Why are we waiting?*

These rooms are set aside to remind us of the absence of god. They call to mind the fact that the Castle was founded to protect the Fourlands while god is away from its creation, and that at some point in the future, god will return. Eszai and Zascai alike look forward to that happening, and the prolonged wait is another reason to want to join the Circle. People find it comfortable to have such a reminder, even if they can ill-afford the space. It's because they feel they have fulfilled their obligation to our departed god, and can forget about it.

I sat on the table and thought about Dunlin Rachiswater. Insects were coming to the Fourlands from the Shift—the world I could reach by drugs, the world that only I knew, no one but me believed.

How could I prove it? Head in hands and in deep despair I racked my brains trying to think of a way to explain it to the Emperor—"My lord, Staniel's dead brother is chasing hordes of Insects into Awia from a land where blue monsters worship entrails." I would be locked up permanently.

Maybe I *am* mad. Pressure from the Emperor's insistent commands and so much scolopendium has cracked my mind and I haven't even noticed. Or perhaps the Emperor has planned the whole situation so he can dismiss me as insane.

The only Fourlanders I have met in the Shift are Dunlin and Felicitia, people I already knew from the real world, so there is no way even to prove to myself that the Shift exists. The first time I visited the Shift, I excitedly recounted my experiences to Lightning, and his solemn countenance told me I had gone too far. He said, "It's just a junkie hallucination. Don't waste my time." It's just a hallucination. Are Insects coming out of my hallucinations and poisoning the world?

A Messenger should be pragmatic. With no way to prove the existence of the Shift, all I could do was trust my intuition. Was I too scared to take a chance to save the Fourlands? No! I would go back to the Shift . . . even if it kills me.

Death from overdose was too dishonorable. What would stories tell of me five hundred years from now?

A shaft of light appeared, increased across my face as the

door opened, and Swallow came into the little room. "Jant? I followed you from the hall. I have to ask you something."

Not now, please, Swallow. "What?"

"Where did you find my ring, and can I have it back please?"

"What ring? Oh. This?" I wriggled Cyan's copper ring from my finger and Swallow held out a hand for it. "Yes," she said. "It's mine."

"I don't think that's possible."

"The dolphin is my standard, as you know. Where did you find it?"

"I . . ."

"I gave that ring to the Archer last year because he insisted on having some token."

"Oh," I said. "That explains it. Well, yes, I found this in the Castle stables; it was lying on the floor and I thought it was pretty."

"Lightning must have lost it. Excellent way to treat a token."

Lightning? No. There is *no chance* Lightning could be Cyan's father . . . He *couldn't* . . . "Mmm. Yes. I was thinking of giving it to Cyan." I passed her the ring.

"Who's Cyan?"

"Ata's daughter, remember?"

Thank you, Cyan. Now I know. Why did I feel so sick? I didn't understand. The world had turned to dirt, heavy with disappointment. Anticipating the anger that would come later, I felt the warmth of gathering dread. "I swear I'll never trust any-one from now on!"

"Jant?"

Why was Swallow changing yet again, becoming ladylike and persuasive? It might be the result of her trauma—I once knew a lord who was wounded by Insects and spent the rest of his life thinking that he was turning into one, that black spines kept growing out of his legs.

I thought, Swallow may look reasonably healthy, but the body heals faster than the mind, and sometimes mind can't heal at all. We all have our private echo of the battlefield.

Mortals change immensely over their lifetimes, but rarely in the space of a few months. Women change incomprehensibly from day to day, but they keep the same themes. Neither mortality nor womanhood would explain what had happened to Swallow. "What's your game, Awndyn? What the fuck are you playing at?" She backed off. I suppose she had a different opinion of me too. How could she view me in the same light when she knows I've seen every bit of her, inside and out, stitches and all?

I followed her out of the gloomy church. "First you're a restless ambitious bitch, then you decide to be content as a Zascai, and now you're acting sly as Tern with frocks and kisses. I'm sorry, but this is confusing the *fuck* out of me."

Swallow tapped her stick on the floorboards. "I'll explain later."

"Explain *now*."

"Now Awndyn is attacked! My home, where I grew up! I need a place in the Circle! I'm so scared, I can't save Awndyn. With immortality and Lightning's help I might reclaim it. I have recuperated, I've had time to think. Something inside me pushes me on, but since the battle I feel worn out. I have no energy to try like I used to for a place. Now I have to fight and I can't; I'm lame. I know the Circle won't give me any more strength than I already have, and my lameness will never be cured, but Lightning will help me. I received a letter from Mist. In fact, you delivered it yourself."

"Yes."

"Mist explained why Lightning loves me. I never considered it before. Mist said the reason was because I look like Lightning's cousin, whom he loved so many centuries ago when his family ruled Awia. He has never forgotten her image—and

I happen to look the same! She was called Martyn Micawater; apparently she was a hunter, and a daring warrior. And she had auburn hair. He thought she was perfect." Swallow glanced down to the folds of her green skirt pooling on the floor. "And she wore silk," she added.

"Having rejected Saker, you're trying to snare him again."

"Well, yes, I suppose I am."

"Damn it, Swallow, hasn't it occurred to you we have more important things to worry about? Vireo and Tawny are marooned in Lowespass! Staniel is making no impact! Eske is at arms! You're holding Insects at bay every day yourself! Has it crossed your mind that Awndyn is the last manor before Hacilith, and if Insects reach the city what the fuck will happen? And what are you doing? Chasing feather. You selfish tart—"

"Don't speak to her like that," Lightning interrupted, lounging in the hall doorway, one arrogant hand on his sword hilt.

I was betrayed, like a kicked dog. None of the Eszai were worthy; my confidant, teacher, creditor, was as flawed as I am. How do we manage to maintain the sublime image of the Circle to which Zascai aspire? I felt more estranged than ever before, even in the bleak mountains.

I pointed at him. "I just found out this is all your doing! How could you sleep with Ata?"

"Oh. No! I—"

"No excuses!" I ran up the stairs and locked the guest-room door.

I sat down on a plain bed and stripped off my shirt, looked at my track-marked skin. When the world around me is falling to pieces and I am powerless in the wake of catastrophes there is still one thing over which I have firm control, my body. Here is a solution for all my troubles: I began to prepare a shot of cat.

Calmly looking at my arms I thought, there isn't any point trying to hook there. Once, probing deeply, I hit an artery, which was an experience I had no desire to repeat.

Swallow tapped on the door and called my name softly, but I told her to go bugger off. I opened a wing, resting it on the white sheets, feeling the sinewy muscles relax. The base where it connects to the hollow of my back is as broad as a thigh.

Lightning has let me down.

I felt between the black tetrice feathers on the inside, bristle-hard and thumbnail-sized. Parting them, I saw the delicate, pale skin beneath, showing the pleats of powerful muscle, hollow bone and healthy veins. I thought, Jant, if you do this you stand a very high chance of never flying again and then you will be nothing but a fated mortal. If the overdose itself doesn't kill me, that is.

How could he?

There's no such thing as honor. Chivalry isn't real. The walls are crumbling.

I didn't have anything to put in a will. Wrought manor belongs to Tern, Rayne could have my books, and Lascanne would keep the Filigree Spider. Goodbye, Tern. I began with nothing, and soon I will be nothing again, but now as the Emperor's Messenger, my highest achievement, I know it's worth the risk for the Fourlands' sake.

Where are we now?

I sat with the needle poised, hating the drug, hating myself, then pushed it in slowly. The skin was sensitive and it hurt so much I had to stop, blinking away tears, but then I found a vein and blood climbed up into the barrel.

I don't want to die. I don't want to do this. Tern, bring your cocoa voice here and murmur me to sleep.

I pushed the plunger down and it started hitting instanta-neously. I just had time to pull the needle out—a smear of my blood in the glass—and dropped it as my coordination packed up completely. A streak of warmth gushed into my back, spreading rapidly down my legs to my feet, and burst in my head like a dark explosion. I lay back, wings open, struggling for breath, and I closed my eyes and fell without end, into the darkness, into myself.

Something moved. A sound. The sound moved in a dance, pale blue curlicues against a blazing white silence. I tried to speak and moaned a row of gray dots. The blue wisp got broader and darker, like a strip of cloth. It filled my field of sound, and tinted rapidly from sky-blue to a hue that was nearly black.

"Mmm," I agreed in resonant rouge.

"Do I *have* to *shout*?" Pale blue, black, pale blue, black—Felicitia's voice. I woke to find myself lying on something green against a hard black surface under a glaringly bright sky.

"He made it," said Felicitia, bluely.

"Yeh."

"It's a hard ride. Take it from me," Felicitia added.

A powerful hand raised me to my feet. I tottered about and fell over. I got up under my own power, rubbed my eyes and looked around. We were on a grassy lawn a hundred meters long, between two immense but graceful black obsidian walls that stretched straight up without blemish into the sky. The windowless walls had no decoration, and no steps were visible on the outside. They curved away, and I could see that at the farthest extent they swelled into round towers, with tall spires piercing the air. The walls were too smooth for even Genya to climb, the soaring pinnacles more slender than anything the Fourlands could sustain. I recognized Sliverkey Palace.

Felicitia on one side, Delamere on the other, walked me over the yielding grass until I remembered how to use my legs. I said, "Is Dunlin here?"

"Let us go see, my persistent lad."

"What about the Vermiform?"

"The Captain of the Guard? They're somewhere around. You have your sword?"

I checked my sword but without much hope for the efficacy of a blade against a million carnivorous worms. We walked around the corner of the building onto more lush lawns, covered with glossy Insects, brown and dark purple with a brassy sheen. Insect bodies were poised immobile on the grass, or frozen chasing in a tidal-wave onslaught on the gatehouse. I caught my breath and hauled at my sword. Felicitia giggled, and I recognized that of course real Insects would not stay still so long.

"The Tine brought those back from the battle," Felicitia informed me, "and they made sculptures out of them, see? They're modeling the battles in Insect shells so that Epsilon will always remember."

We walked to the great entrance, a black archway in the inner wall, and up the stone steps which led through it. On the top step a stripy furry mass lay stretched out. At first I thought it was a rug, perhaps another of the Tine's trophies, but as we approached I saw its massive haunches and shoulder blades, over which rich orange and black fur rolled with the huge tiger's breathing. Its liquid eyes were shut, one paw hung over the top step, its tail was tucked underneath its great bulk.

"Step over him," Felicitia whispered, and as I raised a foot to do so the great beast shot upright, fur on end, and roared, showing a rough pink tongue and a fringe of long white teeth made of string. The tiger was taller than me; as it sat on its haunches, it could look Delamere straight in the eye.

"Who'th there?" it snarled, blinking yellow eyes. "Who approacheth the Palath?"

"If you please," said Felicitia, "tell His Majesty that Aver-Falconet has brought a delegate from Epsilon to speak with him."

The tiger eyed me, its whiskers twitching. "I thall. But thay here till I weturn." It flicked its tail and bounded away noiselessly on soft paws as big as carthorse hooves.

"What was that?" Leigh asked.

"Fiber-toothed tiger. He can't bite you, it's like being mauled by fluff, but I've seen him pounce the length of the courtroom."

I waited, fretting and trying to think what I could say to Dunlin, until the tiger gamboled back and slid to a halt. "Come in! Come in! Fortunate favorite of Hith Majethty."

We followed the tiger, who padded between obsidian columns, its stripy back at the level of my chest and its huge head moving from side to side. I searched the walls to see if Dunlin had added heraldry but there was simply the spotless stone which gleamed as if wet. The passage was so vast I couldn't see the edges; it was like a hall carved from black ice, the floor so well polished that we could see our reflections in it. The tiger's image moved like an orange cloud, the Equinne's bare feet held better on the cold floor than my boots did, but Leigh seemed uncertain of the tiger and hung back behind Felicitia.

At length the Fiber-tooth came to another arch, and sat down outside it. Felicitia raised a hand to its deep fur withers and the beast shook itself. "You may pasth thwew," it said.

Through the arch I could hear lively talk and flurries of laughter. I thanked the tiger and paced in at once, Felicitia and Delamere behind, to Dunlin's court.

Hundreds of creatures looked up as we entered. Tigers and Jeopards lounged on tasseled cushions by the wall, some with velvet collars. They turned their heads as I passed, mesmerized by the flaunting feathers in my ponytail, tempted like kittens to bat them with their enormous paws. Long-haired, well-hung Equinnes stood in a group; they bowed muscularly to Delamere. The Equinnes wore little, impossum-fur cloaks trimmed with platinumpus. They proudly carried their tubular weapons at rest on their shoulders.

Tine with lustrous shells stood in the corners of the room, their scimitars razor-sharp, the hilts wound with tendons. There were women I didn't recognize, with war-painted faces, and blue resin armor.

Leaning against the columns, and round the edge of the stone table, were human soldiers, in mottled green and brown livery. They stopped their chatting as we pushed through, and I was aware of how many were gazing, puzzled, at my wings. A girl with fin-crests fringing her tail, and silver skin like an eel leaned to her friend and whispered; they foundered in bubbly laughter. A gap in the crowd indicated the presence of an invisible creature, a Drogulus. There was a representative of the Sharks, a shabby group of waster-adventurers from Plennish, and eight or nine Market Analysts from the Triskele Corporation.

On the other side of the room were Polyps and some Nasnas—abhorrent beings that look like a man severed longitudinally, and a Hide-Behind, which I can't describe (of course).

An ebony-skinned Fruiting Body of the Chloryll wore a ball gown made of living leaves. She curtsied as we passed, her dress crackling, underwear of fresh flowers visible beneath. An Equinne delegate winked at her.

Flying animals drifted or hovered in the roof vaults. A motionless creature with stiff metal wings surveyed us with one bulbous glass eye. Dirigibles clustered like toy balloons, paper messages tied to their outgrown legs. Problemmings bounced and jostled against the ceiling, their black eyes like beads peering down. These rodents were lighter than air—they gathered in hordes, threw themselves off the edges of cliffs, and floated up into the sky.

The shaved women in Insect-bitten lacquer armor were the last to make way. I already felt the pressure of the curious crowd thronging close behind me. When they saluted and stepped aside, I saw my emerald-ink map spread on the table. Dunlin was seated behind it, on a solid obsidian throne. I bowed. Delamere bowed. Felicitia curtsied.

"Rhydanne," Dunlin addressed me, "you know I have no wish to speak to you." He sat with chin resting on one hand, folds of a mantle pinned at the shoulder, an attitude that reminded me of the Emperor, except for his chain mail and the girth of his arms. A crested helmet sat on top of the throne; a cloth bearing his azure emblem hung there too, its eagle's wing folded over the armrest.

"I've come a long way with an important message," I said.

"From the Fourlands? Is it a long distance away? Or is it as close as one dying breath?"

"I'm sorry, Your Majesty, but—"

"Jant, I find it hard to speak to the person who stranded me here. Although I cannot deny I'm enjoying life in Sliverkey." He raised his voice to the crowd, which rumbled approval.

"You have done very well," I admitted. I had left Sliverkey an empty edifice, and Dunlin's court was now held where my days of dancing and debauchery had been.

"Jant, look closely. I haven't copied the Circle, or instigated a rule anywhere near as absolute as that I held in Awia. All I have done is ask these people to help me, and each realized they could make more impact against the Insects by fighting together than alone. We have saved the city of Epsilon!" he said energetically, to a susurration of agreement from the crowd and a cheer from the ardent Equinnes. "Aver-Falconet, take the weight off that broken leg. Come and sit here." Dunlin indicated an onyx chair at his left side which Felicitia slid onto, smiling broadly. The chair at Dunlin's right was unoccupied. "Give me your message, Comet, and then leave us."

"I have a report from the Fourlands," I said, thinking quickly. "Your Majesty may think of it as a land you've left behind, but Insects run from the Shift to the Fourlands, and maybe between any other world as well!"

"How?"

"I'm not sure, Your Majesty. Instinctively. Like I can go any direction in the air when I fly, Insects scurry between worlds without being restricted by their boundaries. They don't see the difference between them—to Insects, all worlds are one."

"Via the bridges?" Dunlin said.

One of the resin-clad women banged her ugly spear on the ground.

"You can speak at any time, Mimosa," Dunlin told her. "You don't have to ask permission."

"Sir. I saw a bridge at Vista Marchan, before my city fell."

"So, the Insects that I am clearing out from Epsilon are simply running somewhere else. To the Fourlands, is that it? And the Castle is taking good care of them there?"

"He says the Circle's overwhelmed," Felicitia chipped in.

"I do not exaggerate. The Empire will soon be lost. We will be another part of the Paperlands. Thousands have died, Lowespass is finished. Your people in Awia and the Plains manorships are fighting on, but it's a losing battle. The Castle is divided and Insects are running unhindered as far south as Hacilith. So I have come to ask for your help."

"Sent by whom?" Dunlin demanded.

"I come of my own accord."

"Thought so." He closed his eyes, reflecting on the news that his homeland was torn apart, and that he was the root cause. Dunlin tried to let no emotion show, but I glimpsed a second of despair before he masked it. "How *can* I help you? There is no way!"

"I ask you to relieve the pressure on the Fourlands by letting Insects come back into Epsilon."

The crowd gasped and hissed. Dunlin said, "I believe I am

speaking for all here present when I say we have struggled hard these past few months to clear the city and savannah, and the citizens of Epsilon don't want Insects back. These people neither know nor care of the Fourlands, Rhydanne; the world we come from is not so important in their eyes."

"You remember Rachiswater?"

"Of course I remember the Palace."

"The gardens are trenches now. Governor Awndyn was nearly killed there."

"The musician? What drove her to fight?" Dunlin halted as he realized his court might interpret the love of his homeland for a weakness that would put them all at risk.

"If you let Insects back onto the savannah and were ready for them there, you could destroy them before they became a serious threat." No answer. "Dunlin, I rescued you from the battlefield. I gave you this place. You have to help us."

"My brother is now King of Awia?" Dunlin asked, with the tone of one who expects the worst.

"Yes, although Staniel is surrounded, powerless in Rachiswater in much the same way as Tornado is in Lowespass. The front runs through his town and by the boundary of Eske, and our troops are spread too thinly along it. Staniel is called 'weakling.'"

Mimosa said, "Sir. Time is precious. We have other matters to discuss."

Dunlin raised a hand to calm her. "Please attend in the spirit of this court, or Vista is on its own. I listened to your incantations and they didn't work, now let us momentarily concentrate on this Messenger's plea. Jant, tell me how my manor is faring and whether my brother is well."

I described Tanager's flight to Rachis Town, and the wreckage of Micawater. I finished by saying, "One way or another Staniel will not last long. Awia only has days."

"Yes," Dunlin mused. "How will I find out? It's too dangerous to have regular contact between the Fourlands and Sliverkey . . . People risk death every time they Shift through. As did I . . . Jant, where am I in the Fourlands now?"

"Already the stuff of legend," I said smoothly.

"I mean, you took my body back to Rachiswater? I lie in the Lake Mausoleum with the rest of my family and where Staniel will someday join me? Staniel ordered flowers and drapes to be spread on my tomb?"

I said, "Sacrifices have to be made in times of conflict."

Dunlin sprang to his feet, "We will leave this court for half an hour! Please discuss your petitions among yourselves and I promise they will be heard when we reconvene. Aver-Falconet, come with us!" He grabbed the edge of my wing, so that I was forced to follow in an undignified manner, and Felicitia limped behind me, back through the mass of Shift creatures and strangely dressed humans, to the grassy Inner Ward, under the soar-clear sky.

Dunlin sat down on the glassy steps where the tiger had been. "There are no seasons here," he said. "The weirdest thing is I miss winter most."

"Your Majesty."

"You don't have to use titles, Jant. The Tine are in awe of 'Deathless' and I am beginning to see their point. Tell me why I am not at rest in my own domain . . . *Staniel's* kingdom."

I explained about Staniel's flight from the funeral procession. I said that we knew where the coffin was, but we had no chance of retrieving it when Lowespass was teeming. Dunlin listened bleakly to all this, with his assured attention I remembered from when I ran messages between him and the Emperor.

He was silent for some time, then asked, "If there were fewer Insects, would you be prepared to redeem this casket . . . This . . . I'm sorry, Jant, I am more inflexible than you, and this is a peculiar thing to say."

"It's all right."

"Let me say it: this casket containing the mortal remains of Dunlin Rachiswater. And will you convey the same to the Awian capital, to be entombed as it should?"

"It will be the first thing on your poor brother's mind," I assured him.

"Make sure Staniel has a good adviser," he said astutely. "He must have talented counselors if you are to defeat the Insects."

"Brute force is more important at the moment."

"I was coming to that. I agree with what you say. Time and Insects are the only things common to the Shift and the Fourlands. So, here is my answer: I will discontinue my campaign here for four weeks. During that time it falls to you to muster the Fourlands' warriors and launch their force against the Insects. If you push the Insects back I will be ready for them here. We'll exterminate them if we can, but if not I will allow them to dwell here on the savannah for four weeks only—and not cross the bridge, and not build more bridges! I'll tell Mimosa's Bacchantes that we need time for consolidation, but I doubt I can contain the exuberance of the Equinnes for more than a month."

"We need more time," I said.

"No, Jant. One month. If all you've told me is true, you have the hardest work of your long life ahead."

Dunlin got to his feet, the bright armor plates on his legs sliding over each other soundlessly. He scratched his head, saying, "Remember, this respite is solely so Staniel can retrieve my coffin. I would appreciate it if you would tell me when Dunlin's remains are safe in the Lake Mausoleum. When you do return to the Shift, Messenger—and I wish you wouldn't, for the sake of the Empire—but I know you and can't trust you, then come and tell me of the legend of Dunlin Rachiswater. There'll always be a welcome for you here in my Palace."

"Once my Palace," I couldn't resist pointing out.

His eyes sparkled. "Yes. Never trust rich Rhydanne, thin cooks and fat soldiers. Isn't that what you used to say in Hacilith?"

Felicitia grinned widely, and nodded. "Jant *writes* the legends," he said.

"I will make sure you are remembered as the finest champion," I told him.

"We have a deal," he said. He embraced me briefly but strongly; I could feel the steel roundels on his armor dig into my biceps. "Farewell."

"Goodbye, Rachiswater."

Dunlin walked back into the hall, and for long after I lost sight of him, I could hear his spurs clicking on the flagstones. I sighed.

"Well?"

"See you, Felicitia."

Felicitia stamped his stiletto heel in the grass. "Typical! I've been waiting for you for two hundred years! I help you, I bring you to the Palace and, well, you simply ignore me!"

I was preoccupied, looking within myself to try and sense the pull back to the Fourlands. It was beginning, slowly growing. "You're jealous," I told him.

"I *may* be jealous, oh promiscuous youth."

"Felicitia, I'll never forgive you for the way I was treated in Hacilith, back when I didn't have the confidence to escape. So don't hold out hope, Felicitia; you're one of the reasons why I started using cat in the first place."

"If I hadn't died of a flaming overdose I would have won you round, my lissom lad. I know I could. Or I could have had you shot." Felicitia's lips pursed, then he spat, "Shit. The Captain of the Guard."

Worms were pouring in a thick, flesh-colored mass down the

stairs, taking the form of the steps as they slid over them. When they reached the lawn they pooled and coalesced, legs, torso, shoulders, head; and then again to create not one Vermiform, but two, at half the size. The beautiful woman was joined by a male body. For a second his form aped mine, then mimicked Felicitia, and then became neutral. Both occasionally showed gaps that opened and filled, with the worms' fluid movement. They spoke simultaneously with the perfect timing of a choir, but no real emotion: "We see you reached the court at last."

"Despite intimidation!"

"We sit at Dunlin's right hand. We know he doesn't trust you," the lethal creature chorused. "In court today we found how important you are. How useful you may be."

"You weren't in court just now," I said, and for answer the female Vermiform dug her hand into her neck, where it sank up to the wrist, she rooted around and drew out a little worm that looked no different from the rest, dangling from her changeful fingers.

"I see. It just takes one worm."

"That's why they're such a brilliant spy," Felicitia observed distastefully.

The male and female figures wound their arms around each other, and worms crawled from one to the other along the length of their arms, their hair threshed and lashed. "Jant," said the male half, "our world is one of the places where the Insects breed—"

"Think the Fourlands has problems?" the female part added in her myriad voices.

"You should see them swarm—"

"—in mating flights—"

"—above our dying somatopolis—"

"Their eggs are—"

"—hungry. And Insect Larvae—"

"—ravenous—"

"More than we could deal with—"

"—so we came to Epsilon," concluded the Vermiform that looked female. I had a feeling that something was expected of me, so I thanked them for their information.

"You must defeat the Insects," said the male Vermiform.

"Good luck," simultaneously from the female one. I shivered.

"For the sake of worlds not yet infested. Insects will reach fresh places from the Fourlands if your world—"

"—is overwhelmed."

"We do not want that to happen."

"So stay out of the Shift," they said together. The female form raised a hand. "You're needed in Awndyn." Their bodies flowed together.

Felicitia and I watched them unravel and corkscrew down into the grass. They dug into the soil as easy as piss into granular snow. Their faces were the last to merge, the worms behind their faces leaving, their hair sliding off and their faces following, then gone; leaving just the traceless grass.

"I hate that thing." Felicitia bit his lip and glanced up. "Oh, Jant. You're not going as well?"

I felt the pull grow stronger and the black walls of Sliverkey ward began to dim, ever so slightly, and then fading faster and faster out of focus. Felicitia's purple satin and the blazing sky lost their brilliance. I was slack with relief. I wasn't going to die. I wasn't staying in the Shift. I was going home.

"No! Don't leave me!" He ran toward me and I went with the pull.

"Sorry."

"Give my love to the Emperor!" He blew a hasty kiss.

"Goodbye."

G oodbye."

G oodbye? What? Jant! Did you hear that, Saker, he said 'Goodbye.' "

"Good."

Immortals close to death will panic—I can't die now! Can't lose eternity! I fought frantically from the warm depths but only fully gained consciousness when Swallow slapped my face. I sat up in tangled sheets, tried to close my wings but they were too relaxed to obey. Lightning stood by the mullion window, look-ing out, hands in deep pockets. I realized that was where my syringe and wrap had disappeared to.

Well, let him; he could have them. I moaned and Swallow shook me, which cat blurred into a fucking unpleasant sensa-tion.

"Jant? You stopped breathing then! Are you awake?"

"Yes . . . In a few hours."

"We are leaving *now*," said Lightning grimly. I groaned and begged to be left alone, but I think the Archer, appalled, thought it a fit punishment for me to be dragged out into the raging storm.

"It's nearly dawn," he said. "There's enough light to see by." Lightning was tenacious as a hound close to the kill. He was intent on reaching Peregrine as soon as possible, and from expe-rience I knew his anger would not abate.

Swallow was wearing mail, with a leaf-green felt lambre-quin tucked into the neck. With Lightning, she took me down to the stables, at the back of the manor house, where Harrier was waiting with Awndyn horses.

I was propped in a high-backed saddle and my wings shoved into my belt, as they kept concertinaing out and dragging on the floor. Lightning put my sunburst shield at my back for cover and I felt the chill metal through my flimsy shirt. I wound the reins in one limp hand, disturbed by my weakness. My horse followed behind Harrier's on a leash, although Lightning's servant said nothing.

My broadsword in its scabbard seemed weightier than before, and I wished for my ice ax.

Lightning unbuckled the Insect-limb quiver from his back and made it fast to the saddle so that his arrows were at hand. Swallow raised her face to him; he reached down from horseback and gave her a fleeting kiss.

A terrible wind blew from the sea, propelling salt spray and the whistling sleet to the speed of arrows. Spray struck and stung our right sides as we rode north along the coast. Our horses slipped in the mud and their course tended inland, but Harrier kept to the road, guiding my horse along.

Sea-breakers hurled halfway up the cliffs. Windblown foam drifted off and stuck to the grass, which was also blown in waves. The salt water wanted to climb onto the land and it roared with the strength of the fyrd at the failure of each wave to engulf us.

Seen from the sea we were three silhouettes—Lightning carrying his technologically perfect longbow in one hand, Harrier with a scarf wrapped around his ears and a strung self-bow resting on his knees. Me—shoulders bowed from the shield's weight, wishing I could just puke and get the nausea over and done with. My horse pranced, panicking when Insects reared up in front, scurrying in groups from the ruins of Sheldrake. Lightning and the Zascai shot the Insects till their arrows were diminished and then they rode with drawn swords.

I hated the sea air but the pale gray stormy morning was good for me. The bracing wind revived me; the freezing gale cut a smile on my face.

We sped past a kilometer-stone: *Awndyn 19 km. Awiu,*

Peregrine 11.5 km. From there the path dipped downhill, as the height of the cliffs decreased, and I heard the surf on a stony beach. We rode down the incline and plunged into damp woodland. The wind cut off, though I could still taste a tang of salt.

Our horses picked their way more carefully. The soft black path was strewn with blown-down branches and they were uncertain of their footing.

Lightning waited for my horse to catch up. He indicated the track. "What do you make of this?"

"Mm?"

"Forget it."

By the time we reached the Peregrine woods I had begun to take some interest in my surroundings.

By the time we arrived at Mist's manor house, which squatted among the untidy foliage, I had fully remembered who I was, where I was, and the reason for our ride. Gradually I stopped lolling and sat straight in the saddle.

The path had been widened by the passage of a hundred or so men, the leaf-litter was a mash of footprints. The men had walked in the opposite direction, a little time before, since a crumbly, peaty smell still emanated from the broken ground. They had been followed by several packhorses, which must have been well laden; their hoof prints had sunk deep.

Harrier muttered, "We should have lanterns." It was only early evening, but the short days of winter are either dawn or dusk, and nothing in between.

"Were there Insects on the cliff top?" I asked.

"Yes," said Harrier, brusquely.

I rubbed an eye. "I'm sorry, gentlemen."

"Jant dozes happily through Insect attack and the driving bloody snow and then he apologizes!" Lightning informed the forest.

"I am sorry, Saker. But if you only knew—"

"I *do* only know. I know what you are."

We joined the cobbled road, passed through the iron-railing gate, which flaked black paint and rust, up into the shadow of the cream-white mansion.

Lightning dismounted, gave the reins to Harrier, and strolled up to the house. He knocked on the door.

"There's nobody here."

"God's holiday, Harrier, you do have an eye for the obvious."

"Sorry, my lord."

A bird flew up from the white turret, startling us. Lightning's hand twitched, as if he wanted to shoot it down. He turned back to the studded door and hammered on it again. "Is there anybody there?" Silence. "Is there *anybody* there?"

"There isn't," I said. I dismounted gracelessly, my legs numb from the drug, from being pounded on horseback and sodden to the skin. I let the fretful beast feed among long grass and ferns of forest-overgrown gardens.

The Archer stepped back and looked up to a single great window above the archway. A heavy slab of white marble formed the sill; the balcony was deserted, the dirty windows, empty. "Where has everybody gone?" he asked, perplexed.

"My lord, there were a thousand people here," called Harrier. Looked like it, from the state of the muddy, rutted paths, litter and trampled grass; but Peregrine manor was now a deserted shell. Lightning, hands in frock-coat pockets, wandered around the porch, searching for a way in, and muttering how despicable it was that he couldn't get into his own house.

"This is so strange."

"Allow me," I said, and he stepped out of the way, remembering my suspicious lock-picking skill. Instead, I produced a key, fitted it to the lock, where it turned easily, and I pushed the doors wide onto an echoing hall. I presented Lightning with the key. "From Mist's room in the Castle."

He paused on the threshold. "I haven't been inside for seven hundred years."

"May I?"

"Be my guest."

Harrier followed us in; our footsteps resounded in a mansion newly stripped clean. Marble blocks were the pedestals for vanished vases and busts, polished shelves were free of silverware, and brighter squares could be seen on the walls where paintings had been. We walked through to a main hall, a cold black and white, where two staircases converged at the far end. Between the staircases a blue flag draped, hanging on wires from the ceiling. A massive table in the center of the room stood on a blue carpet, the same motif of a caravel in full sail.

Mist and his little band had gone, that much was obvious, and it seemed clear that he did not plan to return. Lightning walked up and down the cold vestibule as if measuring it, gazing at the places where treasure had been. He was looking inward, remembering past scenes when Peregrine was lighted, newly built, vibrant with movement and music. He brought haunting to Peregrine, images of his friends after hunting trips, telling stories over sumptuous feasts. He was remembering the dimensions of the mansion. Whether it seemed larger or smaller in memory, I knew that in reality the manor had changed little since his family owned it—apart from slowly falling into dilapidation. Mist had concentrated on building ships rather than palaces.

While the Archer paced the hall and wandered up and down empty steps to the rooms above, Harrier and I discovered the kitchens. The kitchens were deserted as if abandoned a second before; only the valuables had been taken and we found plenty of food that would just attract Insects. We lit lanterns and brought them through to the table in the hall.

Lightning snapped out of his trance and slammed his fist down on the solid table.

"No, no," he exclaimed. "This shouldn't be here!"

Harrier and I glanced at each other. Lightning threw off his coat and started pushing the table with a great show of effort, but for all his strength he couldn't move it a centimeter. "I'll *kill* Shearwater!"

"Yes, if we can catch him," I said. All the way from the Castle I had been anticipating a duel here in Peregrine and the bird was flown. Lightning had gained the mansion without the satisfaction of a killing and I knew he wouldn't give up the chase. Lightning's kin-worship annoyed me; it was a ridiculous waste of time. I alone knew we only had a month to push the Insects back into the Shift. "Insects are moving south constantly, Saker. We should let Mist go; we haven't enough time."

"Time . . . Ha! Don't . . . talk to me about time," the Archer panted vaguely.

Harrier had realized that nothing was going to happen until Lightning had finished whatever he was trying to do, and so he set to helping.

"You're both mad!"

"Jant, shut up and help."

The three of us heaved and shoved at the table until we had moved it onto the stone floor. Lightning dropped to his knees and rolled the carpet back. It was filthy but he dragged it, threw it aside. Under the carpet was another grimy patch of stone. He rubbed it with the side of his fist, and then with his shirtsleeve, and because that wasn't enough crumpled his brocade coat into a ball and cleaned the stone with it. Harrier leaned close with a lantern and its yellow glow revealed the tomb.

It was a stone slab, three meters long, and it bore the deep relief carving of a square-faced man aged about fifty, broad in shoulder, his feet resting on an attendant hound. He was sculpted in full armor of ancient design, a horizontal-strip cuirass, a helmet with a horsehair plume; he lay on a round shield. I recognized the style of two thousand years ago, before Awians began to use scale armor and before the Morenzians invented plate. A sixth-century inscription edged the slab, punctuated by quatrefoils:

> *Peregrine of the royal dynasty of Micawater lies here at rest, King of Awia 529–587. This manor he founded will always remember. Those he loved and guided will never forget. Lightning Saker caused me to be made.*

We waited respectfully. The silence grew, and Lightning still knelt there, his hands on the deepest engravings, in which fragments of gilt remained.

Harrier drew me aside with an anxious glance over his shoulder and whispered, "What shall we do?"

"I think we should leave him alone."

"Can we help?"

"There's nothing we can do. Come away."

It looked like a midlife crisis to me. I took one of the lanterns and left Lightning kneeling by his brother's grave.

In the kitchens Harrier set out wine in tarred leather cups and bread on scarred platters, and we ate in silence. I tried to enliven the woodsman—if he knew the truth he would realize I'm hardly worthy of reverence. But his ingrained respect and new astonishment got the better of him, and, "I'm so glad I'm not an Eszai," was all he would say.

"We should look for Mist at the quayside next," I said. "That's where the footprints were leading."

"I really want to find my family in Hacilith," Harrier confided. "My wife and son are refugees now. I hate to think what Insects have done to the Palace."

I wondered if Harrier would make a good Eszai; his open, honest face was a true indicator of his tractable nature. How dif-

ferent an Archer he would have been, had he beaten Lightning.
I drew Harrier out by asking after his family; he began to talk
more readily. I found apples and a block of marzipan to divide
between us with more wine. Cat in my bloodstream eagerly welcomed the food, unlocked all its energy and gave me a second
high. I decided to curb my exhilaration when Harrier gave me a
strange look. I may have been speaking a little too fast.

That was why, when the moment came, I thought it was to
do with the drugs. I was just raizing the cup when it hit. It
almost knocked me from the chair. A terrible feeling: disloca-
tion. A million windows blew wide and an ice gale tore through
me. I seized the edge of the table. I cried out.

Harrier's eyes were wide. "What's the matter?"

I don't know. I really don't know. Cat has never done this to
me before. Shift is not like this. For a second I felt cracked open
and all the stuff inside me flooded out. I spread on a plane
through the whole world in view of everything. It was like looking for too long at the spaces between the stars falling faster and
faster up into them a mad sensation of space pulled me out in all
directions paper-thin translucent-thin.

It snapped shut.

It was gone.

I sat there, blinking, surprised to look completely normal.
The fire was crackling in the corner, the taste of marzipan in my
mouth.

"What is it? Comet?" There was an edge of fear in Harrier's
voice. I realized that I had dropped the cup and wine was
spreading out on the table. The impression of infinity had taken
a second. "Shit . . ." I said. "Wow . . . It's *vast*."

Lightning appeared in the doorway, personification of
intense panic. "Jant! There you are!"

"You felt that too?" I asked.

He nodded. "Of course."

"Felt *what*?" Harrier demanded.

"The Circle broke," said Lightning. "One of us is gone. I mean—dead. One of the Eszai . . . For a second I thought it was . . . Thought it was you. Should have known better." He rubbed his eyes, wiping grime all over his face. He looked gray and sick. He had more experience than me. He'd felt it before.

"Tern?" I got to my feet. Damn it, I should never have left Tern. I should be by her side all the time.

Lightning looked distant for a second, sensing the rest of the Circle. He felt for the presence of the other Eszai and our shared time, keeping us all alive. I don't have that ability, it takes centuries of practice.

"It's not Tern. Why should it be Tern?" he said slowly. "Come on, Harrier. Let's go!" He pinched an apple from the table and strode out.

I thought of Tornado fighting to the last of his strength in dark Lowespass, overwhelmed by Insects. I thought of him baited by thousands, the last of his men long fallen, cut to shreds, borne down at last and with his last breath still bellowing defiance at them.

The sensation paralyzed me but Lightning was stung into action. "Jant, you Rhydanne failure. Your help is now *essential*."

"Yes, yes," I said testily, unable to drop the feeling that a part of me had died. I felt lonely, at a loss. I felt like a mortal again, now I knew the sensation of the Circle failing me.

"This will all change!" Lightning promised the mansion, with a glance at Peregrine's sarcophagus, then: "I must take Mist's banner down." He plucked one of his long arrows from the quiver, nocked it to string and flexed both arms, bending the bow. He looked to the flag with instinctive aim, and loosed. The arrow cracked into the wall. The ship flag swung slowly sideways, rippling, until it was hanging like a rag from its remaining wire. Lightning selected another arrow and shot through that wire too. The rich flag fluttered to the floor, draping the white double staircase in dark blue and golden folds.

"Now Peregrine is mine," Lightning said briskly, buckling the nearly empty quiver to his hip. "I hope we meet no Insects on our way to the quay."

The quay was the last place I wanted to be, in reach of those mighty waves. I still thought of the ocean as a gigantic beast, its bulk gray-green, its rabid mouth white with foam. The water had a mind of its own, ever-changing, sometimes lying low, always ready to pounce. I understood the rules of the air and knew its moods, but I couldn't predict what the sea was plotting. With my feathers waterlogged and my acrobat's strength useless in the surf, I would surely drown. The wind was too strong, the ocean too alien. I was averse to horses, lacking an ice ax and I wanted the chance to fly. I had no chance to use my talent here and I was reduced to being hauled along unwillingly by Saker as if I was his flunky rather than an Eszai. Not the best assignment for the Emperor's Messenger and the only being in the Fourlands who knows the truth about the Insects.

I followed Lightning dourly, the horse hooves cracking on cobbles and through panes of ice that were forming in mud ruts on the path. I searched for a way to stop his stupid pursuit but could think of nothing; at least, not while he still had arrows left. I decided that I would stay long enough to find out his next move, of which I could inform the Emperor. I would see Lightning and Harrier to the quayside and leave them there—they could find their own damn way out of the sea's clutches.

The wind was waiting for us when we left the forest, as intense as before. It sped the dissonant seagull cries and the relentless boom and suck of surf on the pebble beach. Insect shells turned over and over on the tide-line. There were fragments of broken wood there too, and stinking clumps of seaweed. Some horses, free of tack, stood on the path. We rode to the manorship's harbor, and there was no one there. The log-built boathouses, stores and offices were deserted.

"The tenders have all gone," Lightning said.

He took his horse up along the harbor wall and onto the main pier, demanding that Harrier and I follow. Impossible. The planks were running with water, doused by waves that licked underneath and covered the horses' hooves. Kelp and limpets encrusted the stacks; the wind blew the water into an opaque expanse of ripples. I kept my eyes on my horse's black mane, and let my mount find her own footing to the end of the pier. It seemed to take hours.

"Look up, Jant."

"Saker, you bastard!"

"Not in front of Harrier." He smiled. His voice was light with triumph. "The sea is for Peregrine!"

Puzzled, I glanced at the gray horizon, and the spectacle held my gaze: a wreck, transfixed prow to stern on the Grass Isle rocks.

CHAPTER TWENTY

Honeybuzzard," I said, remembering the green copper-clad hull. The windows at the stern were ruined holes, the figurehead facing away—the ship had smashed sideways onto the clustered rocks. A tangle of broken spars and snarled rigging washed on her port side, buffeted by the waves. A rent down the other side held her keeling fast to the Grass Isle reef, the deck tilted away from us. Two of the three masts remained, but the first was trailing with the rigging, leaving a splintered stump.

Clear of the water, the caravel seemed the size of a manor house. And silent as the grave. The wind blew the deafening roar of wave after wave crashing onto Grass Isle's shore to us across the strait. It was wild out there, beyond the shelter of the harbor.

"The girl," the Archer said cautiously. "Cyan. Cyan Dei. She will be on the ship." The tone of triumph fell to horror in a second.

"I'm sorry, Lightning."

"Cyan . . ."

"Nothing on that wreck is alive, Lightning. We felt the Circle break; Mist is dead. You must have guessed—"

"I felt it could be him. And I thought Mist would try to run. Wind too strong. Couldn't . . . I suppose he couldn't make it round the headland. Lighthouse or not. But look, Jant, they have been there for hours. How else could the ship be so broken up? So, she's gone . . . I thought I'd find her."

"I have to tell the Emperor."

"No. We will still follow my plan. Fly out to the wreck and see if Cyan is there. See if there are any survivors."

The concept was ludicrous. Lightning took my look of hatred. He saw me take a deep breath and he motioned to Harrier, who goaded his horse round and rode out of earshot to the land. "You take him for granted," I said. "Unlike him I'm no servant, Saker."

"Fly out to the ship," he said quietly.

"How could you be an adulterer? How could you have a daughter? You had an affair with Ata and kept it secret though Cyan herself found a way of telling me and now you're willing to put all the Fourlands at risk for her, not to mention my bloody life, if it hasn't crossed your mind I'm terrified of drowning and the worst thing is I looked up to you, but now I hate you, you seemed to be in love with Swallow so earnestly all this time and now it turns out you were only pretending!"

"No. Not pretending. I am. I always will be. Fly out to the ship."

"You rarely speak to Ata. You've never acknowledged the girl. Fuck it, I'm not hazarding my life for an illegitimate brat."

"I had to keep the secret. I have watched Cyan. Fly out to the ship."

"It's a secret I want to know. I thought you had a blameless past, so giving Ata grounds for blackmail was a doubly stupid thing to do."

"Jant, please. I'll tell you of it later."

"Seduce you, did she?"

"Damn it, stop it. What's got into you? This is not easy for me." A wave of remorse broke in his voice; he sounded bitter. We watched the ship continue its slow disintegration under the force of the waves. "Yes, if you want to put it like that I was seduced. We only had one night together—"

"A *pleasure* cruise."

"Enough! Please. She said it was safe but now I regret it. How I regret it! Eight years is no time at all and I never thought the confidence would become known so soon. That beautiful bitch. I don't know how to cope with her. I have to know what's there on the wreck. Jant, please help me. Fly out."

"Swear that you'll give up Swallow and Ata and any other women for a year, while we turn the tide to obliterate the Insects."

"I swear it!" the Archer declared.

"All right." I clambered from my horse, fighting down a bout of hysteria as the salt water wet my boots. I held my wings open. "Give me some space."

"Thank you, Jant." I heard his horse's hooves backing. The needle-wheal stung on my numb left wing. I will never take cat again.

The gale was so strong I simply had to hold my wings open against it to feel light on my feet. I kicked off and the bay spread out beneath me, the pier shrinking rapidly. A frightening speed of ascent. I leaned forward, pushing all my weight ahead, otherwise the gale would start to blow me backward.

The coast fell behind quickly and I was over clear water. I tried to attend to the shape of the air, but I kept looking down to judge my height from the surface. I didn't want a gust to dump me into the water. My rapid forward flight meant I lost height quickly too, but every time I came within the waves' snatching distance I angled my wings and hurtled up vertically. I faced gusts head on, uplifting and falling between them like waves.

The sea seemed flat dark gray, laced with lines of foam, and it was only when I neared it at the end of each short glide that I saw how broken it was.

Wings knifed the air but my body dragged, aching my prominent carpal bones. It was hard to keep the four long fingers of each wing open against that unpredictable wind. Even the Darkling snowfields have refuges, but the sea is all death. I fought upward desperately as the waves prolonged into crests and grabbing foam fingers. I flew frantically as a drowning swimmer thrashes.

I took a low altitude approach to the sloping hulk, aware that if I overshot I would have to turn with the squall behind me, which would make my flight unstable. I pushed the air down with fingers, wrists, elbows; the whole six-meter wingspan, steered with my legs and skillfully came up to the *Honeybuzzard*'s railing.

Flapping energetically, I made it over the railing and touched down. It should have been a beautiful landing.

My legs slipped from under me, I fell heavily on my backside and slid ten meters across the deck before crashing into the railings on the other side. Winded, I dug my fingernails in. I stood up and looked around. I was standing on a film of white ice-rime, like powdered glass. The deck tilted at an angle of thirty degrees.

Ropes hung from the splintered masts at head height and the rigging and wooden toggles swung and splashed against the seaward side. The side nearest the land was lower, water swirling among massive rocks. I looked over to see jagged black rocks scattered with fragments of planks, impaling the gash in the hull, twenty meters long and ten meters high. Water boomed deeply as it circulated inside the ship. Seeing the high-water mark on the Grass Isle shore, I realized that we were low on the rocks and, come high tide, all this would change. I didn't know enough to tell whether *Honeybuzzard* would be pushed upright, or if it would sink altogether.

A cable from the masthead snaked and cracked. Timbers rasped as waves forced the wreck farther onto the rocks. Quickly I began to walk sternward, keeping one hand on the railings and looking up to the port side. The deck was washed clean of anything not made fast, and I guessed the people, too, had been swept overboard. I searched the land for survivors, but saw no ragged figures, no movement, no signals. Out of Mist's two hundred crew, I saw one body, floating facedown just inside the hull. An Awian man, his wet coat had trapped air that kept the corpse afloat, his sleeves rolled back, skin pale and abraded. His long hair and dark brown wings spread on the surface of the water. I looked for others and saw ripped cloth snagged up on the rocks, which could have been corpses or just cargo.

Everything Mist had taken from Peregrine manor had gone. I couldn't see anything but foam and spray smashing against the headland.

"Where were you taking it?" I said aloud. Then I caught my breath because I saw him.

The body stood against the helm, held upright by a rope passing under its arms and around its waist. Its head rested on the compass glass. Long gray and white rattails of hair were frozen onto the glass and stuck, glittering with ice and salt crystals, onto his shoulders. I slipped closer across the tilting deck. The compass had frozen pointing east-southeast where north was supposed to be.

Shearwater Mist's stocky body hung in the restraining ropes. His arms had dropped to his sides. The skin on his hands was white-blistered and torn. His eyes were open and glassy; he was coated in ice.

Hard skin blue-gray, the skin under fingernails dark purple, folds in his clothes stiff with ice. The hair on his arms was frost-white; the bandages still bound tightly round his ribs and wings. His dagger was hanging on a red lanyard under one arm, ready for use. An ivory shirt was molded over his torso's frozen muscles like a second skin.

It was true to say there had been no Awian hardier than Mist, but why would he take his ship into a storm with only a tricot shirt and denim slacks for protection? I scanned the deck, seeing that his cloak was piled at the foot of the main mast.

In the eerie quiet of this dead little world it began peacefully to snow. The flakes hissed and vanished when they hit the brine.

Shearwater had bundled up his cloak and roped it to the mast. Why? I examined it closely. Cyan's face was peering out of the bundle. I hunkered down and pressed the back of my hand to her blue-gray lips. A little warmth—she was still breathing.

"Cyan? Cyan, darling. You remember me. Can you hear?" I held both hands around her cheeks to warm her, a pointless endeavor because by now my skin was probably as cold as Mist's. I carried on a constant stream of encouraging chatter while sawing through the twisted cable with my sword.

"My dear, everything will be all right. Hold on a little longer, and I'll take you back to dry land." But before we set foot on land there's a short excursion through thin air. I lifted the child; she was far too heavy.

I sat down cross-legged on the ice and proceeded to unwrap Cyan. Mist had tucked his thick sailor's cloak carefully about her, and under that was a shredded sail, then her coat. The girl's dress was cornflower blue. She had gained a belt with peacock-feather tassels. Her feet, though, were bare and dirty.

I unclipped my scabbard so that I could use my belt to buckle the child to my chest. I held her securely against me. Then I wrapped her beaded belt around us as well. I slipped my sword, in its scabbard, under the bindings at my back.

I have never carried a pack as heavy as this eight-year-old. A handful of letters is my usual load. This is hopeless. Not to panic is key. The down-drag will be incredible. If I battle against it I will run out of energy. So I will fly with long, strong beats. I will ignore the pain and stay on a straight path with a solid approach. I'll avoid the fucking pier and set down in the village; Peregrine harbor seemed an immortal's lifetime away.

"We're going to go home. To see your parents and to get some hot drink. Can you open your eyes?" She stirred and moaned. Good. "I know you feel cold," I told her, wildly understanding. "Soon we'll be safe and in the warm. But before that it's going to get very much colder and I want you to hold on. You must not go to sleep. Sing if you can—sing to yourself."

I slid up to the highest point at the stern, and faced Grass Isle. The sea churned and bubbled. I was tense in anticipation of the shock when I, and Cyan, plunge into it. The freezing water will drench my hair and gush stinging salt into my throat. Don't give yourself time to think, Jant. Just go.

"Cyan, don't move. You must stay still." Then I ran into the wind until my feet left the deck, turned toward the shore.

I struggled, confused—I was falling straight down! What a weight! I stretched and beat twice as fast. I maintained an unbalanced flight a meter from the licking waves and then slowly, slowly gained height feeling my muscles tearing. I kept my arms wrapped around Cyan, but I couldn't breathe with her weight on my chest. She pulled me down headfirst.

This pain is too much; just drop her. I kept my eyes on the land, wishing it nearer and nearer, larger and larger. The wind pushed me north so I was at the top end of the village when I eventually scraped in at roof level.

I lost height, turned into wind to land, was blown back up again, pulled my wings shut in desperation and came down with a smack that jarred every bone in my body.

Lightning and Harrier ran from the harbor. Breathless, I gestured for Harrier to cut through the bindings. I lay down in a wide splay of feathers, cradling Cyan in my arms.

The girl's eyes were still closed, her lips blue-gray and her cheeks ruddy with windburn. Harrier leaned over and carefully brushed light blond hairs from her forehead.

"Well done," he said, so impressed that he forgot I was an Eszai.

I wheezed, "Oh, my god. Oh, my *back*."

"Is she dead?"

"No. Thank Mist. Saved her. Look."

Harrier put his hand to her lips the same way I had done; he smiled, his guilt relieved. But Cyan was still in danger. Mortals never allow themselves to think how close to oblivion they or their friends could be, and Harrier was no exception.

I said, "Cyan's very cold. I've seen people killed by cold in the mountains and they look all pale, like this."

Lightning was standing some distance away, with a stony expression, hands clasped behind his back. "What of Shearwater?" he asked.

"I saw him; he's still on the wreck." I described what I had seen, the Sailor frozen to death, the ghost vessel and its shroud of ice.

"He cared for Cyan," Lightning said. "At what cost, I don't yet know. We'll have to bring him back."

My Rhydanne immunity to all but the most severe cold meant I could not warm the girl; she was growing rainbow-colored from exposure and bruises. I passed her dead weight to Harrier. "Give her a hug and warm her up. There are some things I can't do."

Lightning stirred. "No. Give her to me." He scooped his daughter from my grasp and held her close, face down to her face. He gathered the fur-trimmed riding coat into folds and wrapped her so that she was covered completely in brocade, the gray check lining and soft fur.

Harrier still thought the child was Mist's, but not for long. I watched realization slowly dawn on him.

"What are you smiling at?" Lightning demanded.

"I'm happy to see Cyan alive."

"My daughter," he explained, and then said it again, more confidently. He kissed her forehead. "My favorite."

"Please allow me to offer congratulations, Lord Micawater," Harrier said, amazingly calmly.

I rubbed my wings to stop the muscles stiffening. "I have to report to the Emperor," I said. I retrieved my sword, dug in my pocket for the sorry remains of the block of marzipan, which I stuffed into my mouth for energy food. Harrier offered a leather bottle of tan-tainted water. "San must know about this," I added.

Lightning broke off murmuring to the awakening girl. "You're right, Jant. Harrier and I will ride to Awndyn. It's the nearest haven for Cyan, and Swallow needs us—if we can find her. I hope she's still there—she only had five hundred men, and this place is infested."

"It will be dark soon," said Harrier. He had once listened to me complain at length about the labor of flying at night.

"I can go one-twenty k an hour in this wind," I assured him, spidering to my feet and stretching my long legs against the tight leather, extending my wings and arching my back like a cat. I was getting used to the freezing gale; it reminded me of the mountains.

Lightning sent Harrier to fetch the horses before saying, "Offer my apologies to the Emperor. I beg his forgiveness, and I hope I am not too late . . . Beware of Ata; she is dangerous, especially now time is passing for her again. If you have to negotiate with her, mark every word; I've known the lady longer than you have."

"I haven't known her at all," I remarked involuntarily.

"Cease the spite, Messenger; it's dishonorable. I have watched Tern and yourself happily married for a hundred years without showing any of the envy I feel for your happiness."

"But—"

"Go carefully. Go *fast*." He struggled into the unadorned saddle of the larger horse and fussed about, inexpertly securing Cyan in front of him so that he could still pull a bowstring back.

"You could put her in the saddle bag," I suggested. When I was a child Eilean transported me in a papoose. The Archer looked scandalized. "I am going to *carry* her," he said proudly. "When we meet Insects Harrier will just have to fight twice as hard."

I watched them speed away, and then I ran back to the shore. I had to leave the cluster of boathouses that broke up the air-flow, creating lees and bewildering down-currents. Then I sprinted faster, again jumped into the air.

I rejoiced in the lightness; compared to my last flight I was infinitely agile and maneuverable. The sea was there below me and couldn't harm me. I beat the gusts and rode upon their backs, long-winged.

There are some advantages to flying over the sea. Unlike the land there are no people below so it is safe to piss from a height if you are desperate, which I was.

CHAPTER TWENTY-ONE

The lights of the Plainslands villages I used to navigate by—like stars on the ground—had gone out. Diw township was deserted, and Eske town was keeping a blackout in the knowledge that lights attracted Insects.

I aligned my flight west by the constellation called the Mad Sow's Litter, and skimmed close to the forest canopy. I flew all night to the Castle, and arrived in the gray dawn. I loped up the worn stone steps and through the great gate, desperately trying to order my thoughts.

Hundreds of people packed the Throne Room benches. Mortals, governors, fyrd captains and townsfolk. The screen had been rolled back, so the Emperor's gold sunburst dais was in full view from all parts of the hall. I didn't know the screen could be moved, and I had never seen such a crowd of mortals here.

I strode down the aisle and knelt before the Emperor, my hands on the platform's bottom step, salty wings chilled by airflow tense against my back.

The Emperor studied me carefully. "We have been waiting."

His forehead was furrowed, his cheeks were pinched—tiny changes imperceptible in anyone else were significant with the Emperor because in my experience he had always looked the same. Alarmed, I realized they were signs of stress that, even with his powerful will, San could not disguise.

The Emperor began: "The first thing you should know is that Staniel Rachiswater is no longer King of Awia."

"My lord! Has the King been killed?"

San smiled flatly, and I thought he looked tired. "No, indeed. He is a prisoner in his own Palace. Lady Eleonora Tanager seized control last night. She has eighteen thousand men, and Rachiswater's lancers defected to join her coup."

"I only knew she had fled her manor." And she had taken the capital. Eleonora's reputation was fearsome; I had met her once before, in a cocktail party, but she was as good a huntress there as she is in the forest.

"I await my lord's command," I said. King Staniel a prisoner in Rachiswater? Perhaps that's what he always wanted: to be safe.

The Emperor waved his hand, as if dismissing Eleonora's coup as the natural flow of things. "The Princess is defending Awia. Her countrymen rally behind her, and I dispatched Plainslands fyrd to her. I have sent some immortals and promised the help of the rest. Leave the whys and wherefores until the war is won—" He surveyed the mass of people behind me as he left unsaid—if any Awians survive.

I turned half away from the podium and examined the rows of Zascai warriors and civilians. San tapped his age-speckled fingers on the armrest of the throne. "I have made changes. I need their reports; and in return I am giving them reassurance, and hope."

I said, "There are no immortals here."

"They are all in the field. Hayl and Sleat with the Artillerist;

Rayne and the fyrd from Carniss are helping Eleonora hold Rachiswater. The Swordsman and thirty other immortals are holding the front within view of Hacilith city walls. The Architect, Treasurer, Polearms Master and ten more are seeking a way to defend the Plainslands. They lost Altergate yesterday, and Laburnum the day before that."

Maybe I was projecting my exhaustion onto him. Another glance told me that was a vain hope.

San said, "I suggest you give me your news now and your worries later."

I took a deep breath and told him about the Sailor's death. The mortals behind me leaned closer to hear, but after two minutes San cut me short. "I know this—of course! I recovered the Circle! What can you add? About Insects! How close have they come? Cobalt manor?"

I bowed my head. "No. All that is left in Cobalt are corpses. Diw is empty—Bittern evacuated her people to Grass Isle."

"So Awndyn is next. So Lightning is in Awndyn when I needed him in Rachiswater, where half his archers are, the other half on the island! He will answer for this debacle!"

"He asked me to plead forgiveness."

"Comet, what would you do with Peregrine manor? I know, you would give it to Lightning, who regards himself as the rightful owner. So then Lightning would keep indefinitely two of the six manors of Awia. He is breaking a primary rule of the Circle!"

I understood. If Eszai accumulated lands and were able to raise their own fyrd, they could dispute with Zascai governors or kings. And with time they might even be able to challenge the Emperor's authority . . .

"I allowed Lightning to keep Micawater, his birthright. But no new lands. I think he and Ata will choose immortality over property."

"Then who will inherit Peregrine, my lord?"

"Cyan Dei."

"Cyan? She's just a child!"

The Emperor nodded, white hair brushing his thin shoulders. "Yes, Cyan Dei is presently a child of eight. So, tell Governor Swallow Awndyn to protect her and her manor until she comes of age. As regental governor, Swallow has ten years to make Peregrine as productive as it should be, whilst equitably teaching Cyan the Empire's ways. Tell Lightning to salvage Peregrine manorship for Cyan. And he should *listen* to the child as well."

I shut my mouth, because my jaw was dropping. At a stroke the Emperor had brought Lightning and Swallow together. He had burdened Swallow with so much to oversee that she would find it hard to pursue her claim for immortality. And if Peregrine manor could eventually return over twenty thousand men to the fyrd, Cyan would gain the title of Lady Governor.

"Peregrine manor will stay in Lightning's family, which is what he always wanted, Cyan the latest descendant of a long-dead dynasty. He will think it an excellent idea."

"And Ata? She will be furious."

"Tell her to direct her fury at the Insects!" I flinched, but the Emperor continued: "The fleet needs maintenance. Tell Ata that if she is successful, I will bestow point eight million pounds from the Castle's Treasury to that end."

"Yes, my lord Emperor," I said, dazed.

San said, "We must deliver Tornado, or none of this will come to pass . . ." He became lost in thought; I waited, and there was neither motion nor murmur from the rows of battle-worn behind me, although a Sheldrake soldier was weeping silently, clutching his broad-brimmed hat.

Incense smoke rose in thin coils to the vaulted mosaics, the columns behind the throne glittered. Shafts of morning light from the high windows streamed across the hall, illuminating the ancient frescoes of Insect battles and the Castle's founding.

"The fyrd need Tornado," San said eventually. "He is a great symbol of the Empire's might."

I understood. Tornado was the most powerful fighter, the third oldest Eszai, the strongest man in the world in a millennium. The fyrd would rally behind him, if only because it was safer there.

"Comet, you and Ata must liberate Tornado from Lowespass Fortress. What intelligence do you have on Lowespass?"

It was time to tell him. However he reacts, whatever happens to me. I readied myself for the shock of being dropped from the Circle. Dislocated in denial of my own voice speaking I said, "The bridge—"

San looked up sharply.

"That's where the Insects are coming from."

San stood abruptly, called, "Close the screen!" We waited as the ornate partition swung back into place. Now the crowd could not hear us; above the dais, the cupola's architecture damped our voices.

"Tell me," demanded the Emperor.

I hunched up into a ball at the base of the steps. "I resign."

Please render me mortal, so I don't have to tell how I broke the world, and that I don't know how to put the pieces together again. This was like my confession to San and the Eszai in the ceremony when I joined the Circle—easier to die than drag out the details of my past. What was I doing, trying to hide secrets from god's custodian?

"Comet, that is only the easy way. Tell me. Once, then never again to anybody, living—or dead. Do you understand?"

"Y-es. Yes, I do . . . My lord Emperor, there are many other worlds: the Shift. I have been there. Insects cross between them by bridges and they lay worlds waste. They might travel by the tunnels too, if we consider how they first reached the Empire. Insects sense a place where the boundary between two worlds is thin. Then they build a bridge or a tunnel to reach it. They can see a passage through, but to anyone else, the bridge just stops in the air. Insects breed in some worlds; in others, seek food, and the Empire is at the very edge . . ."

"Go on."

"Dunlin Rachiswater, the last King, is still alive—in the Shift."

The Emperor raised a hand, about to ask how this could possibly be. He studied me intently, and read the answer. "I understand," he said. "Go on."

"Dunlin fights Insects there. They escaped across the bridge to Lowespass . . . But I found him! He agreed to restrain Epsilon City's prodigious host for the space of a month. If we push now, we can send the Insects back."

Now I had told the Emperor, I was light and empty. San needed this knowledge; he would know what to do!

The Emperor's face was unreadable. Didn't he believe me? Did he think this was a madman's insane rambling? I pulled my wings tight to my waist.

"If we had the strength to make a push," San said at last. "Hear me, Messenger. Go to Sute and instruct Ata. When she clears Lowespass of Insects she can come to the Castle and join the Circle. I shall give her Mist's title when her campaign is complete, and not before. Now fetch me paper."

I wanted to ask the Emperor how life was, back when god walked the earth. What did it really look like? Sound like? What did it mean to live when everybody knew everything? While San wrote, the pen scratching, I tried to imagine existence with god nearby, enjoying its creation, when there were no

Insects, no Castle—this two-thousand-year-old stone, just lush grass. The Fourlands does not really belong to us—it is god's playground; god gave us responsibility for its creation, which we have failed to defend.

As ever, San read my mind. Almost imperceptibly, he said, "Once there was peace."

I folded the letter, melted the sealing wax, and impressed it with Castle's sunburst.

"Remember my orders. Now go."

I stood and bowed, wings down in a flare of iridescent feathers, then backed and left the Throne Room, watched by the archers on the balcony. As I passed the screen it was opened slowly, and the Emperor called people forward to hear their reports.

Outside, I seized the guard's shoulder. "Lanner's son?"
"Yes, Messenger."

I pointed through the arched arcade to the black sarsen twists of the Northwest Tower. "See my standard? Lady Tern Wrought lives there," I said. "Find her, and tell her . . . Tell her that I love her. Tell her *not* to journey outside the Castle. She is not to leave the Castle no matter what she hears. No matter what she feels."

"I'll tell her, Comet." Shocked by my candor he added, "But won't you be back?"

I masked fear with a swaggering smile, put a finger to my lips and shook my head. "For her sake I'll try not to get myself killed." I desperately wanted Tern, the center of eternity, and if I saw her now, nothing would induce me to leave her again. I stifled the thought; I had to go. Spreading my wings, I vaulted the balcony, fell two floors, righted myself in the air, sped up and over the Castle roof. I lay horizontally in the air, found my pace for five hundred kilometers. Wings touched tips above and beneath me with each beat; the sun setting with a flash, below into the gentle hills of the Awian downland. A band of refugees emerged along the coast road, with fifty covered wagons and laden piebald ponies, they faltered their way south toward Hacilith from Wrought. I passed over the Peregrine cliffs, the land dropped away and there was the coastline.

I flew over the wreck of the *Honeybuzzard* in all its shades of gray and white. Its shattered figurehead reared on my left, a wild-haired sea woman jutting up from the slimy rocks where her wooden dress's cream folds scratched and grated. I shuddered, remembering the corpse helmsman; Mist, stocky and solid, was more terrible than a ghost.

I turned along the coast to the Sute Towers. Men stood on their crenellated tops acting as lookouts. The towers seemed unreal, illusory, frosted yellow gritstone forelit by the winter sunset shining under the edge of the clouds.

I reached the end of the serrated reef, the sea boiling around it. There was the lighthouse, a round stone tower built in the same pragmatic fashion as Ata's towers but with a stone platform and metal roof.

For every night as far back as I could remember, a huge fire was built in an iron cage on the platform to warn ships off the reef. Every morning the flames were allowed to burn down and the ash cleared out. The lighthouse's mechanism had been Shearwater's invention, and the procedure of running it kept several of the island's families in employment.

The lighthouse was useful; I navigated by its blaze at night and the stacks of seagulls carousing its rizing air by day. Even now I could get some welcome lift from it. I flew over the conical black roof, curving slightly to circle into the thermal. Nothing happened. Strange, I thought, and tried it again; nothing happened. I glided lower and tried it a third time but the lighthouse was quite cold. All the missing answers dropped into place. Of course! I somersaulted in the air and hastened inland.

The Sute Tower named August was the only one flying a pennant. The banner was plain white and wind-torn with no insignia, a badge of Ata's self-sufficiency. Lookouts on the battlements scurried down a hatch as I approached. Some wore little bodhrans and wooden flageolets, laced to their belts, which Morenzian men play when on watch duty.

The Sute Towers have no entrances at ground level; their doors are halfway up, with wooden gantries for access. Stealth was not an option, and I could do little in the way of force. Ata frightened me. She caused the Sailor's death, would she have qualms about killing me before she knew my mission? Oh shit. The towers were a web in which Ata sat spiderlike waiting for the fly to appear.

I whipped round, located the highest window, a glassless, shutterless square. I backed with every scrap of strength; even so, it took two laps to slow down and the drag nearly pulled my wings from my back. The window had no sill. I closed wings, drew my legs up and dropped through it without touching the frame, hit the floor and jogged to a halt.

A round room lined with people—men standing against the walls, perhaps fifty pairs of eyes. Click. Click. Click. Click. What? Then I saw four crossbows, in the extremities of the room, braced in the brawny arms of four intense-looking men. Their strings were spanned and the catches off. I spread my hands downward, showing that I had no desire to draw my sword.

"For the sake of the Empire." Ata could dump my body off September Tower pier and sincerely maintain that the sea had claimed me. The unwavering crossbow bolts were sharp, I would scarcely feel the blow; they would rip straight through me. Like a damn fool Rhydanne I had swept in to where Ata was indisputably sovereign of her island and stronger than I had ever imagined.

Ata Dei stood at the far side of the ring of guards, behind a simple table. She had a nearly translucent dress that matched her long white hair, and she seemed most unlike a warrior. She smiled broadly, which made her all the more frightening.

An officious-looking woman was behind her, of similar age and build, with a scraped-back gray ponytail and a hatchet nose. She wore a soldier's coat over her red brigandine and carried a crossbow. A bracing hook hung on her belt and from her assured stance I could see she well knew how to handle it.

"Welcome," Ata pronounced. Her tone was kindly but I didn't trust her. I hated the way the men were staring at me, awe mixed with a greater loyalty to her. There was no way I could reach the window if they took aim. "You must excuse this treatment," she continued. "I don't yet know the reason for your visit."

"Here is a letter from our supreme Emperor," I said, keeping my voice low. "And as an impartial Messenger I am at your service."

"Give me your sword."

I unbuckled my belt and laid it, with sword and misericord, on the bare floor, then took my knife from my boot, and dropped that too. Now I had no defense save a silver tongue. One of her guard took the weapons to her desk.

"I think we must stop threatening the Emperor's Messenger," she said, in Morenzian, and the men removed the bolts from the runnels and lowered their crossbows. "You can leave us now, but wait in the lower room and come quickly if I call. I have much to discuss with Comet, so let there be no interruptions."

The men filed out, creaking the floorboards and with many curious glances over their shoulders. I realized what a weird figure I must appear to them. Apart from my exquisite good looks, I was by now more sharp-set and unshaven, with my damp flight-knotted hair and cat-eyes. The Hacilith men wouldn't wear a silk shirt in the middle of winter. They were two hundred years too late to understand my pewter Wheel brooch but they recognized what was previously a gang patch as Comet's standard. Even the corvine lady behind Ata looked apprehensive, as if she thought that a man capable of flight was capable of any feat. I bowed to her.

"I had better introduce you," said Ata. "This is Carmine Dei, the harbormaster of Hacilith Moren, and my daughter. Before the storm she brought Hacilith's ships to the island, the soldiers San sent her, and several hundred men we employed in the city. The Governor is unaware of the thugs missing from his streets. So our new fyrd are not as finely drilled as the Awians but they do know which end of a crossbow faces outward."

"I see you have a veritable host here," I said.

"Aye, at present. Carmine, you'll have heard of Jant Shira: mad, bad and a pain in the neck."

"Delighted to make your acquaintance," said the human, resting her heavy crossbow at her hip. I understood that nothing would end her support of Ata, but I wondered whether her loyalty was freely given.

Ata dragged a chair away from the wall so I could rest. She took her seat, and her phlegmatic daughter guarded the window. I twisted the chair to see her; being shot from behind without warning was for some reason worse. Ata lit two oil lamps on the table, which gave a comforting yellow glow. "We could hear you flying," Ata said. "Your wings make an awful din."

"Thought it was too dark to hear me," I muttered.

"Start from the beginning," she said.

"You're mortal now, Ata Dei."

"Start at the start and tell me something I *don't* know!"

"San decrees that you will be the next Sailor. You will rejoin the Circle when your campaign is complete." I passed her the correspondence; she sliced the seal and read it.

"No. This must be wrong . . . Jant, the Emperor wants to kill me! I must become Eszai *first*."

"You can't possibly make it to the Castle! There's thousands of Insects in the way!"

Frustrated, Ata examined the letter. "This is practically a death warrant. Fight Insects as a Zascai? Without the Circle to support me if I'm wounded, Jant? Succumb to little cuts and bruises when so much is at stake?"

This woman, adulteress, murderess, was jealous with her own life. I had an idea that San wanted Ata to face Insects on a par with the mortals whose lives she played with so dispassionately.

"Jant, you wouldn't be in the first line if you were a Zascai. You'd run away!"

"Insects bite immortal flesh too." I hid my resentment with a shrug. "Remember the last Hayl was ripped apart at Slake Cross? The Circle was no protection then! If you want immortality, you have to accept San's rule."

Ata collapsed into her chair. "And fight for his favor. Yes, I must . . . I will. A risk of death to gain immortality . . . Eternity is worth it. Do you have any other news?"

I described the wreck of the flagship, her husband's body preserved at the wheel, and the crosstrees sparkling and dripping with nitid ice.

Ata's forehead wrinkled with astonishment. "I knew *Honeybuzzard* had foundered on the rocks," she exclaimed. "I just sent Diw's men to search for salvage! No doubt they'll bring him back . . . Shearwater was from Diw, you know, originally; not from Peregrine at all."

The room was gloomy now, the seascape outside impervious black. Knowing Ata to be callous, I was not surprised when she showed no grief, though it made me hate her. When every other woman I've known would break down and cry, Ata became calm, with steel fortitude. Ice eyes bade me continue, her strong arms folded across her commodious chest. She showed no sign of joy when she heard about Cyan, and guarded her expression when I spoke of Lightning too. Her eyes were emotionless; though there was some strong feeling behind them I could not tell what.

"I felt the Circle strain to hold Shearwater," she said. "I felt it break and I felt him die. I was right here, in this tower, and I knew what I was looking at. It was just the same as when Hayl Eske died, only this time it felt *good*.

"And the clock's ticking for me now. So I'm Zascai, but not for long, either way; I'll be killed, or you will be calling me Mist. I don't like this weight of time, Messenger; maybe you'll have the nasty experience yourself one day."

"I want to know what really happened to Mist." I braced myself for the tearing impact of a crossbow bolt—none came, but Carmine Dei was holding the bow steady.

Ata still let no emotion betray her. Her smile and her sigh were an excellent contrivance. "Jant, you said you were impartial."

"I am impartial, but I do know the truth and I need tell it to no one else if we beat the Insects."

"You're out of your depth, as the seahorse said to the jockey." She smiled. "What in Empire could this accusation be?"

I walked to and fro across the room. Movement might untangle my jumbled thoughts. It helped me to put Carmine's crossbow out of mind and hopefully made it harder for her to aim.

Moreover, the level of cat in my bloodstream was dropping

and I was starting to miss it. Withdrawal doesn't come on immediately but the calm before the storm is a confused paranoia: something is missing, something is not quite right, something awful will happen. Which it will if I don't soon take a fix. In the dullness of encroaching illness I can't think properly. I tried to concentrate, swallowing to clear my hearing. Ata realized that if debate grew difficult all she had to do was stall for time and I would turn into a suffering ruin, glad to agree to anything so I could get out of there.

I said, "Mist wouldn't sail to Lowespass. That's what started all this. There was no excuse for Mist's violence and of course he was to blame, but we assumed you were innocent. No one asked *why* he hit you. I think it was because you told him about your affair with Lightning, and Cyan's origins. A man like Mist wouldn't know what to do, and maybe he felt that violence would make the problem go away. Instead, you asked Lightning for help. He agreed, because you trapped him eight years ago by seduction. Lightning's now full of remorse and a desperate admiration—it isn't love—and he's losing his nerve when the Empire most needs him. Is all this true?"

Ata shrugged. The lamplight colored her white hair and dress a soft yellow, and gave a pleasing roundness to her face. When she shook her head, every hair was illuminated separately so her appearance changed from young lady to mature woman in a second. Then she gestured to Carmine. "Darling, leave your bow, it's making Jant shaky." Carmine complied and, relieved, I continued, convinced by her reaction that I was right.

I sniffed. "You sent Cyan to Micawater, knowing that Mist would attempt to abduct her, as Cyan was now a wonderful tool to use against you. In doing so, he brought Lightning farther into the fight. Damn him, he's so predictable . . ."

"As you are."

"Ata, killing me will not seal your secret while Lightning

lives. You may not have planned Mist's getaway into the terrible storm but he played into your hands there, as well. To escape from Peregrine harbor he had to sail through the strait. And Grass Isle has a tail of rock . . . He was a brave man to make such a move and he didn't deserve what happened to him."

"Shearwater's ship was blown off course and there's an end to it. Many boats come to grief on that coast. The islanders have been picking wood and bounty from it since time began."

"Yeah. So Mist had the lighthouse built and I don't doubt it saved many lives. But the fire wasn't lit, and you are the only person who could have ordered such an omission. I know because I flew over the lighthouse and it was cold."

"It's been a cold day," she said.

"On these dark mornings the fire's always stoked; it *never* cools down."

"Oh, Jant," she said, expressionlessly. The lamplight made her body a compact dark shape within the diaphanous dress. I ripped my attention away from the curve of her breasts. How confusing can the world be, when murderesses have great breasts?

"So you caused Mist's death. You extinguished the lighthouse and he ran into the reef.

"And I'm disgusted and repelled by the way you've treated Cyan. How can you plot eight years ahead? You planned her entire existence! The purpose of her life was for you to use Lightning to fight Mist. I suppose you let Lightning watch her grow, to secure his love for her. Now she's fulfilled her purpose and useless to you, what will you do?" I sought Ata's gaze and held it. "Was every one of your children bred for a reason?"

"Jant . . ."

"Don't involve me in these schemes any longer! I only wanted to fly errands and fight Insects!"

"There's a change from your usual anomie." Ata smiled.

"But if you report such infamy in the Castle it will be your word against mine, and is San likely to believe the word of a junkie?"

I looked away. "Don't use that expression. San believes the reports I bring in every single day."

"They're facts, whereas your tale cannot be proven. Aye, most of the Circle knows Jant is a junkie. Think how it would look splashed all over the front page of the *Wrought Standard*. You would be facing Challengers every day for years! I marvel at your ability to keep the knowledge from mortals. Except Carmine; she knows now, sorry."

I risked a glance at the harridan, who leaned by the window with a mordacious smirk on her face. As an efficient harbor-master she would be well aware of the trafficking that goes on in the Moren docks and I felt a twist of guilt even though I don't do that kind of thing anymore. I tried to reassure myself but Ata knew she had hit a nerve. In fact, all my nerves were beginning to jangle.

"You want your drug now, don't you?" she inquired, guile-lessly.

"No. I'm fine." This will get you nowhere, Ata. I tapped my foot on the floor in a pointless attempt to alleviate the mounting tension. I felt as if all my muscles were starting to compress like springs.

"Go stick a needle in yourself. I can tell you want to. What's that jolt like?"

It's the answer to everything, Ata. The Shift, it's where the Insects are coming from. But of course I didn't tell her that. "Why are you doing this to me?" I asked plaintively.

Ata glanced meaningfully at Carmine, and changed language to Awian. "Because it's the first reason why you will tell no one your strange idea that I caused Mist's death."

"The second reason?"

"Genya Dara."

"What do you know about Genya Dara?"

"I know what you did to her. Rape."

I folded arms, wings, legs tightly and perched on the chair staring at my jiggling foot. Fuck it, fuck it. I was so stupid! How could I have been so possessed? I didn't understand why the mountain girl should turn up now. She had nothing to do with this. Desolate, I said, "I'm not like my father. I'm not. I do love her."

Ata's eyes narrowed in interest.

"It wasn't rape. Rhydanne sex might seem like rape to a flat-lander. It was only a short pursuit; we're both to blame for the affair. In the Scree culture things are very different," I added.

"That won't matter, if Awia learns of it. For all I know, in the mountains you bizarre Rhydanne might chase down girls like deer every day. But people here will not be as understanding. I might just tell Lightning, you know how he puts women on a pedestal. And I will tell your jealous wife; imagine how she would react. With the gates of Micawater and Wrought closed to you—at least for the next couple of hundred years—your life will be more than miserable. Jant, if you slur my name and try to bar me from the Circle I'll bring you down too. In this situation the Emperor would make examples of us both."

"How did you find out about . . . Genya?"

"I just asked her. Men can be so blind. If we get through this you should find her and treat her well as she deserves; see if she doesn't come to you as promptly as a trained hawk."

"Yes, Ata."

"Isn't it strange that Rhydanne will soon be the only people left, even though they have never joined the fight against the Insects? Your kind will discover Insects scaling the Darkling massif only when the last Awian is extinct and the last human in Hacilith is bitten in two."

"Yes, Ata," I said, knowing no one could make Rhydanne

cooperate long enough to fight. It was all too clear I had to take
the only path left open, and become her accomplice.

Ata extended her calloused hand and we both promised to
keep silent. I would have to live beside this lady forever, and I
worried about how long our mutual secrets might last.

"I will be Mist Ata Dei. Immortal again, for good." She stood
up briskly. I sneezed three times in close succession. The tendons
were burning in the backs of my hands.

"Let's end our discussion," she said, returning to Morenzian
vernacular. "It's late, and I perceive you're unwell."

"There's nothing wrong with me."

"Jant, you're smoother when you're lying than when
you're straight! Listen, I have eighty carracks, and eleven
thousand men. You were on the deck of the *Honeybuzzard*
when Shearwater ran my ambush, so you saw what I saw. He
made a castle of his ship. He barricaded the railings and
blocked my arrows. Shame, but I learned from that—how
ships carrying soldiers can be as sound as a fortress afloat. Ah,
look at you! What's the use in talking?"

I wiped my watering eyes with a sleeve. I was having trouble
concentrating; *I need a shot* kept drifting into my mind. I leaned
and rubbed my thighs and shins, trying to stop them aching, but
tension made them stone-hard.

"What about Swallow?" Swallow had ten well-guarded caravels, and her fyrd could sail them. Swallow also had charge of
Cyan. It was essential to know what Ata thought.

"The savante's music is breathtaking. What else?" I could
tell from her hooded tone that if she had any plans concerning
Swallow I would certainly not hear them.

"She's proved herself in battle . . . I think . . . and she will still
try for a place in the Circle; I know she won't ever give up."

"Jant, you're inexperienced. I'll be free of the Zascai in less
than sixty years. She's a genius in music only—"

"The Circle is *based* on merit!" What am I, god's sake, but a specialist?

"Supposed to be," Ata said wryly. "Lightning, the eternal bachelor, will realize one day that what he pursues in all these wild young redhead girls is something he should find in himself. He tries to marry freedom rather than learn it. He should realize he doesn't need their carefree cheer to replace what he's long forgotten, and has to rediscover."

"And Awia?"

"Flags and boundaries mean nothing to me; if we live I'll help the decadent kingdom. But perhaps we'll set the balance right in favor of Morenzia for once." Carmine Dei began to smile.

"Now, Jant, I can tell you're worse now than you were when we started, all curled up like that, so let me give you a bed and see you in the morning." An unintentional lightening of her tone crept in, reminding me again of her hundred children. I was desperately tired and longing, longing to lie down, but I refused her offer. I knew better than to give her the chance to cut my throat. I demanded to stay in the tower room, close to the window, and alone.

From behind her desk, Ata scrutinized me, intrigued, although her manner still appeared kindly; then she called her daughter and they left. The sound of the waves slipped back. Soon I thought it would wear my nerves away.

I lay by the window, on the floorboards like *Honeybuzzard*'s deck, and wrapped myself in the soldier's coat. I began trembling violently, which was nothing to do with the cold. I lay awake all night, sore-eyed with visions of the needle, Insects and ice.

CHAPTER TWENTY-TWO

I relived my first meeting with the girl from the roof of the world. In winter, Scree pueblo nestled roof-deep into the snow, tiny firelit windows by the edge of a sheer gorge. I found the pass and sailed rapidly above the arête, down over a sharp rock buttress. The mountains sped by too fast for breathing. I flew below the level of the peaks, vast black splinters cutting a clear sprinkled sky. I navigated by Polaris and the scent of peat smoke, and I came home to Darkling, to stay in the Filigree Spider for a few days of rest.

A harsh, intensely cold wind blew down from the high peaks, Mhadaidh and Bhachnadich, straight off the glaciers. It dried the skin tight to the bones of my face. I rode that wind in, ice forming on my wings' leading edges. I landed in powdery snow, knee-deep on the pueblo's low roof, slid off in a minor avalanche and hammered on the door of the Spider.

Lascanne opened the top half, and grinned. "You're late."

"I'm *never* late."

"Oh . . . We've already started."

"Free drinks?" I could smell warm whiskey.

"In your honor, Jant."

God, it was good to be back.

There were about twenty people in the little pub, flickered by firelight, quite drunk on gut-wrenching spirits, eating rye bread and smoked goat. Tern bought the Spider as my wedding present because I always used to say I was born in the bar in Scree; the only place where Rhydanne cooperate.

Unlike a human or Awian pub, there is very little conversation, and no music; Rhydanne society is a contradiction in terms. They are not gregarious creatures, each is used to a solitary, independent existence, and so even in the bar they were aloof, keeping distance from each other, and concentrating on drinking. I occasionally told stories, five-minute-long fables—as five minutes heavily stretches a Rhydanne attention span.

The second day was a solid and relentless blizzard, and few people visited. I must have taken too much cat because I stayed awake all night, buzzing with vitality. I checked the Spider's accounts, finding them very out of date. Hollow-cheeked Lascanne couldn't write; he kept all the numbers in his head. Nobody could fault him, he had the best memory for who owed a goat for their jug of whiskey.

Lascanne was tall and stick-thin, with hair cut very short and spiked. The bones of his skull could be seen through it, knobbly and asymmetrical. His long fingers moved in self-deprecating gestures. Lascanne was scared rigid of me.

In the early hours of the morning he was still serving the Spider's patrons, in a lazy, relaxed atmosphere, safe from the snow. A peat fire had burned down to sheaves of white ash, creeping orange sparks. The kilim-covered floor was warm, the room pine-scented.

Gradually I found my attention drawn to a figure sitting at a table, on a rough wood bench by the door. It was strange because people usually tried to sit close to the hearth. Female, although it was difficult to tell. She had her back to me and was drinking vodka steadily, making a pyramid of the pottery cups after downing each shot. I counted thirteen of them. Her very fine black hair brushed off her shoulders and hung to her waist. Her face was away from me and as I watched no one acknowledged her presence. They left her well alone.

Like me she had pale skin, Rhydanne eyes with vertical oval pupils that cut out snow-glare. A very rapid flicker-fusion speed in our vision gives us faster reactions—which a flatlander would call overreactions. Her arms and legs were collections of long muscles, sinewy and toned. Wearing? A black vest, loose and discolored by a thousand stonewashings, pushed out by her tiny pointed tits—I strained to see—and a short skirt, no, a very short skirt, from the same valuable black cotton traded up from Awia. She had leather pumps with string grips, and that was all. As I stared quite openly taking all this in, she kept drowning herself in the house's best vodka.

"Lascanne," I called. "Come over here a minute." He strode across, wiping a horn tumbler.

I pointed at the skinny girl. "Who is that?" He shrugged and turned away but I leaned over the bar and grabbed his elbow.

"Oh . . . just some bitch," he said.

"The name of the bitch?" I prompted.

"Jant, keep away from her. She's not all . . . Well, she's a bit strange." He smiled nervously, with thin lips.

"You're bloody weird yourself, Lascanne, and I do not need

your advice. If you don't tell me I'm going to get angry. Three ... Two ..."

"Genya Dara!"

I released him and he rubbed his bony elbow. "She's a Dara ..." he asserted. "She's Labhra's daughter, so ... my half sister."

"I didn't know Labhra had a daughter!"

"He didn't want you to know, Jant."

Curiosity momentarily stole my attention from the narrow-shouldered girl. "What happened to Labhra in the end?" I queried.

Lascanne shrugged, a gesture he was built for. "Oh ... his wife killed him," he said.

I helped myself to a quaich of whiskey, sinking back onto the bar stool. I felt like I walked on a feather's edge. When fate throws something as delicious as this my way I find it hard to believe I have not strayed into someone else's life. The bar seemed slightly unreal and I was shivering with delight. Lascanne saw the decision set hard in my eyes after a few moments' thought. "Oh, no, you don't," he said softly, with the lilting Darkling accent I so often miss.

"Why haven't I seen her before?"

"Jant, I— Oh. All right. She doesn't come down much ... She only visits in when the weather's too harsh up on the peaks; the rest of the time she's out on Chir or Greaderich."

"Is she, indeed? And what does she do there?" The thin ice of Lascanne's patience cracked and he told me perhaps I should ask her myself. "She's a lone wolf bitch, that's all I know," he said bitterly. He could tell how much I wanted her, I was charged with need. I had thought I would never have another chance since Dellin rejected me. And here she was, my other chance. My last chance. I had to have her.

"She's taller than Dellin," I murmured, thinking aloud. The barman caught the comment, and smiled.

"Yes," he said. "I know what happened back then."

"Mortals can't remember that!"

"Jant, your thorough failure with Shira Dellin is legendary up here."

That was a hundred years ago. This is here and now. "What sort of man does this one like?" I asked, leveling a finger at Genya Dara's scrawny shape.

The bitterness in Lascanne's voice took on a strain of self-pity. "I don't know," he admitted. "She won't let me near her."

Over the next day and night, I put in some hard work. All my efforts were in vain; Genya refused to notice me. Eventually I couldn't decide whether Genya's world was too untranslatable even for me, whether she was just obstinate, engaged, or simply bloody stupid. Two things were clear: she was as beautiful as she was intractable and she was a very dedicated alcoholic.

When in a drug haze I called her Dellin by mistake she simply smiled, showing teeth white as snow. I bought her whiskey and she drank it (as fast as I could bring it) but she never thanked me. I ran through my repertoire to no avail—which only made my desire for her worse. She declined to dance. Cards? She didn't know how to play. Stories of other lands? She was less than interested. Would Genya like me to accompany her home? This caused a flurry of icy laughter, which set in little drifts around my feet.

The Rhydanne girl had a mannish face, although still with high cheekbones and a graceful jaw. She always wore the same clothes, thin vest or a polonaise. She was too leggy, starved and muscular to resemble petite Dellin, but my anger at Dellin, preserved over the years, was now directed at her.

When I lay awake and the rest of the house was sleeping, I thought of her. I was eaten alive by thoughts of her, which I tried to salve with scolopendium. But desire pooled in me like melt water. So much desire. I had to have her. A gram of cantharides would have done the trick in an Awian court, but nothing's aphrodisiac above the snowline.

I wanted to fuck her. What a chase she would give me! I would catch her. Bring her down among the ice formations.

Or I would screw her in a warm bed while snow plumes fell past the window. I wanted her to ride me, muscles appearing and disappearing in those long legs. I was erect again. I was so hard I felt my heart beat blunt in my groin. Genya made me like this. It's what she has to answer for. Lying on the pallet, I cup and caress my balls with one hand, rub my hard cock. My cock is narrow but average long, the tip is smooth. These painted nails are hers. The fist around my cock is hers, tightening on the upstroke. Her body is stretched out underneath me. Little tits, chalky with cold. Cat-eyes, shining with pleasure. When I come, I spurt into her mouth. I sigh. It's just lust, Shira. It's never been "love them and leave them" so much as "fuck them and flee."

On the last night I was at my wits' end. I was expected at the Castle next day and was preparing for a long and uncomfortable flight. My habit was serious, I had run out of money and had no success at all with Genya Dara.

"You've failed, Comet," said Lascanne happily.

"Not yet, struidhear. Not yet, damn it."

"Ha! Try again in a hundred years' time. What do you want the sullen bitch for, anyway?"

Because she's a piece of the mountains, a potential memory. Because she's Rhydanne, quick and feral. Because she looks just like me, Lascanne; she's our kind. I'm a rape child, so is Lascanne Shira; I pity his mother when Labhra pounced on her.

The mountain people considered illegitimacy to be a curse—a curse you can pass on.

I hogged the bar, feeling faint, my movements blurred, and forgot about Genya until she pushed past. She usually avoided contact but wanted to know why the drinks had dried up. She had come in from outside, where people go round the back of the pub to piss in the snow, and her skin was cold although she looked flushed and panicky. I saw her brush her hand down the front of her skirt. "Let me do that?" I suggested. Silence. "Sweet vixen," I said, "I'll probably never see you again."

Dara came close for me to grasp her round the waist, thin enough to encircle with one arm. She didn't pull away.

"I want you," I told her, in all honesty.

"Then chase me!" she said, and ran.

She sprang over a bench, over a pile of skis, and was out of the door before my next breath. Lascanne whined behind me. He looked like he was going to vault the bar and follow her. I slipped off my sword belt, threw it at him. "Stay!" I ordered. And I was gone. Running.

Freezing night air burned my lungs. I sipped at the air, spit gathering in the back of my throat. The road was snow; Genya's footprints led up a little rise. I followed, long-legged. I trod in her footprints, shallow with speed. Genya was nowhere. She had completely vanished. God, she's fast. Without the weight of wings to carry, she was my equal. I hoped she would tire easily.

I ran up the rise and onto a narrow plateau above Scree. She kept close to the cornice. I swept doubt from my mind and concentrated on running. Fast. One foot in front of the other, for hours. My heart thundering on cat and whiskey. Genya slipping always ahead of me like a black ghost. Watch my own thin legs. Desire is a splinter of ice in my mind. Shadows spindly on snow, the frost-twisted trees. She led me between them and I thought she would stop there. She had no intention of surrendering. She was leading to a better place. I wanted to bite her, fast and hard.

We went up a stone chute between sharp rock pillars. Quartz is rock snow, granite froth. We ran on, flight in her mind, fucking in mine. We ran up to the edge of the Klannich glacier, a rearing white wall. Ice crackled as she high-stepped through a frozen stream.

My cock was so hard I could hardly run. I could see her, in the distance, starting the climb of a massive crag. I closed the distance as she gained altitude. At the foot of the cliff, I looked up and she was way above me. I put a hand to the frost-shattered rock. Cold. Detailed in gray. See—this is not a dream. I'm going to fuck that bitch, I thought, as I paused for breath and bent over, coughing and spitting.

Genya had made a mistake. We had run the length of the corrie, into the heart of the mountains. She outpaced me, but she had led to a sheer escarpment, where the hanging valley ended. It stretched up onto a knife-sharp ridge. She climbed with a quick, sure grace, stabbing the hard, pointed nails on her long fingers into every crack. But she didn't have wings and so she had to take care. Falling is nothing to me. I took little heed and climbed faster still. Meagre handholds offered themselves. I flowed my weight each to each and climbed. Fast. I overtook her halfway up that wall of rock, reached the ledge first and gave her a hand over the top.

Wide clear sky. Vertigo view—peaks linked by ridges marching out for kilometers. The mountains were stark, ice-spattered. Their slopes were fir-lined and patched with black shadows.

I clasped her wrist hard enough to bruise and dragged her over the edge. In that vast empty sky I touched her.

She cut at me with her free hand. I twisted her arm behind her back and made her kneel. I would have taken her like that, on her knees, grabbing her flat tits. She kicked me. I didn't slap her; I wrestled her onto her back. She smelled of stone, she was shivering.

That isn't right. She shouldn't be shivering. It isn't cold enough yet. I put my weight on top of her, forearms on her shoulders, forced her to lie supine. She squirmed. I struggled with a cold button and shoved my buckskin trousers down. My cock was so hard it ached. I rubbed a hand over it, in the chill air. Lying between her legs I was already flicking my hips against her. I felt my feathers rustle. My tongue was dry from gulping the cold air but I licked at her neck, holding one hand entwined in dark hair to stop her biting me. So I could look into her eyes. I was desperate for orgasm. I ripped her thin panties, she seized my arm and licked it.

"Is this good?" I said.

"Deyn."

"What do you mean, you don't know?"

She was quite dry. Strange, I thought, and then I realized why. I realized why she was shivering. It wasn't with cold, was with fear. She hadn't done it before. Suddenly disgusted, I sat back on my haunches, hard-muscled belly and prick stuck up in front, larger than ever before. She focused on it, awed.

I rubbed her with the tip of my thumb, and slowly eased two fingers in together, feeling the membrane tear stickily. Her strong struggling gave way to whimpers. She became slick with blood. I wiped a red fingertip over her pale mouth. She spat.

I could feel her heat. I was dizzy with it. Stark with impatience I held my cock and tried to ease in. Bony bitch. I wriggled my hips. Just inside her. Soft, warm. In a hard cold world. One hard thrust and I was as deep in as I could reach. A gasp of pleasure from me, a scream from her. Lust overcame my annoyance and I started fucking her as hard as I could.

I was propped up on stiff arms, looking down onto her sharp-featured face, using her body to rub my cock. I was shoving her body backward on the rocky ground. She was very tight and very hot, lubricated by blood. Her nipples were small and pointed, dragging faded cloth like a ridge between them. She felt better than I had ever imagined. I was elated, had a cat-eyed girl at last. Sex is scrambled with flatlanders.

I spread my wings, to angle my hips better, but Genya wouldn't run her fingers between the feathers tented over her. She put one hand on my arse, to pull me in farther.

I threw my fuck into her, scooping with my hips. I felt a point of heat at the base of my cock. I gasped. She tried to throw me off. That made me more excited. I meant to pull out, but she was too delicious. I emptied myself into her. Fast, and the next few thrusts were slick and squeezed. Her body went limp.

Possession slackened its hold on me. I pulled out and stood up, already guilty. My muscles were aching from the exertion of the chase. I shoved my damp prick back into leggings and buttoned my trousers.

Gradually Genya stood up, pallid, and contemplated the cliff edge.

"You're leaving now, aren't you?" she said.

"Yes."

That's Rhydanne sex.

Genya watched me lift my wingtips from the ground, a look of utter dismay on her face. There was a smear of my come and her blood on her thigh.

I found my bearings; we were on the slope of Stravaig. Mhor Darkling's triple peak was just visible behind its white summit, a sight I had not seen for a hundred years. I lost interest in Dara, remembering my long-lost life in Darkling valley.

Genya set off at a sprint along the ridge—the spur formed a

track leading to Basteir sheiling. She hit a snow patch and slithered dangerously, regained her balance and increased her speed until she was almost flying, running above nothingness. I took a slow glide back to Scree.

Now, in August Tower, as the sickness came on, I spent all night dwelling on my deficiencies. And on Genya.

CHAPTER TWENTY-THREE

Ata returned an hour before dawn, in a heavy woolen shawl. She was wearing her husband's 1851 Sword, that he had so greatly prized. The lacquer scabbard described an arc at her side; rayskin-covered ivory and black silk accents on the hilt. The blade was forged from a charcoal-hardened steel sheet folded one thousand and one times; its weighting was immaculate. Wrought steel is the finest produced anywhere. The sword had never been used; as keen as the day it was honed, it could bisect an Insect without slowing. I lusted after it. It would perfect every fighting move I knew; just wearing it would bring respect and brawlers would steer clear. It was the apex of Awian craft, made for their Great Exhibition, and then presented by the King to Peregrine manor, where it remained in pride of place. Mist kept the 1851 Sword in a glass cabinet. Ata had smashed the cabinet and buckled the sword at her waist.

Ata began to take measurements on a map of Lowespass

Fortress Crag. Out of the window I could see the tapering mainland, which looked as if it was hanging in the air; the sky and the
sea were the same pale blue and I could not distinguish between
them. The wind had dropped, now blowing from the land out
to sea. Where there had been foam-capped breakers, the water
rippled silver like a tray of mercury. I watched the mainland,
waiting for the sun to rise.

Instead, a star appeared on the mainland, shining at the water's
edge. I could see the star's reflection in the sea; it was a pallid, flickering yellow point of light. I squinted at it but couldn't figure out
what it was, and the concentration made my headache worse.

"Mortal," I called, "come and look at this."

"Ah, it does speak," Ata countered. "Thought it just
slumped there and shivered." She gathered her thick shawl and
joined me at the window. I pointed out the bright, unsteady
light. "Do you know what that is?"

"Of course. It's the Awndyn lighthouse."

"We can see that far?" Awndyn was thirty kilometers'
straight flight away. The storm had washed the air clear.

"Aye. It's at the end of the harbor wall. Strange Swallow
should light it by day, eccentric lass."

"It's not strange. It's a signal! Lightning, you're a genius!"

"That's as may be, but it's not a good sign—it's a steady light.
I think they're in trouble; we have to go *now*. Jant, can you
fight?"

"Fight? I can't even stand up!"

Ata ran to the stairs and called down, "Carmine, what's
ready?"

The hatchet-faced hoyden appeared in the doorway.
"Everything. The twenty Great Ships are packed with Hacilith
fyrd. Horses and wagons are on the *Ortolan*; the third-raters and
pinnaces are to carry supplies. The *Tragopan*'s still loading, but
we can't all leave the harbor on the same tide anyway."

"Then we will take the *Stormy Petrel*."

Carmine bowed her head.

"You take charge of the *Tragopan*, my dear, and the other seventy-eight to follow. Meet us at six tonight ten degrees north of Sheldrake Point."

Carmine nodded and ducked back down the stairs.

Ata pressed my sword into my grasp. "Jant, you can do better than this!"

I scrambled to my feet. "Have you got any cat?"

"Cat? You mean scolopendium? No, and I doubt there's any available anywhere in the world now."

"I only have a couple of hours left, I don't want to go—"

She beckoned, sternly, and I followed her down the stone spiral staircase, out onto the wooden gantry and down to the flat rocks at September Tower harbor. I screwed my eyes up against the sunshine. My pupils were so dilated everything was glaring white or deep black shadow. The ocean was just a huge, painfully bright hole. Ata's white slacks and flaxen hair dazzled in the light.

The cobbled quayside bustled with thousands of men, talking loudly. It was a crush, polearms soldiers and sarissai, bands of crossbowmen with the Red Fist blazon of Hacilith on their buff coats, and at least two divisions of Awian Select longbowmen looking worn out, stressed and unpreened.

Stevedores were loading the *Tragopan* with three weighted hoists. Men were pushing dockside carts on their iron rails, full of barrels, pitch casks, piles of arrow sheaves. Chains of people passed along sharpened staves, sacks of anti-Insect salt, creels of food—they were stowed in the holds until the brightly painted caravel sat low in the water.

The harbor wall hugged all the ships in an angular embrace, concrete shining slick with slime. The ships' masts were so close together they looked tangled, and wires clattered against them as the wind blew through rigging.

Hacilith men caught sight of Ata and me from the deck of the *Stormy Petrel*. They yelled, "Look!" to their comrades, pointing excitedly to the quayside. Ata waved demurely, and they erupted in a cheer. I wondered if any would see their city again.

Ata prodded me across the narrow plank over the gap between September Tower harbor and the *Stormy Petrel*'s deck. I hung onto the railings as a whistle called the crew to attention and Ata ordered the sails set.

The *Stormy Petrel* pulled elegantly away from its mooring. I gazed at the harbor wall sliding past.

"Are you still alert, degenerate Rhydanne?"

"I need—"

"Don't say it! Don't talk about drugs—I don't like it!"

"Neither do I."

"Thousands of people are dying in Awia, and we are going to stop that happening."

The *Stormy Petrel* scudded swiftly across the thirty-kilometer-wide strait to Awndyn strand. The square burgundy mainsails bellied out like clouds. Slipstream poured off the lateen rig behind; it ruffled my feathers, making me gag. The sea has definite advantages. You can puke in it if you are very ill, which I was. I retched over the side, for hours until only bile came up; it tasted like Insect blood.

At the wheel, Ata muttered to her ship all the time, "Faster, you bastard." The Crystal Palace blade in its black scabbard hung loose at her thigh.

Awndyn harbor looked deserted. Streams of pale gray smoke rose from the lighthouse, the only movement. But along the seven-kilometer sweep of sand tiny figures milled and churned.

About five hundred soldiers in Awndyn green were fighting in a tightening ring of Insects.

Insects appeared from the town's facade. They darted along the harbor wall and down sea-wrack stone steps, up from the shallow river bed. Insects the size of ponies ran over the grassy machair, jumping onto the sand. They picked their way between the headstones of Awndyn Cemetery, plunged down among the yellow dunes.

Farther back, Insects were nibbling spilled blood on the marram grass. They followed the scent trail down to the beach. I could just make out patches of sand stuck to their gore-spattered chitin.

Some reared on saw-edged back legs, feelers flickering as they closed in. The Awndyn men were being pushed together, losing ground. They retreated toward the sea. The gap between them and the Insects was narrowing all the time.

Adrenaline roused me. "There's a division's worth of men!" I called.

"I hoped for many more," said Ata.

"I can see the Archer!"

It was impossible to miss Lightning. His gold scale armor glittered in the early sun. Bareheaded, and with bindings unwrapping from his greaves, he was waving the soldiers round into a circle, and pushing someone back behind him with the other hand.

Swallow. It was Swallow Awndyn, propped on her spear, and she had Cyan under her arm.

Harrier was shoulder to shoulder with Lightning; he faltered back on the wet sand then flexed his bow again.

Long dawn light cast their footprints as jumbled blue shadows on the yellow sand. The air was very clear, faint shouts carried to us; Lightning trying to keep their formation but men kept breaking away, chancing a run to the sea.

Ata steered starboard, as close in as she could, and *Stormy Petrel* careened parallel to Awndyn strand, almost at right angles to the wind, and lost speed until we stopped opposite the mass of Insects and struggling men.

"This crate is so unresponsive," said Ata. "If I go any nearer, leeway will beach the bastard."

The Insects closed in. Lightning shot straight into them. He was loosing arrows the fastest I had ever seen. The quiver on his right hip was empty, and he was pulling arrows from the quiver on his back. Insects ran straight at him; he shot them down. He kept a distance of thirty meters, twenty meters, ten meters.

I could hear Cyan crying.

"We only have a minute!" I said.

Ata strode onto the lower deck. "We'll have to pick them up."

She shouted the length of the deck, and I heard the thick anchor chain rattle out from the bow. The *Stormy Petrel* drifted completely round before the anchor caught, and the stern anchor was released. Ata's crew began to lower boats in rope cradles, three from each side, into the water.

The boats splashed down simultaneously. Six sailors to each descended neat cord-and-lath ladders and unshipped the oars.

Ata turned to me. "Messenger, wait here." She caught a ladder and lowered herself over the side.

The *Stormy Petrel*'s massive flanks dwarfed the six landing craft. I watched them buck and toss over the waves, oars like Insect legs leaving white tracks in the water.

Most of the Awndyn fyrd were already waist-deep in the sea. Around fifty archers were standing in the waves, bows held above their heads, swords drawn in their free hands. Insects followed them into the surf, holding their abdomens high and gnashing mandibles.

Ata stood in the prow of her boat impassively, while it dipped and heeled, and the oarsmen struggled. The six boats approached the cluster of archers—and nearly capsized as men grabbed the sides and tipped the boats in their haste to get aboard.

Grasping and spluttering, they ignored Ata's cries for order. They surged forward, up to the neck, throwing bows away. The oarsmen reached down, heaved them, belts, wings and armpits, and hoisted them over the gunwales.

As the boats neared shore, they reached men still in their depth, and boathooked them aboard, arses in the air. Laden boat hulls grated against the sand.

Lightning said something to Swallow, who kicked off her leg-armor and plunged in, wisely making for a boat which didn't have Ata in it. Harrier carried Cyan. Lightning removed the silk string from his great bow, held it up and stepped into the surf, the last Awndyn men behind him.

The six boats were so crammed with soldiers—about seventy in each—everyone was standing. The rowers held their oars up out of the locks, Ghallain-style. They fought to turn their boats prow-on against the waves, and began to paddle back toward me.

The coast was left to the Insects.

The landing crafts' return journey took ages. I watched Insects pick over bodies on the sand. An Insect buried its head under a corpse and flicked it over. Two of them took an arm each, and, walking backward, tore a man apart.

I was shaking.

Lightning might give me my syringe back. A soldier might have some medicine—I mean cat—to arrest my decline. I told myself, Jant, don't be so fucking ridiculous. I stopped trying to control the shivering, relaxed, and it took over completely.

I helped Swallow as she appeared from the top of the rope ladder, panting, onto the deck. She had a leaf-green mantle around her throat, and a rondel dagger stuck down her bodice lacings.

I embraced her. "What happened to Awndyn manor?" I asked.

"Awndyn manor!" She burst into tears. "It's *swarming*! God's molt! The Insects have taken the whole Empire, and we'll have to stay at sea forever to escape them!"

"Rachis, Hacilith and the Plainslands are still holding out," I said. "Have courage." With an arm round her, I tried to console her by explaining the Emperor's message, while soldier after soldier climbed the ladder and emerged, dripping, onto the deck.

Lightning was leaning over the prow, picking off Insects on the beach that were beyond any other archer's range. He didn't stop shooting until Ata ordered full sail, and the infested shore shrank out of view.

He turned. "Bring us closer," he commanded.

Ata was banging the compass housing with her fist and swearing. She spared him a glance. "Save your arrows."

"If I can't reach Micawater, I'll die there on the beach!"

"Oh, shut up. You'll have your chance when we get to Lowespass."

"Lowespass? Ata—"

"I want to be Mist Ata. Eighty ships are awaiting a rendezvous at nightfall, full of warriors eager to improve their ranks with the addition of Tornado, the Castle's champion."

Lightning gestured at the rabble behind him. "These are the thirteenth division of the Awndyn fyrd. They're all Select infantry, though there's nothing Select about them now. Do you have the Micawater archers I sent you? Enough to cover the Hacilith men? Their crossbows have no range at all."

"Yes, and I have ten thousand soldiers gathered from Morenzia, counted with those from the island and the coast, who thought wrongly that my island would be the best place to seek sanctuary."

"I see . . ."

"Lightning Saker, you owe me."

He looked at her with undisguised loathing, then mastered it and described a formal bow. "Yes," he said grimly, "I do."

Cyan did not let go of Swallow; cold and terrified, the girl clutched to Swallow's good leg and did not say a word. Swallow hunkered down next to me, wiping tears from her eyes and drips from her nose onto her wet auburn wings. She stroked the back of my hand. I forced a smile and squeezed her arm.

"What's wrong with you?" she asked. She was used to me looking gaunt, but not this defeated.

"He's sick," said Ata. "Will all you armor-clad bastards bugger off away from this compass?"

"Has he been bitten?"

"Not by anything you know about, my lady."

I turned my head away. If I wasn't so fucking weak I could have gone to score. The Circle had not broken again, so the rest of the Eszai must still be alive, with the Swordsman holding Hacilith. I thought of the city's Rowel Alley, Needle Park, East Bank Docks, all the pure quality cat the knife-packing youths sell and cut-down cat in foil wraps the matelots deal between themselves. Zascai low voices, silhouettes at street corners, or a pickable lock on a field hospital coffer full of medical-grade phials. *Anything* to ease the pain.

"Cat-scratched," Ata said.

The Archer looked back to the land.

Ata stared at me as if I was beneath contempt—just above

derision, on about the same level as scorn. She continued to herself, "I thought death was the worst evil, because if it were good
then Eszai would be content to die. Didn't consider that some of
them had chosen a living death."

That was too much for my pride. What did she know? I
tried to stand and only managed to kneel. I heaved a breath,
struggled in a suffocating ocean. Tried to stay afloat.

Ata said, "The Messenger's gone to pieces, Lightning. Hope
you can keep your edge."

Slid into the depths.

I lay on a bunk, shivered and convulsed. My long fingers
brushed the floorboards with each twitch. Swallow did not
find me an easy patient; she put up with being screamed at in ten
languages:

"I can't go through this shit! There isn't enough time!"

"Hush, Jant."

"We only have three weeks!"

"You're delirious . . . He was close to Mist, wasn't he?"

"Yes."—Lightning's voice—"And it was another bad shock
for him to discover that Eszai *do* die."

"Well, I can't understand a word he's saying."

I woke up at a lull point; the cabin was dark. I gripped my
hands between my knees, lay with one wing half-spread,
rigid with stress, shaking with accelerated heartbeat.

I felt the ocean boiling like tar, its surface paved with thousands of faces. A line of blue-gray elephants on cranefly legs
whickered across the pillow. I plucked one from its perspective
tightrope, and it stalked like an insect in my palm.

"Can't believe the sun will rise again," said a voice.

I squirmed round to see, feeling the crustiness where they had mopped vomit away from my mouth. An Awian soldier I didn't recognize sat cross-legged on the floor, his face hollowed by shadows. Harrier, in his long, dark blue waxed coat, stood staring out of the porthole like a sleepwalker.

The soldier was spiral-binding goose feather fletchings to arrow shafts. His splitter-arrows had bodkin-sharp points designed to penetrate Insect shell, and heavy barbs along the length of the shaft to crack the shell open.

The cabin planks creaked. A lantern hanging on a chain from the low ceiling swung with its pattern of shadows. Its light merged with a horrible hallucinatory red glow radiating through the port.

Harrier said, "When god reappears from its break it's going to have a shock." Grisly humor twisted his voice.

"If it comes back tomorrow it just might save us."

"Perhaps it will. Perhaps it will. They say it cares for the Fourlands, holidays notwithstanding. Maybe this is the Return the immortals are waiting for."

"God's supposed to bring ultimate peace and prosperity. Doesn't seem very bloody peaceful to me."

They wished for god's arrival, so they didn't trust in the Castle. I crushed handfuls of the blanket in agony and rage. For millennia the Castle held Insects at bay, kept a stalemate to make the Circle indispensable. Now the balance was tipped, Insects were everywhere, and it was all my fault.

"I doubt even the Emperor knows what to do. Maybe he will leave us."

"Fuck sake, Bateleur! You heard Captain Dei and my lord say that the Circle is strong."

The soldier glanced at me. I feigned coma, which was easy. He looked to Harrier as if to say if that's the strength of the Eszai, we're doomed.

"Did Lightning offer any other revelations?"

Harrier bit his lip. "Have some respect."

"Oh, I'm brimming with respect. Lightning was there at the beginning of the world—"

"Of the Circle."

"Right. Of the Circle. So he might have some idea how it will end."

Harrier began sliding the completed arrows into the spacer holes of his leather quiver. "I'm not my lord's confidant," he said. "I don't hear them discussing the Castle's mysteries. Insects have never caused such devastation south of Lowespass in the Circle's time—Cariama Eske said that they're reaching her manor. If the immortals can't stop Insects in Eske and Shivel, the Castle itself is threatened."

"Will San call the Eszai back?"

"The Emperor San is *not* like Staniel Rachiswater! Damn!" Genuinely upset, Harrier pinched the bridge of his nose and shook his head.

The fletcher named Bateleur continued, "The Emperor founded the Circle, though, and shared the immortality god gave him because Insects defeated his mortal legions. If the Circle is overcome, I wonder what he'll set up next?"

"Daydream all you like."

"Ask Lightning."

"I may not ask my lord anything!"

I pulled myself up against the wall. "Ask me," I said.

"Oh—by god! I'm sorry!"

Bateleur's eyes were like saucers; the soldier was petrified. Weakly, I said, "I have driven myself into the ground for the Empire, and to save your lives, and all you do is speculate. I am sick with exhaustion, and all I hear is blasphemy."

"I'm sorry!"

"The Emperor is in the Castle, and all will be well. San tells us no one knows when god will return, but I can assure you this is no way to prepare."

"We didn't mean anything by it, Messenger!"

I gave him a challenging look. "Will I see you in the ranks of bowmen?"

"Of course!"

"Good. Then pour me some water and get out of here!"

The room stank sharply of vomit. I was fully dressed, my black shirt stained, open to my hairless chest, jeans and bare feet. I doubled my wings up onto the bunk, bones grating, wiped beads of sweat off the Wheel scarification on my shoulder.

Lurid shades dappled Harrier's face and coat; they looked like bruises, but as he stirred the bruises did not move. They were only shadows cast by the sickly red light, through water drops on the porthole glass.

My body shuddered. Pain wrenched; I groaned. Every muscle ached. Was the next wave coming on already? I needed some respite!

Harrier said, "Lightning did entrust me with the real cause of your condition."

"Cold turkey."

"Well, rest assured I will keep the secret."

I told him, "You've seen inside the Circle. I'm nearly well now."

"Yes, you're making sense for a change."

I raised a shaky toast to him with a horn cup of water, sipped it carefully, feeling my innards deciding whether to accept it or not. I was pouring with sweat, my hair plastered to my back. I disentangled it from my earrings.

"Did we make the rendezvous with the fleet?"

"Yes. Four days ago. Comet, I apologize on the fletcher's behalf, but you should know there's a lot of real dissent among the Awian soldiers. They know that Eleonora Tanager is our

Queen now, and they want to join forces with her." Harrier smiled; I could tell he supported Eleonora too.

"Has no one cried treason?"

"Eleonora is not a usurper. They call her the Emperor's friend . . . I don't know about Staniel. Communications are flashing back and forth between the ships that I can't understand. Ata told us: 'Wait, and you can send Tornado the Circle's Champion to Rachiswater, and four thousand Lowespass warriors.' That made them think."

"I bet. What *is* that red light?" Harrier hesitated, peered through the porthole again and lost his chance to answer when Ata came in through the low cabin door.

"Ah, the physical freak's recovered," she said. She passed me a wooden bowl full of soggy pasta. I started guzzling handfuls— I was ravenous.

"If San ever decided to make an Eszai best in the world at being feverish and puking all over the place, it would be you. Lying in a pool of your own vomit . . ."

Well, it's better than lying in a pool of someone else's. An amazing feeling of accomplishment was dawning on me. I'm kicking it. I really am. I'm really going to be *free*.

"And you rave about some very interesting things, Jant Shira."

"What's the red light?" I said through a mouthful.

"We are sailing along the coast of Wrought."

"Wrought? Oh, no—Insects?"

"I think you should come above and see for yourself."

I ate, washed, and followed her up to the deck, awash with the terrible light. I joined Lightning and Harrier at the stern. The brick-red glow stretched into the sky on the western horizon. It hung in a gigantic arc, one single body of rising air, like a red bubble.

The town of Wrought, Tern's gothic manor house and Sleat's Armorer's Society Hall were out of sight, below the horizon. All I could see was the flat black landmass. I rubbed my dry eyes and just made out two thin black pylons in the center of the glow. The steelworks was burning.

One of the massive coal stores overheated and exploded. We ducked instinctively as a dull rumble like thunder toppled over the marshland.

In an untended steelworks it would only take one spark—or a furnace left burning when workers flee from the Insect assault—and now it was utterly out of control. No building could survive the conditions in that inferno.

Around the mad glow, the sky lit dark blue. Everywhere else was completely black. Blue, red and black, the colors of Wrought.

"What are we going to do, with no armory?" asked Harrier.

"We'll have to rely on Morenzia."

I moaned. No scolopendium to stroke me, I only thought of Tern. Everything she owned was in that manor house. She had to be safe, within the Castle's walls. I didn't want Tern to face this; too much for her to manage, it would change her forever and her voice would lose its softness.

Lightning traced his scar compulsively. "I watched that town being built. I witnessed Awia's achievements over fifteen hundred years. It *cannot* stop now . . . Insects are eating their way to the core of my country and, by god, I will kill every last one of them."

I watched Tern's manor. My responsibility, the town I knew so well.

"The Chatelaine Diamond. Esmerillion's crown . . ."

All the people. All the people's homes.

"The glass sculpture by Jaeger . . ."

I hope our steward has made it safe to Rachiswater.

"Conure's poetry. Wrought katanas . . ." came the voice from the golden age.

At least the children were evacuated.

"Donaise wine. The Pentice Towers. Micawater Bridge . . ."

Ata said, "Saker? Saker! Snap out of it."

Ata took the wheel and adjusted the horizon glass of her sextant; she looked impassive and ethereal. Harrier's long brown hair was tangled, he had sunken eyes. And me, a pale blur. And faces lined the port side of every deck of eighty ships. I never knew eleven thousand men could make so much silence. Nobody spoke. Nobody slept. We all just stood there watching Wrought go up in flames.

CHAPTER TWENTY-FOUR

The fleet sailed in a crescent formation up the coast to Summerday bay. There, the great caravels and little pinnaces entered the mouth of Oriole River.

Immediately, a knot of six pinnaces got stuck on a sandbar. Ata could do nothing to dislodge them; we offloaded the soldiers and supplies, and left the boats.

A clock still running in abandoned Summerday town chimed five in the morning as we passed through the ruins. I saw burned thatched roofs above the town wall, a snapped rooftree shedding stone tiles, an unstable weather vane teetering on flaking charcoal timbers. Crows flapped above derelict shop courtyards.

Half an hour later, another clock chimed five, and bitter laughter rippled over the troops. The Hacilith soldiers wore baggy trousers tucked into half-length boots, daggers on chains looped at their hips, and their hair cropped short. Most looked even younger than me, at fifteen or twenty, although a few among them had grim experience. Their polearms and armor were mass produced, but painted, scrawled with slogans—personalized—so that the city fyrd gave me more to look at than the Awians in all their plumy panoply.

Gray-green estuary water became clearer as we sailed upstream. Through Midelspass the eddying river was broad, the tide was on the flow, and we made good progress.

A team on every caravel dropped lines, taking depth measurements.

"Fifteen meters. Twelve meters. Seven. Five meters."

"A sandbar!" said Ata, and swung the wheel round hard. The keel scraped through the mud. I held my breath. Ata found a deeper channel, and we sailed on.

"The river's not tidal from here, the passage's too narrow. If one ship gets beached none of the ones behind it will be able to sail round. We'll have to leave them, only have half an army, and never escape."

"The wind won't be with us on the way back," Harrier pointed out.

"It blows offshore at night," I said.

"We can drift back downstream," Ata explained. "For god's sake trust me."

Our ships slipped into the Paperlands.

"It's so quiet," said Swallow.

White paper buildings covered the ground, as far as I could see from the river banks up to the tops of the valley sides. Insect tunnel arches, scaly paper passages, the roofs of cells. No green fields were left, no trees. The river bank mud was dark with decomposing matter; its putrescent stench wafted over the ships.

I imagined Insect mating flights twisting up above the Crag. I thought of fat, pupa-pale maggots large as a man but soft-bodied on stubby legs, lying in damp nests glowing with decay, belching silent chemical demands for food. I shuddered; I blame my father for my Awian imagination.

My Rhydanne instinct, on the other hand, was telling me to quit now and go get drunk. "God, this place is totally flyblown."

"It's another world," Swallow whispered, not aware how close to the truth she was.

The bridge loomed.

"The river winds between its legs," said Ata.

"We're going *underneath*?"

"Aye. Soon," she said shortly. It was getting harder for her to steer.

The *Tragopan* misjudged a bend in the river and smacked into the mud.

Ata yelled, "Concentrate, Carmine!"

The caravel ran along the bank and veered off into the center of the river, with mud smeared up to its railings.

An Insect was drinking from the river. Its abdomen pulsed; it stood on the tips of its claws, mandibles opening and closing underwater. A second Insect joined it, glistening light gold brown with darker dorsal stripes. It stretched up; they stroked their antennae together; four front legs rasped against thoraxes. They lowered their heads to drink.

Cyan pointed. "Look! They don't even care we're here!"

"This is their land now," Swallow said.

"I'm not scared," said Cyan. "Imnotscaredimnotscaredimnotscared—"

Swallow spread her wing around the girl.

Oriole River looped round and led under the bridge's white legs. The spindly, impossible construction reared higher than the Crag. It leaped at the sky like a frozen fountain; swept up and vanished cleanly at its height. Its long shadow cast on the Paperlands cut off too.

"It's so vast!"

"Look up!" I said. The bridge's shadow fell over us. Small as nutshells, Ata's great ships threaded beneath it.

Ata shivered. "How do brainless bloody Insects build something like this?"

"They start at the top and work down."

Ata grimaced when she saw I was serious.

Maybe these animals aren't so mindless; Vireo said that they organize themselves, speaking in gestures or scents. Infuriated, I thought: a language I don't know, in a medium I can't even perceive. I felt the weight of two centuries more keenly as I thought no matter how long I study them, the way they communicate with each other and the way they see the world are far too alien for us to understand.

The men pointed, muttered, looked up. They rubbed aching necks and gaped up to see the walkway's underside, a hundred meters above the topmost reach of our masts. The bridge's legs shouldn't be able to take that weight; they're only as thick as the masts. Closer, pale gray laminations showed on the surface. It looked like a wasp's nest, with striated curves, brittle but amazingly strong. The walkway was wider than the Grand Place. It hung from thousands of Insect spit cables, liquid set hard. Some fine strands trailed out on the wind.

I could soar through and around it, fly between the cables, explore the structure in three dimensions, see it fall past me, survey its depth—

"No Insects on the bridge," Lightning said.

Without thinking I said, "There probably aren't any more to come through."

"What?"

"We have to destroy it."

Lightning said, "That's beyond our capability."

"We have to!"

Ata put in: "Jant, shoot some cat and look at this from your usual level of consciousness. While you were being impressively sick, Lightning and I worked out our plan of attack. I rallied the men until I had no brave words left."

"The bridge is key! No matter what we do, if the bridge stays the Insects swarm in!" I demanded, "What will burn? What can we sacrifice?"

Ata gestured to the flotilla behind us. "There are wagons. Barrels of tar we prepared to heat-crack Insect walls."

"Then to work!"

On twenty pinnaces I had men cutting spare sail into strips and packing all the cloth they could find around tar barrels, transferring them to the *Ortolan* and lashing them tight to the wagons with ropes.

I clipped my tertiary feathers shorter, the ones nearest my body; sculpting my wings sharp to maneuver like a falcon. Soaring would be difficult, but it was worth it for the fine control and gain in speed. I buckled my sword to my back, and long cuisses and poleynes to my legs, customized to my shape, the only armor I could carry.

As we sailed we drew Insects from every part of the valley to the river bank. They ran alongside us, on the mud and claw-deep in the water.

Five Insects snipped branches off a felled tree, dragged them to where others crouched, building up a passageway. They cemented the chewed pulp onto the end of the tube. Insects infested ruined villages; as the ship carried me past I saw the wall of a burned-out cottage collapse, rust-brown claws thrashing under the rubble.

The Crag came into view. Solid Insect spit veiled the gray stone fortress; it jutted from rings of white walls. I could construct Tawny's and Vireo's struggles from the concentric walls, holding out and falling back, until Insects sealed them in. White paper structures washed over Lowespass's outer defenses, but the Inner Ward looked clear.

"They're in there."

"It's like a maze," said Lightning.

I spread my wings. "I can direct you."

From the sailors' noisy swearing and despairing it was clear they thought the terrain mountainous. Humans choose to live shoulder-width apart in the crowded capital of their flat country. The deserted Paperlands affected them—they tried to fill it with sound. Shouting stridently to each other, boasting, encouraging, captains organized the fyrd divisions on the main decks. Lightning made them check and recheck their equipment, keeping their minds occupied as much as possible, to lessen their fear.

The Circle broke. Faster than with Mist. For a split second I filled infinity, fell to nothing. The Circle reformed.

"No!" Lightning cried out.

I picked myself off the deck. "Who's gone? Who's killed?"

Lightning paused momentarily, gray gaze on the surface of the water without seeing it, concentrating on the faintest external feeling. "The Blacksmith, I think."

"In Rachiswater! What the fuck is going on back there?"

"Two Eszai dead, forty-eight to go." Lightning turned away.

Perhaps it's a good thing I'm too inexperienced to feel the Circle. I don't want to know just how much my drug abuse had been stretching it.

As the ships slowed, a hundred more Insects sprinted to the swarm on both banks, packing in around the ships, hungry, desperate to get to us.

"Steady yourselves," called Ata. "Here we go."

The depth-finders at the prow were hollering. "Ten meters! Eight meters! Five! Three!"

Stormy Petrel shuddered along her length as she ran aground. The caravel behind us nearly ran on to our stern.

Ata yelled, "*Tragopan*! Steady! Steady . . . We need you to get away." *Tragopan* dropped anchor and slid back in the current. I could hear the river trickling past the hull, pooling up as so many ships blocked the flow.

The landscape came alive. Insects teemed down from Fortress Crag, two kilometers away. Watching them, I didn't trust my strength to fly up there. I saw myself falling onto thousands of razor-jaws. Hitting the ground and breaking my legs. Faceted eyes plunging toward my face, whiplike feelers whirling.

Lightning approached Swallow, and lingered to compose himself. "Stay here, stay on the ship. Some of us will return. I . . . If I do not . . . ah . . . you will take good care of Cyan, won't you?"

"Yes," Swallow said. Cyan toyed with an arrow. Insects massed on the shore.

"If I survive, will you join me in the Circle?"

"Repeat to fade," Swallow murmured.

"I can still offer you immortality. Will you marry me?"

Worn down, lamed, overwhelmed, Swallow's glorious ambition just buckled. "Yes," she said.

Lightning swept an elegant bow, gold-blond wings spread; he received Swallow's hand and touched his lips to it. "Kiss?" he said hopefully.

"No. I think under the circumstances . . ."

Insects waded into the river's edge and scraped mandibles on the ships' sides.

"Under the circumstances it would make me feel much better."

Swallow threw her arms around him, fastened her lips to his, and gave him a really deep, long kiss that seemed to go on forever. Lightning reciprocated, burying his powerful hands in her red hair.

"The longer we wait the more arrive," said Ata; she drew her Wrought sword.

"There's *hundreds* of thousands!" I shouted.

"Hurry!"

Each ship lowered a gangway, splashing down in shallow water. For a second, every fyrd captain waited for another to make the first move. Archers, pikemen and those leading the horses, all delayed.

"Go!"

Lightning said, "Ata, raise flags to tell them I will shoot anyone who refuses to leave the ships." He nocked an arrow to string and stood on the steps in view of all.

Ata agreed. "Comet, do something useful! Into the fortress and speak to Tornado. If he can, ask him to start breaking through. It'll save time when we reach them." She pointed up to the Crag.

I hesitated, and Lightning leveled his bow at me. All right! For Wrought. For Tern.

I went from standing to top speed in three strides. Launched from the deck, fell till I gained windspeed. Hurtled low over the Insects' heads.

They jumped up, jaws snapping.

Can't catch me!

Insects appeared from every crevice, streaming down into the colorless valley. Their red-brown bodies scrunched into one great mass around the ships.

I found no lift in the bumpy, dead air. I beat my wings fast, keeping just above the festering swarm.

I worked my way low up the profile of the hill to the summit. Lowespass Fortress, like a model, spun below me. A trace of green—some grass still in the Outer Ward. I swung round low over the tower tops. Concentrating on flying, I was surprised at my agility. I stretched, feeling braver, glided in with my wings held below me. I leaned right, tipped the skyline crazily, and dropped into the fortress.

Faces peered out from arrow-ports in the gray bastions. There were more people than I expected, their packs dotted all over the ground. The filthy soldiers looked sullen, sitting in their curved square shields. I spotted Tornado looking up, surprised.

I flared wings, hit the grass, dropped to my armored knees and slid to a halt; flicked sickle wings closed.

Tornado seized my jacket and shook me, bellowing, "You should have come earlier!"

I struggled for breath. "We had a lot of trouble at the coast."

Tornado's shaved head was bristly. He stank of sour sweat; he was covered in cuts, his canvas trousers slashed. Fragments of chain mail strung on his belt hung round his loins and buttocks. Armpit hair stuck through his overlarge leather waistcoat, open at the sides with crisscross binding.

I said, "I want you to break through the wall. Here . . . to here," pointing out a space where the Insects' defenses were one wall deep.

Tawny raised his arms and a division of five hundred fyrd clattered to their feet. They wrapped scarves around their faces as protection from splinters. They fetched picks, mattocks and trench-spades and started to chip at the wall. Its surface began to shatter like porcelain; it broke away in lumps from the objects suspended within. Bones, petrified branches, dented armor all emerged and broke off as the Lowespass men hacked.

"Many more survivors than I thought . . ." I said.

"There's nine thousand six hundred of us," he answered. "Fighters sought refuge here from, like, every town north of Awia."

"Get them armed. Saker and Ata are here; we brought food. We brought *ships*. They have eleven thousand fyrd—but I don't know how many will make it up the hill."

"Then who died?"

I realized Tornado had felt the Circle break as well, and how terrible it must have been for him, incarcerated here without any news.

"Sleat the Blacksmith. And Shearwater Mist—in a storm."

"It was an accident?"

I nodded.

"Eszai don't die in accidents," he said bluntly. "Mist was Plainslands, and he could look after himself. Jant, I tried to fight my way out of here, people were dying round me all the time. Vireo said better to sit and wait if there's a chance we could save them."

"Do any of the big catapults work?"

"We ran out of ammunition a long time ago. Just about the time I ate the last horse." He raised his voice: "Vireo! Vireo! All of you—prepare to fight!"

Vireo ran from the spur-buttressed gatehouse. Her armor was styled to look like an Insect—big eye bulges on the sallet, a keeled breastplate like a thorax. She carried a spiked warhammer on a meter-long pole.

"Is this it?" she asked. "Comet, we had given up on you!"

"What did I tell you?" Tawny berated her. Then the muscle-bound maniac actually grinned. He was truly gigantic, living proof that Plainslanders fuck oxen.

Wondering how Tawny could have any men fit to do battle, I looked about and noticed a great heap of burned shell stacked by the stables. The shells were smashed, reddened, pale inside. It resembled the remains of a massive seafood feast.

"You've been eating *Insects*?"

"Little one, I don't want to talk about it."

But Insects eat people! "Aren't they poisonous?"

"I said I don't want to talk about it!"

Back at the caravels, archers were pouring arrows in almost solid arcs onto the Insects, and akontistai on the decks hurled javelins. Under this cover, fyrd divisions in tight formation left the decks together, marched down the gangways onto the river bank, where they joined ranks with men from ships on left and right.

First out were spearmen, with their backups carrying bundles of spare spears, and pikemen with square shields beside them. With the bombardment from the vessels, they made space on the shore.

Their spears became clogged with skewered, contorting Insects, yellow fluid running down the shafts. They dropped their spears and were passed new ones. Then followed untrained polearms men with axes, pole-cleavers, and gisarmes. They wore helmets with aventail and latten plate armor over padded shirts. The crossbowmen had discarded their brigandines for cuirasses, and to their scale armor the Awians had added plate protection on their limbs. All were behind the heavy wall of square shields, the spears bristling like a Shift creature's spines.

Ata left the gangway on her steel-clad courser. Too aware of her mortality, she kept three ranks of axmen in front of her, and I recognized one of her sons on either side of her chestnut horse. She was head-to-foot in polished, fluted plate with no crests, but its shine marked her out; she flourished the Wrought sword's phenomenal blade.

With everything Ata knows about me I hope she doesn't survive; in a battle any accident might happen, and it will if I get chance to pick up a crossbow. But Ata was keenly aware what I'm capable of, and I thought her sons were here not to protect her from Insects, but from me.

I drew my sword, searched for a space in this defensive phalanx, landed next to her. "Hear Tornado breaking the wall?" I shouted.

She gave a brief salute. "How many Insects?"

"Can't count them! Thousands! Swarms!"

Ata could not see what I saw. It was like being in an anthill. Insects drained out of the whole valley toward us. They sped down the valley sides, out of the tunnels. Ata's men were a knot of color surrounded for a quarter-k by a vast red-brown Insect tide.

I said, "It'll be tight through the walls; follow me."

A dark red Insect clawed at my face. I sliced its foot off.

The Hacilith men set up a howl, cut forward twenty meters; Ata made good use of the advance and directed the archers out from their positions on deck.

I flew up to see Harrier's archers on the left, Lightning on the far right. Lightning was mounted on a heavily armored hunter-clip white stallion, the one other horse. He only looked ahead; he had a dent in his cheek where the arrow nocks had pressed. The archers shot twelve flights a minute. How long could they keep up that rate of bombardment? There were more Insects than we had arrows!

Insects fell, cut apart, Insects ran madly away, arrows sticking out of them, but more crammed into the space they left.

Under cover of the archers fyrd surged forward and left the river bank. It took an hour to gain the foot of the hill.

Ata kept her men in one wide column, surrounded by shields in two staggered ranks. Then polearms men, chopping at Insects that got through. The sarissai's spears were used up by now. Archers shot from the column center, but Lightning and Harrier's divisions cleared space out in front. The crossbowmen were shooting to the rear. All attacked the climb full of energy, but were out of breath after the first few hundred meters. Breathing heavily, shouting less as the gradient increased, they plowed up, slashing at Insects.

A river of Insects descending the crag charged headlong, antennae waving. Lightning's archers loosed, a hundred Insects dropped and the rest came on. I plummeted down, only thinking that I should aid the Zascai.

I landed by a Hacilith soldier, who had a black bandanna under his helmet and broken-off mandibles embedded in his round shield. He brandished his poleax out at arm's length, keeping two Insects at bay. The smaller one pounced at his throat; he swiped and cut through a feeler. The damp white nerve strand that ran down inside the antenna flopped out over its eye. It stumbled, scraping over his armor. The second Insect stabbed its jaws under his breastplate, between his ribs. It braced itself with six legs and pulled, dragging him forward.

I reached him as it tried to open its mandibles inside him. I smashed my sword into the globular knee-joint of a middle leg, shattering it. As the Insect shifted its weight onto the other five, I leaned back and with one long overhand swipe took its head off.

The soldier panicked when he recognized me. I took his hand; he coughed and tried to fend me away. His jagged chest wound sucked as he breathed in, then an artery ruptured. A blood cascade erupted from his mouth, gushing over breastplate, dead Insects, the ground. It frothed from his nose. With a look of terror, he mouthed through the bright red gouts. He fell to the ground and that was it—he bled to death in ten seconds, blood filling his lungs.

Twenty Insects scented the blood and closed in, clustered over him, heads moving, munching. I spread my wings and got out of there. After witnessing that, I will never take hallucinogens again.

Our host spread out to either side, spanning the hill. The vanguard was a mass of struggling, falling people. The rearguard bunched up away from the river. The column continued to advance, leaving spiky arrays of dead Insects and severed human limbs. Insects pounded down from every lair in the landscape, eager to feed.

"Ata!" I shouted. "Go left here, around the edge of this wall. Go along the wall. Then right. Climb up to where you see a gap."

Ata urged her horse on.

I said, "For god's sake don't let them move apart. The gap is very narrow."

I watched as the columns passed between low, broken Insect walls. Teams of men between the columns planted sharp stakes in the ground, until every breach bristled with staves. The first charging Insects impaled themselves, the rest had to slow to pick their way through.

Harrier's archers on the left dropped their rate of shooting to ten per minute, then to six. Insects gained ground on them and started preying on their line.

"Go see Harrier!" Ata shouted to me.

"You want me to be everywhere!"

"Yes! *Be everywhere!*"

Volleys of arrows flew up, tilted at their zenith, dropped onto the Insects. Another cloud of arrows buzzed beneath me, and another.

Harrier raised a hand, fingers spread. "Comet! Five minutes! Five minutes' worth of arrows left! That's all! Help me!"

I turned back, found the captain of the Hacilith crossbowmen behind in the column, and directed the whole crossbow division through Harrier's ranks, to spread out in front of them, "Make way! Move down—let them through!"

"Out of arrows!"

"Out of arrows!" Harrier's voice.

Harrier's five hundred men simultaneously dropped their bows behind them and drew their swords.

Insects slammed into their ranks. The archers' solid line flexed, then Insects intermeshed into their edge like into a forest. The ranks disintegrated, Insects moving through and over them. Men were shoved together; the line dissolved into single men against Insects. Archers were struggling, disappearing. The crossbowmen started up.

I heard cracking as the Insects fractured archers' bones. Awians have hollow limb bones, which are tough, but cracked with a higher tone than human bones and splintered to shards in arms, legs and wings.

An Insect pulled the man next to Harrier out of the line, ripping his cheek open to bone and teeth. It raised a sharp claw, and unzipped his stomach from hip to chest. The archer screamed, wrapped both arms around his waist, his long coat slick with blood. Harrier slashed the Insect's abdomen to gluey yellow ruin; it lunged at him, quivered and collapsed.

The crossbowmen found their pace. The first line shot, stepped back, kicked their bows down to span and reload. The next two lines came forward and loosed, sending a barrage of bolts against the swarm.

Harrier looked, bewildered, to the scattered dead, the surviving longbowmen, then up at me. "Thank you," he said.

The Awndyn fyrd at the rear were under a lot of strain from
Insects running uphill, and they didn't stand it long. I know
what their blank faces meant. Suddenly Insects are the size of
god. They have god's power. Fighting is not an option. "They're
not invincible!" I shouted desperately. "Don't run!"

I stopped and soldiers ran straight on underneath. A handful
reached the river bank, and disappeared into a villagers' pitfall
trap that was already full of Insects.

"Shit."

I reached Ata. "We've lost the Awndyn division!"

"They'll draw Insects away. Order a crossbow division back;
I don't want the rear to degenerate into skirmishes. Keep going
up!" Ata called for the troops to stay together as the slope
became rocky. Vireo's archers inside the keep were shooting
from the towers' wide windows high over our heads, thinning
out the Insects reaching us.

I led the column up onto the saddle of the hill. It narrowed
as the men marched between two low walls, which swept round
in a long curve. The outer wall ended in rubble, leaving the
inner wall an unbroken white surface. Tawny's men were hew-
ing a hollow out of the far side.

I circled, wings beating furiously. "Break through here."

The front of the column milled around, calling over the wall.
Shouts answered from the other side:

"Hello?"

"Yo! Hello!"

"We're nearly through!"

"I don't think they can hear us."

"Hello! Hello, hello, hello!"

"Are you from Rachis?"

"From Hacilith! How many is there?"

"All of fucking Lowespass, mate."

"Lightning is here. Eszai are here."

"Watch out for Insects they come up the ditch!"

"Get back in your *places*!" Ata screamed. "Keep the shield line!"

Lightning ordered his archers to the peripheries of Ata's wall-breakers. Her crossbowmen formed a semicircle around them, two hundred meters wide, facing outward with their backs to the wall. I spiraled up, directly above.

A mighty crash—the wall-breakers burst through—the wall began to collapse. Men shouted—hands appeared from the other side and grabbed Ata's hands frantically. They started to widen the breach.

Ata left her horse and pushed her head into the gap. "Make space! Come through here! Spread out on the hill! Fall in; we'll start back to the ships straight away."

Part of Tornado was visible through the breach. "No," he said. "Not yet."

"But? We're here to get you out!"

I landed by him. "What are you planning?"

His Lowespass fyrd emerged in a long thick chain, carrying arrow-sheaves out of the breach. Those inside chucked sheaves over the wall to distribute among Lightning's fyrd. Tornado and Vireo squeezed through, surveyed Ata's host excitedly as the fortress troops jostled out to join them. "Look at all these warriors! Just think what we can do with so many, Vireo!"

"Who's the leader?" Vireo asked.

"I am," said Ata.

Vireo regarded Ata as a fellow mortal. "We won't forget your courage. But Tornado's in charge now."

"You can't do that!" Then Ata saw Tawny and me agreeing, and she let the giant take over without another word.

The fyrd, a sagging crowd, all heard Tawny bellow, "Now you'll see what it's like to have a real leader!" They looked at each other, and they stood a little more proudly.

"My god," I said, awestruck.

"You have a few minutes' rest," Tornado announced. "Any more time, and the Insects start their wall-building. We don't want them to build between us and the boats! I need a few more hours' work from you this evening. Drink water from the well. Let Comet see the wounded; those too injured to fight can stay here."

Vireo turned to me. "We have some too faint from hunger—the ones that refused to eat Lowespass Lobster. Pass them into the ward and instruct a captain to look after them while Tawny regroups the host, and we'll leave some archers here to protect them."

Twilight was growing rapidly, the afternoon becoming evening. I was low on energy from so much non-glide flying, but I attended to the maimed, traumatized and starving. There were fewer badly wounded men than I expected; they fell behind on the march and Insects don't spare them. Still, I had my work cut out in the keep, while Tornado marshaled the troops up behind the shield wall in preparation to march out en masse. "How many have we lost?" he asked me.

"Above fifteen hundred in all, I think," I said.

Ata said, "We've gained eight thousand, then."

"They're knackered, what did you put them through down there? Well, I suppose they're ready as they'll ever be."

Vireo raised her crow's beak hammer. "Tawny, you're the best weapon the Emperor has!"

"Love you!"

"For Lowespass!" she howled. The Morenzians and Lowespass fyrd swarmed to her.

Ata shook her curved sword. "For the Empire!" she cried. "For Sute! To me, Islanders!"

"For something!" yelled Tawny as he pounded past me.

"Survival," I explained. I outpaced him, took off.

They charged down the hill, and the fortress fyrd followed. Tornado's two-handed ax decimated Insects at each stroke.

Lightning had not set foot inside the fortress wall. He had spread his archers along the crag summit, behind linked pavises brought out from the keep. Two divisions each toiled for thirty minutes, shooting nonstop, sending ten thousand arrows per minute down into the valley. I had never seen such desperate effort; Lightning kept them working at utmost strain. His hair was wet with sweat, he was bare to the waist but for the bracer on his left arm. His horse's white neck was covered in bloody prints from the blisters even on his hardened hands. As Ata went past Lightning stopped the shooting, then spurred after her, furiously protesting. "I *said* we can only cover three hundred meters!"

"Tawny won't go out of range. Look! They're going to sweep round the hill."

"Crazy! It will be too dark soon to see that far!"

"I'm going after them!" Ata leaped her horse down rocky outcrops. Her men peeled off in a long, formless line behind her.

I circled the archers. "Look! Insects are crossing back over the bridge!"

Groups of Insects, and then a whole horde, began to run from Tornado. Other Insects wavered antennae, sensed the panic, and joined them. They bit at men they passed, tussled with halberds. The bridge teemed with them scurrying from Tornado's scything attack.

"Keep ranks," I shouted, but a great wordless euphoria broke over the tired troops. Carried away, they began to chase Insects to the bridge, Tawny and Vireo marching ahead of the shield wall.

Now scarcely pausing to bite, Insects swarmed up to the apex and vanished into the air. They departed in a flood. Going back into the Shift; taking the line of least resistance—fleeing to safety. They think they're safe. But Dunlin Rachiswater is waiting, worlds away at the other end.

I shouted, "They're going!"

Vireo beat Insects back before her. Tornado was on her left, towering above the normal-sized men, nineteen thousand warriors fighting behind him. Vireo put a foot on the white walkway, strode up onto the bridge itself.

A gigantic black Insect turned from the stream to face her, Insects running past it on both sides. Head down, jaws gaping, it struck forward. She embedded her hammer between its multifaceted eyes. With an agonized movement it swept its claw into her shins and knocked her over. She cracked her head on the edge of the walkway and lay still, facedown.

I swooped over. Vireo was unconscious. "Tawny!"

The big Insect crouched and brushed its antennae over Vireo's compound-eye helmet and metal-covered shoulders, trying to figure out what she was. Then it raised its sharp foreleg and jabbed it neatly into the nape of her neck.

"Tawny!" I yelled. "Here! Can't you see?"

Tornado realized what was happening as Insects started to tear at Vireo's armor. He roared. He ran to her, picked up the black Insect bodily, and threw it through the air. Writhing, it crashed onto the swarm, fell between rounded backs and disappeared under their claws.

He shook her gently. Her face was calm; blood was pooling on the rough gray paper. He put her over one shoulder and began to fight back down off the bridge. He hewed Insects as he strode, casting their shell carcasses aside. The shields parted to let him through at the bridge's base, while the stampede kept on around them. The Insect crush became a river, a trickle, and after an hour complete silence.

I touched down heavily onto the scarred ground behind him. "She's dead, Tawny."

"No . . . I just have to get her to Rayne."

"She's dead!"

Tornado bounded to his feet and took a menacing step toward me. I fanned my wings out hastily.

"I won't leave her!" He picked Vireo's body up onto his shoulders. "Rayne can save her!"

The hooves of Ata's mare boomed, her armor reflecting darkness and the wide, empty land. She spoke quietly, full of respect: "Tornado, will you order the fyrd back to the ships? Sun's setting, tide's turning, and no one should remain in the Paperlands after dark."

The ships got under way at nightfall, caravels and pinnaces packed with fyrd. We abandoned the *Stormy Petrel;* it was lodged upright even-keel in the gravelly river bed. Ata took command of the *Ortolan*. Tornado, standing at its stern, still carried Vireo's corpse; no one dared approach him.

Swallow and Harrier helped me with the wounded. Men sat on the steps between decks, hammocks were hung in the hold where arrow-sacks had been. Cabins stank of human grease, muddy river water and wet feathers. Food was passed around: bread, smoked cod and samphire broth, black coffee and flasks of water. Men and women laid their packs on the decks and slept there.

I brought a bowl of chips up to the stern, and Tawny told me to get lost. "You can't avenge against Insects," he said. Vireo's blood was dried across his back, her hair hung down, twisted around a quill.

"Come help me build a pyre," I said. Vireo was Lowespass, I knew their tradition. Unlike Awians, the practical Plainslanders do not want to take up space forever in opulent tombs. "Tawny, I will ask the Emperor to raise a memorial for her, where the bridge was."

"Where the bridge *was*?"

"That's the idea."

While the line of ships passed in the darkness under the bridge, I began sorting and laying out pieces of tubular steel scaffolding, elastic straps, piles of nuts and bolts on the stern deck of the *Ortolan*, to rebuild one of the Lowespass catapults.

"That contraption is far too dangerous," Ata protested. "I won't allow you to play with it on my ship."

"Lightning—leave Swallow alone! Remember your promise. Will you help me with the trebuchet?"

"I think Jant's right." Lightning strode up to us, hiding his fatigue with willpower, clear voice and upright bearing. "We should be able to shoot safely from the stern."

"I liked Jant better when he was on the drug salad," Ata said.

Lookouts kept watch for Insects, as Tornado and I led an armed expedition to shore, with horses drawing wagons full of pitch barrels. We piled fifty barrels in pyramid-shaped stacks around each of the bridge's four nearest legs.

I hunkered down and touched a match to the sailcloth on one of the stacks, and called to my captains to do the same. We stepped back and watched flame lick up around the barrels. The fire took hold quickly, barrels bursting open and the pitch seeping out.

Tawny walked into the flames, shrugged Vireo's body from his shoulders and laid it down.

"Goodbye, love," he said.

We watched the flames wrap round, until roils of thick smoke covered her shape. Intense heat drove us back little by little as the bridge's legs began to burn.

"Let's go," I said. We returned along the river bank, through the alien scenery. Although I was still wary of Insects, their absence was dramatic—quick as blowing out a candle, they had fled and we were actually walking without attack in their noise-less landscape.

"There'll never be another like her," Tawny said gloomily, as we reached the *Ortolan*.

"In all immortality there might be."

"Vireo. Vireo . . . I should've made her Eszai. God knows why I always hang on until it's too late."

We heard Lightning's clear voice instructing the catapult crew with an authority he must have been taught at an early age. The catapult loosed. A burning barrel of pitch arced high over our heads, crashed onto the bridge's walkway, dropping gobs of flame. Trust Lightning to get the trajectory right first time. Two more followed, spread throughout the walkway, and the bridge caught fire along its length.

From end to end of the ships' procession, men were cheering. They waved swords, helmets, cups in the air. The uproar grew as the bridge lit the night, Swallow's voice leading the applause, until men were gasping for air to cheer with.

The bridge blossomed bright yellow. Its nearest legs split open from the ground into the sky. They unfurled along their length in sheets of flame, and the whole thing started to collapse. Cables snapped, the walkway crumpled. It went down slowly, sinuously; debris raining down, ash flecks twirling into the air.

I thought of the citizens besieged in Rachis Town, and molten glass creaking as it set in the cooling ruins of Wrought. "That'll show them," I said to myself.

I watched the Paperlands lit flickering amber and black,

seguing into empty fields and the Summerday town wall. Dunlin's coffin was buried somewhere in that mess; would I ever be able to find it? I determined to send search parties when soldiers began to smash the cells, fill in tunnels, and rebuild the town. Staniel knew the exact location where the metal coffin lay; I would drag him out here to give us directions, and examine every centimeter of ground. I would recover the King's remains and, no matter what happened, I would find a way to report the truth to Dunlin, as I promised and as he deserved. Now I'm clean, addiction's prison seemed distant, and it was strange to think that the Shift still exists, and Dunlin is alive.

"I must search for Dunlin." I turned to Lightning. "The King's bier has to be retrieved."

Lightning nodded, as if this matched his thoughts. "It will be built into a wall. When we destroy them, we'll find it."

"Insects or no, it will take months to break up the Paperlands," said Swallow. Cyan was quiet at her side; she still did not stand close to Lightning.

"Yes, but it can be done," the Archer told her.

Tornado said nothing, his face was lined with grief. I didn't want to give him time to dwell on it. I said, "Tawny, we need you in Rachiswater. There are still Insects to clear out; Eleonora Tanager needs help."

"Eleonora's revolution," Ata said, leaning on the ship's wheel.

"And her coronation," said Lightning graciously.

I sighed. "It never ends, does it?"

"Consider yourself lucky that it doesn't, Messenger."

Lightning understood. He clapped my shoulder, face radiant. "Don't worry, Jant," he said. "Times will pass, and we'll survive. We'll live long enough for all these trials to become satisfying memories and the best tales."

STEPH SWAINSTON was born in 1974 and comes from Bradford, England. She studied archaeology at Cambridge University and then worked as an archaeologist for three years, gaining a masters of philosophy from the University of Wales.

She also worked as a researcher in a company that develops herbal medicines. Her current job is in defense research.